The Man

who Loved

Landscape

and other stories

Barbara Lennox

Dedication

To my late parents, who gave me that greatest of gifts, a love of reading.

Table of Contents

Foreword

T he stories in this collection were written over a twenty year period and range from tales set in the deep past to those that take place in a post-apocalyptic future. They have been influenced by myths and legends and by the landscape and history of Scotland. They explore the nature of what it is to be alive. Many deal with loss of one sort or another: the loss of a loved one or of love itself, innocence, youth, integrity, faith, self-respect. They invite us to believe that loss can be met with wry humour or determination and, ultimately, overcome or accepted.

The collection has been divided into four sections: stories influenced by mythology, stories set along the shores of the River Tay, historical short stories, and stories about relationships, good and bad. Inevitably, there are some overlaps between these categories. *The Washer at the Ford*, for example, in the historical section, is set at the time of the Boer War but was based on the idea of the *Ban Nighe*, a spirit from Gaelic folklore who washes the clothes of the dead. *The Eagle in the Serpent* is another historical short story which could have been included in the River Tay section, since it's set in a Roman fort on the banks of that river. And, of course, all of the stories in each section explore relationships of one kind or another.

There is further information about each story in the Appendix, where you will find details of when each was written, when and where it was published, if that's the case, and what inspired me to write it.

I hope you'll enjoy reading the stories in this collection. I certainly enjoyed writing them.

Myths and Legends

Introduction

I was brought up on myths and legends, so it isn't surprising that many of my short stories have been inspired by the creatures of myth. Indeed, the very first short story I wrote, back in the early 90s, was a retelling of the Beowulf legend from the point of view of Grendel's mother.

The title story, *The Man who Loved Landscape,* is about a nameless spirit of the wilderness. This spirit was also the inspiration for *Am Fear Liath Mór,* a tale about an encounter with a creature said to haunt the Cairngorm plateau.

Many of my stories were inspired by the Greek and Roman myths that are so full of larger-than-life gods, demi-gods and heroes. *Going home* is a reinterpretation of the tale of Persephone. Both *Eurydice* and *Icarus* use the ideas from these particular Greek myths to explore, from diametrically opposite standpoints, the consequences of obsession. *What's in a Name* takes a light-hearted look at the myth of Perseus and the Gorgon. *Heartwood* is the tale of a wood-turner's relationship with a dryad, the spirit of a tree.

Fairy tales are also a rich source of inspiration, and *The Gingerbread House* is based on the story of Hansel and Gretel, but with a horrific twist.

The Arthurian legends are a wonderful body of tales, and the legend of The Grail was the inspiration for *The Lyall Bequest,* a story in which an old man comes across this treasure in an antique shop.

Myths and legends are still being created, and *The Skies of Kansas* was inspired by the modern myth of the superhero.

There is further information about each of these stories in the Appendix.

The Man who Loved Landscape

J ames McCloud loved landscape, and I loved James McCloud – but not as a man might love another man. This was different, although I didn't understand the nature of that difference until many years later.

We were both loners, I suppose, me from a certain awkwardness with other people, him from a self-sufficiency I profoundly envied. But, whatever the reason, we were both drawn to the mountain park with its empty valleys and high cloud-wreathed peaks. It was a place where you could be alone without awkwardness, where you could walk for miles, or days, and not see another soul, a place that drew you back time after time. I took to spending my weekends tramping the tracks that led to the park's interior, camping beside shadowed lakes and climbing up to the high snowfields. When I returned from these expeditions I'd usually had the loneliness beaten out of me, and a longing to be with other people would take me to one of the inns that surround the park: watering-holes for the rangers, walkers, trekkers and climbers who're drawn to the hills and crags and wild empty spaces. It was in one of these inns that I first saw James McCloud among a group of climbers poring over an old map beside the fire.

I've always loved maps myself, and in winter, when the weather forced me indoors, I'd take up my own maps of the park and read them as another man might read a novel. I'd trace the routes and follow the contours, giving shape to the places I hadn't seen and memory to the places I had. Perhaps all who walk the wilds feel the same fascination, and the crowd around the fire was large and noisy enough for me to join their outer fringes without being noticed.

The scraps of conversation were familiar; *that track . . . this ridge . . .* Most of those around the fire had a story to tell of this place or that, of this occasion or the other. It was the usual sort of thing: weather closing in, the wrong ridge descended, a long walk back or a night spent in the open. I heard tell of days of wind and rain, of clear winter sunshine, of fog blinding the sky, of snowfields as hard as ice beneath the moonlight. One man, however, had nothing to say. He alone remained silent, his face lightening in recognition or darkening with memory, like a slope swept by wind-blown breaks of sunlight. And all the time he touched the map with faintly trembling fingers, tracing the soft swell of the foothills, as a man might trace a woman's breasts.

I stopped listening to the bragging tales and stood at the fringe of the group, as was my practice, silent, as was my nature, and watched James McCloud. Eventually he looked up, and his fingers stilled for a moment as a brief lift of recognition flickered across the sunlit coruscation of his expression.

You too? he seemed to be asking.

We didn't speak that night. We never did speak until one evening in October, the night that was to change me. But after that evening in the inn I began to listen for his name, to collect stories about him and weave them into a legend. He hadn't spoken that evening, but on other occasions he could be persuaded to talk, although the things he spoke about weren't the usual tales of adventures in the hills. Instead he'd tell of older times, of ghosts and spirits and strange lonely creatures, stories that were remembered and repeated, tales that glinted in your memory like the surface of a lake stirred by fish ascending from great depths. Sometimes, trudging down a track, heading for the high peaks, I'd repeat the stories out loud to myself until I caught the timbre of a voice I imagined and the lilt of an ancient tongue speaking the names of the places that had trembled beneath James McCloud's fingers: *hill of the stag, the yellow slope, corrie with the wing of snow*, phrases that would roll over the tongue like cold clear water with the tang of peat at the back of it.

But for all the tales and stories, true or imagined, I came no closer to the man himself until I met the girl. Oh yes, there was a girl. Isn't there always? Ellie was her name, and I wanted her almost as much as I wanted to be alone.

I'd seen her occasionally, had noticed her immediately. Her presence was enough to lure me to the outer margins of whatever group she was in. I didn't speak, of course, but I watched and listened. I began to nod a greeting to her, and, after a moment of puzzlement, she'd nod back.

You too? I'd ask her without words, but I didn't get an answer until one night in June when the nod was followed by a smile, a chance drifting away of her companion, a shift along the bar and the end of my pint. Diffidently, I offered her a drink. She accepted and indicated a vacant table in the corner of the room. Heart racing, I thought of so many clever things to say they knotted themselves together at the back of my dry throat. But it didn't matter because she wasn't interested in me at all. She just wanted to talk about James McCloud, and, over a drink or three, the reasons came spilling out.

They'd met by chance at the end of the season, midweek, both expecting to find a particular camp-place deserted. Instead they'd found each other. It was the end of a trek, and the tug of other people was strong, so they'd made the most of things. A shared campsite had led to a shared meal, a shared half-bottle of whisky leading, in its turn, to another sharing.

'But it was *strange*, you know,' she said. 'It was like I reminded him of someone. No, that's not right. It was as if I made him think of a *place*, somewhere he was trying to find.'

She laughed as if she'd said something foolish and began to talk of other things, but I'd stopped listening. I was remembering those trembling fingers tracing out a route and imagined how the hollow of her neck might have reminded him of a corrie he knew, how the ridge of her spine was recognised and named, how the angle of her elbow recalled a bend in a particular river. A place, she'd said, a map to be explored, its contours followed then forgotten.

After that, whenever I saw her, a faint flush and a turning away told me she regretted saying anything at all. Later she stopped coming to the park, and I never saw her again.

Perhaps it was because of the girl, but I paid more attention thereafter to the tales about James McCloud, although I didn't see him myself for months. Yet others did and they spoke of a strange dichotomy in the man. If anyone met him as he trekked into the park, he would, like most walkers, stop to exchange plans and weather forecasts. But he seemed distracted, they said, excited even, with some compulsion tugging at him that went beyond the usual pull of the unexplored.

'A woman,' one suggested, but I was sure it wasn't that. I barely knew the man, and yet I seemed to know him as well as I knew myself. Better, even. No, it was something more compelling than a woman. Yet, whatever it was, it seemed to be something he was unable to find, for those who met James McCloud on his return from those trips spoke of a different man entirely, a morose uncommunicative man who'd lost his knack for language, a man disappointed by something, or someone, yet relieved by his own disappointment, as if what he searched for was also to be feared. This I also understood, for I was at the age when you search for something you've no name for, something you're afraid will hold disappointment in the finding. Or the not finding.

I've always found autumn a troubling season, a time when fires are banked down and sap sinks, when days contract in the cold that seeps from the North. It's a time of last chances, and that was what took me deep into the park that October weekend. The days were blue and calm, the low golden light picking out the yellow flags of the birches that still held their leaves, vivid against the pines that had turned winter-black and inward-looking. In two weeks it would be Samhain, the old end of the year, and, as always in the park, the sense of ancient times was strong. With each step I felt as if I was travelling into the past James McCloud would sometimes speak about, a past peopled by the lonely spirits of wood and water and wind. So, as I walked, I thought of James McCloud, and when I came across the man himself it seemed as if it had been meant.

He nodded, recognising me, and might, I think, have passed on, but he was returning to civilisation, and his longing for company warred with his need for solitude. I nodded in return, tongue-tied as ever in his presence, so perhaps it was the prospect of a silent but listening ear that decided him. The long night was drawing in, the place we met an ideal campsite – a dry meadow sheltered by a stand of stunted alders – and so we pitched our tents for the night and shared a meal and a fire.

Later we spoke, of little things to begin with, of journeys, routes and waymarks, of herds of deer seen in the distance, a pair of eagles soaring over a ridge, a crag where ravens bred. I asked no questions and offered no opinions, fearful of breaking our nascent brotherhood, and eventually, as our fire burned down to ash, he began truly to talk, in a different sort of sharing.

I've never forgotten what he told me that night, of how he'd headed for a particular peak, thinking to descend a spur that ran away to the south, but long before he'd done so the cloud had dropped, and, in spite of his years of experience, he'd lost his way and found himself descending in the wrong direction. There was a trackless slope, a stream that flowed from beneath a black cliff-face, a river gathering other waters to itself and coiling cold and silver in the pale green meadows of a valley. A single rowan clung to the rocks above a bend in the river.

'The valley's a day's walk from here,' he said. 'Right in the heart of the park, between the two peaks.'

I was confused, for between those peaks lies a high plateau of sere grasses and rocky outcrops, of wind and emptiness. I knew of no such valley, but his certainty made me reach for my map and a torch.

'You won't find it there,' he said, taking the torch from me and switching it off. 'How could you? It's a place I'd never seen before, a place I couldn't find on the map, and yet it was utterly familiar. It seemed as if I'd known it all my life, grown up there, grown old there, and never left it. Have you never come back to a place you know and felt it claim you? Been aware of every slope and slant of it as if was another person? As if it was *yourself*?'

He said nothing more for a long time. The fire burned down, and the cold of the October night was bitter, and yet we both remained by the glowing ashes, listening to the quiet of a night that was not truly silent. Out in the dark I heard the mournful piping of a plover, the purl of water between rocks, and alders creaking in the wind.

'I don't know how long I stayed,' he went on eventually. 'Moments, perhaps. Or it could have been days. It let me go in the end, or I let myself go. On the way back I met a girl. I forget her name, but it doesn't matter. All that mattered was that she was something other than what I'd seen, experienced . . . been. And yet I couldn't forget it. In the darkness, all I could see, and feel, was that place – the spurs, the slopes, the bend in the river. I've searched for it since, so many times, and never found it. But it's there, waiting for me, calling me back. Listen! It's calling me now . . .'

I listened, hearing nothing at first. But when I did the hairs rose on my arms. It was the sound of rock and water and the dry rustle of grasses, of wind in trees, wind that had swept through a vast forest – not the patchwork woodlands of the park but the greater, denser forests that lie far to the north, empty, mysterious, and treacherous. It was the sound of wind on rock, on ridges that scar the clouds, in black chimneys of cliffs that reach up into mist and down into shadow. It was the sound of grasslands, of steppe and tundra, where only the cries of geese break the endless whine of the wind. And yet the sound was not only the wind, for at its core was a wordless cry of uttermost wilderness, profoundly lonely, impossibly ancient, yet startlingly familiar. It was the voice of a man, or something other than a man, who loved landscape more than he loved people.

In the morning I woke to find James McCloud gone, with no more evidence of his presence than a depression in the grass and a still warm smoor of ash. I never saw him again. No-one did. They never found his body. An enquiry concluded that he'd made one further trip back to the mountains about two weeks after I'd seen him. The weather had been bad, rain turning to snow. There are many ways for a lone man to die in the mountains in winter. People nodded sagely, and the case was closed.

But he's not forgotten. He's still there; I'm certain of it. The man who'd loved landscape had been claimed by the thing he most desired, had become the place he'd so longed to find. He'd searched for something in the wilderness and found, perhaps, only himself, or a semblance of himself. A fetch. There are such things in the world, in the empty places, and we give them names in whatever tongue we speak: dryad, sidhe, uraisg, the big grey man. We give them a shape too – our own – although they have neither shape nor form. Only a voice. Only a folding of the land by mist or moonlight. A creation of the self's searching heart.

I stopped going to the mountains. Time overtook me. Or life. That's what I told myself. There was a motorcycle accident, a long period of convalescence, a physiotherapist whose name, co-incidentally, was Ellie. We married and later – for life is rarely straightforward – divorced. I'd found the thing or person I'd been searching for, but the fear of disappointment proved to be its own terror. He lay between us, James McCloud, his hand on her cheek, her breast, tracing out the contours of a place that didn't exist.

It's autumn now, October, a few days from Hallowe'en, the name they give Samhain these days. The Night of the Dead. Children of the more old-fashioned sort carve turnip lanterns to frighten away the spirits. But they can't hold back the night. Or the voice on the wind, a voice that is oddly familiar. I hear it as an echo in my own ears.

I have a few days off, and the forecast is good. I get out my old maps and trace the contours of a high plateau where no valley is to be found. I imagine the shape of it: the curve, the ridge, the valley falling away to silver, one rowan clinging to a rock. It's a place shaped by my own longings, a place that calls to me with my own voice. I trace the contours and feel my fingers tremble.

Am Fear Liath Mór

'Ye're no feart, then?' Archie asked as they walked up the track at the back of the Linn of Dee carpark.

'Feart? Why should I be feart?' Duncan looked at Archie in surprise.

'Well, it's Ben Macdui we're heading for, and the cloud'll be down on the top the day.'

'So what? I've not forgotten how to navigate, even if you have. Come on, man! The forecast's good; we've plenty of time. What's the worry?'

'Ye mean tae tell me ye dinna ken about Am Fear Liath Mór?' Archie shook his head in disbelief.

Duncan eyed him sourly. Archie was full of daft stories. Half the time he made them up, like that time on the Aonach Eagach when he told Duncan the last pinnacle was haunted by a climber who'd fallen to his death, and how the ghost would grab hold of the legs of unsuspecting scramblers and pull them over the edge. Duncan hadn't half-hollered when he'd felt a hand on his ankle, but of course it had just been Archie playing the fool. This 'Ferly Mor' would likely be another of Archie's pieces of nonsense.

Duncan decided to ignore him, and he put his head down and strode out along the land-rover track to Derry Lodge, heading for the bridge over the Lui. It was early still, the day cold and fresh. The clouds were high but, according to the forecast, they'd drop in the afternoon. It was all the more reason to get a move on, so they stepped out along the gently rising and falling track above the flats of the Lui, past the ruins of the old shielings and along the edge of the new plantations.

From time to time Duncan pointed something out: a heron down by the river or a group of stags high on the hill, but, apart from nodding in appreciation, Archie didn't have much to say, which was unusual. Duncan was the one who liked to look around at things and think his own thoughts, but he didn't often get the chance because Archie was aye blethering on. So this silence, no matter how welcome, was uncharacteristic and oddly unsettling, and by the time they'd reach the pine-wood at the foot of Glen Derry and were tramping towards Robber's Copse Duncan was beginning to wonder what it was he'd said. Archie didn't even manage a grin when Duncan reminded him of one of the stories Archie had told at that particular point on a previous occasion.

'Mind the Gold Tree?' he asked, nodding up into Coire Craobh an Oir where a single pine clung to the upper slopes. 'Mind you telling me it was where that Lord Thingummy had buried his gold, and all them plans we made to come back with a couple of spades? You had me going then!'

'Aye, I mind,' Archie said distractedly. Normally he wouldn't have been able to resist the urge to poke fun at Duncan's supposed credulity. Something was definitely wrong, and, by the time they'd struck off from Glen Luibeg and were heading up Sron Riach, Duncan could stand it no longer.

'What is it then, this 'Ferly Mor'?'

Archie stopped abruptly, and Duncan almost ran into him. 'Ye really dinna ken?' Archie asked with a glance up the ridge that led to the great plateau of Ben Macdui.

'No, I really dinna ken! But see if this is ane of your stories . . .'

'It's no *my* story!' Archie protested. 'You can read it for yourself in the Cairngorm Club Journal. It was Professor Norman Collie that seen it first.'

'Who?' Duncan asked suspiciously. Archie, when he wasn't telling wild stories, was a bit of a name-dropper. 'Friend of yours, is he?'

'He's dead, you daft pillock! You mean you've never heard of Norman Collie? Collies' Ledge?'

'Oh, *that* Norman Collie! Sure I've heard of him,' said Duncan, who hadn't.

They headed on up the track and were high on the shoulder of the Sron by the time Duncan had got the whole story out of Archie. 'Ferly Mor' – Am Fear Liath Mór – was some sort of ghost, by all accounts. Professor Norman Collie first reported it back in 1925, although his encounter had been thirty-five years before. But others had seen or heard it since, mostly on Ben Macdui: huge footsteps in the mist, crunching on gravel or snow. Sometimes voices could be heard, and there were those who'd seen a great grey figure, twenty feet or more tall. Everyone, whatever they'd seen or heard, had been gripped by an intense feeling of dread and an overwhelming desire to run, to get off the mountain, to get away at any cost.

'You believe all that?' Duncan asked, looking up at the wide scree-strewn slopes of the hill above them.

'Of course not!' Archie scoffed. 'I'm just telling you so you ken what to be feart of.'

'I'm no feart,' Duncan said stoutly.

'Nor am I,' Archie said. But he was, Duncan realised. Archie, leg-puller extraordinaire, was feart.

Time to get his own back, Duncan decided, although he didn't know how. Not yet. He thought about it all the way up the ridge but still didn't have any ideas by the time they'd reached the cliffs above Lochan Uaine. The clouds, as forecast, had dropped, and the track was swathed in a grey mist.

'Maybe we should head back,' Archie said suddenly.

'What? We're almost there. We've just to skirt these cliffs and then we'll hit the Etchachan track. Listen, you can hear other folk on it.'

The mist magnified sounds, and Duncan heard a voice in the distance before it was blown away by a wind moaning up from the loch far below. Then all he could hear was the sound of wind and water and, once, the harsh complaint of a raven, tumbling on an updraft. Archie jumped at that and looked around wildly.

'What was that?'

'Come on, man! It was only a raven.'

Before long they reached the track and turned west, heading up the shallow slope that would bring them to the summit. Archie hesitated and seemed reluctant to go on, but continuing with Duncan was evidently preferable to staying behind on his own, and he followed closely, jumping at each sound, his breathing faster than the gradient warranted. Duncan realised Archie was listening to the sound of their own footsteps in the granite gravel, the steady crunch, crunch, crunch. There had been something about footsteps, hadn't there? Duncan stopped, unshouldered his rucksack, took a swallow of water from his bottle and, when Archie wasn't looking, scooped up a handful of gravel and stuffed it into his jacket pocket.

After twenty minutes or so they reached the cairn and triangulation point. They were alone, which was strange, for Duncan was certain he'd heard a voice on the track ahead of them. Whoever he'd heard must have carried on north.

'Right,' Archie said, touching the cairn briefly as he always did. 'We'll get away down now.'

'Already? Come on, let's have a breather, eh? Look – the cloud's breaking up.'

Sure enough, it was becoming lighter, the mist more luminous. With any luck the clouds would lift completely, and they'd be able to see Braeriach and Cairn Toul across the great gash of the Lairig. But the mist continued to form on the downwind side of the summit, even although the sun was shining from the south east. Duncan stood up to peer through the forming mist to see if he could make out the distant peaks, but what he saw instead, with an unpleasant loosening of his insides, was a huge grey figure.

'Christ, Archie! What in God's name's that?'

'Bloody hell! It's Am Fear Liath Mór!'

'Christ! What'll we dae?'

'Act casual. Try no tae look feart! Wave at it.'

'Wave at it!?'

'Aye, go on. Wave!'

Duncan raised his arm and waved. Amazingly, the great grey figure waved back. Then Duncan heard a snort behind him, and he turned in alarm – only to see that Archie was doubled up, tears of laughter streaming down his face.

'Ye daft pillock!' Archie gasped when he'd got his breath back 'It's a Brocken Spectre! An optical illusion. Anyone would think ye'd never seen one before!'

Duncan, his heart rate slowing, raised his other arm and watched the great grey figure do likewise. Archie came to stand beside him, and then there were two grey figures waving back at them.

'Well, bugger me! So that's all it is, eh? Just our shadows on the mist?' Duncan was annoyed with himself at being taken in and even more annoyed with Archie for pretending to be scared just to get Duncan's wind up. He'd been had, once again. But then he remembered about the gravel. He slipped his hand into his pocket and squeezed the gravel rhythmically in his palm. It ground together with a crunch, crunch noise, like footsteps in the distance, footsteps that were coming closer.

'What's that?' Archie whispered, grabbing Duncan by the other arm. The blood had drained from his face. 'Run!' He took off across the plateau. 'Run, man!' he yelled as he disappeared.

'But –'

It was too late; Archie was already out of earshot. Duncan began to laugh. He could hear Archie's footsteps as he ran down the hill, great bounding footsteps that tore down the mountainside. Oddly though, the sound of the footsteps didn't disappear; instead, they seemed to come closer. The mist closed in and it turned colder. Duncan's laughter shrivelled to a gulp, and he felt an overwhelming desire to run, to get off the mountain, at any cost.

'Wait, Archie! Wait for me!' He'd better catch up with him, since the daft bugger could run off the cliff if he wasn't careful. But it was Duncan who nearly ran off the cliff as he tore down the mountainside as if . . . as if something was after him. He swerved at the last minute, skidded along the edge, and ran on and on, not stopping even after he'd emerged from the mist, not even after he'd overtaken Archie on the way down the track. He kept running until he reached the bottom of Sron Riach and could see the woods of Robber's Copse ahead. Only then did he ease up, wait for Archie who wasn't far behind, and stop to catch his breath. Neither of them could speak for some time.

'You thought it was yon ghost,' Duncan said accusingly.

'No, I didnae.'

'Aye, you did,' Duncan insisted as they walked on. After a moment he squeezed the gravel in his pocket once more and had the satisfaction of seeing Archie turn as white as a sheet. 'Aye, you did,' he said. 'But it was just me all along.' He pulled out his hand and showed Archie the gravel.

'You . . . you . . .' Archie was speechless, steam practically coming out of his ears. Then he began to laugh. 'All right, you bastard, you got me there! I admit it. See when I heard thon footsteps . . ?' He bent over clutching his ribs, gasping with laughter. 'And see when I saw that third figure in the mist? I dinna ken how you did that, though!'

'Third figure? What third figure?'

Duncan looked at Archie and Archie, sobering, looked back at him. Then, together, they turned and peered back the way they'd come, up the Sron, up into the mist. The cloud was dropping now, a long tendril of fog reaching down the track, lifting and falling as if it was running in huge bounds. Something dark and dense was forming at the leading edge. Something huge and grey and utterly terrifying . . .

Going Home

'**I** 'm going home to Mummy,' I say. I've said it many times before. Sometimes I've shouted or screamed. At other times, my voice has dripped with ire, or ice. On this occasion, however, I'm quite calm.

My husband says nothing and continues to work, moving figures from one column of a ledger to another. He gives no sign of having heard me, and I begin to wonder if I've spoken at all, but then I hear him sigh.

'The usual reasons, I assume?' he asks, neither looking up nor altering his steady rhythm of shifting millions from one column to the next.

That, of course, is one of the reasons – his work. It flows, like a dark tributary, into a swollen river of reasons: his reserve, my boredom, his coldness, my need for light and warmth, his self-possession, my guilt. That last above all the others.

'Yes,' I say, still calm, matching my mood to his. 'The usual reasons.'

'Then there's no more to be said.'

He is, of course, correct. Everything that could be said has already been said. We've thrown insults at one another, accused each other of crimes neither has committed, said things we've both regretted. We've spoken in tones that have ranged from anger through disdain to a feigned indifference, and if that implies some sort of progression or regression in our relationship then it's a false impression, because it's all quite, quite random. On this occasion we've settled on a chilly inevitability. The next time, perhaps, we'll rant and shout, but the reasons will remain the same, as will the outcome. There is, as he points out, no more to be said.

Nevertheless, I feel I must make the attempt.

'You could come with me,' I say.

That breaks his rhythm. He pauses, his pen poised over one column. Then he lays it down, replaces the cap, takes off the half-moon glasses he uses for reading, gets up and comes to stand beside me. The door to the balcony is open, and I'm leaning against the frame, half in the room, half-out. At times like this I'm drawn to places of transition, but now I move to the balustrade. He comes to join me, and together we look down over the City.

It's dusk, a time of transition also, but this too is a false impression, because it's always dusk in the City. The sky is overcast, and the clouds have lowered almost to the top of our tower. A brown murk smogs the river and gathers in the plain, and the buildings rise from the gloom like jagged teeth. Some are crumbling, some burnt-out shells of girders and flapping sheets of rusting metal, others raw with new cement. Our tower is the tallest building in the City, and we look out from the penthouse suite, as is appropriate. It's his City, after all, his responsibility, an empire whose extent I've never quite grasped. Only the river marks its margins, a wide black river that winds sullenly in a shadowed valley down by the shanty town. How many people live in the City? Millions? Billions? I've never known, but I believe it increases by the second. New buildings rise and spread. Old ones collapse. Expensive hotels become slums. Palatial mansions are subdivided into over-crowded boarding houses. Only our tower is immune from the disease and decay that permeates the City, and it stands inviolate, gleaming with steel and glass, implacable. It reflects its owner, and so, of course, I know what his answer will be.

'I think not,' he says, looking down at the City, his City, seeing . . . what? An empire? A prison? Does he ever long for freedom? What does he feel in the brief moment that falls between my offer and his inevitable rejection? Does he even consider the possibility? I think not.

I've already packed. I don't take much. Mummy keeps my room exactly as it was when I left, despite my protestations. My old clothes hang in the wardrobe, and my dolls lie on the bed. I'm past the age for dolls, but they're comforting nevertheless. I long for comfort.

He walks me to the bridge. We're silent, but the City isn't. It's never silent. It hums and roars and moans. Police sirens wail, and there are shouts, gunfire, and screams, but not necessarily in that order. There's laughter too, although it has a hysterical edge to it. Music, subversive sultry jazz, oozes from dark cellars, and heavy rock throbs from the high-rise flats. I used to listen to that music from the far side of the bridge. I used to think the City sophisticated and exotic.

They watch us, the inhabitants of the City. They stare then vanish. I've lived here for ages, and yet I know little of the people, since I mix only with my husband's servants and functionaries: accountants, lawyers, officials from the higher echelons of his various enforcement agencies, never his subjects. They seem afraid of him, although I don't understand why. He's powerful but never quixotic, and yet they avoid us as we walk to the bridge, and the streets are empty for once, the bridge cleared of the stream of refugees. They mill in confusion on the far bank, searching for relatives and children. Some stare at us, passing our names from one to another in shuddering whispers. But they look disbelieving, disappointed even. They think of us as celebrities, yet all they see is a normal couple taking the air on a dull afternoon. My husband is dressed in his dark business suit as usual, a slim gold watch on his wrist. He isn't handsome, but I think him distinguished. I'm not beautiful but am dressed elegantly in taupe silk, and I wear only the one diamond, small but of good quality, set in the wedding ring he gave me so very long ago.

'Do you remember –?' I begin as we reach the middle of the bridge.

'Yes,' he says before I can go on. I am rebuked. This is no time for reminiscences. We stop, look down at the river, at the old ferry that still plies its way from bank to bank. It's no longer economic, because the bridge has made things simpler, with its coin-operated barrier, its guards and guard-dogs. There are still those who like the old traditions, however, so he keeps the ferryman on as a kindness.

'It doesn't have to be this way,' I say, turning to face him. He's pale. The light is brighter here, and it makes him look older than I imagine him to be. His face is drawn and lined, but he smiles the twisted wintry smile I know so well.

'I've always loved your optimism,' he says, before leaning forward to kiss me on the cheek, a fleeting touch of cold lips. There's an audible intake of breath from the watching crowd. 'Give my regards to your mother,' he says, then turns and walks away.

The crowd surges forward across the bridge, and I'm almost swept back into the City. I almost allow myself to be swept. Almost, but not quite, and, when the flow falls away to a trickle, I pick up my suitcase, walk up the road and climb away from the mists of the river valley. The day grows brighter, the fogs lift and the clouds part. It's not long before I'm blinded by the sunshine and develop a splitting headache.

'Darling!' Mummy enfolds me in a fierce embrace before pushing me back to peer critically at me. 'What has that terrible man done to you!' she exclaims, measuring the depredations of the City in my face. I don't think I've changed that much. I'm a little thinner perhaps, paler certainly, but I'm shocked to see the magnitude of the changes in her. This is no longer the golden mother I remember but an ill-kempt and dull-eyed old woman with straggling hair. And nor is the house as it used to be, a warm and shining place of glowing fires, burnished copper, vases of lupins and the scent of new bread. It's cold and dusty, as un-cared for as she is herself, and is much as I'd feared. As ever, in my absence, she's let herself go, but I know how to deal with that. I tell her I'm fine but confess to the headache.

'Headache!?' She straightens and pulls herself up to her full height. The light of battle brightens her eyes, and she goes into action. Hot-water bottles are filled, milky drinks brewed, fires lit and curtains drawn. Before long I'm ensconced in my old bed, warm and drowsy, my headache soothed by cool hands on my forehead. I'm Mummy's little girl again and we both love it.

It's several days before she mentions him. We're sitting in the kitchen by the Aga, companionably sorting through seed-packets. A basket of kittens purrs by the hearth, and a soup of spring greens and barley bubbles on the hob.

'And how is that husband of yours?' she asks, not meeting my eyes. She's never been able to bring herself to call him by his name.

'Fine. He sends his regards.'

She sniffs disapprovingly. It's the old story: a family feud between three brothers who, even after all this time, are still wrangling about their inheritance from their father. The oldest got that exclusive mountain-top resort and the second son a big shipping concern, while my husband, the youngest, got the City with its slums and tenements. It was hardly a fair distribution. Mummy, social climber that she is, naturally sides with the oldest brother, and, although she emphatically denies it, I suspect that at some time, in her rather murky past, they have been lovers. She was furious when I ran off with the youngest of the three sons and used to tell anyone who'd listen that he'd abducted me. But it wasn't like that at all.

The City had always fascinated me, and I used to walk down to the bridge to listen to the sounds of jazz and smell the exotic foreign spices from the street vendors' stalls. Sometimes I'd see a man at the far end of the bridge, a tall distinguished looking man wearing reflective sunglasses and black biking leathers, his gleaming Harley Davidson parked by the kerb.

'Do you like jazz?' he asked one day, when I plucked up the courage to venture closer.

'I think perhaps I might,' I replied, and, of my own volition – I must stress that – I climbed on the back of his bike. It was hardly an abduction, and nor was what followed what Mummy describes as the seduction and ravishment of her innocent young daughter. In the first place, I wasn't as innocent as she fondly imagined, and, in the second place, it was neither a seduction nor a ravishment. He isn't at all like his brothers, whose morals leave a lot to be desired.

'Do we have to go to their party?' I ask a couple of months later. Midsummer is drawing near and, with it, the annual celebration up at the mountain resort.

'But darling, we always go!' If there's one thing Mummy insists on it's following traditions. We always go; therefore we always will go. And she does so love it: the exclusivity, the flowing champagne, the charming young men I suspect are shipped in for the occasion. She likes to flirt with her old lovers too, my husband's brother included.

'So this is my little brother's little wife!' he says, patting my hand with his great paw. 'You're not a patch on your mother,' he adds regretfully, casting a merry eye at my golden-haired, large-breasted mother, who blushes pink with pleasure. I decline the invitation to sit on my brother-in-law's knee, since I know from past experience that those patting hands are far from avuncular. The other brother is just as bad, passing himself off as an old sea-captain and pinching any bottom within reach. I make my escape and wander around, and, for the first time since I left, I begin to long for my tower in the City with its echoing silences and cool marble, its elegance and sophistication. There's little sophistication at the party; the cocktails are multi-coloured and sickly, and the buffet of stuffed dormice and satayed larks' tongues is distinctly tacky. Inevitably, it's fancy dress, and a fair number of the women are dressed improbably as nymphs and are screaming with delight at being pursued by visibly aroused satyrs. It's all quite tasteless, and I make my excuses and leave before the night descends into the usual bacchanal. Mummy doesn't get back until the next morning, dishevelled, slightly tipsy, and languid from goodness-knows what encounter in one of the many arbours.

It's the beginning of my disenchantment. I love spring. I love wandering in the meadows picking flowers, watching the little lambs gambolling about the fields, and lying on my back in a patch of sunlight to dream away the day. But summer is less pleasant. It's too hot, the nights too bright. Mummy organises picnics, forgetting that I've never liked al-fresco food. And the worst of it is that Mummy, growing accustomed to her little girl being home, begins to take me for granted.

'Just nip down to the lower meadow and refill the trough for the cattle, would you darling? And, on your way back, can you pick some peas for supper?'

I hate shelling peas. The trouble is that Mummy's a farmer at heart. She doesn't think twice about hauling on her wellies and setting off through a sea of sewage to assist in the birth of a sheep or goat, but, to be honest, that sort of thing makes my gorge rise. We begin to have the usual arguments, and the onset of autumn deepens the rift.

'Why do we have to do harvest-thanksgiving? Can't someone else do it for a change? Why does it always have to be us?'

'But we've always done it, darling!' And that, as far as she's concerned, is that. No matter that it's an immense amount of work. No matter that plaiting all those wreaths of corn and poppies completely ruins my nails. No matter that it would be much easier to get in a catering company. No matter that I'm *tired*.

'A daughter of the house should set an example,' she points out. 'You don't see me lying around when there are apples to pick or corn to thresh.'

'I'm not the daughter of the house any more.'

She opens her eyes wide in mock surprise. 'Of course! You're a married woman now. I'd forgotten. Silly me! Of course, darling. You just lie there and paint your nails. It's all right, I can manage. I'll just take a couple of pain killers for the backache. And who cares about my heart?'

She goes on and on until, eventually, I give in. But I don't enjoy being at home with Mummy any more. I begin to think longingly of my nice cool penthouse with its black marble floors and silk sheets, and I begin to yearn for someone who will leave me to my own devices and not nag at me like Mummy. Even boredom is preferable to this, and I begin to worry about my husband. He won't have gone to pieces like Mummy does – he's made of sterner stuff – but I know he'll be missing me. I imagine him looking out of the Tower and searching the faces on the bridge for mine. He'll be throwing himself into work and making himself ill with it. He'll be short-tempered, demanding, intolerant, perhaps even quixotic. Guilt grips me.

'I'm going home to my husband,' I tell Mummy one morning as the leaves are falling in the orchard. I'm standing in the doorway, looking down the path that leads to the gate and thence to the road that runs down to the valley where the river flows black and cold.

Mummy takes it badly.

'Go then!' she sobs. 'Leave me here, all on my own, with all this work to do. But don't you worry about how I'll manage. And don't you worry if I'll be lonely. I'll get used to it. I'll probably just waste away with grief, but don't you worry about that either!'

'That's emotional blackmail, Mummy,' I say firmly, snapping my case shut. 'You have to learn to let go. I'll come back to see you when I can.'

'No, you won't,' she says bitterly. 'You've eaten the fruits of that evil empire and are lost to the world of sun and hope.'

She should be on the stage. I've always said so.

He's waiting by the bridge. Somehow, he's known when I'd be back, but there's no effusive welcome, no relieved embrace. He kisses my cheek, the usual touch of cold lips on my skin, then bends to pick up my case. Together, we walk back to the City

'How was your mother?' he asks when we're back in our cool dim penthouse. He snaps his fingers, and a servant brings a tray with two glasses of pale wine, frosted with moisture.

'Much the same as ever,' I say. 'She'll never change. Her parting words were that I'd eaten the fruits of your evil empire. It's what she always says.'

He laughs. It's a strange unfamiliar sound in these echoing spaces of polished chrome and black ash. He hands me a glass of wine and a plate on which lie six blood-red seeds. It's an old and very private joke between us, and I'm pleased he's remembered. I smile and eat them one by one. They're sharp and acid on the tongue.

'I'm glad you're back,' he says.

'I'm back to stay,' I tell him. I mean it this time, as I mean it every time, but he touches a finger to my lips.

'Don't make promises you can't keep, my dear. We'll see how it goes, shall we?'

We touch glasses to toast my return. For however long it might prove to be this time.

'Welcome home, my love,' he says. 'Welcome home, Persephone.'

Icarus

L eighton Travis-Browne had a fondness for white. It could even be said to be his favourite colour.

'White isn't a colour,' objected a friend. 'It's an absence of colour.'

'Nonsense,' said Leighton, who held strong views on this, if on little else. 'White light is a combination of all the colours of the spectrum. White isn't an absence of colour; it's a presence.'

The friend thought there must be a flaw in this argument but couldn't quite place it and so said nothing. Let Leighton think what he liked. He was rich enough to be allowed any number of crazy ideas. If he thought white was a colour that was up to him, and, given his appearance, it was hardly surprising.

Leighton was one of those washed-out, fair-haired individuals often encountered in the English upper classes – lanky with over-breeding and parental expectations. He was someone who, in the days of Empire, would have risen before dawn, dressed himself in tropical whites and strolled off into the jungle to tame the savage breasts of lesser folk with tales of Queen and Country and the importance of playing the game – at some risk, quite probably, to his health and, almost certainly, to his milky northern skin. In his own time, however, such exigencies were no longer required, and he was more often to be found in cricket whites on the playing fields of England.

He was, surprisingly for the scion of such an old and respected family, quite ridiculously wealthy, a fact that embarrassed him from time to time and irritated his less well-off friends who, had they possessed his wealth, would have thought of something better to do with it than indulge what they considered an unnatural obsession.

His car was white. His shirts were white, and, in summer, his suits were white. His towels and sheets and bathroom porcelain were white. He lived a simple life, by his own lights, having consigned the crumbling family mansion to the tender care of the National Trust. Instead he'd installed himself in a house of modern design set on a shoulder of the Downs, a house made of glass and steel and bleached stucco. It had white curtains and white blinds and the floors were covered with thick white carpets that were the despair of his housekeeper, Mrs Stonewall. He had a fondness for the works of up-and-coming artist Maximillian Talbot, and had purchased at vast expense his seminal work, 'White on White', which now adorned the large wall of his sitting-room.

'Very nice, Mr Travis-Browne,' said Mrs Stonewall, gazing up at the expanse of glossy white paint, privately thinking that it was bound to show the dirt and that her Ronnie, given a sheet of plywood and a tin of Dulux, could have run up something just like it for a fraction of the price. Unfortunately, in Mrs Stonewall's opinion, all-white interiors were all the rage that year, and so Leighton Travis-Browne had little difficulty in persuading the interior designer he hired, one Rufus Bond, whose foxy muscular name was quite at odds with his manner, to create a space of cool calm purity.

'I just adore sterility,' claimed Rufus Bond – whose lifestyle perhaps ensured it – when he and Leighton surveyed the results. 'So elemental. One could even go so far as to say atavistic, could one not? It just needs a touch of colour to point the scheme up,' he went on. 'Fuchsia or maybe lime green. Linen scatter cushions. What do you think?'

Leighton regarded Rufus Bond with a fresh eye, and it occurred to him that the man's suit, a creation of grey silk with narrow stripes of – could that really be turquoise? – was quite unsettling in his otherwise cool and calm interior. What did he think? That he no longer required the services of an interior designer. He knew what he liked, and it was white. No more, no less.

So, when it came to the garden, he hired a team of gardeners and told them exactly what to plant in his chalky soil. They sighed but carried out his instructions and created a garden to rival Sissinghurst, also all the rage that year. They consoled themselves with the expectation that, come the following year, they'd be summoned back to replant the garden with the new year's fad – hot borders and black tulips or the like. But Leighton was faithful to his favourite colour, and so his garden matured into a restful place of white flowers and pale foliage. In spring it was a mass of white cherry blossom, and in summer tall campanulas vied with phlox and roses. In the autumn his borders were bright with Shasta daisies, and even in winter he had white flowers in his garden: Christmas roses, white cyclamens and, after the last snows, the nodding bells of snowdrops.

Naturally he liked winter best of all: days of snow falling on snow and the sky heavy with more snow to come, days when he could sit in his white interior and look out on a world that was also white, when he could watch the margins of one blur into the other. At times like that, he might, if Mrs Stonewall had left for the day, take off his clothes and stand naked in his living room, enfolded in white. If he half-closed his eyes everything merged together in a wash of light until, dissociated from the world and floating in a haze of sky, he felt much as Icarus must have felt when he soared too close to the sun. But Leighton Travis-Browne wasn't burned by that white-hot light, and, unlike Icarus, he didn't fall to earth. Instead, laved in the pure high notes of his favourite colour, he smiled and drifted gently back to earth. He put his clothes on again and became himself once more, with only a half-regretful sigh for the white enfolding spaces he'd imagined.

'Why don't you move to Switzerland?' another friend, who was keen on skiing, suggested. Leighton tried it one winter and was content enough for a while, except for the suspicious blueness of the sky. There was snow on snow right enough, but when spring arrived the snow melted, and plants began to bloom in the high meadows.

'The flowers!' enthused his friends.

'The flowers!' he complained before heading home to his house on the Downs that lay beneath a sky more often than not a shade of grey that approached the colour he'd come to love. Grey was a compromise, of course, but unavoidable. As were other compromises. There wasn't much he could do about the regrettable biological requirement of plants to have green leaves, the occasional obligation he felt to wear a dark suit, or the impossibility of finding something to spread on his bread (never wholemeal, never toast) once white-currant preserve proved to be a disappointment.

Love too was a compromise. Oddly and unaccountably, love seemed to be a requirement in his life, and there were times when the purity of his existence wasn't quite enough. At times like that the burning of the flesh assailed him, a burning that could be relieved, if necessary, in solitary if distasteful ecstasies, or else satisfied by encounters brief enough to barely sully the purity of his crisp white linen sheets. But the burning of the spirit, the desire not only to share the flesh but the soul of another being, was harder to dismiss.

He met her at the party of an acquaintance, a noisy affair he regretted attending almost as soon as he arrived. It was garish too, inevitably, an assault on the senses he could only relieve by resting his eyes on one other guest, a girl wearing white. She was small and slight, her skin the bleached ivory of a red-head, and her hair was pale too, but neither red nor blonde. Rather it was an intriguing silver, the white hair of an old woman, which she most decidedly was not. She'd gone prematurely white in her early twenties, she informed him with a smile. But, rather than try to hide the fact by dying her hair, she'd decided to celebrate it. White was such a beautiful colour. Didn't he agree?

He had a brief enchanting vision of this alabaster woman naked on his white linen sheets with her hair spread out on his white pillow-slipped pillows. Simultaneously he also saw her clothed in lace from neck to ankle with orange blossom in her hair and the light shining on her as she walked towards him down a cathedral nave to the sound of organs. And then there was another vision – the same woman, clothed in white, her eyes closed, lying on a bier with lilies at her breast. She was, in that one confused vision, all women to him.

'Shall we leave?' he suggested. She smiled and put her hand in his. Her name, it turned out, was Fiona, which, she explained, was Gaelic for white.

He rarely took women to his white-walled house in the Downs. Such overtures as he'd made to fulfil the distasteful, if possibly unavoidable, requirements of an ancient name and, more importantly, ancient money, had proved to be a disappointment. Such women had either been frankly horrified by his house and garden – 'All that white, darling! So bad for the complexion!' – or, with his money on their minds, had tolerated it for a while but in the end had tried to change him. He'd return home to find that, in his absence, the purity of his decor had been sullied by the appearance of a green-shaded lamp, a pot of red geraniums or a blue towel in his otherwise white bathroom. The spectre of lime-green scatter cushions swam before his eyes, cooling his relationships until the women left him, much to his relief, allowing him to live his clean white life once more.

But with Fiona it was different, and her reaction to his house was neither horror nor a grim resolution to quietly put up with it but a wide-eyed joyful delight.

'Leighton! How beautiful! It's so pure, so white! Doesn't it make you want to tear off your clothes and just bathe in it?'

And she had. Moments later he'd joined her.

So this was love, this merging into one another's spaces. She began to blend into his background and he into hers, until, snow-blinded by their love, they could no longer see one another clearly. But where there is white there must also be black. And where there is love there will always be doubt.

'Do you really love *me*?' she asked. 'Or am I just an accessory in your colour scheme?'

'Of course not!' he replied, hoping she wasn't thinking of dying her hair.

'Would you love me if I looked different?' she demanded, reading his expression if not his mind. 'Or if we lived in a different place?'

'Would you love me if I was poor?' he countered. 'If I didn't own a place like this?'

Doubts thickened like snow-clouds in a winter sky.

Am I a freak? he wondered. *Am I only half a human? Is white really an absence of colour after all? Is the life I lead an absence of life? Do I live here in the way I do because I can't cope with living life to the full? Am I afraid to experience the red of anger? The green of jealousy? The black of despair?*

'Dye your hair then,' he challenged her, a flicker of displeasure crossing his face at the thought.

'Give your money away,' she suggested, glancing regretfully at the luxury of silk and linen and the cleanliness and order created by the indispensable, but expensive, Mrs Stonewall.

Gradually, they grew fearful of each other. *What colour is fear?* he wondered.

It was blue, he decided a week or so later when, late at night, she called him into the bedroom, his cool calm bedroom of white linen and pale gauzy draperies. It was cool and calm no longer, however, for his bed was covered in royal blue sheets, and her hair, now a fan of red, was spread over daffodil yellow pillowslips.

He stepped back, appalled.

'It's a test,' she said, beckoning him. 'Of our love.'

'I can't!' he whispered.

'If you love me, you can. Close your eyes if you have to.'

But, even with his eyes closed, he still flinched from the assault of blue and red and yellow.

'I'm sorry,' he said in the end. 'It's too much, too soon.'

She turned away and wept like a woman betrayed.

He couldn't stay in a house wounded by such colour, in a house that bled blue cotton and red hair. He got into his car, his blessedly white car with its white leather upholstery, and drove off into a night in which the first flakes of snow were beginning to fall. The snow soothed him, and he drove further than he'd intended, high up into the Downs where the snow lay deeper, and the roads, unfrequented, soon succumbed to the weather, losing their glossy black surface and merging in his headlights into fields and uplands. Inevitably, he ran off the road. White could betray him too, he discovered, as his car plunged into a drift and stalled.

He tried to get it going again but the car, chosen for the colour of its panels and upholstery rather than the reliability of its electrics, refused to start. All around him, in the light of a torch, the snow fell harder. Yet he was close to the road, wasn't he? He had legs. He had the spirit, he rather fancied, of the Travis-Brownes of Empire, and so he turned up his collar and set off towards the road. But, unused to walking in snow at night, what he took to be the road turned out to be a track across the uplands that led to a waste of tussocky slopes down which he fell.

Shaken, he got to his feet, groped for the torch and found himself to be in a wilderness of white swirling flakes with the cold edge of crystals. His hand, cut open when he'd fallen, bled profusely. In the fading light of the torch the red was startling, and he stared at his own blood in amazement.

It had been years since he'd bled, so many years that, if he'd thought about it at all, he'd have imagined the liquid that pulsed through his veins to be neither red, nor even blue, but of some pallid shade. However, it now appeared that he could bleed like any other man, and it occurred to him, for the first time, that, family and money notwithstanding, he could die from the cold like any other man too.

What colour is fear? he'd wondered earlier and had decided it was blue. Now he realised it was white, and he thought back to the world of colour from which he'd fled. Now he longed for blue sheets and yellow pillowcases, for the warmth of Fiona's newly red hair and what it symbolised – a love that could change, could shift its wavelength within the rainbow's meld of light. Things would be different when he got back, he decided. He'd no longer love white with the same obsession. He'd begin with pastels and see how it went. Eventually, he'd learn to embrace colour and be able to walk out of his cold white spaces. Just as he was going to walk out of the snow.

He began to move through the deepening drifts, into the strengthening wind. His torch was all but useless now, and he threw it away then stumbled blindly on in the dark until, beyond cold, his blood withdrawing to his core of self, his brain sluggish, his body slowing and huddling inwards, he began to understand that he wasn't going to be given a chance to change. He'd embraced white, had loved it to distraction and, like a jealous lover, it wasn't going to let him go. White embraced him back, claiming him in a selfish single-minded love that permitted no other colour, no pastel-tinted plans for the future, no future at all.

He'd made a choice. Now he himself had been chosen, and, as if to confirm that choice, to reveal it more clearly to his freezing mind, he began to see light. It grew all around him, glowing at the edge of sight, merging with the darkness into a shade of grey that brightened to an argent luminescence. So cold now he could barely move, he watched the light merge with the snow in a blizzard of white. All around him was a dawn in which there existed only himself and the white and killing wind.

He smiled in recognition and, moving slowly but deliberately, he took off his clothes until all the surfaces of his body were bathed in white. Everything fused together in a wash of light and cold, and he felt as if he was floating, drifting in the hazed enfolding space he'd imagined so long before. He sighed without regret.

Then, like Icarus, he fell from the white-cold sun. Smiling, he fell to earth.

Eurydice

From the moment she was born, she loved the dark.

Her mother blamed it on the month and time of her birth, since it was in December at three o'clock in the morning – a dark time at a dark time of year. Yet hadn't there been sufficient light, an excess even? So perhaps it was the nine months she'd spent in the womb exploring her senses. She'd tasted the warm salt of amnion, smelled the inner woman smell, touched the liquid lining of the vessel in which she lay and heard the thudding of a heart that wasn't her own. But she'd known nothing of light until the moment of her birth. Perhaps the sudden awareness of a fifth sense had been too much for a creature not yet ready to adapt.

But this explanation didn't satisfy her mother, for her other children had been born in similar circumstances and had the usual liking for bright colours and vivid images. They hadn't shown an inclination for shadow.

Not that it was a problem. A quiet child who refused to sleep in the light could be accommodated. A child who reached out to the shadows of her cot, who laughed as the light was switched off, wasn't something to worry about. And nor was there reason for concern when, a little older, she'd point not to the pictures in her books – bright things in primary colours – but to the letters that described them, letters that invariably were black. She'd trace their margins with a questing finger as if she sensed a meaning in their dark shapes.

Later, when she could speak, her preferences didn't alter.

'Look!' She'd point to a bird as it flew across the garden, but it was neither a bluetit, nor a rosy chaffinch. Rather, it was a creature with glossy feathers and a gleaming eye. 'A crow!' she'd exclaim, matching action to word.

'See!' she'd say in awed tones, looking out of the window on a moonless night. 'How dark it is!'

She was a girl who liked the dark, who loved the winter for its long nights but hated the snow that fell to bleach her world, who preferred sticks of charcoal to coloured crayons, who liked her fires unlit, her toast well-burnt. Simple idiosyncrasies perhaps, but they required reasons at the very least, treatment if at all possible.

'There's no colour blindness that I can detect,' said the specialist reassuringly, having privately examined her for stigmata of the devil.

'Sibling rivalry,' decreed her teacher, who was all for it, hoping this child would be brighter than her older sister, a pretty creature with a fondness for pink and an inclination to tears, and less cocky than her older brother, conventionally drawn to blue and the sharpness of weaponry.

'Bring her back again next week,' suggested the psychiatrist, since he'd taken a fancy to her mother, a red-haired generous-breasted woman who stirred oedipal urges he considered unhealthy to repress.

'It's just a phase she's going through,' said her mother's friends with pragmatic psychiatry of their own.

'Leave her alone,' said her Aunt, a third child herself and thought to be eccentric.

This was divergent advice, and so a compromise was reached. She was left alone but watched. The phase, if it was one, was measured. The psychiatrist gave her a book of Rorschach blots to amuse herself with and detained her mother for an unaccountably long time in the large room with the couch.

And so she remained herself, as contained as a cat, as quiet as a winter's night, imaginative and probably clever, a girl who loved the dark.

'What will become of her?' wailed her mother, thinking how easily her conventional pink daughter would find it to marry, how her conventional blue son would find himself a job in the city, and wondering, as the affair began to dwindle, whether she should find another psychiatrist.

'She'll do well!' announced the teachers, relieved to find one child at least who might improve their standing in the league tables.

'She'll grow out of it,' her mother's friends said complacently, glad their own daughters were pastel-coloured and compliant.

'There's nothing wrong with her,' said the psychiatrist who, having satisfied his urges, had tired of the mother.

'Let her do what she wants,' demanded the Aunt, wishing she'd been allowed to do so.

No-one, however, neither the psychiatrist, nor even the Aunt, thought to ask the simple question, 'Why do you like the dark?' And by the time the question was raised it was too late, since she'd learned to hide behind a slow smile that spoke of secrets, and ring-fenced herself with a rebellion that led her to question in return.

'I just do. What's wrong with that?'

Yes, what *was* wrong with that? It just didn't seem normal. And yet she showed no hint of obsession. Given the choice, she preferred the shadows to the light, black to any other colour but, failing that, purple would do, or navy or the dark green of a starling's wing. She was willing to compromise and took delight in confounding expectation and avoiding labels. She slipped like a shadow into the spaces between categories and ran like ink from pages of theory.

She was serious without being sombre, intelligent but lacking sense, confident yet introspective, languid yet with an active mind. She wasn't strange, precisely, but out of focus with the world, someone it was difficult to put one's finger on. Which, had anyone thought to ask her, was exactly as she wished. Gradually, she changed from an odd child into an eccentric adolescent, with long black hair that hung down over her face and concealed eyes that were darker than the spaces between the worlds, as remote as the black holes about which she began to read.

It was the first of wonders that trapped her in the end and allowed her to be pinned to the board of life and labelled. It was that first intrigued tracing of letters and numbers on a page that she'd sensed, long before she could read or count, had meanings that went beyond their shapes. The spell of logic and symbol was a private enchantment, and she found joy in the strangest of places: in the subtle symmetry of algebra, the cool logic of a differentiated equation, the perfect impossibility of the square root of minus one. Beyond these lay other things, half-glimpsed, half-grasped, as inexpressible as light to one who's always been blind, or darkness to one reared in the light. Her love of shadows refined itself, reduced and focused to the simple wish to fill a page with symbols, to heal the empty whiteness of the paper with the balm of black and, in doing so, to explain her world. She ceased to be nothing more than a girl with an odd liking for the dark and became someone as defined as her beloved equations, as explicable as she believed the world to be. She became a mathematician.

'She's clever!' moaned her mother, thinking of all the clever people she'd known and how little she'd liked them.

'She's clever,' sneered her teachers, who thought her too clever by half.

'She's clever,' murmured her mother's friends, thankful that their own daughters were not.

'She's clever!' exclaimed the Aunt, since she had aspirations to cleverness herself.

She was clever enough to care for no-one's opinion but her own, and so she continued in her own contained way as seasons came and went, seasons not only of the year but of the generation. She immersed herself in the more arcane regions of mathematics, the matrices in more than four dimensions, and chaotic equations that defined the effect of one beat of a butterfly's wing on the weather two centuries hence. She dealt in paradigms, breathed propositions, and had such a familiarity with probability that she shouldn't have been as surprised as she was when the unpredictable, the unequatable happened.

He was shorter than her, short-sighted too, hair thinning on a high forehead. He was a physicist who specialised in galactic origins and spoke only Italian. Naturally, she fell in love.

'It comes from being brought up in a dysfunctional family,' complained her mother, who didn't like the man and who'd learned this concept, if little else, from the long-gone psychiatrist.

'She'll live to regret it,' said her mother's friends, seeing a man with a string of degrees and not much else.

'His thesis is unsubstantiated,' sneered her Professor, since there's as much snobbery in the world of physics as in any other.

'I'm sure she'll learn Italian in time,' said the Aunt, but doubtfully, for she'd never, herself, fallen in love.

She ignored them all, failed to learn Italian and, for a brief season, took pleasure in the grey of a certain pair of eyes, the flesh tones of olive skin, the brown of untidy hair. It was colour of a sort, neither vivid in hue nor light in tone, but colour nevertheless. But, after a season, the initial flare of excitement was gone, the cresting wave ebbed back into the tide, and the intrigue of symbols overwhelmed her transient interest in exploring sensations not hitherto aroused. And yet the physicist offered more than that. He had a poetry that went beyond the mere tumescence of the flesh, beyond the confines of language. He spoke of supersymmetry and duality states, of unifying theories and the microsecond after the creation of the universe when everything had been dark. He plucked the harp-strings of a mind that began to sing with the music of the spheres.

The two of them had their own duality state, a reflection of ideas and a shared love of something that was inexpressible in terms of current mathematical models. They pledged themselves to one another's expertise and set off hand in hand for the bowels of the earth, to a place carved deep within the mountains near his native Italy, a torus enveloped by vast magnets and cooled to degrees unimaginable. There, fragments of atoms were cleaved still further and bombarded into elements too dense to have survived the creation of the world. There, like Orpheus and Eurydice, they lived out a span of years deep below the earth, in a Hades that was heaven at least to her, where she could not only live, when she chose to, in a world entirely dark, but could explore its very nature.

And so she did, this strange girl who loved the dark and wanted to understand it from the moment of its creation – for it was older than the light – to its ending, sucked back into the black hole of its own birth. But birth and life have their own inevitable end, and, when she found time to look up from her contemplation of the season of the Universe, she found that her life had its own season too. Time, however it might fold and twist in the curved plane of space, for her ran straight as a die towards its end. She realised there were limitations to what she might achieve, that time itself might trick her, that she might never have enough of it to solve the mysteries that so enchanted her. Belatedly, she realised she wasn't immortal. And so, sensing that time was running out like sand in an hourglass, her love of the dark turned to obsession.

Her lover shared it for a while but, like Orpheus, sweet singer of theorems and hypotheses, he began to long for the light, for the adulation of his peers, for the adulation, more specifically, of a certain red-haired graduate student who liked beer and had an uncomplicated smile. And so he left.

'I knew it,' said her mother with grim satisfaction, remembering how often she herself had been left.

'It's probably for the best,' murmured her mother's friends, a sentiment echoed by the Aunt.

And perhaps in one sense it was, for in freeing himself her lover had also set her free to follow her own course, to explore the creeks and inlets of the dangerous coast that lies between the high lands of physics and the deep ocean of advanced mathematics. She visited territories as yet uncharted, mapped their shoals and over-falls, and finally, one day or night, in what might have been December, or could equally well have been June, she let slip the anchors of her mind and set out for the deep ocean, for the distant possibility of land. She left no word of her going, no record of her course, just scribbled notes, a diary filled with symbols and, here and there, the occasional word that might have been poetry, or music, or both.

'I loved her best of all!' wailed her mother, not certain if she'd loved her at all.

'She was such a clever girl,' mourned her mother's friends, implying as they did so the cause of her demise. *Too clever*, they thought, *for her own good*.

'It is as I predicted,' said the psychiatrist with private satisfaction, since he still had the case notes and scented a possible book, film rights, fame.

'I hold myself responsible,' wept the physicist in Italian, finding solace in the arms of the red-haired graduate student.

'Can I see her?' asked the Aunt, the only one of them not to regard her as dead.

She visited her in the place they'd taken her body, her mind hanging by a thread, a quiet place in the foothills of the mountains not far from the great chamber in the earth. She was vacant and seemed far away but was as calm and contained as ever. The Aunt, thinking to spark some pleasant memory, handed her the notebook with its symbols and words, and the girl who loved the dark picked it up, leafed through it page by page, traced the symbols with a questing finger and stroked the pages, once white, now healed by the balm of black. And then she smiled.

The Aunt didn't return the smile and never again visited her in the alpine sanatorium. That smile haunted her until she died, for she'd looked into the eyes of one who walks forever far from the light, who has travelled in her mind to the outer reaches of the universe, to the beginning and ending of eternity. Who has seen what lies there.

And understands why.

What's in a Name?

'My name is Perseus,' said Percy Henderson on his first day at Rockwell Junior School.

'Perseus?' Mrs Braithwaite looked down at him over the top of her glasses, and Percy's heart sank.

'It's Greek,' he said desperately, although he could see that his name had already been written at the bottom of her list. *Percy Henderson*

'It's my Dad,' he explained, lowering his voice. The rest of the class were staring at him, and they didn't look a friendly lot. 'He teaches at the University,' he whispered. 'And my mum . . .' Mrs Braithwaite bent forwards. '. . . she *reads*.'

Actually, Percy read too, but he wasn't going to admit it to Mrs Braithwaite. Just imagine if she announced to the class, 'This is your new classmate, Percy, who *reads*.' He'd die! It was bad enough being shorter than average, having ears that stuck out and needing to wear glasses, without getting a reputation for being brainy. It was bad enough being called Percy.

'It's a very good name,' his Dad had said when he'd asked if he could change it to something else such as Wayne, or Scott or Virgil. 'It dates back to the middle-ages.'

'It doesn't matter what you're called, Perc,' said his Mum. 'You'll still be you.' Which just went to show that, in spite of all that reading, she knew *nothing*! It *did* matter what he was called! If he turned up at his new school calling himself Percy, he'd be for it. Percys always came to a sticky end in all the books he'd read. Usually they were eaten by wolves. So there was only one thing for it, he decided; he'd have to look for a new name. Eventually he found just the thing in 'Boys' Own Book of Myths and Legends' – Perseus, who was a hero and who might have been called Pers for short. So Percy borrowed his name, and all he had to do was convince Mrs Braithwaite there had been some mistake.

She looked at him and Pers looked back, his heart thumping, his mouth dry. Eventually, however, she smiled, scored out 'Percy' in the register and wrote 'Perseus' instead.

'Well, Perseus, I suppose you'd better sit beside Jason, since he's named after a Greek hero too. Although I don't imagine his mother was thinking about Greek mythology . . .'

Percy, now officially Perseus, eyed the boy he was introduced to. He was taller than Pers and looked tough.

'My friends call me Jase,' the boy said coolly when Mrs Braithwaite had gone back to her desk, making it clear that Pers wasn't being invited to call him Jase just yet.

'Mine call me Pers,' said Pers nervously. 'Jason was a Greek hero too, wasn't he?'

'Was he?' asked Jason, interested now. 'What did he do then, this Jason?'

Pers thought back to Boy's Own Myths and Legends and remembered it had something to do with a sheep but didn't think that would go down too well. So he improvised. 'He fought lots of battles and won them all.'

'Cool!' said Jason. 'What did Perseus do then?'

Pers didn't think it would be wise to claim to be a winner of battles as well. 'Oh, he just fought a monster,' he said modestly. 'And saved a Princess. She was called Andromeda.' Then inspiration struck him. 'My sister's name's Andromeda, but she likes to be called Andy.'

Jason rolled his eyes. 'Girls!' he sniggered, and Pers sniggered with him. They were best of friends after that.

His sister was actually called Andrea, but she did indeed like to be called Andy, which was stupid since Andrea was a perfectly good name. But then his sister *was* stupid. She wasn't like him at all. Her ears didn't stick out and she didn't wear glasses. She didn't read either but that was OK apparently because she was 'gifted'. She played the piano and took lessons from a scary woman called Mrs Gordon, who had a big hooked nose and hair like the steel wool he cleaned his bike with. She smelled funny, like Great Aunty Dora. Pers was glad he didn't have to do piano lessons, and he knew Andy was scared of her.

'One, Two, Three! One, Two, Three!' Mrs Gordon would shout out, keeping the beat with her walking stick. He'd listened at the door and heard her telling Andy off for sloppy fingering. Andy had rushed out crying, just like a girl.

Pers' Mum had calmed her down, but later that day Pers had overheard his Mum and Dad discussing it.

'Poor Andy!' said his mum. 'I wonder if we shouldn't try to find another teacher. I know Mrs Gordon is meant to be good, but she is a bit of a gorgon.'

Pers' ears pricked up. A Gorgon? Of course! Why hadn't he realised? He got out 'Boys Own Book of Myths and Legends' and checked the details. Yes, he'd been right; Perseus had saved Andromeda from a Gorgon, a fearsome creature who turned anyone who looked at her to stone. So Perseus had to save his sister from Mrs Gordon who was obviously a Gorgon in disguise.

It wasn't going to be easy, he discovered, for according to the story he was going to need lots of equipment. In his book Perseus had been given it all by some Goddess, but Pers didn't know any Goddesses – except maybe Mrs Braithwaite, and he didn't think he could ask her – so he was forced to improvise. The reflective shield wasn't too difficult – a chopping board covered with aluminium foil. He also found his sword in the kitchen – his mother's best carving knife, which he knew to be extremely sharp, for hadn't she told him never to touch it? He put both shield and sword into a plastic bag. The winged sandals were more of a problem, but the budgie hadn't been dead all that long and he could always bury the wings again later.

Thus equipped, he sallied forth, keeping a low profile (in the absence of a helmet of invisibility), but Mrs Gordon's garden, when he reached the house, had lots of bushes, so he was as invisible as it was possible to be. He approached the house and skirted around the side. 'I'll just have a quick look,' he told himself, trying to ignore the butterflies in his stomach. Gorgons, according to his book, were tricky creatures.

He'd just about convinced himself that it might be best if he came back another day, or when he was older, when he spotted an open window. He hesitated, tempted to run, but he knew Perseus wouldn't have run away. Pers had borrowed his name, after all, so he'd have to be brave. He crept closer and peered over the edge – and there she was! The Gorgon sat at the window, her back to the garden. An easy target.

It turned out, however, that looking at the Gorgon in the crinkled surface of his mirrored shield wasn't as easy as he'd expected. He knew, of course, that if he looked at her directly he'd be turned to stone; the book had been quite clear about that. The fact that not only he but his entire family had looked at Mrs Gordon lots of times without even the slightest feeling of stoniness just showed that even Gorgons had days off. Today, however, he'd come upon her alone, so he wasn't taking any chances.

Manoeuvring himself with his makeshift mirror, he took aim at the head and raised his sword. It should just take one good sweep of the blade. She'd grow her head back again later, of course. Gorgons did that; his book had said so. But it would put her off for a bit, he thought. She couldn't come around to their house with no head, couldn't shout out 'one, two, three, one, two, three,' with no head. He gritted his teeth, closed his eyes, and wondered, for a brief guilty moment, if it would hurt, then took one tremendous swipe. He felt the head topple. There was surprisingly little blood and no sound at all. His sword must have been just as sharp as his mother had always warned him.

'Cool!' he said, pleased that his first slaying of a monster had been such a clean kill, and wondered if he might be a dragon-slayer when he grew up. Still looking in his mirror, he reached out to pick up the head. The snakes felt horrible as they coiled themselves around his fingers, but he plunged the head into his plastic bag and ran home as fast as his legs could carry him.

The head banged against his leg as he ran. It was remarkably light, and, remembering a lesson about dinosaurs, he wondered if Gorgons kept their brains in some other part of their bodies. He'd cut the head open when he got home, he decided, just to see. Then he'd stuff it, mount it on a board, and take it to show Mrs Braithwaite. She'd tell the class the story of Perseus and the Gorgon and get out the head at the end. 'And here's one Pers brought in to show us,' she'd say casually. Pers could imagine the muffled gasps of horror and admiration. He'd just shrug, he decided, and say nothing. Scott Pritchard, whose father was a taxidermist and who was always bringing things in, would be as sick as a parrot. Pers clutched the bag tightly, imagining these future pleasures, and hoped the snakes wouldn't escape.

'What have you been up to?' demanded his Mum when, breathless, he arrived home with his trophy. 'Mrs Gordon has just been on the phone!'

How had she managed that, Pers wondered, with no head? Surely she couldn't have grown it back already? He glanced at the bag, which turned out to be a mistake.

'What have you got in that bag? And what's that on your trainers?'

'Nothing,' he muttered, edging back towards the door. His mum had been fond of the budgie.

She gave him an 'I won't ask' look. Relieved, he loosened his grip on the bag – another mistake – and she snatched it from him.

'Don't look!' he yelled, knowing the penalty for staring at a Gorgon's head, but it was too late. His mother looked into the bag and turned to stone. She remained, not moving, for a very long time. Finally, however, she looked up, took in the wings stuck with superglue to his trainers, the foil-covered chopping board, and the carving knife Pers was trying to conceal behind his back, and sort of choked.

'Well done, Percy,' she said in a funny sort of voice. Then she pulled his trophy from the bag. 'But how am I going to explain this to Mrs Gordon?' She held up to Pers' fascinated gaze a polystyrene head, slightly damaged around the neck region, crowned with a wig the texture and colour of steel wool.

His Mum's explanation must have fallen on deaf ears, or perhaps it was because she couldn't stop laughing, because Mrs Gordon decided that Andy's talents – or lack of them – would be better suited to another teacher, and they never saw her again. So Perseus saved Andromeda from the Gorgon after all.

His Dad, a stickler for detail, explained that he'd got the story all mixed up, then gave him a lecture about the importance of being able to tell the difference between stories and reality. He made Pers promise not to go in for any more heroics. Pers promised and handed over 'Boys' Own Book of Myth's and Legends'. (He'd finished it anyway.) Instead, he started reading 'Tales from Shakespeare', which pleased his Mum. The histories were dead brilliant!

'My name is Percy,' he announced on his first day at Rockwell Senior School. 'Harry Percy, but you can call me Hotspur . . .'

Heartwood

H e stands in the open doorway of his workshop and examines the bowl in his hands. The light is better there, and he tilts it to and fro to catch the pattern of the grain. The shaded lines mark the seasons of the wood, thick ones and thin ones that tell of wet summers, harsh winters, or mild extended springs. But the look of the bowl isn't the only thing that's important. He judges it also by touch, and so he feels for rough places in the flow of the grain or the curve of the rim, but finds none. It's as good as anything he's made.

Yet still he stands in the doorway, turning the bowl between hands that tell their own story. There are chisel cuts on his fingers and raised lumps, made by hammers, on his knuckles. His skin is dry from the wood-dust, his nails split and stained with oils. Idly, he wonders if there are deeper invisible marks inside him. Does he, like the wood he works with, have rings to mark the setbacks and triumphs, the seasons of joy, that one stark discontinuity and the years of grief that followed?

He goes back into the workshop and lays the bowl beside the others. They are made of beech and walnut, elm and ash, and all are smoothed to a gleam and marked with the sign of the acorn by which he's known. It was a hobby once. Now it's a living, if not a life. No, not a life.

He wraps each bowl in tissue paper and places them in a cardboard box, intending, later in the week, to take them to the gallery in town that sells his work. When he's finished, he goes back to the doorway, empty handed now, to watch the evening fall. As the autumn day draws to a close, the shadows slide from the canopy of trees beyond his garden and slip down their trunks before running swiftly across the lawn towards him. He stands there, night lapping at his feet, waiting for the girl to come.

The cottage is set back from the road that loops around the forest before heading for the village, some five miles away. Further on, out of sight beyond a low rise of hills, is the town. So the cottage, while peaceful, isn't entirely isolated. 'Conveniently situated', the estate agent had declared, 'with extensive outbuildings'. These had proved to be two draughty leaking shacks, but nevertheless a cottage close to an ancient forest, with enough space for a workshop, was too good an opportunity to be missed by a wood-turner with no-one to please but himself, and he'd taken up residence in the spring. By the end of summer he'd sorted the place out and had begun to produce the turned wooden bowls for which he has a small but growing market. He's content, he decides. Not happy, but then he doesn't expect to be. He's lonely at times, but that doesn't concern him. It's safer to be lonely. You have less to lose.

He hadn't thought much about it when he'd first seen the girl, other than regarding it as odd to see anyone at all in the forest – *his* forest, as he's come to think of it since he seems to have the place to himself. Actually, that isn't so surprising. Apart from the track to his cottage, there are no roads or paths that lead to the woods, and it's too far from the village for dog-walkers or ramblers. And so the forest remains a charming wilderness of ancient trees clothed with moss and festooned with lichen, where vague paths wander aimlessly, disappearing when he least expects them to and never seeming to be in the same place twice. Not long after he'd moved into the cottage he'd set himself the task of making a map of the forest and had begun to chart the glades and little streams, the stands of holly and pine. Eventually, however, he'd given up. Even the glades seem to shift with the paths, and he still comes across them unexpectedly, from strange directions, and, having found them once, can't always find them again.

The first time he'd seen the girl he'd been in one of those glades, a sunlit lawn starred with orchids. An old oak, dark and leafless, stood in the centre, stark against the summer greens of the rest of the forest. A little birch grew close by, stretching its pale trunk up into the oak's leafless crown. The oak was a huge specimen, hundreds of years old in all probability, but quite dead, its trunk hollow and cracked open. The heartwood had gone completely, and all that remained to support the vast canopy of branches was a layer of thickened bark. It was probably dangerous, but nevertheless, obeying some urge he couldn't explain, he'd clambered into one of the openings and found that he could stand upright in the centre of the tree. He'd stayed there for some minutes, bathed in a strange underwater light from the sunbeams that filtered through cracks higher up the trunk and moved and shifted with the wind. Maybe it was that odd shifting light, or perhaps it was the powerful smell of woody decay, but, whatever the reason, he'd felt faint and claustrophobic, as if the tree was closing in on him. Breathlessly, he'd climbed out of the oak, and it was then that he'd seen her.

She was standing beside the birch, one hand on its trunk, staring at him. She must have been surprised, frightened even, to see someone clamber out of the hollow oak. He'd felt foolish standing there, fighting to get his breath back. He'd tried to think of something to say, but he'd been alone so long that words no longer came easily to him, and, after a moment, the girl had whirled away and vanished. In some ways, he'd been relieved, and he'd gone back to the cottage, having made a mental note to return to the glade after the next gale to see if any of the bigger branches had fallen. Oak was always useful. That was before he'd realised how difficult it was to find his way around the forest. That was before the girl started to come to him.

He'd never been a ladies' man. Indeed, the very expression made him smile wryly. There had only been one woman in his life and always would be, even although she was gone now. He didn't want another. He didn't need that sort of complication, and, to begin with, he'd been annoyed when the girl had turned up. He'd come out of his workshop one evening and had seen her standing at the edge of the forest. But she didn't approach. She just stood there, looking at the cottage – at him? – before turning and vanishing into the trees.

That had been the beginning, but now she comes sufficiently often that he's taken to watching for her, although she still comes no nearer than the edge of the trees and never stays for long. He calls out to her, but he's not sure she understands. There's never a reply, and if he steps towards her she takes fright and backs off into the trees. She's a strange creature, thin and pale, with dark luminous eyes, in her late teens maybe, although it's hard to tell. He wonders where she lives, given that there's no house nearer to the forest than those in the village. He makes a few diffident enquires but learns nothing, and so she remains nameless, without history, without home. He comes to think of her as *his* girl, just as the forest is *his* forest, and he begins to look for her each evening and to worry about her when she isn't there, for she wears a flimsy dress and thin sandals, even although the nights are growing cold. He begins to feel responsible for her.

Tonight, after he's packed the bowls away, he waits and watches as usual, but she doesn't come. Oddly disturbed, he eventually gives up, since it's too cold to wait by the door any longer. Throughout the day, the wind has been rising, and now, with the fall of darkness, it begins to whine around the cottage, to roar in the canopy of the forest and make doors and windows rattle. It's the first storm of the autumn equinox, and he realises that there hasn't been wind of this strength all summer. He hopes the girl's all right.

The cry wakes him. Later, recalling the sound of it, he'll wonder why he thought of it as a cry. It's more like a groan of falling timber. He jerks awake, pulls on a dressing gown, and goes to the back door. The night is wild now, the forest roaring, the sky wind-torn, a half-moon riding the clouds. He sees the girl standing at the forest margin, but not as she normally does. This time she's agitated, wringing her hands, stepping forward a few paces then retreating again. And all the time that cry. He goes down the garden, and this time she doesn't turn and vanish, even when he opens the gate and walks towards her.

'What is it? Are you afraid of the wind?'

He's close enough to touch her now. The moon flashes through a rent in the clouds, and he sees her clearly. Her pale skin has a faint sheen to it. Her dark eyes seem to be all pupil, and her limbs are as thin and awkward as those of a new-born foal. He reaches out to take her arm, but she backs away and runs into the wood. He follows. He's followed before and always lost her, but this time she runs ahead of him then stops, looks back, and only sets off again once she's sure he's following. He stumbles over fallen boughs, tussocks of grass and trails of bramble, but each time he stumbles she stops and waits. He follows her until the night opens in a wash of moonlight, and he finds himself in the glade with the dead oak.

It's begun to break up. Even as he reaches the edge of the clearing, one of the upper branches crashes to the ground. The forest floor is littered with broken twigs, and one mass of broken branches lies hard against the little birch, crushing it against the oak. She gestures towards it, but he shakes his head. He can do nothing without the tools to cut away the branches.

'Come,' he says, holding out a hand. 'Come home with me.' Hesitantly, she puts her hand into his outstretched one. It's smooth, as if polished, the ridges of her skin as fine-grained as pear-wood. She lets him wrap her in his dressing-gown and lead her home. It's the first time he's thought of the cottage as home.

She stays all that winter. He makes no further effort to find out who she is. Loss will come. He knows it already, but, for the moment, he's content. He's even happy. She doesn't speak, doesn't seem to understand what he says, but she's not deaf. She likes to listen to the sounds he makes when he talks, and she makes her own sounds in reply, strange humming songs that make him want to weep. Her mood alters with the weather, he finds. The wind agitates her, the snow delights her, but the bitter cold turns her pale and listless. At those times, he wraps her in a blanket and lies down beside her in front of the fire. It's a coal-fire now; she can't bear it when he burns logs. She doesn't like his work either and never stays long in the workshop, but she's fascinated by the finished bowls and holds them in her hands, her fingers tracing the smoothness of their surface, much as he traces her limbs, searching for flaws and finding none.

It can't last, of course. He's known that from the start. Seasons come and go, leaving their rings behind in the heartwood. Spring comes. One day, feeling the warmth in the air and seeing the bulbs begin to push through the earth, he goes to his workshop and takes down his tools. This time he has no difficulty in finding the dead-oak glade. The winter has brought down more of the tree, but he clears the tangle of fallen wood away and cuts down the branches that lie against the birch. It's young still, little more than a sapling, and it springs back to stand tall again, pale-barked in the sunlight. The girl steps out from the edge of the glade and puts her hand on the trunk, holds another out to him. He shakes his head, his eyes blurring. By the time he's blinked away the tears, she's vanished.

She doesn't come again. He hadn't expected it, but he'd hoped. The cottage seems emptier than ever, more lonely. His work no longer contents him. He finishes his orders, wraps the bowls in tissue paper and takes them to the gallery as usual, but when he returns to the cottage that's no longer home, he doesn't begin his work once more. Instead, he collects all his off-cuts, his apple-wood and burr elm, his pine and beech. He judges the direction of the wind then builds them into a bonfire.

Later, they said it was asking for trouble – an open fire left unattended right next to a workshop full of wood. The fire burns out of control and spreads from the workshop to the cottage until it too is ablaze. The forest looks on impassively as the wind blows the sparks away, and by morning all that remains is a pile of smoking ash. He was a quiet man, they said, kept himself to himself. What was his name again? No-one had seen him all winter.

In the forest, should anyone go there, they might come across a glade with an old oak and a young birch and notice that the oak has begun to sprout once more, its twigs and leaves lacing through those of the little birch that grows close by. The great crack in the hollow trunk, into which a man could climb, has sealed itself up again, and slowly, patiently, the heartwood is growing back. It's a strange sort of living.

But it's a life.

The Gingerbread House

'**I**'m hungry,' said Greta, bursting into tears. 'And tired,' she wept, sitting down abruptly on the trunk of a fallen tree. 'And frightened,' she sobbed.

Hans wished she hadn't said that. It might make him feel frightened too. Although, of course, he wasn't. He was a boy, after all. But girls? One moment they were singing and picking flowers, the next sobbing uncontrollably. There were times when he envied them that simplicity. Times like this.

It was dark in the forest, even although the moon, high in a black sky, shone down through the branches of the trees that wove together in a cage of twigs. Thorns and brambles tugged at their clothes.

'And I'm cold,' announced Greta, slipping a hand into his. 'But we're not lost, are we?'

Hans wished she hadn't said that either. *Lost*. It had a frightening sound. Lost in the great forest that lay all around them, dark and still. Except it wasn't still. The moonlight deepened the shadows, made faces in the bushes and eyes in the undergrowth, eyes that watched and waited. An owl drifted from a branch, and Greta shrieked. There was a silence after the shriek, a listening silence into which sounds seeped slowly: the crackle of twigs, the cry of some night creature, the trickle of water between mossy banks and, far in the distance – or so Hans hoped – the howling of a lone wolf.

'We're not lost,' he said. 'We'll just follow this little path . . .'

'And then we'll be home?'

But they were leagues from home. Their grandfather had taken them deep into the forest and, unusually, had let them play in a clearing while he chopped and gathered firewood. The sound of his axe had grown more and more distant until it disappeared. He hadn't come back, even although they'd called and called.

'It's just a game,' Hans had said staunchly, knowing it wasn't. The villagers had been giving them strange looks recently. Men and women had turned away to hide their faces or had looked at them harder than usual. Their grandfather had listened grimly to their grandmother's whispering and turned silent. And now they were lost, as others had been, other children on a moonlit spring night such as this. Hans had always wondered why the lost children hadn't been able to find their way back. Why hadn't they followed the little paths as he and Greta were doing?

'We'll soon be home. Look! The path's wider here!'

Indeed, the path was no longer a fox run. Instead it was a track made by a larger animal that had left a strange elusive scent: not the musk of fox or deer or boar but something sweeter than those. A trail of moisture gleamed in the moonlight and edged leaves and twigs with crystal. The smell grew stronger and seemed to come from the ground itself, spongy sticky earth beneath last year's crackling leaves.

Greta tripped, fell down, and got to her feet crying, her thumb going to her mouth. Then, to Hans' surprise, she stopped crying and proceeded to suck her other thumb. Then she licked both her hands, stooped to the ground, scooped up a handful of earth and crammed it into her mouth.

'Gingerbread,' she said, her mouth full.

He pulled her hands away from her mouth. 'Don't be stupid!'

'But I'm hungry!'

'If you eat earth you'll die,' he said. Sometimes you had to make things very clear. 'Come on. There must be a clearing up ahead. It's brighter there.'

He pulled her along the track that was now broad enough for them to walk side by side. Perhaps, when they reached the clearing, he'd find enough wood to light a fire; he still had his tinderbox. There might even be a charcoal burner's hut to shelter in, or a house with kindly people who'd let them sleep in a barn. Perhaps they'd give them something to eat. Hans' stomach growled at the thought, and the spicy smell that filled the air just made it worse. Gingerbread? What nonsense! He pushed his way past a bush, stepped into the clearing – and stopped in amazement.

'Gingerbread,' said Greta. 'I told you so.'

In the clearing stood a little house with brown walls, a brown roof, brown chimney pots and a little brown door. A mist hung about it and drifted towards them, a cloud of cinnamon and ginger, nutmeg and cloves. There was a caramel taste in the air that made Hans' stomach rumble even louder. Moonlight glinted on what looked like snow on the roof, but it was crispy white icing dusted with sugar. The children gazed entranced at the house and saw that it was made not only of gingerbread but of all the sweets they could possibly imagine and a few more than that. There was a little fence around the house made from barley sugar canes linked by ropes of liquorice. The twisting path was paved with slabs of toffee, and from the bushes hung bunches of cherry lips and sugared jellies.

Greta darted through the mint-crisp gate and, before Hans could tell her not to, broke a piece of chocolate from the edge of a window-frame. The snap of chocolate was loud in the sudden silence, and a shadow seemed to pass over the clearing. In its wake light blinked from the windows, and the door, that had been shut when they'd arrived, now stood a little ajar. Greta, having crammed herself with chocolate, was busy picking jellies from a bush.

Just one, Hans thought. *And then we'll go.*

But one jelly led to a little taste of liquorice rope, then a mouthful of barley-sugar, then a slab of toffee and a chunk of chocolate, and, before long, Hans was gorging himself with sweets so single-mindedly it was some time before he noticed that the door stood fully open.

He wondered who lived there and felt guilty about eating their house. But he and Greta were lost and hungry, and surely no-one who lived in such a wonderful place would begrudge them a few mouthfuls of cakes and sweets. He imagined an apple-cheeked woman with flour on her apron, a rolling pin in her hand and a warm oven in her kitchen, and he stepped through the door, intending to apologise for eating her house.

The door closed gently behind him, leaving him in near darkness. Little light penetrated the red and yellow windows of glazed fruit boilings, but what light there was shone, not on the room he'd expected, but on a cave, a place more magical, if anything, than the outside of the house.

The walls were made of nougat, studded with nuts and cherries and other fruits, and there were stalactites of buttered mint and horehound hanging from the roof. Syrup dripped down the walls, together with treacle, honey and molten butter. The floor was as shiny and translucent as a wine-gum, and it sloped downwards to a dark opening at the back of the cave, into which the liquids flowed and from which came a breath of air that smelled of violets and mint and aniseed.

Hans looked around in wonderment as his eyes adjusted to the faint light. He saw gobstoppers lying on the floor, blue and green and brown, and there were jelly-babies, bigger than any he'd ever seen, their faces finely detailed. He peered at one; the face reminded him of a girl from the village. But she'd vanished many years before . . .

Hans ran for the door and tried to pull it open, but the door was shut fast, and the chocolate handle just melted in his hand. Then the floor heaved beneath him, throwing him to the ground. He landed in a pool of butter, rolled towards the wall of nougat, and found himself face to face with . . . a face. It was embedded in the nougat with the cherries and nuts and . . . other faces. He pushed himself away, but the floor bucked and tilted as he tried to get to his feet. He began to slide down the stream of butter and syrup towards the back of the cave, into the darkness of sugar and spice. He scrabbled at the floor, trying to stop himself, but his fingers gripped on nothing but rolling gobstoppers. One was bright blue, like an eye.

Something hard dug into his chest; it was his tinder box, still in his pocket. He grabbed hold of a horehound stalactite, pulled himself to his feet, then opened his tinderbox and struck a spark. The cave flinched. Once more, he struck a spark, and this time it fell into a pool of molten butter which caught light and began to smoke. The cave shrieked, and the floor trembled beneath him. He struck another spark and started another little fire. Smoke bloomed, acrid and overpowering, and Hans hoped he wasn't going to suffocate. He lit a fire close to the door, then another. The flames began to melt the chocolate, and eventually the door became soft enough for Hans to force his way through. He grabbed Greta by the arm and dragged her down the toffee path, through the gate, across the clearing and into the safety of the cold dark forest.

'I feel sick,' said Greta, who did indeed look very pale. Her face was smeared with chocolate, and her lips were stained with cola drops. Hans too felt sick but not because of what he'd eaten. It was because he knew where all the children had gone, the children who'd been lost and hungry, who'd eaten from the magic house and been eaten in their turn. He wondered how long the house had been there, how long the villagers had been sending children into the forest to feed it. In the centre of the clearing the house gleamed in the moonlight, trembling a little, puffs of smoke coming out of the door, but the fires had gone out, blown away by the house's breath. The windows glinted maliciously.

'Come on, Greta. Let's gather all the wood we can find!'

They gathered fallen branches, twigs and dried grass, and piled it in a big circle around the house. Then Hans set fire to it with his little tinder box. The fire flickered and caught, swept around the circle and sprang high into the night sky. Within the circle, the house shrieked and shook, but the children fed the flames, and, slowly but surely, the house began to melt, toffee and chocolate flowing into a sticky pool until that too caught fire. Eventually there was nothing left but a spitting boiling mass of burnt sugar and a cloud of smoke and spice and heat.

'Let's go home,' he said. They set off, following the little paths, and by daybreak they'd found their way back to the village. Their grandfather cried when he saw them. His eyes and nose were red, as if he'd been crying for a night and a day. But their grandmother just looked grim.

'We'll have to send another two,' she muttered.

'No. It's gone,' Hans said. 'I . . . I killed it. I burnt it to the ground. There's nothing left.'

'All of it?' demanded his grandfather. 'Every last scrap?'

'Every last scrap and crumb.'

His grandfather cried again then went to tell the villagers they were free at last of the thing in the forest that for generations had demanded its tithe of their children.

'Free at last!' they shouted, clapping Hans on the shoulder and kissing Greta who didn't understand. But then, she was a girl.

'When are we going back to that nice house?' she asked.

'Never!' Hans laughed. Greta's face fell, but after a moment she brightened, remembering something, and turned to their grandfather.

'Here, Grandfather,' she said, putting her hand into her pocket. 'I brought you a piece of gingerbread.'

But it slipped out of her hand and fell to the ground where, beneath their horrified gaze, it shivered and trembled for a moment, then slowly dissolved, seeping its way into the earth.

Where, with a sigh of spice and sugar, it began to multiply once more . . .

The Lyall Bequest

T he day had come, the day on which my life was to change. I'd known for
months, years even, had been conscious of it hanging in my future,
approaching gradually to begin with, then with surprising speed. But the
details had been blurred, and I'd never known what shape it would take,
whether it would be a day of shadow or of light. In the end, however, what
happened was so different from my imaginings that it acquired the
insubstantial, drowning quality of a dream. Or nightmare.

You'll have heard, of course, of the Lyall Bequest, the largest collection of
mediaeval artefacts in Europe. It was *my* collection, my life's work, but on that
day I was to sign away my treasures into the hands of strangers. This act of
cession had been long in the planning, for I was old and had no heirs. The
thought of death had plagued me in recent years, so perhaps the bequest was
my one bid for immortality. With that in mind, I'd chosen the museum to be
the recipient of my gift, a gift so hedged about with conditions that they'd
grown reluctant. In the end, however, they'd agreed to all my demands: the
annexe they'd build for my collection and my power of veto over every detail of
its construction. It had been a long and bitter fight, but now it was over, and
that day I was to see, for the first time, my collection in the setting I'd fought
for. There was to be a lunch to celebrate and a private view. Naturally, I was to
be the guest of honour.

I should have been triumphant, and yet I wasn't. A sense of loss depressed
my spirits and made me reluctant to take that final step. So I dismissed my
chauffeur and set out to walk the short distance between my house and the
museum, hoping that air and action would allow me to come to terms with
what was now too late to change.

It had been many years since I'd walked those narrow streets, and they
were unfamiliar now, darker and dirtier than I remembered, full of unexpected
alleyways and turnings. Within minutes, I'd lost myself in the labyrinth of
lanes and passages, and my footsteps slowed and faltered, until I found myself
turning, as if by instinct, towards the one place that had any meaning for me in
all that squalor – an antiques shop.

It was an unprepossessing place, with paint peeling from the door in long
strips like the bark of a maple. The old and uneven glass in the windows,
silvered with grime, reflected the grey street with a queasy shimmer. The
placed appeared to be unfrequented, judging from the stiffness of the door,
and I wondered how long it had been since anyone else had crossed the
threshold. A bell jangled somewhere in the shadows, but no-one came, so I
was free to look around the dusty chaos of leaning chairs and stacked frames,
of boxes of books and piles of fabric. Almost without thinking, I put a price to
everything I saw and concluded that I could, had I wished, have bought the

entire contents of the shop for less than a thousand pounds. This had been a waste of time, I decided, and, as I was in danger of being late, I turned to leave.

It was then that I saw it, perched on a pile of books and gleaming in a fitful ray of light. One glance and my life was torn from its smooth and gentle slide down the slopes of comfortable old age and forced into a new and thorny path that led I knew not where. I felt as if I'd been borne down by a childhood fever, that a virus was spreading in my blood, multiplying cell by cell until I was reduced to a burning seethe of infection. I had one thought, one need – to possess this object – and I knew, with a clear knowledge born of that conflagration, that there would be no relief from this, no cure, no dulling of the pain. I felt, quite simply, that were I not to have it, I would die.

Yet it was nothing more than a simple wooden bowl worn smooth with age. It was encased in a network of silver into which were set crude pearls and garnets, topazes and jet: cheap jewels in a cheaper setting. It was neither beautiful nor functional; the wood was cracked and it sat unevenly on its silver stem. It was of doubtful provenance, a late copy of an earlier artefact no doubt, and, having no intrinsic beauty, could be of little interest to someone of my educated tastes. There was no reason at all for me to want it, and yet I did, most desperately. My eyes grew soft at the lines of it, the curve of stem and bowl, the gleam of pearls and the baleful wink of garnets. I felt my arms stretch out, the skin on my palms burning and clammy with the ache to touch, to cup it in my hands.

'May I be of assistance?'

The voice, thin and reedy as if long unused, came from behind me. He must have been standing in the shadows watching me, a man older than myself, small and dark-skinned, with the high cheekbones and prominent nose of the Ashkenazi Jew. He seemed oddly familiar, and his face teased at my memory as if I'd seen it in another context.

'What is it that you want?'

He limped towards me in a slow arthritic shuffle, until he was close enough to reach out and touch my sleeve. Suddenly I was afraid, but not of him, for he was old and frail. I was afraid that it wouldn't be as simple as it ought to be. I knew how it should go, the pavane I'd danced so often, the side-stepping and weaving around price and provenance, the advancing and retreating, the hints of compromise and resignation, the final shaking of hands. It was a process that could take the best part of the morning with, at its heart, the assumption that I wouldn't care too much, that I was prepared to lose. But, on this occasion, I wasn't.

'The bowl,' I began, breaking the first of my rules by mentioning it at all.

'Ah!'

'How much do you want for it?' With that I broke the rest of my rules. But I'd pay anything and had no wish to bargain. I was rich enough to buy it ten times, a hundred times, over.

'You know what it is?'

In truth I'd given no thought to that. I, who can date most objects to within a decade, was unsure even of its century.

'Yes' I lied, not caring that my impatience would be doubling the price. 'How much?'

He made a gesture, an elaborate shrug of sorrow and resignation. 'It's not for sale.'

I tried to laugh. 'I'm sure I can make it worth your while.'

He peered at me with red-veined eyes, taking in my cashmere coat, my silk scarf, the heavy gold on my wrist. He was pricing me up, or so I thought.

'I'm sure you could. If it was for sale. If it was mine to sell.'

At his words, hope glimmered.

'Does it belong to someone else?'

He laughed a dry laugh that sounded like twigs burning in the heart of a fire.

'No-one *owns* it!'

He wheezed with laughter as if the idea of someone owning the bowl was unbearably funny. He laughed so much I began to think he was not right in the head. Then he turned away, still cackling, and began to drift back into the shadows of the shop.

'Wait!' I tried to stop him by clutching at his arm. 'I'm really very . . . interested in the bowl. Look, it can only be worth a couple of hundred at the most, but I collect this sort of thing, so I'll give you a thousand. That's more than generous! What do you say?' I was past pride, ready to beg if I had to, but he slipped out of my grasp as if he was made of smoke and disappeared into the shadows. Only his voice remained.

'It's not for sale. It can't be *bought!*'

In his voice was the same agony that flexed its way through my blood. We were like the survivors of a train disaster, bound in some way to the object of our pain. I knew that he'd once felt what I felt then, the terrible desire to possess the bowl, a desire that had consumed him and dried him to a husk. The bowl possessed him, not he it. I was no longer afraid. I was terrified.

I fled that place, running as I'd not run in years, only stopping when I neared the museum and the wheezing in my chest reminded me that I was no longer young. I'd forgotten why I was there, had fled merely to a place of familiarity, had sought out faces I'd recognise in the board room where we'd arranged to meet. I was trembling and pale and felt so unlike myself I thought everyone must notice. But no-one saw anything beyond their own concerns.

The Director, Mansfield, and his staff were visibly nervous at my late arrival. A couple of members of the Arts Council chatted together, deliberately ignoring me. An MP, whose name I couldn't bring to mind, looked pointedly at his watch, and Travinger, my lawyer, eyed me speculatively, judging my lateness to be some last-minute ploy he couldn't quite fathom. Their self-obsession calmed me somewhat, and I was able to mutter some excuse and wave Travinger on. And so the business began, but I listened with little attention to the words I'd paid him to twist on my behalf and signed without a glance the documents so carefully crafted to a labyrinth of words. Gradually, as I listened to clause and sub clause, I recovered my poise and almost began to believe I'd dreamt the whole thing – almost, but for the viral pulse of desire in my veins.

I beckoned Travinger aside before we went in to lunch. 'There's an antique shop on the corner of Church Lane and Willow Passage. Find out who owns it or rents it, would you, who holds the mortgage, any debts. The usual sort of thing.'

I don't pay Travinger to have scruples, and he'd acted on my behalf in similar circumstances, but on this occasion he looked at me in surprise.

'That's just a piece of waste ground. I believe the Council have plans for a car park, but I'll certainly find out if you're interested.'

I felt sick. It must have shown in my face, for he put a hand out to me, but I waved him away and allowed Mansfield to usher me into the room in which we were to have lunch. For a moment, I considered making my excuses and leaving, but I was afraid to go past that place, to find out that the shop was no longer there. Or that it was. And so I stayed, allowed wine to be poured into my glass and food to be placed on the plate before me. But I ate little and drank less, for the food, so carefully chosen, was like ashes in my mouth, and the wine, rare and perfectly balanced as I knew it would be, tasted of vinegar. I toyed with the wine, turning the glass in my fingers, oblivious to the babble of conversation around me, and thought of the smooth curve of the bowl I so longed to hold in my hands.

It couldn't be bought, he'd said. Perhaps, then, it was only a question of waiting. He was an old man, fragile with age, close, surely, to death. But, feeling the ache of desire in my veins, I wasn't sure I could wait that long. I stared into the blood-red depths of the wine and wondered what it would take to stop the beating of an old and ailing heart. I crumbled a piece of bread between my fingers and thought of bones and skull and how easily they might be crushed. I knew then that the bowl and the wanting of it had changed me more than I'd imagined. It was drawing me towards an act so formidable it unnerved me. I swallowed the last of the wine, hoping it might give me courage.

'Are you ready?' The words came from a long way off. I supposed I was as ready as I ever would be.

'It's the only way.' I tried, without success, to excuse myself.

'You won't regret it, I assure you.'

Then I realised it was Mansfield speaking, that he was waiting for me to lead the way to the private view. This was to have been the culmination of the day, my hour of triumph, and yet I felt more hopeless in that moment than I could ever imagine feeling. The loss of my treasures, which had so occupied my mind that morning, now seemed of little import, so changed was I by the day's events. But still I led the way, grateful, for the time being at least, that I needn't confront whatever it was I'd decided to do.

I don't know what I expected. To me the mediaeval period is both terrifying and exalting, a time of baseless poverty and high ideals, of legend colliding with history, a period when all the colours of pageantry emerged like flowers springing from the sombre earth of the Dark Ages. My collection was a reflection of those times, objects unearthed from a bloody past with traces of their history still clinging to them. To me they breathed the spirit of the age, and that spirit had been captured in the room that held them.

It was a high-ceilinged space set with windows inlaid with stained glass, and the air was pierced with spears of light, amber and ruby, emerald and sapphire. Within this airy network of colour were placed all the objects of my collection, and they seemed to float, gleaming and glowing with gold and ivory. Painted banners hung all around the walls, and I found myself standing within a circle of figures. Men and women from legend brushed shoulders with kings and bishops, saints and sinners. Mythical beasts entwined themselves around their legs, and in their hands they held objects that mirrored the collection beneath their feet: gold-chased swords, ivory bound missals, and manuscripts, their colours fresh and bright as if newly painted. The room whirled in a circle of treasures until I was dizzy and stupefied with wonder.

Then my eye was caught by a tableau of figures, knights by their dress, their arms outstretched towards an object that floated before them. Sunlight streaming through the red glass of the windows suffused it in a ruby glow until it appeared to be filled with blood. It was the bowl, my bowl.

It was the Grail.

I knew what legend said it to be: the chalice of a dying Christ, a symbol of the Eucharist, the one unattainable object. I'd no belief in such things and knew it to be a Dark Age myth appropriated by a later century, a strange fiction consigned to folklore by my more reflective age. Nevertheless, I was familiar with the story, for no student of the mediaeval can afford to discount its influence. It was the one great quest, the search for truth. I could see it in the faces of the men who gazed towards it, willing to risk their young and hopeful bodies and adventure themselves in its pursuit. None, according to the legend, had been pure enough to succeed and live to tell the tale. So what chance had I – long past the age for questing – of succeeding where they'd failed? I'd tried to buy it with gold, that being the only currency with which I was familiar, and of course I'd failed in that. Now, God help me, I was planning to take it by force. That course too must be doomed to failure. But what other way was there for me? Why had it called to me and filled me with a longing that couldn't be relieved?

I stared up at the tableau, searching for answers, and noticed, half-hidden in the group of heroes, a figure who didn't gaze, as they did, at the Grail, but who looked back to watch who came, as if he was on guard, an old man, small and dark-skinned, with the high cheekbones and prominent nose of the Ashkenazi Jew.

I think my heart stopped as I gazed up at him. I knew now why he'd seemed familiar, for I'd seen, as I'd demanded, all the sketches of the artwork for this room. I remembered being puzzled by that figure, not recalling at the time the older tale that now rang like a warning bell in my memory. There was nothing Christian about that story, the myth of a king wedded to a broken land, guarding in his failing years the one remaining symbol of power, while he waited for one to come who'd know how to use it, who could make the land whole once more. I recalled that, as each guardian grew frail, another would appear . . .

My bowels turned to ice, and my heart pounded in my throat. I knew then why I'd been called. My whole life had been nothing but a preparation for this moment, this place in time, this one decision. I felt the fever of desire leave my blood and transmute itself into something more remote. I became, in that instant, more than human. No-one tried to stop me as I left.

'You know what it is.' It was no longer a question.

'Yes.' I wasn't lying this time.

'I've guarded it for years, centuries. I forget how long.' His voice was thin and exhausted.

He picked the bowl up in his claw-like hands. It was dark in the shop, and yet his face was illuminated as if by the cold clear light of morning falling through red glass.

'Will you let me guard it now?' I asked, saying the words to bind me, words to set him free. I held out my aching hands.

It had neither weight nor texture, but the touch of it flared through my body like that first fire of desire, blinding me with its history, changing me cell by cell, molecule by molecule, into what I'd prepared myself to be – its Priest, its Guardian, its Fisher King. And when that transformation was over, when my vision returned, changed so that I saw the world only dimly as if through coloured glass, I found that he'd gone, that the shop had disappeared, that I stood by a pile of rubble behind a broken fence with litter blowing on the chill winter wind. In my hands I held an undistinguished wooden bowl, roughly set in silver and studded with crudely cut gems.

I took it back to the museum and insisted with what was left of my waning temporal power that it be included in the collection. And there it remains, an odd addition to an otherwise outstanding collection. It excites as little comment as does the old man who stands beside it, as if on guard. They say that giving up my treasures cracked my mind. They think me touched in the head but harmless. Gradually, they cease to notice me, and I fade from sight, as does the world to me, slipping behind tinted glass, until there is nothing but myself and the Grail.

But I have not gone. I have my own immortality, here in the shadows, while I watch and wait. Perhaps, in my time of guarding, one will come who knows its power, who will take it and wield it and restore the damaged world. Somehow, I think I'll wait in vain, but still I must remain, waiting and watching, until I can watch no longer. Another will come then, to take from me my burden and my delight. Another with gold in his eyes, fear in his mind, and an emptiness in the heart big enough to contain the Grail.

The Skies of Kansas

Martha stares up at the cloudless sky and thinks she sees a speck in the far distance. It's too big to be a bird, too small to be a plane. But when she blinks it's gone, leaving the sky empty and enormous.

She spends a lot of time looking skyward. Everyone does in Kansas. The sky has more life in it than the land, those great plains of fenced dust that green only briefly before bleaching themselves to ochre in the sun. It's as if the land has been crushed by the vastness of those skies, much as the Kansas folk are trampled by summer's heat, winter's rasp and the storm-clouds that tear apart the nights. But there are no storm clouds today, although it's the season for them. There's not a cloud in the sky. Not a speck.

In Kansas, change comes from the sky, not the land. It brought the dry wind that thickened Jonathan's lungs to rheum and shrivelled his body. The wind left nothing of him but a cage of bone blowing about the farm like tumbleweed. They'd buried him yesterday, the wind gusting out of an empty sky and drying up any tears Martha had been planning on shedding. The boy had wept though, his hand on her shoulder, and later they'd talked long into the night of what had been and might be, of the unnamed grave beneath the cottonwoods and the fenced-off hollow in the paddock where he'd never been allowed to play. It was an ending, that tale, a letting go that was a beginning too, one they'd both known had been coming. The farm's been failing for years and now it's time to let it go. She's sold the land to Garret Tucker, who owns the adjacent farm. He'll be over later to sign the papers, and then only the house will be hers, an ancient clapboard dwelling that sprawls in the shade of the cottonwood trees like an old yellow dog.

If one talks to God in Kansas – and Martha often talks to God – it's to something formless and less than benign, a being to be placated rather than praised, one who's only deigned to notice Martha once in the course of her life, the day she'd buried her son in that unnamed grave beneath the trees. She'd prayed on her knees in the dirt, the rain falling from a slate-coloured sky. They'd waited so long for this child, and it had lived for barely an hour.

Dusk had come early that leaden day, the heat of summer driving thermals high into the atmosphere, and clouds had towered in tumbled masses, bellies flashing and rumbling, rain driving from their trailing skirts. Lightning had struck close by, missing the house and the trees where she knelt and tearing a great hole in the paddock. They never spoke about what happened next, her and Jonathan, although in later years he'd point out reports in the paper of strange occurrences on the Kansas plains, of twisters that could lift a whole house into the sky and set it down in pieces half a county away. Sometimes living things would be carried – frogs and fish – scooped from some creek to rain down miles away in the middle of a field. Never a child though. That was never reported, never spoken about. The child was a gift, the impossible answer to a prayer, and not to be questioned.

Garrett Tucker arrives later that day, his pick-up stirring up the dust on the track to the house. He's a grey little man, gritty with the Kansas soil that gets into your skin and eyes, into your soul, a dry stick of a man with whom Martha has exchanged only a few words over the years. But he's not ungenerous; Kansas folk are like that. He's given her more for the land than it's worth. And now, after they've signed the papers, he lingers uneasily.

'You'll manage here on your own, Mrs Kent, you and the boy?'

'Oh, we'll manage just fine!'

Neither says what they think: that this parched land of dust and sky and horizons is no place for the young, that the City, a dark Metropolis of towers, will take her boy away.

'Thought he'd be here today,' Garrett Tucker says disapprovingly as he eases himself into his pick-up.

'Oh, he's around somewhere . . .' She smiles and glances up at the matte white bowl of sky. Later, when Garret Tucker's pick-up has turned off the driveway and onto the track, her smile fades.

Is it always like this? she wonders. *The setting free?* They don't tell you about that in the stories. They never mention the mothers, the ones who stand in doorways pretending to smile as they wave farewell to the sons they've sent away to war, to adventure, to unimagined horizons. But then aren't all sons their mother's heroes? No matter who they are or where they come from? Even those who're the answer to a prayer? Who've come from the sky itself? Or further than the sky? And just as on that rainy night, when she opened her arms to a stranger to take him into her heart, she'll open them once more to let him go, knowing something of his destiny and his strengths, which are superhuman, and his weaknesses, which are all too mortal.

She glances once more at the cloudless sky, which is no longer empty. A speck is hurtling through the air, too fast to be a bird, too small to be a plane, a speck that resolves itself to a boy who's a man now, ready to right wrongs, ready to take on the world.

'All settled, mother?' he asks, landing lightly beside her.

'All settled, Clark,' she says, patting him on the arm. Then she waves and holds her smile as he disappears once more into the great Kansas skies.

Tales from a Riverbank

Introduction

I grew up on the banks of the River Tay and still live there, so many of my stories are set along that river. They range from *One Gold Ring,* which takes place at the very source of the river, to *Fairway,* which is set at the mouth of the estuary where it meets the North Sea. The first three stories, *One Gold Ring, Feckless as Water* and *Being a Tree,* are linked stories which explore the interplay between members of the same family. *One Gold Ring* is about a man's relationship with his son following the death of his wife. *Feckless as Water* takes up the story of the man's son-in-law as he struggles to reignite his relationship with his own wife, while in *Being a Tree* we hear his wife's side of the story.

Imagining Silence is also set near the headwaters of the Tay and follows a composer as she walks the West Highland Way in an attempt to find herself following a separation from the man she loves. The story in *Backwater* takes place further down the river and is about a man trying to make sense of the loss of a child. Both *The Outing* and *Room with a View* take place in the City of Dundee. The former explores the difficulties a pensioner experiences as his memory begins to fail him, while in *A Room with a View* a young woman comes to understand the nature of her relationship with a much older man.

The last three stories in this section take place near or at the mouth of the River Tay. Like *The Outing, The Tower* is an exploration of memory, while in *A Bobble Hat in Blue,* a pensioner finds an unlikely solution to the cracks that are appearing in his marriage. *The Fairway,* the last of the River Tay stories, is set on a yacht sailing to the last buoy of the river and follows a woman as she tries to re-connect with her husband.

There is further information about each of these stories in the Appendix.

One Gold Ring

*O**nce upon a time there was a king who had a great love of gold . . .*
That's how it began, the story in the big blue book with the gold lettering, *Boys' Own Book of Myths and Legends.* It was my book once, before it became Michael's. The colour had faded with the years, and the spine had turned to grey. The letters were so worn you could barely see that once they'd been gold. But the stories were the same.

'Once upon a time there was a king who had a great love of gold,' Ellen used to begin. 'Just like your father.' She and Michael would look up to see if I was listening, and they would laugh, not cruel-like or critical, but indulgently, as if it was I who was the child, not Michael. They were close, Michael and Ellen. Perhaps too close.

It was nonsense, of course. I wasn't like that old king. I didn't want everything I touched to turn to gold. Not that a few gold bits and pieces wouldn't have come in handy in those days, the price we got for sheep being what it was, and the cost of living so much more. Although it was true that I loved gold, it wasn't for its value. No, I loved the metal for what gave it value, its gleam and colour, the way it was hard yet malleable, the way it didn't corrode but remained forever itself, and the fact that it was so rare it took hours of panning to collect even a few grains. I loved gold enough not to begrudge the hours I'd spent up to my knees in freezing water in the river that lay five hundred metres below where I stood, waiting for Michael to catch me up.

He was making heavy weather of it, but eventually, panting and gasping, he reached the crest. He was thirty years older than the boy who'd first been read that story, and I was thirty years older than the man who'd listened. Ellen would have been sixty.

'You need to take more exercise,' I said. 'Fancy letting your old Dad get ahead of you!'

'I thought I was going to die on that last bit.'

He stopped beside me, bent over and put his hands on his knees, trying to get his breath back. He was overweight, not badly but enough that you noticed.

'Tell you what,' I said. 'We'll come out every day you're here and climb the hill, and I guarantee that after a week you'll be back in shape.' He didn't reply, and I grew suspicious. 'You're staying the week, aren't you? You said you had a week's holiday.'

'Yes, but . . . well, you know how it is.' He peered up the ridge, into the sun, carefully not looking at me.

I didn't know how it was and didn't want to know. But I knew the reasons he'd give, because I'd heard them before. He'd made a commitment; he had responsibilities; I wasn't the only person in his life.

'I thought I'd come up next weekend,' he said, still peering into the sun. 'On

Sunday maybe.'

'All the way from Glasgow? Just for the day?'

'I like the drive. It's OK.'

'You don't have to, you know. I'm all right. I can manage. Julie will drop in.'

My children had been good to me since the funeral, coming to see me when they could, 'making sure I was eating', as they put it. But it wasn't my daughter I wanted, the daughter who lived just down the road with her three boys. It was my son, the one who lived and worked in Glasgow now, the boy who used to love the stories I'd loved, who'd seemed so like me, a chip off the old block, as the saying goes. Except it turned out he wasn't like me at all.

'I know you can manage,' he said as we headed up a grassy slope. 'I want to come. As long as you don't drag me up this hill again!'

'You used to like coming up here,' I said as we reached the little lochan and sat down on 'our' rock beside the outflow of the water.

'I like *being* here. I don't like the process of *getting* here. Helicopter me in and I'll come as often as you like.'

He was being flippant, although he knew I didn't like it, not here. This had always been a special place, Ben Lui's northern corrie where all the waters that seeped out of the hillside gathered in a little lochan before trickling over a rocky lip into a stream that collected other waters along its way. The stream fell noisily down a series of pools to the valley far below where it finally found itself a name – the Allt an Rund. Later, swollen with other waters, it was called the Cononish, then the Fillan, then the Dochart. Only when it had plunged into the loch at Killin, and headed eastwards from Kenmore, did it find its true name, the River Tay. Once, when Michael had been a boy, we'd gone to Carnoustie, and, gazing across the widening estuary with its banks and tides, I'd told him that the waters from our nameless lochan ended up there, flowing into the North Sea.

Now, close by the river's source, Michael bent down and scooped up a handful of gravel from the stream bed, spread it out over his palm and picked it over. There was granite in the gravel, and the planes of mica glittered in the sunlight, but it was fool's gold, not the real thing.

'You won't find gold like that. Not up here,' I pointed out.

'And how much gold have *you* found over the years?' He tilted his hand to let the gravel fall back into the stream.

'Enough,' I said, reluctant to tell him just how little 'enough' was.

'Flakes!'

'Flakes add up.'

'How much?'

'Two grams,' I said, stung by his scepticism.

'Two grams! Wow!'

I almost told him then. I shoved my hand into my pocket, reached down through the rubbish I carry with me – the rusted knife, the stub of a pencil, a hank of baler twine – to the thing that, heavier than the others, had sunk to the bottom of my pocket. The gold ring.

'It's enough,' I said, fingering the smooth curve of the ring, not realising I'd given him a way into the conversation I'd so far managed to avoid.

'Enough for what? Dad, you don't have a pension. You don't have any assets, not since you let the farm go. And you can't say panning for gold has made you rich. All you have is the house, and it's too big for you. You must be practical now that Mum's . . . passed away.'

'I'm all right. I can manage.'

'I know, but for how long? Julie wants you to go to live with her and Jake, but you wouldn't be able to stand it. The boys would drive you mad within a week.'

'They're good kids,' I protested, although they were nothing of the sort.

'They're little bastards! Just like their father, I'm sorry to say.'

I nodded. I'd never seriously considered going to live with Julie, Jake and the boys. But neither had I considered the alternative Michael had suggested. Not in the circumstances.

'You haven't even *thought* about it,' he said bitterly.

I didn't reply. Instead I looked down at the valley I used to farm and the river where I'd panned for gold when I'd had the chance, always hoping for the big find that had never turned up. Hidden beyond the cliffs on the far side of the valley was the old worked-out gold mine. The gold had long since gone, but the rocks remained, and other streams flowed into the Allt an Rund out of gold-bearing hills. I wasn't daft, just unlucky. I'd been unlucky with the sheep too, but I hadn't been the only one, and young Jimmy Farquharson, who had the farm now, wasn't making a profit either.

Not that there was much satisfaction in that, and, from time to time, I regretted having sold the place. My father had farmed it, his father before him, and I'd always imagined my son would farm it after me, and his son after him. But times change, or so Ellen kept telling me. *You have to move on. You have to adjust.* It was as well Ellen had been the adjusting sort, since I hadn't been and still wasn't. It was Ellen who'd managed to make a go of the Bed and Breakfast, but I didn't know if I had the heart to carry on with it on my own. So Michael's suggestion of coming in with me on the business should have been welcome. Except it came with strings attached.

'I wish you'd accept it,' he said after a while, his voice quiet, his gaze following mine down to the valley and the hills beyond. I wondered what it was he saw, what it was he thought and felt. 'It would mean a lot to me, you know. I understand why you're reluctant, but you should try to look on it as a business proposition. Although it's more than that to me. This is my home, the place I grew up.' He swept his arm out to encompass the whole valley. 'I'd like to come home, Dad.'

I couldn't look at him. I knew by the sound of his voice that he was close to tears, and it made me want to cry too. I'd wanted to cry since Ellen . . . well, since then. But I hadn't let myself. I had to manage. If I had to make myself hard, well, that was how it was.

'But not on your own,' I said. In spite of myself, I felt my own voice begin to break, and I gritted my teeth to stop it. 'Not on your own!'

He got to his feet and brushed grit off his trousers. 'I guess that's a no, then,' he said after a moment, still a little shakily.

'We'd better be getting down,' I said, getting to my feet too and leading the way down a sheep track into the corrie. The going was rough, and it made the silence easier to excuse, but I wished I could have been kinder. So, once we'd reached the river and a broader track where we could walk side by side, I tried to make us friends again.

'Your mother's ashes; I was thinking of scattering them here by the river. Maybe, when you come up next Sunday, we could do that? I could ask Julie and the boys.'

'Good idea,' he said, but he sounded tired and unhappy.

I touched the ring in my pocket, the two grams of gold garnered through the years. I'd had it made into a ring for Ellen, had planned to give it to her on her sixtieth birthday, but long before then it had no longer fitted her, since the disease had wasted the flesh on her fingers as violently as it had the rest of her body. It had slipped off her finger as soon as she'd put it on.

'Give it to Michael,' she'd whispered, pressing it back into my hand.

'To Michael? Why?'

'You know why.'

It had been her last wish, and yet I'd not even mentioned it to him. Perhaps that was why her voice haunted me now. *Give it to Michael!* I could hear it in the sound of the river beside us, in its muted tones as it ran through deep places by grassy banks, the soft voice with which she'd read stories to our son. *Give it to Michael!* I remembered the blue book with the gold lettering and one particular story.

'What was his name, the king who turned everything he touched to gold?' I asked him.

'King Midas. Why?'

'Oh, no reason. I couldn't remember the name.' *Give it to Michael!* I pulled out the ring and showed it to him. 'There it is. Two grams of gold.'

I looked at the ring glinting in my palm and remembered every flake and fragment I'd strained from the river. The thing about gold is its weight. That's how you find it, since even the smallest grains sink deep into the gravel and you can sieve them out again, each gleaming fragment, and fuse them back into a whole once more. That was why I liked gold. It remained forever itself. For ever.

'It was supposed to be an eternity ring. But . . . well, I left it too late, didn't I?'

He stared at the ring, then at me, as if he was seeing me for the first time, as if he suddenly understood everything.

'Mum was right, you know.' His voice was clipped and angry. 'You're just like that king. You want everything to turn to gold. You've spent your life panning in that bloody river, letting the farm go to the wall, leaving Mum to do all the work, letting Julie take up with that waster, and, as for me, you never even *tried* to understand!' He was shouting now. 'You want everything to last for ever, to be perfect, and when they're not perfect you turn your back on them. You'll end up rattling around that house on your own, a lonely old man, poring over a few scraps of gold. Go on, prove me wrong. I dare you! Throw it back in the river!'

I almost did it. I held the ring between my thumb and forefinger and imagined it spinning through the air and splashing into the water, sinking into the gravel of the river bed where it would quickly become worn and scratched, as if a woman had worn it for a lifetime. But, sooner or later, sooner if the gravel was granite or quartz, it would wear right through, be ground into fragments, each fragment sinking deeper into the river bed, shrinking as it was ground still further into grains of dust. Gradually, as each year went by in a spate of water, each grain would roll downstream. Centuries later, some of the grains would reach the sea, and my ring would be scattered so far along miles of banks and shorelines and backwaters that it could never be gathered together again. Just like Ellen's ashes.

'No, I'm giving it to you.'

'Why?' The anger had drained out of him, but suspicion remained.

'Just take it, Michael. I gave it to your mother, but she wanted you to have it.'

'That's not the reason.'

He wasn't making it easy for me, but I couldn't blame him. I hesitated, thinking it through, facing up to it, not liking it any more than I'd expected to, but facing up to it. Trying to adjust. Trying to understand.

'You're wrong, you know. I don't want everything – everyone – to be perfect. Just special.'

'And what do you expect me to do with the ring?'

'Give it to someone else. To someone special.'

I grabbed his hand, pressed the ring into his palm and closed his fingers over it. 'I want you to have it, Michael.'

He opened his hand and looked down at the ring. I couldn't bear to see his expression, and so I turned away. 'We'd better be getting back. It's late. Come on if you're coming.'

He caught up with me a few minutes later. He said nothing, but the silence between us was different now. The river ran along beside us on its way to the sea, muttering and murmuring to itself. *Silly old fool. Did I not tell you? But would you listen? Not you! Up to your knees in water. You'll catch your death. Once upon a time ... Everything he touched turned to gold ... Just like your father ...* The river carried on down the valley on its long journey to the sea and wherever it goes after that. And yet it would always be there. Some things *do* last for ever. Or as for ever as is ever likely to matter. We walked on in the speaking silence until the house came into view, pale against the forest down at Dalrigh. It was a good house, far too big for one, but perfect for what Michael had suggested, a small country house hotel. Michael had always had good ideas. I could trust him in that. And it seemed to me now that I ought to be able to trust him in other matters as well.

'That business about turning the house into a hotel.' I cleared my throat resolutely. 'We'll talk about it next weekend when you come up. And –' I went on in a rush in case I lost my nerve and didn't manage to say it. '– maybe you should both come up. The two of you. You and ... your friend.'

There was silence now, and I was afraid I'd left it too late. But then he answered.

'He has a name, Dad. I've told you his name.'

I swallowed hard. 'Patrick then.' It wasn't as difficult as I'd expected. 'Bring Patrick with you. We'll scatter your mother's ashes by the river. The three of us, the four of us if Julie comes too. And the boys maybe . . .' I was babbling now, much like the river running along beside us. But he understood. He clutched the ring tightly in his hand and smiled.

Behind us the sun broke through the clouds and shone down on the high corrie where the Tay rises and all along the river as it flowed, murmuring approvingly, to the sea. For a moment, all the waters in the valley gleamed as if they'd been touched with gold.

Feckless as Water

'Tell us about the monster, Daddy.'
'Well, now –' I begin, then stop when I notice Jamie's scowl. Ewan, however, is looking up at me in keen anticipation, and if Mikey isn't listening, well that's not unusual.

So I tell them the story of the Water-horse, the *Each Uisge*, of Loch Iubhair. '...this very loch as is,' I say with a wide sweep of my arm to encompass the loch we're sitting beside. Ewan knows the story by heart, gestures and all. So does Jamie, and he sighs and moves a little away, far enough off to pretend he's not listening but near enough to still be in earshot. Mikey, sitting next to me, is doing calculations on his phone and is oblivious to everything else.

I tell my sons the story as if it's true, but on an over-bright Saturday morning, with the loch a blinding sheet of silver and only the whirring damsel flies to give it life, it's difficult to imagine that deep below its placid surface there might live a Water-horse.

'How could it breathe under the water?' Jamie scoffs when I've finished. He's eight and no longer believes in Santa Claus.

'Because it's magic,' says Ewan, who still does.

Jamie grunts. 'I'm bored. I want to go home.'

So do I, but I've been given strict instructions to keep the boys out of Julie's hair for the morning at least. She has work to do, accounts or something, and if she doesn't get them done she'll be in even more of a mood than she already is. Jamie takes after her in this, as in other things.

'Come on, lads. Let's go and look for the Pike.' That's enough to interest Jamie, at least for a while – the prospect of a real monster, the big pike that's supposed to live in the loch and has been known to take a duckling or two. Not that I've told Jamie that since, although he's stopped believing in magic, he finds reality a little too . . . realistic. Ewan, a tough little nut, would just shrug, and, as for Mikey, no-one ever knows what he thinks.

'If we carry on at this rate –' Mikey announces, '– we'll be back where we started in exactly one hour and thirteen minutes. Except . . .' He turns back to his calculations, struggling with some variable which has just occurred to him and which he's not yet taken into account. God help us when he discovers differential equations! His younger brothers ignore him as usual, and we carry on to the far end of the loch which, at this time of the day, is shadowed by the trees, and where, a year before, we'd all seen something.

'The Water-horse,' Ewan had announced. 'The Pike,' Jamie had corrected him. 'A shadow,' suggested Mikey after turning to measure the angle of the sun. The memory of it is enough to occupy them for a while, and they sit very still, waiting for whatever it was to re-appear. I envy them their single-mindedness of purpose, the lack of which, according to Julie, is one of my many failings. I don't have staying power, and that's a failing too. But I'm easily bored, like Jamie, and today, in spite of my very real desire to see a pike, or a Water-horse, or even a shadow that could be of something more mysterious than either, I can't concentrate, and my attention wanders, flitting about like the blue-tailed damsel flies that haunt this end of the loch.

A little wind ruffles the surface of the water. A heron stalks in the shadow of some willows, and the waterlilies lift their faces to catch the sun. On the far side, by a stand of alders, a man is fishing half-heartedly. I'm desperate for a cigarette but am supposed to be giving up so didn't bring any with me, something I'm beginning to regret.

'There isn't really a pike, is there?' Jamie demands after five minutes of fruitless watching. He's lost any belief he might once have had in its existence, but I assure him I've seen it many times, a big pike turned cannibal, a great eater of its own children. I lick my lips and grin at him, but he isn't amused, having acquired his mother's habit of regarding everything I say as nothing more than a story. Most of the time he's right, and yet he still wants to believe me, then blames me when he can't. 'That's all rubbish!' he says.

Your father's a dreamer, Julie used to say with a smile. She still says it, but no longer smiles as she does so. Dreams and stories no longer appeal to her as once they did. I wonder if she'll ever move back into our bedroom. She's been sleeping badly since her mother died, and, what with her having to make an early start for work and me getting in so late from my job at the hotel bar, it makes sense for her to sleep in the spare room. Or so she tells me. I rarely see her these days. Only at weekends, and even then the boys and I are banished from the house.

'Can we go to the hotel, Daddy?' Ewan asks, craving crisps and coke for lunch rather than the sandwiches and juice Julie has packed. The thought of going to the hotel brings on my own craving for a cigarette, but I manage to resist temptation.

'No. We're going to eat our sandwiches by the bridge.'

'I'm cold,' Jamie moans.

'That's because of the Water-horse,' says Ewan.

'Don't be stupid! Anyway, I'm not really cold.'

Jamie and Ewan bicker all the way to the bridge but settle down once the sandwiches are unpacked. Cheese, I notice. I'd intended making them myself, but I'd slept in so Julie made them. I could have done it later, so I suspect a point was being made. We feed one of the sandwiches to the mallards who're nesting in reeds near the head of the loch then lean over the bridge to drop twigs into the water and race them to the far side. Jamie and Ewan compete furiously, but Mikey wins as usual. He can tell from the patterns on the surface of the water where the river is running the fastest and throws his sticks accordingly.

It's funny how the loch can be so still and yet run so swiftly here at its outflow. No doubt Mikey could explain it to me, but I prefer not knowing. That's another failing, I expect. I'm the sum of my various inadequacies. Julie's old man thinks I'm feckless, and her brother Michael considers me a waste of space, but I let their disapproval flow over me like the river and conclude that it doesn't matter. If I have a talent at all, it's for concluding that nothing really matters.

'What will we do now, boys?' I ask once the sandwiches have been eaten, the juice drunk and the ducks fed.

Inevitably, an argument ensues. Jamie wants to go back the way we came. Ewan wants to go to the far side of the loch even although the prospect of going to the hotel – something he's not quite given up on – is greater if we go back directly. Mikey, after a lot of thought, decides he wants to go on. If he subtracts the time spent eating our lunch from the overall time, he explains, and adds the extra time it will take to get to the woods on the far side, we should still get back in one hour and twenty eight minutes. No-one asks what I want to do and so, it being roughly two to one, we go on around the loch. The track is fainter here and muddier. If I take them back muddy, Julie will be furious. Her temper is uncertain these days. I understand why but, bizarrely, that just makes things worse, because she can't bear being understood. She wants to be strong because she believes I'm weak. I'm not actually. It's just that my strength is in other things, but they're no longer things she values. I have a talent for contentment, you see, for being as placid as the loch. Perhaps I'm as deep. Perhaps I too hide within my dubious depths a Water-horse or a pike.

'What are we going to take home for Mummy?' Ewan asks. It's become a bit of a tradition, taking Julie something from our walks: a smooth pebble, a snowdrop, or a polished chestnut, depending on the season. I began it, but the boys have continued with their inevitable rivalry. Her smiles are so rare these days we all compete mercilessly to win them. I usually end up at the back of the pack in a field of four, if I haven't already fallen at the first fence.

'This is all a bit primitive,' she'd told me when we'd taken her the first primrose of spring. Meaning I was a bit primitive, I suppose, but actually I quite liked the idea of being some sort of throw-back. In the old days I would have been someone.

'You?' she'd laughed. That had been in the days when I'd amused rather than disappointed her. 'You wouldn't have lasted long in the old days! You'd have starved to death! You can't even skin a rabbit!'

The rabbit, I have to admit, had been a mistake. After an unpleasant hour of skinning and gutting I'd eventually given the poor thing a decent burial under the forsythia. Ewan had been chief mourner. We still put flowers on the grave.

But it's best not to mention graves at the moment. Julie would have preferred her mother to be buried. She wanted to tend the grave, I suppose, as part of the letting go. The cremation came as a bit of a shock for her, but it was the old girl's wish, apparently, so there was nothing more to be said. It made the funeral a bit . . . uneasy, so when it came up in conversation that Michael was gay and I said, 'Oh, good!' everyone thought I was being sarcastic. I wasn't actually, but it didn't go down well. So best not mention graves or, to be on the safe side, flowers. I even have my doubts about stones.

We continue around the loch past the big house. We're probably not meant to be there, which always gives this route an added frisson. Eventually, we come to the wooded promontory on the far side of the loch and take a fisherman's track to the shore. There are waterlilies close to the edge, and Ewan's determined to take one back to Julie. But I think of the trouble I'll get into if he falls in, as is likely, and persuade him she'd rather have a nice clean pinecone. It's time to go back now, but we stop for a moment, looking out over the loch. The fisherman has gone, and we have the place to ourselves. And so, of course, that's when we see it.

On the far shore, close by the trees, down by the water, stands a horse. A single horse, grazing the lush shoreline grasses, a horse who could almost – so very almost – have stepped straight out of the loch. I put my hand on Ewan's shoulder, say nothing, but turn him in that direction. I feel it when he sees the animal, the quiver of shock, the almost disbelief, the way he holds his breath before letting it go in one spoken word.

'Water-horse!'

They others see it now and are transfixed by the same breathless awe, until Jamie, unable to bear the believing he already knows will turn to ashes, turns away and looks out over the loch – and gasps. Out beyond the lilies, a deep V is forming on the surface, as something big, something very big indeed, swims idly by close to the surface.

'The Pike!'

Then it's gone. We look back at the horse, only to see that it's vanished too, possibly into the trees, possibly back (surely, back?) into the water. A shadow passes over the sun, the light flattens in its wake, then everything clears. Mikey glances up at the sky and smiles faintly, satisfied with what will no doubt prove to be his own complicated explanation.

'Well, now . . .' I say with a satisfaction that eludes them all.

Julie's out when we get back, even although it's late. I'd taken the boys to the hotel to celebrate, and they're hyper on coke and crisps, still excited about what they've seen, still arguing. And when they see her car pull into the drive they're straight out there, all talking at once.

'A Water-horse, Mum! – and the Pike must have been six foot long! – you see, the angle of incidence –'

It takes her some time to sort it out. 'Well, you boys seem to have had a good time,' she says dryly. Can she smell coke on their breaths? She doesn't come close enough to smell the cigarettes on mine.

'One of your stories?' she asks later, flatly.

'Two of my stories,' I tell her. 'One for Jamie, who needed one, and one for Ewan who wanted one.'

'And Mikey?'

'Mikey makes his own stories.'

She nods and pours herself a drink, although she rarely drinks these days.

'Michael's coming home,' she tells me eventually, still in that flat voice. 'I've been to see Dad. You know about the hotel business? Well, Michael's coming back to run it, with his friend. He's called Patrick.' She takes a deep breath, leans her head back and closes her eyes.

'Good,' I say hesitantly, not wanting to inadvertently sound sarcastic.

'So Dad will carry on living in the house at Dalrigh, but he won't be on his own now. I wanted him to come here, you know, but it wouldn't have worked.'

She opens her eyes and looks sharply at me, as if trying to catch me out in some infelicitous expression, but I manage to keep my thoughts out of my face. She would have had to move out of the spare room, wouldn't she?

'Anyway,' she continues, apparently oblivious to the matter approached but retreated from. 'We're going to scatter Mum's ashes on Sunday, by the river. Dad wants everyone to be there, including you.'

I'm sure that's not true, and I wonder who it is who's doing the wanting.

It's not a bad day on Sunday, fair and with a light wind. The boys are cowed into silence for once by the solemnity of the occasion, Jamie white-faced and looking a little sick, Ewan curious, Mikey thinking of something else. Patrick's OK, I suppose, not my taste, but then I'm not Michael. Michael's being his usual fussy self, but the old man's less crabby than usual. Julie stands with her arm through his, but I don't think he's aware of her. It's as if he's listening to someone else speak.

The three of them – the old man, Michael and Julie – take turns to throw the ashes into the water. The river's swift after a few days of rain, and the grey dust is taken quickly away, but they carry on standing there, like rocks left behind in a flood.

I wonder if Julie understands it yet, the strength I have that is so unlike her own: contentment, not ambition, going with the flow, not enduring. She's the rock, and I'm the river, slipping feckless as water between her fingers.

We all stroll back towards the house. The old man seems more at ease with himself than I've seen him in a long time. He even tells the boys about how he used to pan for gold in the river we're walking beside. They've heard it all before but listen politely enough and, thus encouraged, his story turns into something else, a tale about a ring, and a king who wanted everything to turn to gold. I'm astonished. I hadn't thought the old man had a single story in him. Of course, one story leads to another, and Ewan starts telling him about the Water-horse, then Jamie butts in to talk about the Pike. Beside us, all the way back to the house, the river chatters away, telling its own tale. Mikey strikes up an unlikely conversation with Patrick about cars, horsepower, torque, mpg, that sort of thing, and Michael joins in. Gradually, Julie and I fall behind.

'I didn't really want Dad to move in with us,' she says in a low voice. 'I didn't want someone else to worry about.'

'I know,' I say soothingly, because I do.

'All you do is tell stories,' she says with the beginnings of a smile.

'Stories are important.' I nod at the old man with the boys. Jamie, who's always been a little afraid of him, is telling him just how long he thinks the Pike really was. Julie laughs suddenly, for no apparent reason. It's a laugh that's been crushed beneath a boulder but has finally worked its way free.

'Do you know, I used to think you could make your damn stories come true? What an idea!'

I smile but don't reply. I'm thinking of the Pike and the Water-horse and the shadow, and how they reappeared just when they were needed. I have talents of which even I am unaware. Who knows what lies beneath my placid feckless surface?

Julie doesn't move back into our bedroom that night, but I notice the door to the spare room isn't quite shut. I wonder if it's ever been quite shut, and I push it open. The boys aren't the only ones who need stories, and all that night I tell her one without words, about the river and the rock and the deep places of the loch, about the Water-horse and the Pike and the Shadow. All that night I am water, washing her away.

Being a Tree

T here's a bang followed by an ominous rhythmic rumble. The car lurches towards the ditch, but I manage to steer into a grassy clearing next to a gate and stop just before hitting a tree.

'Stupid, bloody, sodding car!'

I'm not given to swearing, or at least I wasn't until recently, but when I get out of the car and confirm I've had a blow-out, I kick the offending tyre, stubbing my toe in the process, and swear even more inventively.

Then I take several deep breaths, limp back to the driver's side, fish out my phone and try to call Jake. He ought to be at home right now, but the only reply I get is my own voice inviting me to leave a message, so I throw the phone down in frustration, swearing once more.

I really must stop doing that, but it's been one thing after another, and my temper is a little fragile these days. Just that morning I'd snapped at Jamie over nothing, and although I've forgotten what it was about Jamie won't have. Mikey doesn't notice criticism, and Ewan doesn't care, but Jamie minds. Like me, I suppose.

Come on, old son, Jake had intervened, flowing between us and dampening down the fire that always seems to flare up between Jamie and me these days. *When your mother's in a bad mood I find it's best to keep a low profile.* That's typical of Jake, taking sides with the boys rather than me, a pal and not a father.

She's always in a bad mood, Jamie had muttered as he'd followed Jake out of the room. *Is it because we had to throw Granny's ashes in the river?*

The door had closed before I could hear Jake's reply, so later we'd been able to pretend that nothing had been said. Nevertheless, there's a little coolness between me and Jake right now. However, since I can't think of anyone else to call, I take another deep breath and try again.

'Jake, it's me!' I say brightly to the answering machine. 'The bloody car has a flat. Any chance you can track down someone from the garage and see if they can stop by and fix it? I'm on the back road to the village, but I can walk from here. I'll call you at home later.'

I sound unfazed, annoyed but resigned. Normal. I deliberately don't say I'll call him at the hotel, since that's another source of friction between us. He isn't supposed to work there until the evening, but he has a habit of going over around lunchtime to help out if he's needed.

They take advantage of you, I complain. *They should pay you for the hours you actually work, not the hours you're supposed to work.* He agrees with me but does nothing about it. He likes working behind the bar and is popular with the customers, what with all his stories. Full of stories, is my Jake, always has been, but I've stopped listening to them.

Why don't you do a management training course or something? I've asked him on more than one occasion. *Maybe I will,* he says and doesn't. He never will, and we both know it, so I suppose I'd better get on with winning the bread in our family. I call the client I was supposed to be meeting, and he agrees to being rescheduled but doesn't sound pleased. I've probably lost the chance of a big chunk of commission on the financial services I was planning on selling him. I feel like swearing again, but instead I toss the phone onto the seat, get out of the car, push my way through the gate and walk down the little track that leads to the edge of the river where there's a convenient boulder to sit on. Then I burst into tears.

I've never been a weeper, not until recently, and I'm not very good at it. I'm not one of those women who goes dewy eyed and fragile as they sob gracefully on the nearest manly shoulder. Instead, I do the whole red-nosed, swollen-lidded, hag-like transformation, and, in spite of looking efficient in my smart suit and uncomfortable shoes, I don't actually have any tissues with me, so I'm forced to wipe my face on the sleeve of my jacket, a thing I'm constantly telling Ewan is a disgusting habit.

Eventually I pull myself together and think about walking into the village. But it's not a prospect that appeals to me, not in these shoes, so I carry on sitting on the boulder, looking out over the river while I wait for Jake to rescue me, and wonder why I'm crying.

The car, obviously. I don't want to have a flat tyre. I don't even want the car, a sleek silver thing that's more powerful than I'm used to. But it goes with the job, which I don't want either. I'm fed up selling money to people who have too much to begin with, but one of us has to have a proper job. I don't want a husband with no ambition, who can't even answer the phone when, for once, I actually need him. Horrifyingly, I'm not sure I want my children either. What I want – the thought comes unbidden – is my mother.

I start crying again, because my mother is the one thing I can't have. We scattered her ashes in this very river two weeks ago and they'll have long since washed away. I didn't want a cremation. What I'd expected was a proper funeral with a grave and a stone with her name on it, somewhere I could go and talk to her, even although I knew she wouldn't reply. She was never much of a talker. She'd just been there, the calm centre at the heart of our family, the rock on which I'd always relied, although I didn't realise it until after she was gone.

Now I seem to be the rock, because who else is there? My father, wandering aimlessly about that big empty house? My brother Michael, with his boyfriend in Glasgow? Jake? Certainly not Jake, who can't be relied upon, Jake who runs like water through my fingers, Jake with the stories that flow in and out of my life, leaving me behind, grounded like . . . like a rock.

I don't want to be a rock, the person on whom everyone depends, the one who's in control, who knows what has to be done, when to do it and how – if not always why. I want to be –

'Julie? Is that you down there?' I recognise the voice, a woman's voice, and swear at Jake under my breath, because of all the people he could have sent to rescue me the last one I had in mind was Aurora, his mother. But I can hardly pretend it isn't me, so I wipe my face on the sleeve of my jacket again and make my way up to the road where she's standing beside her bike. 'Jake got your message and asked me to come along to help you,' she announces, peering at me in some concern.

'Goodness, Aurora! I didn't know you could change tyres!'

There's a flicker in her green-lidded eyes that tells me she knows I'm being sarcastic, but she pretends not to notice.

'Of course I can't, dear. Jake's gone off to look for that nice man from the garage who's going to do marvels with jacks and wheel-nuts, I believe. Not my style at all! No, I've come to take you to lunch while those men-folk do all that manly stuff.' She peers more closely at me. 'Are you all right, dear?'

No, I'm bloody not all right! But I manage a thin smile. 'Hay-fever. I forgot to take my anti-histamines this morning.' I stare at her defiantly, daring her to ask whether I've been crying.

It's not that I dislike Aurora, precisely. It's just that we've absolutely nothing in common. Her name says everything about her. She's a relic from the seventies, a widow of indeterminate means and indeterminate age, who still dyes her hair an unlikely shade of red and dresses in long hand-woven skirts and shawls. She lives a couple of miles down the road in a rambling untidy house on the edge of the village with a man she refers to as 'my dear friend Theo'. She breeds chickens and wears sandals, even in winter, and she's probably a pagan in a wishy-washy, mother-goddess, tree-hugging sort of way. She certainly has enough trees to hug in that overgrown garden that runs down to the river.

To my relief, she doesn't ask any questions, although she continues to look closely at me in the rather too clear sunshine and sees more than I want her to: my tear-stained face, my soiled sleeve, my scuffed shoes, the shadows beneath my eyes. Then she nods decisively as if she might have the answer to all these things.

'Right,' she says briskly. 'Best take the bike. The door's open. Ask Theo to fix you something to drink. I'll walk back.'

I do the 'couldn't possibly' routine, but she insists, and, since it's a toss-up between my dignity and a long painful walk in unsuitable shoes, I allow myself to be persuaded. Moments later, I've hitched up my skirt and am pedalling along the road. It's been years since I've been on a bike, but, after a wobbly start, it comes back to me. I stop feeling ridiculous and begin to enjoy myself as I sweep through insect-hazy summer air that smells of cut grass and warm tarmac, with the river running to one side, sparkling and full of sound. It's not long before I reach Aurora's house, the one with the gate hanging off its hinges. A nail on the signpost is missing and the name of the house hangs vertically. *Fearnan* it says, a common name around these parts. Something Gaelic, I've always assumed. Typical of Aurora.

'Julie, how nice!' Theo greets me, looking a little startled, but then he always looks startled. Aurora's 'dear friend' is middle-aged and rather portly and, like Aurora, he's distinctly odd, what with his earrings and tattoos and the long grey hair he wears in a ponytail. He's the founder and sole member of an Iron Age re-enactment society and is probably a pagan too. But he nods sympathetically as I explain about the flat tyre and makes the clucking noises he uses to soothe the chickens.

'Lemonade,' he announces with decision. 'Just made it. Down there on the patio.' He nods towards the river down through the trees. 'You go ahead. I'm making lunch, omelette with herbs. I'm just off to pick them. Fascinating things, herbs. Indeed, back in the Iron Age –' He breaks off at my expression. 'Well, best get on,' he says and wanders back into the house.

The patio is actually a patch of badly laid paving slabs in a clearing near the riverbank, with a couple of rickety benches and a tree-stump for a table. But it's in the shade and there's a jug of cloudy lemonade and a couple of glasses standing on the stump. I fish out several drowned insects, pour myself a glass and taste it suspiciously. But it's delicious, and, rejecting the benches, I wander down to the river's edge where I find yet another boulder to sit on.

Sitting there, sipping the lemonade, I begin to feel guilty about Aurora. I think of her tramping down the hot road in her sandals and wonder how long it will take her to walk the distance I whizzed along in a few minutes. Probably ages, I decide, so I relax and lean back against a sapling that's growing next to the boulder, its roots down in the river, its leaves fluttering peacefully and dappling the dusty light. The house is just above the falls, and the river, picking up speed as it drops down towards the loch, is turbulent with creamy water that plunges into dark pools between mossy boulders. Being summer, the water level's low, but in spring, when it's in spate, the river will lip the boulder on which I'm sitting. It's smooth, worn down by all those springs of snowmelt. I know how it feels. A prickle of self-pity starts the tears again, but I brush them angrily away.

'I sowed that tree, you know,' says Aurora from behind me. She's standing with her sandaled feet planted widely, her various shawls and scarves lifting in the breeze. 'Just a seed it was, and now look at it.'

And I know she's thinking about the last time I was here.

Let's all pretend to be trees! Aurora had said. It had been a Sunday, a duty visit. I hadn't wanted to go, but someone had to keep an eye on the boys because Aurora lets them run wild, and Jake doesn't stop them, in spite of the absence of a fence to stop them from falling into the river. And now I was expected to 'be a tree' was I? I'd felt my lip curl.

What sort? Mikey had wanted to know.

A poplar, she'd said promptly. *Something tall with its head in the clouds.* I'd laughed dutifully.

I'm going to be the biggest tree! Ewan, the shortest, had announced, throwing his arms into the air and waving them about frantically.

I suppose I'd better be an aspen, Jake had said. *Something insubstantial with fluttering leaves.* He'd shaken his hands about until Ewan had fallen about in hysterics.

What about you, Jamie? Aurora – being an oak – had asked. *What sort of tree are you going to be?*

But Jamie had looked at me and some of his enthusiasm had died in his face. *I don't want to be a tree*, he'd said, coming to stand beside me and distancing himself from the others. Jake and I had argued about it later.

You could at least have pretended to enjoy yourself!

I don't do pretending! What a liar I'd been even then.

Now that day comes back to me and, with it, the thought that had been interrupted when Aurora had arrived to rescue me, the one about the rock and the water. I'm not like Jake, all flow and slippage. But I don't want to be a rock like my mother. I want to be something that has the qualities of both, solidity and change, something rooted in the water, something that bends and sways but doesn't break.

I want to be a tree.

'It's an alder, isn't it?' I ask Aurora, turning away from her too-penetrating gaze to lay my hand on the smooth bark of the sapling. 'I like alders.' Then, after a moment, still not looking at her, 'Thanks for rescuing me. I was feeling a bit low when you came along. I was thinking about Mum.' I try to sound matter-of-fact, but my voice cracks open and rebellious tears, never far away, spill down my face. I sniff and wipe my cheeks with the back of my hand, and Aurora, efficiently, finds a clean handkerchief in one of her many pockets and hands it to me.

'We all miss Ellen,' she says simply. 'I'll go and see where Theo's got to with the lunch. Stay here. We'll eat *al fresco.*'

An alder, I think, kicking off my hateful shoes, taking off my snagged tights and stepping gingerly down to the edge of the water, gasping as the cold grips my toes and ankles. *I'm going to be an alder*. I stretch my arms up to the sky and squint against the sun. Up by the road I see a flash of silver through the trees and hear a car pull up. Moments later there's the sound of children yelling and a deeper voice telling them to go into the house to wash their hands and not to annoy Uncle Theo. Then footsteps on the path.

'What are you doing?' Jake asks, not critically but curiously.

'I'm being a tree,' I tell him, wondering if Theo has put one of his weird herbs in the lemonade. But if he has I don't care.

The boys burst out of the house, shouting and yelling, and come running down the garden.

'Quiet, boys!' Jake says peaceably. 'Your mother's being a tree.'

'What sort?' Mikey wants to know.

'An alder,' I tell him.

'Fearn,' says Aurora, coming down the garden with a tray of glasses, Theo in her wake. 'It's Gaelic for alder. I named the house after the wood.'

'I'm going to be an alder too,' Ewan announces, tugging off his shoes and socks and clambering down to stand beside me. For once, I don't tell him to be careful. Mikey joins him, then Jake, until we're all standing in the water stretching our arms up to the sky like madmen. I look up at Jamie, poised uncertainly on the edge of the bank.

'Come on, Jamie,' I say. 'We need you to make a wood.'

He grins, pulls off his shoes and socks and scrambles down. Everyone laughs, Jamie, Jake, Mikey, Ewan, Aurora, and Theo. Even me. I'm laughing and crying and hugging my little wood of trees.

Beside us the river runs fast and furious, beating itself on the rocks that split the stream into foam and whirlpools as it pours over the falls towards the bridge, heading for the loch. But in Aurora's garden, in the shallows, we're safely rooted to the shore, our feet in the water, our heads in the sky. We're growing together into the future, bending to the bad times that life throws at us.

Bending, but not breaking.

Imagining Silence

F irst, I imagine silence. A silence as black as a wet December night, as soft as the fur behind a cat's ear, a silence that tastes of water and smells of the wind. I imagine a silence like this, and only then can I begin . . .

~~~

We're gathered together in a circle next to the first way marker. We are to introduce ourselves to the others, announces the leader, a fussy little man with the voice of a piccolo. I'm worried it will be like those encounter groups I've read about. *My name is Ethel and I'm an alcoholic.* I edge backwards, which is difficult when one is in a circle, and wait for someone else to begin.

We have an investment banker, a florist, a physiotherapist, a charity worker, an English teacher, a joiner, a retired company director . . . I stop listening because I'm no longer hearing the words. Instead I'm concentrating on the voices: the timbre of one, the light fluting tones of another, the way a third drops his voice a register as he tells us that he's always wanted to walk the West Highland Way. He doesn't know why.

That'll do, I decide when my turn arrives.

'I'm Sophia Barton,' I announce. 'I teach musical composition and, like – Fred, wasn't it? – I've always wanted to walk the West Highland Way. So when an opportunity came up, I jumped at the chance.'

All of this is true, but none of it is the truth. I'm a composer who seems to have lost the knack of imagining and filling silence. I'm a woman whose husband has left her for a younger colleague. I'm convinced the two things are related, but I don't know how or why. I need to make the connection for myself, and I think best as I walk. So surely, at some point on the ninety-five-mile hike from Milngavie to Fort William, I'll be able to find the answer?

The introductions are followed by some awkward conversation, some forced laughter and a lot of photography, both singly and in groups. Then come the inevitable quotes: *One small step for man . . . A journey of a thousand miles starts with a single step . . .* And then we're off.

The journey is part of it. It's the old cliché; a journey is always one of discovery. *Discovery of what?* the devil's advocate part of me wants to know. *Anything*, another part replies, *anything at all*. But it doesn't feel like a journey just yet. There's a light drizzle, and the route north through the suburbs of Milngavie is depressingly urban. Perhaps that's for the best, because the city part of me isn't ready for all this and is wondering what I'm doing here. Why *here*? But, like Fred, I don't know exactly. All that matters is that I feel the need to travel from A to B, rather than from A to A. A guided walking tour seemed to make sense. Being with other people. I'm told I need to get out more.

'I've always loved music,' the English teacher offers in a breathless fluty kind of voice. 'I was going to study music after school, except . . .' She smiles apologetically.

Quite. Music is unreliable.

'I used to play the piano,' she continues. 'But I wasn't very good.'

'Neither am I,' I tell her. 'I just use it to –' I almost say compose. '– to teach. My husband's a violinist. Nicholas Barton. Maybe you've heard of him?'

I'm pleased with my use of the present tense, but then I have been practicing. My husband (is he?) doesn't cease to be a violinist merely because we don't live together any more, or because I no longer write the pieces that were for him alone, his voice threading through them like a river through a dusty plain. Perhaps that's why he left me.

'How marvellous!' the English teacher flutes, and it's a moment before I realise she's answered my spoken words, rather than my unspoken thought. I'm out of the habit of speaking to people, but in ninety-five miles, by the time I've reached B, I'll surely be better at it.

'Oh, yes. I'm his biggest fan!' There was a time when he was mine.

I mention some of his concerts and his favourite pieces, and the conversation, thankfully, becomes more general. She confesses to a weakness for Schubert and adores Beethoven, of course. The retired company director, whose name I've forgotten, falls back to walk with us and, while agreeing that Beethoven is all very well, maintains that the only real composer is Bach. He's a big man, overweight and already sweating in spite of the cold. The drizzle has eased, and the sky's lighter, but the wind's picked up.

'Bach has shape,' he says, as if this clinches the argument, then disarms me by glancing down at his own portly form and smiling ruefully. I can see him thinking *Unlike me,* but what he actually says is 'Unlike your modern music. That 'shouting into pianos stuff'. Can't abide it.'

I find myself drawn to the defence of twentieth century music in general and the 'shouting into pianos' school of composition (with which I don't actually agree) in particular. He's more knowledgeable than he pretends and is aware that someone who teaches composition must also be a practical exponent. 'You compose that modern stuff?' he demands.

'Occasionally,' I confess, although it's been ages since I did.

'How marvellous!' the English teacher exclaims. 'How exciting to actually *compose* music! Where do you get your ideas from?'

First, I imagine silence . . .

'Oh, all sorts of places.'

'Maybe you'll compose something about our little walk?' She trills into laughter. 'Our *big* walk!'

'Maybe,' I say and change the subject. She doesn't speak to me thereafter but nods encouragingly, convinced I'm busy composing and not wanting to break my concentration. The company director, however, continues to speak. He's a man who likes to argue, who takes ridiculous stances in order to force others to attack them. I don't much like his voice. It's harsh and raw with a lifetime of smoking, which he's given up for the trip, as he informs everyone at great length. He's like a chain-smoking tuba, I decide, unkindly.

This is a habit of mine, and a bad one. I don't listen to what people say. I'm more interested in what they sound like, and I picture each of them as an instrument. The English teacher is definitely a flute, the walk leader a piccolo, the physiotherapist a bassoon, the florist a xylophone, and so on and so on. None of them, thank goodness, is a violin. That's Nicholas. His was the voice that filled my head, the solo to which everything else was merely an accompaniment. But I no longer hear his voice, no matter how much silence I imagine.

The miles slip by and my feet start to ache, but I begin to hear the things I hadn't noticed in the city: wind and birdsong. The city itself slips behind us remarkably quickly, and we're soon among woodland. But I can still hear the sound of traffic in the distance, and it isn't until the second day that we leave it behind as the 'Way' climbs through wooded slopes and up the steep track over Conic Hill. This second day is harder than the first, the weather more unsettled, the wind stronger, the sky a tumbled layer of bruised stratus. I talk to some of the others and find that my tongue, like my legs, is initially stiff but eases off as the day goes by. The hill has spread everyone out, with the tuba bringing up the rear, so we wait down near the shore for the slower members of the group to catch up. I move a little apart and listen to the sound of water on the shore, waves on pebbles, a stream in a culvert, the soughing of wind in the pines. I begin to feel the shape of music forming.

Perhaps you'll compose something about our little walk?

I'd laughed off the idea, but now it comes back to me as I imagine the route ahead, the way it will rise and fall, the narrow way beside the loch, the ascent to the watershed, the valley that leads to Tyndrum, the climb out of the village then the descent, and later the section we all talk about in hushed tones, the zig-zags up the Devil's Staircase. I think of horns, a high piercing crescendo of woodwinds, a single violin carrying the theme.

I've not imagined silence, but nevertheless the music takes form as we walk north. The loch is on my left, woods on my right, the way behind already shaped into notes: a slow beginning of single minor chords, a drumbeat that imperceptibly changes rhythm, the hum of traffic in the strings. Ahead, everything is possible, and the music dances through my mind as the charity worker (a cello) tells me of the plight of the Nepalese hill-farmers and what he thinks the government ought to do about it. And, before I know it, we've reached the hostel at Rowardennan.

Is this the answer? The finding music once more? Is this why I'm here? I consider calling Nicholas. Yes, we still speak, although not as much as we used to. How ironic that a violinist and a composer can, between them, make such silence! But I have a voice now, and all I need is his, the violin refrain for which this journey is just the pretext. I'll phone him, I decide, and ask for some technical advice. I'll say little as yet of what I'm doing, but I'll sound happy and other than I've been. In the end, however, reception is poor, and I think better of it. I resolve to wait and surprise him with my West Highland Way study when it's complete. After I've reached B.

It fills my head all the next day, a wet showery day with flashes of sunshine that follow brisk chilling showers. Slopes rise all around and the water gleams like burnished steel. There will be two themes, I decide: the journey shaped by the land, with its counterpoint the weather that shapes the land into a journey. A thunderstorm on the Devil's staircase might be an appropriate passage, I think, but it seems tactless to mention this desire to the others.

The group is growing closer, more defined, and on the following day I fall in with the bassoon and the xylophone. I nod conspiratorially with the flute. I avoid the tuba, who irritates me, but feel comfortable with the cello. These people with their various concerns and histories, are a third theme, their voices the instruments that will give my music life. I find myself becoming uncharacteristically sociable, flitting from one group to the next, eavesdropping, interjecting, encouraging everyone to speak so I can capture the precise tone of their voices.

'How marvellous!' the English teacher declares. *Exactly*, I think.

Reaction sets in. It's a mixture of relief at finding something I'd begun to think lost for ever and hope that its return will herald other changes. Or perhaps it's just that I'm not used to the exercise. I grow breathless and think it's with the melodies beating in my head. I go faster than I ought because what I'm hearing lies just ahead, just out of reach, and if I don't hurry it will all slip away. I feel dizzy and light-headed, and there's a darkness at the edges of my vision that's like the low blare of trumpets. Then, on a hillside above Crianlarich, I cross the last stream that flows west and begin to ascend a slope beyond which all the waters run east. *This is the watershed, folks. Just one last push then it's all downhill!* That's when I faint.

They're kind, all of them. Maggie, the florist, makes a pillow of her fleece jacket. Her husband, Dennis, offers me some hot tea, Fred a biscuit. Andrew, the charity worker, turns out to have medical training and puts a confident hand on my wrist. Judith, the English teacher, pats my shoulder and murmurs consolingly. Even Roger, at the back as usual, puffs up and wants to know what's all this then? Then he, Andrew and Joshua, the group leader, confer quietly while I give way to shameful tears. The voices all around me are reassuring, not impatient or disdainful, but warmly human. There's no flute, no bassoon, no cello, not any more, and the music that had danced along the track ahead of me, just out of reach, carries on up the hill and down the other side, a descant fading with distance until all I can hear is wind and the sound of water running east.

My fate is pronounced. I'm to be taken to Crianlarich and will stay in the hotel. If I feel better the next day I can continue. Two of the others will go with me. We'll meet up later if all is well. If not – but let's not think about that! – we'll definitely keep in touch. And do it all again next year. Wouldn't that be nice! I object but am gently overruled. I want to go on, I say. I want to catch up with the music, but I don't say that. In the end I'm helped to my feet, my rucksack handed to Andrew and my poles to Roger, both of whom are to go with me.

I begin to feel better as we make our way downhill, then enormously guilty at breaking up the group and delaying everyone. But my apologies are brushed away. Roger declares that he'd just about had enough and it should have been him up there, collapsed with a heart attack. He'd been looking for an excuse to give up. Andrew, it turns out, was only going as far as Crianlarich in any case. He has business in the area, he tells us later that evening at dinner. In spite of everything, it's quite a jolly occasion, and I listen with more attention than previously to Andrew's stories of the work he's done in Nepal. Roger and he argue happily about politics, and then we turn to music, and I find myself telling them about what I do, or did. I tell them about Nicholas and how he's left me to live with a young Chinese cellist.

'Lucky devil,' Roger says enviously then blushes when Andrew kicks him under the table. I smile and say that she's very gifted, then find myself laughing because I understand now it had nothing to do with my own silence. It was just Nicholas' need to hear another voice. I still feel the loss of my music, but now it's for myself. My journey's over, although I haven't reached B, but I've discovered something I hadn't expected. I tell Roger and Andrew that I'm going back to London, that I'll take the early train to Glasgow in the morning. We promise to keep in touch. We might even do that.

The next day I leave in time to catch the train, but I don't head for the station. I feel strong and fit and have decided to go on to Tyndrum, to catch up with the others and continue my journey. I've asked the hotel to order me a taxi to take me there. It will arrive in thirty minutes, they tell me. The morning's fine so I walk down to the river. It flows strongly here, running from the north then curving east, since I've crossed the watershed and all rivers run east from here. I get out my map and trace its route as it heads for the North Sea, changing its name as it goes. It's the Fillan here, but downriver it's called the Dochart before it falls off the edge of my map to become the Tay. The river runs swiftly in its deep channel, almost silent in the power of its flow. First, I imagine silence . . .

I shoulder my rucksack and take up my walking poles. The taxi will wait in vain, and I feel vaguely guilty about that as I head along an old railway track that follows the line of the river, heading east. It's all downhill from here, as I set out on my journey, no longer from A to A, or from A to B, but from A to an unidentifiable C that lies somewhere off the edge of the map. I walk, strongly now, past a loch full of water-lilies, but I barely notice because I'm imagining silence and filling it with the harmonics of a river in all its moods: of water and wind and the unselfconscious singing of the birds. It isn't music, but as I walk I will make it so. Music that's true to itself, not just an accompaniment for the voice of a man who no longer sings just for me. Music that isn't orchestrated from the stolen voices of others but – remarkably – from my own voice.

First, I imagine silence. Then I begin.

Backwater

I don't know why I'd left the invitation where I knew Alice would see it, laid out on the kitchen dresser with my keys and wallet. Some actions are like that, and I might have called it a challenge flung in the face of fate if I'd been the poetic sort. But I'm not, so let's just say it was an impulse.

'What's this?' she'd asked, picking it up and spending rather too long reading the details, a little catch in her breath when she'd noticed the date, the 25th of May. It's Toby's birthday, when he'll be nine. But neither of us had said anything about that, because we won't be with Toby to celebrate it.

'Oh, the usual invite,' I'd replied with the casual lack of interest I've perfected in the past few years, and she'd carried on looking at it for longer than was necessary just to lay the thing down and forget about it. Not that the annual summons to the boss's summer barbeque was something to be ignored lightly.

'We'll have to go,' she'd said eventually, turning the invite over and over in her fingers, a half-question in her voice.

'Of course we'll have to go!' I'd said sharply, and that was the end of it. A challenge had been flung down, like a mailed glove, and accepted. Of that I was certain. What was less certain was what the challenge actually was and who'd been doing the accepting. But, whatever the reason, the thought of a challenge helped me keep my nerve, and so here we are, on Toby's birthday, the 25th of May, driving down the road that lies between the river and the woods to Fred and Margaret's house, in anticipation of an afternoon of unrelieved misery.

'Who else is going?' Alice asks as we get closer to the house. She's been careful not to ask until now.

I list them for her, my colleagues with their various wives or partners. '. . . and David and Irene . . .' I slide them into the middle of the list as if I don't know that David has been her most recent lover, if that's what one calls it. But, whatever it's called, it's over now, ending, as these relationships generally end for Alice, with a shrug and a metaphorical girding of the loins. I can tell, you see, not from her – because she's become adept at hiding such things – but from him, poor chap. He has the exhausted relief of a relay runner who's just passed the baton on to someone else, and I wonder, with very little curiosity, who's taken it up now.

It's not long before we arrive at a big house in its own grounds on the north bank of the river. Family money, I understand, but, if so, it's been well-spent, and the house is a gracious place set among mature trees and flowering shrubs that on a summer's evening will be loud with birdsong. Today, however, on Toby's birthday, any birdsong there might be is drowned out by the sound of people enjoying themselves, and there's a moment when I want to get back in the car and drive away and keep on driving, to follow the river upstream until it's nothing more than a trickle. I want to trace its roots back to its source and stay there forever, as far from the sea as it's possible to be. But another part of me wants to stride down into the laughing mass of people and start yelling and screaming. *Don't you see?! Didn't you see?!*

I do neither of these things, however, because I've perfected the art of compromise, and we walk down to join the crowd then go our separate ways.

'All right, mate?' David greets me uneasily. He's standing with his wife, Irene, who smiles distractedly before running off to remonstrate with their youngest son who's all set to help himself from the big bowl of punch that's set out under an awning. 'Little devil,' David mutters, even more uncomfortable now he's alone with me. 'Takes after his dad, I'm afraid. Bloody good punch though. I'm going to get some more.' We walk down to the drinks tent together. 'So,' he says bracingly once we each have a full glass in our hands. 'Who's driving today? You or . . . Alice?' There's just the slightest hesitation, but I recognise the subtlest of signs these days and feel the usual wash of irritation with Alice. David used to be a good mate, and now she's spoiled it. Still, we can go on pretending, go on not saying the things that will never be said. I listen to the murmur of conversation around the barbeque and think what a clamour there would be if everyone said all the things that will never be said.

'Alice is driving,' I tell David, helping myself to more punch as Irene leads their chastened son away. 'How old is he now?' I ask, nodding at the kid. I'm obsessed with the ages of children.

'Five on his next birthday, little devil,' he says affectionately. Toby had been five once, but he's nine today. I want to tell David this but restrain the impulse. He doesn't know Alice and I have a child. No-one does. Perhaps David thinks Alice's behaviour is because we don't, that it's some desperate desire to fill the ache of absence. He wouldn't be entirely wrong.

We chat idly about the day, the weather, the house and garden, Fred and Margaret, about our various colleagues. Others come to join us, and I go off toward the barbeque with Tom and Hannah, then meet Adrian and Penny and start chatting to them. I move from one group to the next, never spending long with any of them, never falling into anything more than a superficial conversation. I'm good at circulating. I only see Alice once, when our paths cross briefly near the marquee. She has two plates of salad in her hands but doesn't offer me one, and I conclude it's for someone else. *So, it begins again,* I think sourly, Alice risking her heart like a man holding a revolver in which there's only one bullet. One of these days there will be a bang rather than a click, and our fragile little world will blow apart as it's been threatening to do for the last four years. No-one will be surprised. They will all have seen it coming, but, personally, I would rather not see it at all.

'Don't . . .' she begins, and, for a moment, I think she'll say one of the unspoken things. *Don't judge me. Don't you dare judge me!* 'Don't drink too much,' is what she actually says, and disappointment makes me savage. 'Don't . . .' I snap back and let the moment draw out until she opens her eyes wide in fear. *Don't fuck yet another of my colleagues,* is what she's afraid I'll say. 'Don't nag,' I say instead, and she turns on her heel and walks away. No, no-one will be surprised.

Later, once the afternoon has lengthened towards evening and the sun is less blinding, I manage to make my escape. Fred and Margaret's garden is a place designed for escape, half wood, half garden, with odd little paths that lead to secret clearings in which stand crumbling statues or benches dappled with lichen. I wander aimlessly, down halls pillared by yews, bright openings slanted with shadow, and past beds of azaleas with their acid yellow flowers and where the scent is overpowering. The noise of the party is deadened by foliage, and the promised birdsong pierces the canopy. A thrush is pouring out its liquid song, and I can hear the piping of goldcrests in the as-yet leafless oaks. But I'm only half-listening. I'm only half-aware of the plume of the green spring woods, because I'm seeing Toby, whose birthday it is today. I'm wondering if there will be balloons and whether he'll get the new football strip he's bound to want. He used to love balloons, but perhaps he's outgrown them now, and, with a chilling shaft of loss, I realise that I don't know what football team he supports these days. As he grows older, he drifts further and further away, swept from me by a current of time into backwaters I couldn't have predicted.

I'm so caught up in my thoughts that it comes as a surprise when yet another of those odd little paths brings me out at the remains of an old jetty. I'm about to turn back when I hear the distant murmur of conversation and realise that my wanderings have brought me close to the house, just along the river from the lawn below the terrace, and I step up onto the jetty to see if I can spot a footpath that will take me back to the house.

The sun, low in the sky now, burnishes the surface of the water to a sheet of beaten steel, and the river slips soft as a snake between its banks. Downriver, however, there must be rocks, because I can hear the growl of falls, but here by the jetty the water's deep, and I feel the usual irrational panic at the thought of those depths, the same irrational panic that makes me unable to look at the sea, the same panic that made me give up everything in the south and take up a job as far from the coast as I could get. It wasn't to do with the publicity, although that played its part, nor the swing of hope and disappointment every time I saw Toby walking by with a stranger. Because it never was him. How could it be? Toby is nine now, living some other life.

So it seems unfair that today of all days and here, far from the sea, from the beach with its grief of gulls, I see Toby once more. He's wandering down the lawn to the edge of the water, walking between the people who're all chatting and laughing, oblivious to his determined little figure.

Don't you see him? I want to yell at them all. *Didn't you see him?*

But *I* see. I see what I've seen in my imagination over and over. Toby's playing with a pebble close by the water's edge when someone, a man or a woman, bends down to speak to him, hands him an ice-cream, then takes him firmly by the hand and leads him away. Over and over I've seen it happen. If only I'd looked up. If only I'd been there to tear the stranger's hand from his. But this time it isn't too late. If I dash off the jetty and run along the path, I'll be in time. I'll shout and yell until everyone looks up, looks around and sees the stranger bend down to him. Surely I can make them understand that a five-year old boy is being led away?

Except Toby's nine now, not five, and that's why, instead of dashing off the jetty, I climb over the handrail. Because that's not Toby. And that's not what happened.

Even as I jump into the river, I see the bending figure straighten. I see that it's Alice and that she takes the boy – David and Irene's youngest – by the hand to lead him away from the water's edge. I see her attention caught by a movement further down the river. It's a man leaping fully clothed into the river. I see her hands go up to her mouth in horror. Then there's a bang and I'm under.

The shock robs me of breath, the cold of movement, and I feel myself being swept downstream in the peat-brown grip of the current. Something touches my hand, a strand of weed perhaps, as the pillars of the jetty streak past me. Then I'm pulled down, tumbled in an eddy, my lungs burning now, my mind filled with shattered images of sands and gulls. Once more I hear the screams of children laughing, see the ripple of the sea in the sunshine, the dark current that tears around the headland, the warning signs down on the beach. I never saw Toby again, but somewhere, in the home of a stranger, he's nine today. To think anything else would be . . . unthinkable. Somewhere, Toby is happy because Alice and I are unhappy. That's the deal after all. Or I'd thought it was.

Because now I see how it really was: the ball rolling down the beach with the wind behind it and into the sea where it's snatched by the waves. I see Toby following, forgetting our warnings about not going in the water. It's only a step after all. That won't count. But the beach slopes steeply here, and perhaps, between one moment and the next, when no-one on that crowded beach is watching, he stumbles and falls and is dragged under for the current to take him out to the sea that will horde his body and his bones and keep its sullen silence. *Didn't you see?* I'd yelled. Now, at last, I do.

The realisation sends me kicking frantically for the bank, but the current has me in its grip, and I'm flung downriver to follow Toby down to the sea. Eventually, however, the river relents, and a quirk of flow throws me to the surface in a welter of foam, and something hits my shoulder.

Things are confused after that. Rocks scrape against my arm, a bank sweeps by, and I'm swirled into a backwater and hurled across a boulder to which I cling. Hands help me out, and Alice cries as she tries to dry me with a tissue. Later, I'm in Fred and Margaret's house, in one of their spare bedrooms, dressed in some of Fred's too-big clothes and wrapped in a blanket. Tactfully, I'm left alone with Alice, and, once the door closes, we clutch one another and sob uncontrollably.

'I thought I'd lost you,' she says over and over.

I thought I'd lost everything.

'Toby . . .' I begin, and she looks away and bites her lip. 'He would have been nine today.' She looks at me then, really looks for once. Because of what I've said. *Toby would have been nine today*. Past tense. Finally.

'I know,' she says quietly, and that's all that will be said on the matter. There are some unsaid things that need not be said; that we don't know what happened and never will. But we have to agree on just one ending to believe in, or there will never be an ending at all. Alice knew that long ago, but I've only just understood it. So now I will believe what she believes: that his bones lie somewhere in that bay on the south coast. I will no longer think of him living his life apart from us, growing up out of our knowing, growing out of balloons, being either happy or – unthinkingly – unhappy.

'You're lucky to be alive, you know,' Alice tells me.

And sitting there, in Fred and Margaret's spare room, with Alice's hand in mine, I realise that I am.

The Outing

'Are you looking forward to it?'

The woman, who looks oddly familiar, beams at Charlie in the way they all do.

Looking forward to what? he wonders. *Lunch?* As if it's likely to be edible. *Going home?* When they keep insisting that this is his home. *Death?* He scowls at the woman.

'You've forgotten, haven't you?'

Forgotten? They tell him that's why he's here, that he keeps forgetting things like what he had for breakfast, or where he lives, or when to take his pills. Unimportant stuff. If there's something he *wants* to remember, he'll remember it. He keeps telling them that, but they never listen.

'The Outing,' the woman prompts him. 'To the Botanic Garden.'

The Botanic Garden? Why would he want to go there? And yet something stirs. A memory slides to the surface of his mind like a fish rising, but it doesn't break the surface and disappears back into the depths once more.

'Never liked fish,' he states.

There's a look in the woman's eyes that reminds him of a dog he used to have, a dog with eyes like that, disappointed and suspicious. Cross-collie, it was. What was its name? If he tries to remember it will be gone, but sometimes, if he thinks sideways-like and pretends he doesn't care one way or the other, a name will pop into his head.

'Jess,' he says triumphantly. Who says he can't remember things? But the woman's expression becomes, if anything, more whipped-like.

'Lydia, Dad,' she says. 'I'm Lydia.'

Lydia? That was his daughter's name. Bright little thing, always running. Young, she was, but this woman's old and has the look of someone else, and, after a moment, he remembers who. This woman looks like his wife, Mary, but not in a good way. This woman is old and lined and tired. Is it possible that little Lydia grew up and turned into her mother? What happened to time? Some days, when Charlie wakes up, he's startled to find himself occupying the body of an old man.

'Lydia,' he acknowledges grudgingly. 'I *knew* that! Well, I suppose I'd better put my coat on . . .' He struggles to his feet, the woman Lydia's hand under his elbow. 'I can manage! You find my coat. I'll catch my death else.'

Eventually his coat is found and struggled into, and he shuffles out of his room. He goes down a corridor that smells of pee and into a hall where a gaggle of old folks mill about aimlessly while they get everyone aboard a bus. It turns out he's not the only one on this 'Outing'. There's whatshisname with the wart on his nose, thingumabob with the gammy knee, whatshisface who always calls Charlie Bob. Charlie doesn't bother to correct him and calls the man something different every day. Small things amuse him these days.

'Well, Peter, all set for a bit of gardening?' Charlie asks whatshisface once they're finally all settled in the bus.

The man looks confused and plucks at his knees. 'I've not got my gardening trousers on.'

'Don't you worry, Mr Winstanley,' the woman calling herself Lydia says, patting the silly old fool's hand. 'You won't have to do any gardening. But God help any weed my Dad catches sight of, eh Dad? He was always a great gardener, my Dad. Won prizes and everything.'

Did I? You'd think a man would remember a thing like that. 'Flowers,' Charlie says, hazarding a guess.

'Cauliflowers, more like.'

'Cauliflowers *are* flowers, you silly girl!'

The whipped look is back, and he feels momentarily guilty, but she shouldn't be pretending to be his daughter.

Eventually the bus gets going, and it's not long before they pull up at the Botanic Garden. Someone at the front wants to go to the toilet, and whatshisface is still going on about his trousers. Probably wet them. It takes an age to get everyone off. For some reason, they'd put the less abled at the front, so they all have to wait for the wheelchairs and Zimmer frames to be marshalled. Then half of them toddle off for a 'nice cup of tea' in the cafe, but Charlie doesn't join them. Instead he makes for the entrance to the Garden.

'Let's get this over with,' he mutters at the Lydia woman. 'Don't know why I came in the first place.'

'You used to love coming here! Come on, let's go into the glasshouses.'

Once through the door, a wave of moist warmth hits him. His glasses steam up, and all he can see is green. It's like being under the sea. Has he ever been under the sea? Branches hang, clothed in unfamiliar leaves. A flowering plant of some kind riots up the glass. A pool opens out, studded with huge plate-like leaves and fat white buds.

'Waterlilies,' he announces, surprising himself. 'Water lettuce,' he adds, pointing to a fringe of fleshy-leaved plants growing along the margins of the pond.

The woman Lydia looks at him oddly then bends to read a label. 'You're right!' Then she gives a cry of delight. 'Look, Dad! Goldfish!'

'Carp,' he corrects her. 'They're called carp. We had them once.' He's almost certain of it. The fish begin as golden glimmers in the depths of the pool, then swim upwards, taking shape as they do so, before lipping at the surface of the water with their soft mouths.

Lydia gives a breathy laugh of surprise. 'So we did! I'd *forgotten* that. But you remembered!'

'Of course I remembered! Nothing wrong with my memory. Keep telling everyone.'

Oddly, or perhaps not, it's as if the appearance of the fish in the pool has stirred the mud in his own brain. Memories begin to rise and turn, scales glinting, fins cutting through the surface of his mind before they disappear back down into the depths.

'Impatiens,' he says, pointing to a plant. 'Frangipani,' he says to another, welcoming them as if they're old friends. He's been to the Botanic Garden before. He doesn't remember, but he *knows*. More old friends press forward to greet him as they move along the path. Hypoestes, Mimosa, Begonia, a Kapok tree.

'They used Kapok in lifebelts,' he explains. 'When I was in the Navy –' He stops. Had he been in the Navy? Another fish rises out of cold depths to a surface glazed with ice, and there, in the heat of the tropics, Charlie finds himself shivering and doesn't know why. But the Lydia woman does.

'– when you were in the Arctic convoys.'

'A long time ago,' he agrees, although in truth he remembers nothing except for the cold that still lingers in his bones. Sometimes it's good to forget.

'Do you want to go outside, Dad?'

He nods and, once they've left the glasshouse with its exotica, Charlie feels better, because he finds himself in a proper garden with neat raised beds that are planted with vegetables. This is more like it! There are leeks and kale, carrots and beetroot, peas and beans.

'Bolthardy,' he murmurs, bending down to the beetroot. 'Always was a reliable variety. Early Nantes was a good carrot if you could keep the root-fly off it . . .'

He spots more old friends in the raised bed, blue-tinged Musselburgh leeks and a few late salad bowl lettuces. Further up the garden is a row of recently planted apple trees, one of them laden with fruit, some having fallen to the ground. Charlie picks one up, smells its sweet green scent, and bites into it.

'That's not clean, Dad.'

But it's as clean as it needs to be, clean and fresh and oh-so-familiar.

'James Grieve,' he says happily.

'Did you know him?'

'It's an apple, you fool!'

But she's not a fool. She's his daughter, and she's doing her best. She's brought him to his place of old friends and fishes rising out of the dark, because she cares.

'You don't forget an apple,' he says. 'Or you do, but not forever, not for always.' He looks away, clears his throat. 'Can we come back again? Just you and me?'

'Of course, Dad!' That smile is just like her mother's, and in a good way this time.

'You'll have to remind me,' he warns her. 'My memory's not what it was, you see.'

'I know, Dad.' She tucks her hand through his arm and they make their way back to the bus for the journey back to the place he now accepts has become his home.

Later that night, when he's asleep, neurons burst into life in Charlie's brain, little lamps flickering in the dark. Some flare and die, but others go on shining. Like the carp in the pool, they rise out of the depths to glimmer back into the light.

A Room with a View

'This is Deborah Marshall in room 18. No, there's no problem – except there isn't a view. Yes, I know there's a window, but I'd expected a view of the river. I'm sure Professor Brinkley would have asked for a view when he booked. He didn't? Then is there another room? Oh, I see. All right then, I suppose it will have to do. I'm sorry to have troubled you.'

Deborah sets the receiver done and sits staring at it for a moment. *I'm sorry to have troubled you?* How pathetic! Julian would have made more of a fuss, but she's not the complaining sort. Yet how strange he forgot to ask. It's become a private joke between them; whenever they meet in an out-of-the-way guesthouse, or remote country hotel, the first thing she does is go to the window and look at the view. It's something he always laughs about.

'Does it matter about the view? That's not what you're here for, is it? Come here, look at *me*! God, I've missed you . . .' And for the rest of that snatched day or night, that occasional stolen weekend, she'll not look at the view again. She'll do as he asks and look only at him, make herself a refuge from the world, a place he'll never want to leave. But when he does – since he always has to leave – what she remembers most vividly of those days and nights is that first view from the window. Each one is hoarded in her memory: an autumn hillside near Dunkeld, a meadow running down to a river somewhere in the Borders, the winter lights of Edinburgh sprinkled across a carpet of night.

But on this occasion, this special occasion, all she has are the blank windows of the tenement building across the road. All she sees are hard edges of stone and metal when what she wants is the river with its tides and green distances. How could Julian have forgotten? Doesn't he realise it's been two years to the day since that first time? Two years since everything changed for them both? And now she wants everything to change once more, to move forwards, as life is supposed to.

He's at a conference in the city, has been here for a few days already, but it's due to finish today, and he's arranged to meet her in this hotel. It had seemed an odd choice: an old-fashioned building, cluttered about the roof line with a cluster of little pointed windows, like the paper crowns you used to get on lamb chops in the old days. She'd thought it rather endearing, but that was before she'd discovered the room didn't have a view.

It doesn't matter, she scolds herself. *Not really.* She looks around the rest of the room, searching for some feature to redeem its lack of view, but it's as bland as most city centre hotels, with pale wood and pastel colours imposed on an ornate interior. The plasterwork is rather fine, the ceiling higher than she's used to, and there's the usual disparate collection of pictures: a couple of mass-produced prints of vases of flowers in the impressionist style, a glossy photograph of a three-masted ship, and a large gilt-framed mirror on the wall opposite the window.

She hadn't noticed the mirror to begin with, but now a shaft of sunlight from a chance break in the clouds brightens the room, reflecting from the mirror so that it seems to be a window itself, a window on another world. Instinctively, she steps towards it and is startled when a woman springs out at her, a woman wearing the face of a stranger. Less than a heartbeat later she realises it's herself, and she's taken aback by her expression, a strange amalgam of joy and terror. But then it's gone as she rearranges her features into the face she knows, the face Julian loves. Because that's all that matters.

She isn't beautiful. She knows that, even although he tells her she is. She knows it's just his love for her that transfigures her in his eyes. So she smiles and doesn't disagree but is aware that her nose is too long, her lips too short, her eyes an undistinguished brown, her dark hair neither one thing nor another. She runs her fingers through it now, sweeping it back from her face. She wears no make-up, because he doesn't think she needs it, but the perfume she wears is the one he bought her at Christmas, a hot sultry scent, heavier than something she might have chosen for herself.

She looks at her reflection and thinks it strange that he sees a different person from the one she sees. She wonders, for the first time, how he sees himself, how others see him. But she prefers not to think of the others: his wife, his grown-up children, his colleagues, his friends. They, surely, see only what he wants them to see, not the whole man she knows, and she dismisses her thoughts of those others with a quick shake of the head. He'll be here soon, and they'll have eyes only for each other. The view won't matter, nor the strange unworldly image in the mirror. But still she sits, looking at her reflection, trying to catch that first sense of unreality, or reality. Was the woman she'd seen so briefly her true self, caught for a second in the purity of silver? She's looking so hard that, for a moment, she doesn't realise the phone is ringing.

'Julian?' She snatches up the receiver. *He's here*, she thinks. *He's down in the foyer*. But he isn't. He's not even calling her. It's the hotel receptionist with a message from a Professor Brinkley to let her know the conference is overrunning, but he'll meet her after dinner. Does she want to book a table?

'Sorry?' Deborah asks in confusion.

'A table, madam,' the woman says patiently. 'We're very busy tonight. You'd be advised to book.'

'Oh . . . Yes, please.'

Later, sitting at a table next to the serving door, something Julian wouldn't have tolerated, she wonders why she'd agreed. Perhaps it was because she hadn't wanted to stay in the room with no view and that too observant mirror. But, now she's here, she doesn't want dinner. She doesn't like eating on her own and doesn't feel hungry. Her heart has sunk. It's an old cliché, but it really does feel as if her heart has settled heavily in her chest and is pressing on her stomach. So she toys with a glass of wine as she flicks unenthusiastically through the menu, distracted by the noise from the bar. There's a wedding on, she realises, judging by the number of overdressed men and women who've squeezed themselves into the bar and begun to spill into the adjoining restaurant. They all seem to be enjoying themselves, as she would have been if

Julian had been there. She wouldn't even have noticed the other people, but now, sitting on her own, all she can think about are all the other times this has happened, when he's been late because of some crisis or other, and she's been kept waiting, her stolen hours running away like sand in an hour-glass.

'Bride or Groom?'

The voice startles her out of her introspection, and she looks up to see a man looking down at her, his head tilted to one side like a blackbird hoping for a worm. He pulls out the chair opposite her, sits himself down, plonks his elbows on the table, props his head in his hands and continues to look at her with more than a passing interest.

'No, don't tell me. I'm rather good at this sort of thing.'

Surprised rather than offended, she stares back at him. He's older than her, judging by a face that looks decidedly lived in, and he's rather scruffy. His thick dark hair, which falls across oddly pale grey eyes, is in dire need of a cut, and he's not shaved for a couple of days. She's just beginning to be a little worried by that persistent stare when he smiles a rather engaging smile. His teeth are large and white but uneven, and one of the front ones is chipped. It's a smile that takes years off his face, and, in spite of her heavy heart, she smiles back.

'Bride!' he announces with a snap of his fingers. 'Definitely not Groom since –' He squints meaningfully at her left hand. '– you're not married, or with anyone, so if you were a friend of the groom there's no way his now-lady-wife would have asked you to the wedding. So you must be a friend of the bride, but a distant one, and you've outgrown one another. Or else you'd be over there with the others.' He jerks his head at the bar. 'Unless you're escaping? Like me?'

'I'm not with the wedding party,' she says. 'I'm here to . . . to meet a friend, later on this evening.'

But he doesn't seem surprised, or even embarrassed, and just grins.

'All right. I confess I didn't really think you were with that lot.' He tilts his head towards the noisy bar and gestures at the crowded restaurant. 'It's just that you have the table I had my eye on. Should have booked but . . .' He shrugs. 'They tell me I'll have to wait an hour and I'm starving. So . . . I was wondering . . ?' He smiles his engaging smile once more, a small boy not only asking to be forgiven but expecting a treat into the bargain. She glances around, sees that he's right, and feels unable to say no. Although she dislikes eating on her own, she's uncomfortable with strangers. *What will we talk about?* she wonders. But it turns out that she needn't have worried, because he talks enough for both of them and, between mouthfuls, explains that he's a photographer, here to cover the wedding of the happy couple who're having their reception in the hotel that night. But he's finished, thank goodness, so he's off duty now. His name, he tells her, is Robert.

'Robert,' he repeats. 'Not Rob or Bob. I can't abide contractions.' He raises an eyebrow at her.

'Deborah,' she tells him. 'Not Debbie or Debs.'

'Excellent choice of name,' he says approvingly. 'Well, Deborah, let's not beat about the bush with unnecessary social chit-chat. What do you do for a living?'

She tells him she's a radiographer. It's not a profession that normally excites much interest, but he raises an impressed eyebrow.

'Wow! A woman who sees below the surface, while my good self only catches the superficial.'

She's never thought of it like that before, and she looks at him quizzically, trying to see below his surface to the man beneath, to see him as he might if he'd caught his own reflection in an unexpected mirror. She sees a man who's been disappointed in life but who's not quite given up on hope. She sees a man who dreams but who's capable of laughing at those dreams. She sees . . .

'Don't!' he exclaims with a nervous laugh. 'You're giving me the creeps! Next thing you'll be telling me I've got a crack in my left shoulder blade and that my nose was broken a long time ago and healed out of line. Although I expect you can tell about the nose without an X-ray!' They both laugh since his rather long nose is indeed distinctly crooked. 'Seriously, though,' he goes on. 'I envy you, being able to strip away the flesh and get down to the bones. I suppose that's what I try to do when I take pictures, to get below the skin, to see the bones and sinews, the structure of a person, what they were born with rather than what they've added over the years, or what's been added to them. When I look at someone I want to photograph, that's the reason. It's because I catch a glimpse of the person under the skin and I want to see more, so it's a pity you weren't with the wedding party, because I'd like to have taken your picture.' Then his dreamy expression vanishes and he looks mortified. 'Oh, God! I know what you're thinking. It's a classic chat-up line, isn't it? But I promise you I'm not trying to chat you up. Wouldn't dream of it! Anyway, I'm off in the morning, catching the 9.10 back to Edinburgh, to deal with the consequences of a rather messy divorce. And let's not forget you're here to meet a friend.'

'Yes,' she says, and, to cover his embarrassment, she begins to speak of Julian, telling him he's a consultant cardiologist, that's he's very eminent, that she's known him for two years. She makes it clear that they're very much in love, that he's distinguished and cultured and, in her opinion, couldn't compete with any other man. She doesn't tell him that Julian's a great deal older than her, that although he's married to a woman interested only in her horses, and that his children have grown up and moved to London, the question of a divorce, messy or otherwise, has never been raised. But it will, she thinks. This weekend, their second anniversary; somehow, the topic will come up. She doesn't tell Robert that either, but she has the uncomfortable feeling he understands these things, that although he's a man who normally has difficulty guarding his tongue he's being unnaturally restrained on this particular topic. She's glad, therefore, when, as the meal comes to an end, she looks up and sees Julian standing in the doorway of the dining room.

'Who was that?' Julian wants to know as they leave the room together.

'The photographer for the wedding they had here. He shared my table since they were so full. I expect that's why they couldn't let us have a room with a view. But it doesn't matter. Let's go up.'

But he wants a drink in the bar first, wants to tell her about the conference, how his talk had gone, whose arguments he'd refuted, what people had said to him afterwards. He's still high with it and doesn't apologise for being late. *Being in love means never having to say you're sorry.* She wonders if that's really true, but the thought's gone as quickly as it surfaces. He's here now, with her. He has so many claims on his attention – she understands that – and yet he's made time for her. Only a little time, but if she's calm and quiet and understanding, if she makes herself a place to rest, then surely he'll keep turning to her until the habit of turning becomes so ingrained he'll realise there's no need ever to leave. He'll understand it could always be like this. He could divorce Charlotte and marry her. But Deborah can't make demands. It's part of their unspoken pact, part of what he values in her. All she can be is her loving self, and so she smiles and listens, patient and undemanding. She's had enough practice at being both.

Later, in their room, she lies awake with his head on her shoulder, listening to his breathing and watching the lights of the traffic gloss the walls in red and yellow. The mirror catches the light and throws it back into the room, as if it's watching them both: the man, his face relaxed in sleep, looking older than she thinks of him, the woman holding him uncomfortably, his weight pressing her down. Earlier, his absence had been a weight on her heart. Now his presence is a weight on her bones, on the self that lies below the skin. Lying there, cramp developing in her arm, she thinks of radiography and photography, and of mirrors that are windows into another world. She thinks of how these artificial means can capture the truth of things, of how a magnesium flare can burn down to the bone, of how radiation can speed through flesh as if it's no barrier at all. Briefly, in the restaurant, she'd seen beneath a stranger's surface to the man beneath. As here, in the mirror, she sees beneath Julian's. She seems to have caught the trick of it, and now, beneath her closed eyelids, in the silver of her own imagination, she begins to see herself.

'Breakfast?' she asks brightly the next morning. It's early still, the traffic outside in the street a distant hum. She's been up for an hour already and is standing by the window, looking out at the view.

'Mmm,' he says, still half asleep, opening his eyes to squint at her across the room. 'Phone reception, and tell them to send it up.'

'No, I'm going downstairs to order it myself. I want it to be a surprise. It's our anniversary, after all!'

He laughs indulgently then closes his eyes once more. 'My sweet Deborah! Tell them to make sure the coffee's strong, and get them to send skimmed milk, not the usual stuff. But I don't have to tell you . . .'

Downstairs, at reception, she orders breakfast. She's uncharacteristically firm because it's a special occasion. The coffee must be strong, the orange juice freshly squeezed, the eggs poached rather than fried, the tomato grilled properly.

'Yes, madam,' the receptionist says sullenly. 'And the same for yourself?'

'No, it's just for one,' says Deborah. She picks up her overnight bag and sets off down the steps and out into the street, glancing at her reflection in the glass doors as she goes. She sees a stranger there, a woman she doesn't recognise, but the woman's expression no longer startles her for it's one of joy and no longer of terror. She smiles and checks her watch. If she hurries, she'll just make the 9.10 to Edinburgh.

The Tower

H arry wakes to find he's been dreaming of the island, the island with the tower. But perhaps it isn't a dream. Perhaps it's a memory. He can no longer tell one from the other.

He's heard it said that memories are the stories we tell ourselves to make sense of the world, but he's not convinced. Life, he thinks, is the story. It has a beginning, a middle and an end. It's dreams that are the true reality.

He opens his eyes, and everything's white. The sky's white. The sea's white. The sand's white. It's summer, the golden white summer that lasts for the whole of the school holidays. The sun shines all day and every day, and the nights are hot with sunburn and the smell of calamine lotion. There's sand between his toes and in his shorts and tea-shirt. There's even sand in his sandwiches.

And what would you like for breakfast today, Mr Wainwright?

Breakfast? He doesn't remember breakfasts. All he remembers are the picnics, the lettuce and tomato sandwiches, the pan-loaf bread as soft as a cloud, the black and bitter crusts.

'Lettuce,' he says. 'Tomato.'

You can't have those for breakfast. Maybe for tea, the voice says. *Let's try again, shall we?*

There was lemonade too. Glass bottles with heavy rubber stoppers. Lemonade and orangeade.

'Orangeade,' he says.

Orange juice? That's better! And maybe a bit of porridge?

Orangeade staining his lips and tongue. 'Look at you!' his mother says. 'You've got an orange smile!'

That's a lovely big smile, Mr Wainwright! Porridge it is then!

The bubbles in the orangeade prickle up his nose, painfully acid, making him sneeze.

'Nose!' he says, fretfully.

Is the mask bothering you? It's helping you breathe. There . . . Is that better?

He dreams again, or remembers. White becomes black becomes white. There are voices he doesn't understand, faces he doesn't recognise, sounds he doesn't like. *Beep, beep, beep. Drip, drip, drip.* When the white changes to black there are lights flashing. *On, off, on, off.*

'It's an old lighthouse,' his mother tells him as they wade towards the island, splashing through the shallows, being careful not to stand on the razor shells. The wide expanse of sand and mud is steaming in the hot sun. Some of the sand is hard, like corrugated iron. Some is soft and glutinous, and, if he stands still and wriggles his toes, his feet gradually sink until the sand grips his ankles. 'I'm stuck,' he said, holding out a hand.

'No, you're not,' his mother says, pulling him free. 'Come on. We're almost there.'

The island is tidal. It's part of the land, then part of the river. The tower stands, impossibly high, but it's a ruin, the doorway black, the windows empty. It scares him, and he starts to cry.

Is something wrong, Mr Wainwright? Are you missing your family? Maybe someone will come to see you later on today.

'Come on, Harry. There's nothing to be frightened of. The tide's still going out and, anyway, we're almost there.'

'Tide,' he says, in the white place. The tide changes too. In, out, in. Everything changes from one thing to the next and back again. White, black, white. Day, night, day. Summer, winter, summer. Young, old, young. No, not that. 'Tide,' he insists, groping for certainty.

Time, Mr Wainwright? It's half past three, almost visiting time. Can't you make out the clock? Shall I see if I can find your glasses?

He doesn't know this woman. He doesn't recognise her face. His eyes, fogged, drift about the room. There's another face, on the wall. Is it a clock? No, it's a sundial, a compass. Half-past three. South. East. Southeast – yes, he's got his bearings now.

And here's Tracy to see you! You remember Tracy, don't you?

Hello Grandpa!

We're a bit confused today, aren't we, Mr Wainwright? But we gave everyone a lovely big smile this morning. Can you manage a smile for Tracy?

Someone takes his hand.

'Take my hand, Harry. The water's not deep.'

But it looks deep. 'Water,' he says, doubtfully.

Are you thirsty, Grandpa? That'll be the oxygen. It dries you out. Here, let me help you. There we are . . .

'Here we are!' They crunch up the little beach through the drifts of fine shell shingle, and they're on the island, the island with the tower. 'Let's explore!'

The grass is sharp to his fingers. Carpets of plants sprawl through the pebbles, grey-leaved, starred with the yellow flowers of silverweed. *Potentilla.* He still remembers the name. There are shells and stones, a deserted nest of dried reeds, the carcase of a seal. 'Don't touch that, Harry, it's dirty.' There's a picnic rug and lemonade and sandwiches wrapped in waxed paper. The river's on one side, and there's a mile or more of tidal sand on the other. The north shore of the river is closer than he's ever seen it, the boom of traffic louder. A train rushes past, heading for Carnoustie, and he can hear a car-alarm.

Beep, beep, beep.

'Turn it off,' he says. It's spoiling everything: the sound of the river, the waves on the shingle beach, the cries of the gulls and plovers and curlews. 'Turn it off,' he says, but there's a hand over his mouth and no-one can hear him. 'Turn it off!'

But you need the oxygen, Grandpa. No, don't . . . Please . . . Nurse! Nurse!

The island's gone, and the tower, but he can still hear the car-alarm. *Beep, beep, beep.*

'Car,' he says querulously. 'Car.'

Yes, I came by car, Grandpa. The one Mum and Dad gave me for my eighteenth. Don't you remember? It's new, well almost new, and it only cost . . . Beep, beep, beep . . .

Car,' he says, closing his eyes and reaching for the island once more, for that perfect summer's day, for that perfect childhood.

'Isn't this lovely, Harry?' his mother says, lying down on the picnic rug and closing her eyes.

'Mother,' he says happily, reaching for her too.

Mother's not here, says the voice with the car. *She comes on Fridays. Don't you remember?*

Of course he remembers! He remembers everything – the stones and the shells, the skull of a bird, bleached by the sun. He remembers his mother pointing to the river, the buoys, red and green. 'They guide the ships up-river, Harry. So do the lighthouses. Do you see all the lighthouses? They've got lights on them, so even in the dark the ships know where to go. They just need to find the light and it will take them home. But the river changes. That's why there are old lighthouses. Look – over there on Buddon, and there, at Tayport. And this one, on the island.'

He doesn't like the thought of the river changing. He doesn't like change. But he likes the white towers, the ones with the lights, and he likes the idea that, no matter where he is, a light will guide him home. But he doesn't like the dull lightless towers, and he's still afraid of the tower on the island with its black doorway and empty windows.

'Come on,' his mother says. 'Race you to the top of the island, and I'll show you another lighthouse.'

The island isn't big. It's a curve of shingle lying between river and beach, a cast up mound of pebbles, seeded with grasses. The top's barely above sea-level, but when they reach the highest of the shingle banks his mother picks him up and points at the long flat line of the seaward horizon. 'There! Do you see, Harry? Follow my finger.'

He screws up his eyes, and eventually he can make it out, a little chip of white between blue and blue, a lighthouse on the edge of the world.

'That's the Bell Rock Lighthouse,' she tells him. 'It marks a rock out beyond the mouth of the river. That's an island too when the tide's out.'

'Tide,' he says.

Time, Mr Wainwright? It's half-past six.

She means south, of course. Silly woman!

So it's time for tea. Do you fancy a sandwich then? Now, that's a lovely smile! Have you got your appetite back?

But there's no sand in the sandwich. It's not real.

'No,' he says, pushing it away. 'No.'

You have to eat. You'll waste away if you don't eat.

Wasting away. Washing away. Tide and river, washing the island away, eating at the foundations of the tower. It's all gone now, island and tower. Change came, and it's all different now. But that's just a story. That's just life, and life doesn't matter. In his dreams, in his memory, the island's still there, the island with the tower. It will always be there, and he'll always be on it, and his mother will still be lying there on a picnic rug in the sunshine, her eyes closed. He starts to cry again. Eyes closed. A box with the lid screwed shut, lowered into earth, not sand. Eyes closed . . .

Eyes open. 'Goodness, is that the time! We'd better get a move on. The tide will be coming in. Come on, Harry.'

'I want to stay.'

'So do I, but if we do we'll be cut off by the tide, and we'll have to spend the night here. You don't want that, do you?'

But he does. He wants to see the lighthouses guide the ships up-river. He wants to see the buoys blinking, red, green, red, green.

'I want to stay,' he says. 'I want to *live* here.'

'Maybe you will, one day. Now, come along. Race you to the shore!'

It wasn't until later that he understood how close it must have been, the tide coming in, tearing across the flat expanse of tidal sand, the woman and the boy racing ahead of it, his mother's laughter odd and sharp before softening into a relieved gasp as they reach the dunes and the forest. Sometimes he dreams of a tide racing behind him, the water rising, from ankle to knee. He dreams he's striding through water, but it's not water. It's mud, and he's trapped, and there's no one holding out a hand. In his darkest times he dreams he's standing on a rock at the edge of the world, a rock that's crumbling beneath his feet. A tower rises above him, its light blinking, off, on, off, on, but the walls of the tower are smooth and white, and there's no door, no stair, and the tide's coming in . . .

I don't think it will be long now . . .

'I wanted to stay for ever,' he tells his mother, looking back at the island, already vanishing behind the first veils of a streaming summer haar.

'We'll go back one day.'

He's not sure if they ever did. Events slip between the fingers of his memory like soft summer sand, and all he's left with are details, pinpricks of lights in the dark. He sometimes wonders if it's all just a story he's told himself. Was there ever an island? Was there ever a tower? But if it's a story it must have had an ending, so perhaps he did return when he was older, and alone. Perhaps the water only came up to his ankles, not his knees. Did he reach the island? He doesn't know. Perhaps he lost his way, mired himself in mud and was too afraid to continue. In the white place he no longer knows what to think, but in the dark, in the dream, he does.

In the dream, he finds his way by bank and channel and climbs up the shingle beach to the marram grass and silverweed. In the dream, the tower still stands with its black doorway and empty windows, but this time he isn't afraid to go in. Shadow falls, black after the white, and he hears birds, high up in the tower, the clap of pigeon wings. A feather, dove grey and barred with black, drifts past his face. Only birds can reach the top of the tower now, the place where the light once burned, for although a stair spirals up the inside of the building its lower part is a litter of rubble lying at his feet.

But, in the dream, he's a bird. He's a gull, a plover, a curlew, and he's rising, spiralling up into the dark, to the place where the light burns, where the sun rises, a great ball of light on the edge of the world. In its centre, a pointing finger, is a tower, until it vanishes in the blaze of light, and the horizon is a perfect line once more.

Beep, beep, beeeeeeeep . . .

'Car,' he says and sighs because, finally, it stops and everything is quiet once more as the light guides him back home.

A Bobble Hat in Blue

He's dreaming of the river, of banks and buoys, of sand and silt, of a river rushing to the sea. Sometimes, in such dreams, he's running, stumbling knee-high in water that has all the fluidity of porridge, and he's late for something: a plane, a meeting, the rest of his life. At other times, however, there's nowhere to run, because he's standing on a sandbank far from the shore, the water rising to his ankles, his knees, his crotch, his throat, washing over his head. But he never drowns, and instead finds himself on a beach, fingers clawing at wet sand, with the sea behind him, sucking and hissing. Usually he discovers that he's naked, but no-one notices. He is, in such dreams, invisible.

Gradually the dream recedes, leaving him beached on the edge of the day. He opens his eyes to blue-green shallow water, rippling in the wind. He sees acres of sand and doesn't know where he is or when or even who. He seems, in these moments, to be nothing but himself, with everything ahead of him, full of promise. But the feeling never lasts for long, and reality closes around him, brick by brick, bar by bar.

He's in his bedroom, and the sun's shining through closed curtains that stir in a draught from the partly open window. The curtains are the blue-green of algae, the walls the brown of wet mud. No wonder he dreams of the river and the sea. He can still hear it, the hiss and suck of breakers on gravel, the sound of breathing.

That will be Stella, he thinks, pleased to remember his wife's name, to remember that he has a wife. He squints at the light beyond the curtained window and wonders if he's late for something. A plane perhaps? A meeting? Surely he ought to be going to work? Then another brick mortars itself into position. He's not late for anything. He has no need to get up today or any other day since all days are the same. Weekends don't mean anything, not even holidays, because, as Stella keeps telling him, *every day is a holiday, Gerald, now we're retired.*

Gerald. That's his name. Odd how it comes back to him last. Gerald. Not Gerry. He hasn't been Gerry for years. He's sixty-five. *Life begins at sixty-five,* Stella tells him, but he's yet to be convinced.

The bedroom used to be magnolia. His dreams, in magnolia, were as light as air, insubstantial and without meaning, but now they're as murky as the room that presses in on him. Stella tells him a bedroom should be dark and intimate, but to Gerald their bedroom is as intimate as a slice of mouldy bread. He keeps that thought to himself, however. There are no warning buoys in a marriage, but Gerald has learned to navigate this particular river. He knows where the shallows are, the over-falls and rocks, and whether the tide is flooding or ebbing. He knows when to keep his mouth shut.

Stella has taken up interior decorating since they retired. She has taste, she explains. Gerald says nothing, because what does a man who prefers magnolia know about taste? Stella has taken up a great many things since retiring. *We're free now*, she tells him. *We can do all the things we always wanted to do – take up new hobbies, make new friends, take an interest, Gerald.* Staring into space in his slippers is *not* an interest, apparently. He needs to get out more, she tells him. She doesn't want him under her feet all the time. Why doesn't he join a club, go to a class, take up photography? Surely he has friends he could meet up with?

But he doesn't. His friends were blokes he used to go to the pub with after work. He's met up with them once since leaving and discovered that they're no longer his friends. A river lies between them now, and they stand on opposite banks, each envying the other. He doesn't want to make new friends. He wants to be friends with the woman he married.

But Stella's just too busy. She's joined a book group, taken up Tai Chi, meets other retired women for lunch, and goes to lectures on improving subjects. She rattles cans for various charities, does a stint in the Oxfam shop and is thinking of joining a political party. She gets her hair done with alarming frequency, wears jeans and heels and too much lycra. She drinks Pinot Grigio and tries one diet after another. She tells him she prefers herbal tea.

'What time is it?' she asks when he brings her a cup. It's half past eight, as it happens. It's a Tuesday in October, and in a week or so the clocks will go back. But time won't.

'What are you up to today?' he asks, as he might enquire of a guest.

'I'm going to finish my book,' she replies, indicating the slim volume on her bedside unit, a grim tale of a political refugee struggling with what seems to Gerald to be overwhelming disadvantages. 'Then I'm meeting Marjorie for lunch. You remember Marjorie? From Tai Chi?' He doesn't. 'We're going to that little café on the square. They do a lovely ciabatta. And after that . . .'

After that, Gerald stops listening. He's wondering what happened to the woman who liked sweet sherry and steak pie, who had fallen arches and love handles, who cried at Barbara Cartlands and never, ever, missed The Archers.

'. . . and then you and I are going to that restaurant I told you about, before we go to see the Chekov. So don't be late, whatever it is you're doing today. What *are* you doing?'

Now isn't the time to confess he'd intended doing nothing, so he improvises. 'Thought I'd take a walk, get a bit of fresh air. Out to the Point, maybe. I haven't been there in ages.'

He walks down the road and into the estate, then takes the track by the farm that runs down to the beach. The track skirts forest and heath, following the shore, bounded in places by the concrete blocks of the old shore defences. The tide's well out today, but it must be on the turn, since the Pool buoy's tilting to the current. Beyond, in the channel, the pilot boat is powering up the river, rushing back to port like a collie let off the lead.

Gerald has suggested getting a dog. He'll have time to walk it now he's retired, and he's happy to be the one to pick up all that shit. Stella, not recognising irony, vetoes the idea. She doesn't want them to be tied. So Gerald walks alone along the edge of the sand, crosses the nature reserve fence at the stile and heads for the dunes at Tentsmuir Point. He doesn't see anyone, but doesn't expect to. Most people don't go much beyond the carpark in the forest, and the dunes at the Point are a long walk from anywhere.

There's a cold wind today, an easterly, blowing in his face, and the air's gritty with sand, but he gets some shelter from the dunes. They're bigger than he remembers, but this is a transitory land; sand is scoured from one part of the river and deposited in another. Grasses take root. Dunes form. He crosses a muddy area of dune slack, only flooded now at the highest of tides, and climbs up through a scrub of marram and thistle to the top of the dune. To the west is the river, narrowing down to Broughty Ferry. To the east, beyond the sandbanks that lie on either side of the channel, is the sea. He counts the buoys out: the Pool, the Inners, the Abertay. The rest are lost in the haze.

'Aye, aye.'

Gerald jumps. He'd thought he had the beach to himself, but a man is sitting cross-legged on a picnic blanket in a hollow of the dunes just below him. Beside him stands a small rucksack, a flask and a steaming cup. He has a pair of binoculars in his hands, and he's just lowered them to look up at Gerald. He's wearing a ridiculous bobble hat.

And nothing else at all.

'Black-tailed Godwit,' the man says, jerking his chin at the shoreline where some greyish birds are poking about the tideline. 'Want to look?'

He means at the bird, with the binoculars. He doesn't mean 'do you want to look at me?' although Gerald is doing just that. He can't help himself. He hasn't seen a man this naked in he can't remember when, and the only time he himself is truly naked these days is in his dreams. So maybe this is a dream. Maybe he's still asleep in that river-coloured bedroom, still dreaming of being invisible.

'They're not that common,' the man adds. 'Could be your last chance.' He holds up the binoculars, and Gerald takes them and looks at the birds.

'Marvellous,' he says, because he has to say something. He wonders if not wearing clothes is allowed, if it's even legal. Should he report it to someone? But the man seems harmless enough.

'Fancy a cuppa?' the man asks. 'I've got more than I can get through, and it's a pity to waste it. There's a bit of sponge left too; the wife's a dab hand at a Victoria.' He shifts over a bit on the blanket, leaving space for Gerald, who sits down. It seems churlish to just walk away. They sit side by side, looking out at the sea, drinking tea and eating Victoria sponge. Stella used to make it before she went on that flour-free diet, he tells the man, whose name turns out to be Humphrey.

'Gerry,' Gerald says. 'I'm Gerry.'

Humphrey tells him about the birds, points out waders and gulls, ducks, and geese. Gerald tells him about Stella's aspirations as an interior designer. They both laugh. 'Wives!' Humphrey says feelingly. Neither, at any point in a long and rambling conversation, mention that Humphrey isn't wearing any clothes. Eventually Gerald's bird-watching companion gets to his feet and packs away his flask, binoculars, and the picnic blanket. 'Better get going or I'll be in trouble. She lets me out on Tuesdays though, so I'll maybe see you here again.'

And then he's off, wending his way down the beach towards the carpark, still wearing the bobble hat, still wearing nothing else at all. Gerald stays on the dunes, watching the birds, wondering what just happened. Eventually he realises he'd better get going or he'll be in trouble too, and he walks back the way he's come.

Stella's ready to go and champing at the bit. She's been to the hairdresser again, and her hair is sticking up in spikes. She's wearing a purple tent thing that hangs off one shoulder, tight shiny leggings and high heels in an unfortunate shade of puce.

'How do I look?' she asks coquettishly, giving a little twirl so he can see the full horror of her outfit.

He thinks she looks like a prostitute, but he's not fool enough to say so. Nevertheless, something has to be said. 'You look . . . lovely.'

A few moments later she's banging about in the kitchen, slamming doors, and she's tight-lipped all through the meal. On another occasion he might have told her about the man from the beach, but he knows that anything he says tonight will be the wrong thing. Later, at the play, she digs him in the ribs when he falls asleep and hisses that he's a philistine. They go home in silence, go to bed in silence, and Gerald dreams of the river again, of dunes and birds, of a picnic blanket and Victoria sponge. He dreams of creamy flesh, of blue veins just below the surface, of being naked, of being visible.

He goes for a walk most days now. *Getting out of your hair, dear.* He walks up the river, around the farm or into the forest. He doesn't go back to the Point, but occasionally, in the course of the next week, he surprises a smile on his face. And so, when Tuesday comes around once more, he packs a rucksack, fills a flask, and tells Stella he's going for a walk, that he might be some time.

The day is milder than before, the wind gentler, the tide well up the beach, the banks deep in tidal water. The river has become the sea. Humphrey is sitting there with his bobble hat on and nothing else at all.

'Aye, aye,' he says.

Gerald sits down, stands up, then sits down again. Things are briefly awkward, then less so. Some time later Humphrey wanders off in the direction of the carpark, leaving Gerald alone. He needs to be alone, to think. A line has been crossed here, the bar of a river, and he's in deep water now, black depths, beyond the power of any tide to draw him back to the safety of the shore. He feels as if he's half-dreaming, half-awake, that everything lies ahead of him now, full of promise. He puts his clothes on again and goes home.

It's the beginning. He goes every week, rain or shine, gale or snow. One day it's not Humphrey who's there but George. He's younger than Gerald, an unemployed cabinet maker, good with his hands. They shouldn't have anything in common, but it seems they do. Later there are others. Sometimes they light a fire and huddle about it for warmth.

Eventually, he tries to tell Stella. He explains that he's joined a club, that they meet out at Tentsmuir Point. He admits ruefully that there's a name for men like him. She stares at him, surprised. It's been a long time since he's surprised her. Then she laughs.

'You're a *twitcher*!' she exclaims. 'Who'd have thought it?'

When his birthday arrives, he receives 'Birds of the British Isles' and an expensive pair of binoculars. Stella does up the spare bedroom as 'Gerald's Den' and buys framed prints of puffins and scatter cushions that match their beaks. As a reward for finding a hobby, joining a club, taking an *interest*, he's allowed to choose the colour of the walls. He chooses magnolia. He sleeps better these days and, although his dreams are still disturbing – since what dreams aren't? – they're disturbing in a different way. The décor of the bedroom no longer bothers him. The walls make him think of sand, darkened by rain. The curtains remind him of marram grass with its blue-green razor edges.

Life goes on, running between banks. Stella redecorates the sitting room in 'Wild primrose' and 'Bright apple'. *Spring colours, Gerald.* Tuesdays are his 'birdwatching' days now, and sacrosanct – until one particular Tuesday in March.

He'd warned the others he might not make it that day. It's Stella's birthday, and it doesn't begin well.

She holds up the blouse he's bought her between finger and thumb, and her face has that closed pinched look he's learned to dread. He'd had the happy thought of asking Marjorie what Stella might like. The blouse cost him an arm and a leg, a skimpy badly-made little thing, but if it's what Stella wants . . . Turns out it isn't.

'She put you up to this, didn't she?' Stella snarls. 'She told you to get this size, didn't she? Bitch! But I'll show her. I'll get into this if it kills me!' She marches into the bathroom, and for some minutes he hears grunting. Then silence. Then sobbing. Eventually he plucks up the courage to go in. She's standing in front of the mirror, half into the blouse, half out. It's torn down one side, and she's distraught.

'I'll take it back,' he says. 'I'll get it in a bigg– . . . another size.'

'Oh, what's the use?!' she wails, ripping the thing off. 'Look at me! Go on – look at me! Tell me I'm lovely!'

Gerald says nothing.

'You can't, can you?'

No, he can't because, right now, she isn't. Her body is trussed with straps and elastic. Lycra panels squeeze her flesh like a toothpaste tube, sucking it in in one place only for it to bulge out in others.

'I'm fat,' she declares. 'I'm old and fat and tired. My feet hurt and I *hate* Chekov! I hate those bloody books. I hate wine. I hate *myself!* But you don't care. You have your friends, your club. I don't have *any* friends. Marjorie's a *bitch!*'

Eventually he coaxes her out of the bathroom and makes them both a cup of proper tea.

'Let's go for a walk,' he suggests.

He packs and shoulders a rucksack, and they walk through the village, past the estate and down to the beach. They head for the dunes at Tentsmuir Point.

The wind's from the east, and the tide's out. It's March and the clocks will be going forward soon, and maybe, just maybe, time will too.

The others are surprised, of course, but recover quickly.

'You must be Stella.' Daphne comes over, one hand held out, batwing arms wobbling, breasts slapping against her chest.

'Gerry's told us all about you,' George says, his beer belly bouncing as he too comes over. Stella stares open-mouthed, looks away, then looks back.

'Fancy a cuppa?' Humphrey asks, putting his binoculars down. 'There's a bit of Victoria if you fancy it.'

The others gather round, Gloria and Daphne, Humphrey and Edna, George and Lewis, Isaac and Noah, and they introduce themselves. Quite a few are wearing hats. After all, you lose ninety percent of your body-heat through your head, so it makes sense. They surround Stella with their bellies and their rolls of flab, with their scrawny arms and their dimpled bottoms, with the flaws of a lifetime and the marks of their age, with their pure unclothed humanity. Gerald slips to the back, unnoticed, unpacks his rucksack, gets out his picnic blanket, takes off his clothes and folds them neatly, then puts on his bobble hat. Stella sees him and stares. The world stops. The tide stops. The river meets the bar. There are no buoys here to tell him which way to go. He has to navigate back to land by instinct.

'Care to join me, birthday girl?' he asks.

She goes on staring at him, pale, then red, then pale again. She's on her toes, ready to run. But she doesn't. She pulls down the zip of her jacket in one swift defiant movement. She shrugs out of the jacket, tugs off her jumper, kicks off her shoes, steps out of her trousers and wrestles her way out of her underwear. The others look away politely, but then one of them claps and Stella gives a gurgle of laughter as she flings her bra into the wind.

'How do I look?' she asks, standing there, as naked as the day she was born, her flesh as creamy as the petals of a magnolia, pale blue veins pulsing below the surface of her skin. There are red marks where the straps and lycra panels have constrained her flesh, but they're beginning to fade.

'You look beautiful,' he says and hands her a bobble hat in blue, the colour of her eyes.

The Fairway

V ariable, becoming westerly 3 to 4 later . . .
Sarah groans when the early morning shipping forecast wakes her. She's heavy-headed from the sleep into which she'd finally fallen after spending most of the night listening to Martyn pretending to be asleep. Now she just wants to roll over and sink back into oblivion but forces herself to listen to the rest of the forecast. It will be clear, cold perhaps, but fair. It's not a bad forecast for the time of year, so she isn't surprised when Martyn gets up, goes into the kitchen and comes back with the tide tables in his hand.

'It's a spring tide,' he says. 'We could get away by eight.'

Once she might have resented his assumption that she'd fall in with his plans. But not this year, especially when it might be their last sail of the season. So, half an hour later, they're down at the harbour, sniffing the air, Sarah shivering, Martyn muffled up in his waterproofs and the ridiculous hat he's taken to wearing. Everything is damp from the mist that had run up the river at dawn after a clear night, and the handrail is beaded with moisture, the deck slippery, the sails stiff. There's barely enough breeze to lift the pennant.

'For 'Variable' read 'Flat calm,' she complains. 'The forecast was right.'

'The forecast usually is,' Martyn says gravely and, with a sinking heart, she sees his mood plummet. They get away quickly, however, and he seems to recover his spirits. At the beginning of the season they're all fingers and thumbs, but by the end of the year they're a well-oiled machine, with everything to hand, the engine purring evenly, their speed and momentum carefully judged. If it wasn't for the cold and her slip of the tongue, she might even have taken pleasure in their seamless slipping away.

They cut the engine once they're out in the channel, shock the sudden silence with a squeal of winches, and then, with a turn of the wheel, there's quiet once more. Not silence, of course, but the small sounds of water running along the hull, the fluttering luff of the foresail, the log ticking slowly as they drift down the river, caught by the tide, the wind barely strong enough the fill the sails.

Sarah always likes the moment when the confusion of slapping canvas and loose ropes gives way to the controlled tilting to the wind and the feel of the tide catching the keel. She likes to watch the banks recede, houses merge together then fade, farmland give way to forest then to dune and bank. Ahead, the light is rising above the thinning mist, a lemon-coloured light washing the leaden sea, and the whole estuary is open before them.

But today the quiet holds other things, a silence and a tension, a sense that things that have not been said will now be voiced. Martyn seems to be waiting for her to speak, to begin something he's afraid of beginning himself.

'Shall I make coffee?' she asks brightly to break the silence.

'We've only just had breakfast.' Martyn is a creature of habit. Coffee is taken at 10.30 and not before.

'But I'm cold,' she says, and goes below. There isn't much gas left, and the drinking water, after a few weeks of absence, is stale. The biscuits have gone soggy in the tin. The coffee, as most things made on the boat, tastes faintly of bilge water, but it's hot and wet and makes her feel warmer, if no less of a coward.

'Martyn . . .' she begins, after they've drunk their coffee and he's poured his dregs into the river, but he turns away and the opportunity evaporates.

'Listen!'

She hears the gurgle of the wake, the creak of ropes, the distant boom of the city, a train announcing its departure, a dog barking. Nearer, from the banks and mudflats, comes the whirling trill of curlews. Then, high and clear, she hears what Martyn's heard, the honking of geese. They're directly overhead, the veins of their flight caught in the tilting angle of the mast. Stella and Martyn watch them wing their way upriver, and by the time they've disappeared, their calls fading, Sarah no longer has anything to say.

Martyn leaves her to steer and goes forward to stand by the mast, holding on to the shrouds. The wind picks up a little from the west, but the river is smooth and untroubled. The land slides past them, and their progress is effortless. It's easy, at such times, not to think of the return – the wind on the nose, the long beat to windward, the day darkening. But today, with each passing mile, Sarah thinks of going back, and, her mind having strayed into the future, finds herself also wandering in the past. Another boat, but the same river. A different channel but the same abandoned lighthouses. Over the years the forest has encroached on the dunes, the dunes on the sea. The banks are wider now, the channel narrower, and the bar at the river mouth, marked by two buoys, can be a troubled place. She wants to share these changes with Martyn, but he remains resolutely apart, swaying to the growing motion as an old swell heaves its way over the bank from the south east.

They pass the place where the lightship used to be. 'Do you remember . . ?' she might have said another day, another season. But on this day, the last sail of the year, she remains silent and forces herself back into the moment. She will make Martyn do the same. She will offer him tasteless coffee at the wrong time, soggy biscuits and a silence he can fill with the sound of geese if he wants to. She will offer him the wind and the river, and then the sea.

The transition is imperceptible: an opening out, the banks to the north and south falling back. Surf gives way to breakers, breakers to troubled water and then . . . nothing. It's clear now. The mist has lifted, and the rim of the world is sharp and cloudless, notched by the white finger of the distant lighthouse. 'Do you remember . . ?' she wants to ask again. But once more she doesn't.

They're over the bar now, a wild place in a storm, but today the two marker buoys just swing uneasily in the cross-seas. The waves steepen, and the sail slaps in the troughs, but the tide draws them through the angled waves, and, before long, they're free. The water darkens as the seafloor falls away, until it takes on the blue-green damasked quality of great depth. Sarah leans over the side, watches the light spearing downwards, and imagines, as she always does, that she can see creatures with no shape and no name swimming far beneath them. Out there, beyond the edge, she has a sense of other worlds, and draws back, afraid that her imagining of such things might give them life.

'Only the Fairway to go now,' Martyn says unnecessarily. It's about a mile off, a pillar buoy blinking its semaphored message – warning or greeting. This is the place where ships are gathered in: oil rig supply boats coming south from the North-sea oilfields, past Scurdie Ness and the Red Head. Or tankers coming up from the Forth past the Isle of May and the Carr Light. Some even come from the east, past the low black rocks on which the Bell Rock Lighthouse stands. All of them come here, to the Fairway, where the little pilot boat will chivvy them up-river on a rising tide, passing them from one buoy to the next until they reach the wharves and docks of the City.

But today no-one waits to gather her and Martyn in.

'I like it here,' he says, looking around. The wind has dropped away completely now but there's still a little tide taking them north-east towards the Fairway. Yet, sitting on the oily tilting water, it seems to Sarah as if it's they who are tethered and that the buoy is sliding slowly towards them, blinking lazily in the pale afternoon sun.

'The land's last holding,' Martyn says, a quote from something she doesn't recognise, as the Fairway slides past them. Sarah watches it rocking in the swell and imagines the chain that binds it, rusting and weed-slimed, descending through darkening water to impossible depths. She shudders at the thought.

'There should be music here,' Martyn says, his voice sharper now. 'There used to be, didn't there? This was a whistle buoy. Remember how you could hear it from miles away? And there were foghorns on the cliffs. Remember how we sailed below the cliff once and how they boomed out like . . . like wolves? And a bell. There was a bell out on the rocks.'

The tide breathes its last, but Martyn has found his own tide. 'Remember?' he demands, cuffing moisture from his cheek. Appalled, Sarah can think of no way to stop the flood she's seen coming for months and knows she mustn't even try.

'Now, what is there?' He sweeps his arm out to encompass the whole horizon, holding on with the other but so lightly she half-rises, afraid he'll lose his balance and fall. 'Nothing! Nothing but chaos. Listen to it!'

She listens. She hears what he hears – the slap of the sail, a shackle rattling on the shrouds, a gasping flutter from the luff. But then, when she can bear it no more, and knows he's borne it too long already, there's a breath of wind, and the sail snaps full, dragging the boom back. The boat tilts a little and a ripple catches hold of the keel. The log, silent until now, slowly begins to tick. Martyn laughs in a shudder of sound that's half a sob.

'Sorry,' he says. 'Sorry!'

It's all right, she wants to say. She longs to go to him and bend his head to her shoulder. *Everything will be all right*. She wants to hush him like a child but knows she mustn't.

'Chaos, indeed!' she says sternly. 'Well, what now? Where are we heading? North? South? East? Or back home?'

'You choose,' he says, turning away.

'No. You choose,' she snaps, fighting his defeat. She lets the tiller go, and the boat swings into the wind, the sail slapping irritably. 'You choose.'

He comes back to the cockpit. She knows he hates this, the noise, the lack of control. Especially that. He grasps the tiller and pushes it hard down-wind, then winches in the fore-sheet on the other side. The boat heaves-to, the sail pulling against the rudder, and they're drifting now like the buoy, tethered to the land's last holding. It's an option that hadn't occurred to her.

'I said I like it here,' he says, evenly. Not angrily now, not anything. Just calmly. She feels cold all of a sudden. The boat surges into the breeze then falls off again with a hiss.

'We can't stay here for ever,' she points out.

'Why not?'

'Because . . . because we've only got soggy biscuits to eat.'

It's such a stupid reason that they both laugh shakily, and Sarah begins to think they've drawn back from the danger into which Martyn had taken them.

'All right,' he says eventually. 'I'll choose. It's our last sail after all.'

He steps up to the deck and looks to all points of the compass. Close by, the buoy still blinks away. The day is darkening, clouds closing in from the east. In the distance the lighthouse flashes.

'The reason I like it here –' he says, '– is that you can go anywhere. Until you choose, all things are possible. This is the place where you cast loose.' He looks down into the water, the impossible depths, blue-green shifting light and the chain leading downwards.

She sees the possibility cross his mind, and the tears she's beaten back for so long – so long – prickle at the back of her eyes. She'd thought this was a place of gathering in but understands now that he sees it quite differently.

'I wish you'd take off that stupid hat!' she says crossly, brushing a tear away, angry that she's broken at last, that they've both broken, in spite of the promises they'd made to each other.

'I'll take the hat off if you stop pretending it's going to be all right, Sarah.'

'I'm not pretending. I'm just . . . hoping.'

But that's the one direction in which he's not prepared to go.

'Let's go home, Martyn,' she begs.

They both turn towards the West. Clouds have built up over the land and the sky is slate and sullen-looking. The wind has picked up; it's due west now, as forecast, dead on the nose. Sarah imagines their return, beating between banks, the day fading, light from the city confusing, the rush of water in the dark, the cold landfall.

'All right,' he says, loosening the sheet and pulling back the tiller. The boat swings and catches the wind. He pulls off his hat and tosses it into the sea as they pass the Fairway. His scalp is pink, the hair fine where it has begun to grow back. It will take a while, they'd told him. It might never grow back properly. What they haven't told him, but which they both know, is that it might not matter. Sarah imagines the months ahead, beating from one appointment to the next, the setbacks, the rough places where hazards come out of the dark, the buoys that blink their unintelligible warnings, and the cold, cold landfall.

The wind strengthens, as predicted, but as it does so it veers into the south. Martyn eases the boat to windward, adjusts the ropes and turns his face to the wind, his fine hair blowing back from his thin drawn face as the boat plunges home, sweetly now, on a close reach, picking up speed as the wind continues to veer. They rush through the darkening river, the shrouds taut and humming, their wake chuckling under the stern. There is music here after all.

'You see?' she yells against the wind and the rush of water and gestures to the pennant at the top of the mast. 'Forecasts *can* be wrong!'

She's crying openly now. He's thrown his hat away, so she mustn't pretend any more. But she can still hope. Hope, surely, is allowed.

A Glimpse of the Past

Introduction

I have a keen interest in the history of Scotland and am particularly fascinated by the Dark Ages, the period in which my longer fiction is set, but I enjoy writing historical short stories set at other times in the past. The stories in this section are arranged in roughly chronological order. The first of these, *Caught Knapping*, takes place in the present day but is about a man who's convinced he belongs in the Stone Age. *The Eagle and the Serpent* is set in the first century and is my attempt to explain the abandonment of the Roman fortress of Inchtuthil on the River Tay. *The Knowing* takes place a little later, after the departure of the Romans, and follows a Pictish boy as he faces the initiation test of his tribe. *Nechtansmere* is a time-slip story that explores a modern-day sculptor's relationship with the Picts of the 7th century. *A Bohemian Christmas* was inspired by a 10th century Bohemian saint and a well-known Christmas Carol. *The Orb-weaver and the King* is told from the point of view of Robert the Bruce's spider and is set in the 14th century. The final two stories in this section, *The Washer at the Ford* and *The Sparrow*, date from the beginning of the 20th century and both tell the story of young girls falling in love on the eve of wars.

There is further information about each of these stories in the Appendix.

Caught Knapping

U ntil the day I met Bob at the British Museum, about a month after Shirl upped and left me, and everything went tits-up, I'd never had much time for bankers.

I know what you're thinking. *British Fucking Museum! Have you completely lost it, Barry?* And you'd be right. Them as knows me – and there's a fair few who do down Watford way – know I've never been one for museums, galleries, wine-bars – all that crap. Dyed in the wool philistine, me, and proud of it. Give me a Hornets' game down Vicarage Road, a few jars down the boozer and a side-order of Ginster's pasties, and I'm a happy man. Or I was.

So what happened, you're asking? What happened to Barry of Barry the Ballcock fame? (*Barry the Ballcock for all your plumbing problems. Give Barry a bell and it's sorted!*) Had a van, me, and two trainees, nice lads, promising. Business was on the up, Shirl not complaining all hours of the day for a fucking change. Everything was rosy – until the day IT happened. IT. Note the capitals.

It was a Tuesday in May, and the day began as most days begin, in that I woke up. So far, so normal. Except I hadn't woken up, not really. You know them dreams where you think you're asleep and you wake up but weird stuff keeps on happening, so you know you're still dreaming after all? It was like that. So, I was lying in my bed under the blankets, and I was thinking *this isn't right.* That's the only way I can describe it. That it wasn't right. So I gets up, puts my feet on the ground and thinks, *what the fuck!?* Because the grass is softer than usual, and isn't grass supposed to be green? And since when was there grass inside the cave? So I walk over to the mouth of the cave across that soft blue grass wondering why I can't see out, and what's this stuff hanging across the entrance? Spider's webs? I brush the webs aside and put my hand out then – bang! – my hand hits some magic invisible barrier. I push and push, but I can't get my hand through it, so I turn around to see what the fuck's going on, and it isn't my cave after all.

Then I wake up for real, and I'm in my bedroom, my hand against the glass of the window, and Shirl's still asleep, her mouth hanging open. She's snoring like a woolly rhinoceros, which freaked me out because what the fuck's a woolly rhinoceros when it's at home, and how the fuck do I know what one sounds like when it's asleep?

It passed, of course, like wind, but, like wind, it kept coming back at the most inconvenient moments. One minute I was down on my hands and knees sorting out a blocked u-bend, and the next I was staring at a pipe-wrench without a clue what it was or what you were supposed to do with it. Once, I was looking out of one of them square things with the invisible barrier, and I saw something big coming for me.

'Hide!' I yelled. 'It's a mammoth!'

'Think it's a number 72, boss,' Darren said, exchanging a look with Tariq, because this wasn't the first time I'd had one of my 'turns'.

IT had become THEM. My Turns. That's what I decided to call them, because then they sounded medical, like they could be sorted. Not that I went to the doctor or anything. He'd just think I was off my trolley. I could sort it out for myself, I decided. What's the interweb for if not for working out what stuff is when it happens? By this time, though, even Shirl had noticed, which was scary because Shirl isn't the noticing sort.

'What you doing on that laptop?' she kept asking me.

It wasn't until she turned up one night in a little black lacy number that I realised she thought I was into pornography.

Now, I'm no prude, and I like a bit of how's-your-father as much as the next man, but I'm not adventurous. I like it straight, in the dark, me on top, none of your women's magazine crap with scented candles and the like. Shirl, bless her, is a big lass, and that black outfit did nothing for her.

'You look like a right slapper,' I told her, so she went off in the huff, and we were back to the winceyette after that, thank Christ. Didn't stop her though. She started plying me with wine of an evening (and me a pint of mild man!) and inviting me to 'talk'. *What about?* I asked. *Anything at all, Barry.*

Turned out 'anything at all' didn't include Watford's chances in the championship league, and she went off in yet another huff, which put paid to 'talking', but that suited me just fine. I didn't want to talk, especially about IT, because I couldn't see that talking was likely to sort what I was suffering from.

I knew what it was by then, see. I'd been born into the wrong time. It's not uncommon, especially in men at my time of life. Yeah, I can hear all you fuckers laughing! *Barry's having a mid-life crisis!* Well, maybe I was. Maybe it was a, you know, a wotsit – 'an attempt to make sense of an increasingly pointless world'. A cry for help. Because by then I really did need help. But there was hope. All that late night interwebbing had told me one thing that had me sobbing with relief, although I'm not proud about that. You see, I wasn't the only one. I wasn't alone. There were other men out there who'd also been born into the wrong time, and some of them had taken matters into their own hands. You can't go back to when you were supposed to be, but you can re-create the world you should have been part of. You can re-enact it.

I got quite excited when I found out about re-enactment groups, and then I got a bit scared. I've never been one for clubs and societies, and some of these sounded suspiciously like weightwatchers or the AA. You know the sort of thing – 'Is there anything you'd like to share with the group, Barry?' – and me sitting there like a muppet telling everyone about the mammoth and the invisible barrier, then bursting into tears, and everyone being touchy-feely and understanding. Thank Christ, though, it wasn't like that, and the groups were fun to begin with, the blokes friendly enough, real enthusiasts, some of them, real nutters. But none of the groups felt right. Sealed Knot? Too modern. Pax Romana? Too modern. Sparta Mora? Too fucking modern. It turned out there was no society for people like me because I hadn't just been born in the wrong century. I'd been born in the wrong age. The time I belonged to – the time I needed to get back to – was the Stone Age.

That's when things began to fall apart. I'd never felt lonely before, but I did now. Shirl talked about antidepressants and counselling, but I didn't want to pop pills, and I didn't want to talk. I just didn't want to be here and now. The business suffered, of course, and, not long after the mammoth episode, Darren and Tariq both decided plumbing wasn't for them and buggered off. Around the same time, Shirl decided marriage to me wasn't for her either and buggered off as well.

To be honest, though, it was a relief to be alone, to be able to do my own thing. I could sleep on the floor under a mouldy old sheepskin and feel comfortable for once. I could dig food up from the garden and eat it raw and it tasted better than anything from M&S. I spent a lot of time hunting in a nearby wood (snails, mainly) and gathering. I had bonfires, grew a beard, and went barefoot. I was happy, I suppose, but I was still lonely.

And so, from time to time, I'd fight it. I'd shower and shave and put on proper clothes. I'd take a train into town, let the crowds wash around me and tell myself I was one of them. On one occasion I even let them sweep me into the British Museum. Which brings me to Bob.

Now, I've never been one for culture, so this was a first, and I wandered about aimlessly for a while until my attention was caught by a display of stone tools: hand axes and socketed axe-heads, delicate little flint arrowheads, almost translucent, and flakes of flint – microliths they called them – that looked sharp enough to cut flesh. You know how it is when Lewis McGugan scores a particularly good goal? When all the passes work like clockwork, and he slams it right into the back of the net, and you're thinking *Sweet!* and you feel like bawling like a little kid you're so happy? Well it was like that looking at them tools.

'Beautiful . . .'

I hadn't noticed the man standing next to me, and I don't think he'd noticed me, because he was speaking to himself. It was as if he'd seen that perfect goal too. I turned to stare at him, and he stared right back at me.

You know that 'eyes meet' thing you get in Barbara Cartlands? Not that I've read any but Shirl was an addict, always banging on about 'romance' and 'true love', and how you just have to look into someone's eyes and you know. Well I knew. That bloke and me, we recognised one another. Not that it was anything weird, no stirring of the old wotsit, because this man was definitely a bloke, although he wasn't what I'd call a bloke's bloke. He was a little ponce of a chap, designer suit, designer glasses, designer shoes, probably designer fucking underwear. We must have looked a right pair, what with me in my jogging bottoms and trainers with my gut hanging out the way I like it. But it didn't matter. *Beautiful*, he'd said, and so they were.

'Fucking marvellous!' I said, looking at the tools. I could imagine the hand-axe fitting into my palm like a glove, and I wanted to feel it for real. But, short of breaking through the glass of the display cage, there was only one way. 'Reckon I could make one of them,' I said, because, being a plumber, I'm good with my hands.

'Could you really?' he asked.

'If I could get hold of some flint . . .'

At this point, you understand, I didn't know what flint was. I thought it was prehistoric, like dinosaurs, and you couldn't get it any more except in museums.

'You find it in chalk,' the man explained. 'If you're interested, I've a little place on the Downs – chalk country. I'm sure we could ... that is ... my car's just outside.'

And so it began, me and Bob. Turned out the 'little place' was a big fucking estate, that he was rolling in it, being a merchant banker and all. He lived with an architect; Jasper was his name. A couple of, well, you know what. Bob was everything I hated – not just a banker, but an upper-class tory-voter with an enthusiasm for opera and wine. He loathed football in general and fans in particular. *Scum of the earth*, he called us. But – get this – none of that mattered. We were the same. We weren't alone any more.

Jasper hated me of course and couldn't understand what Bob saw in me. 'I haven't told him,' Bob whispered when Jasper flounced off in a huff. 'He wouldn't understand.' He didn't, of course, couldn't see why me and Bob went off to visit Stonehenge or Avebury, didn't see why we chose to camp in Bob's extensive woods when there were several perfectly decent en suites in the house. Eventually it came to a head.

'It's me or him, Robert! You choose! Me, or that ... that *caveman!*'

No contest. Jasper left that very day, leaving Bob in tears. *Soft fucking muppet*, I thought, but I put my arms around him all the same and gave him a hug. I can do touchy-feely when I put my mind to it. 'Never mind, old son,' I said. 'Let's go and do a bit of flint-knapping. That'll make you feel better.'

He sniffed and smiled, and we've been doing it ever since, me and Bob – flint-knapping that is. We're a Stone-Age re-enactment society of two, and we're living the dream.

The Eagle and the Serpent

'**D**eeper.'

I looked up. The helmeted head of Tiberius Claudius Vitalis, Centurion of the Third Century of the First Cohort of the Twentieth Legion of Rome, was a black shape against the sky. I was standing at the bottom of a hole in the ground that was deeper than my own height. And, since there's not a single legionary shorter than six good roman feet, that made it a bloody deep hole. It was raining. Did I mention it was raining? So I was up to my ankles in mud.

'Deeper,' he repeated.

'But Vitalis –'

'That's Sir to you, soldier. Dig it deeper.'

That was how it ended. And this was how it began . . .

'Well, lads, here it is. Your new home.'

Vitalis waved a meaty hand at the expanse of tussocky grass that lay in the bend of a river. There was nothing to be seen but clumps of thistles, a few scattered bushes, and the posts the surveyors had put in place to mark out the fort. It was clearly going to be enormous, but then this was to be no ordinary fort. This was the Twentieth's new Legionary Fortress. We'd built the fort at Deva. Now we were going to build another fort at – where was this exactly? No-one could tell me. And it was raining. Did I mention it was raining?

'Something bothering you, Silanus?' Vitalis asked me, seeing I was looking less than impressed. 'You don't like it? Not flat enough for you?' He kicked at the ground, sending a spray of mud into the air. 'Ground not soft enough for you? You got one of your 'bad feelings' Silanus?'

Someone sniggered. Bugger was in my squad too.

'You want me to write to the Governor and tell him Lucius Valerius Silanus has a bad feeling about the place, and maybe we'd better call it off? The place that Agricola – *Agricola* himself! – chose for a legionary fortress? You want me to do that, Silanus?'

I'd turned red by then. The truth is that I often get these feelings, and sometimes – more often than not – I'm right. And I did have a bad feeling about the place, although I wasn't going to admit it to Vitalis now.

'Right then, you lot, since Silanus has given his gracious permission, perhaps you could all get to work?' He whirled around – eyes in the back of his head, has Vitalis – and caught a couple of the lads smirking. 'What are you waiting for, you useless bunch of cretins?! Get the fucking spades!'

I can count on the fingers of one hand the number of times I've wielded my weapons in earnest. So I'm no expert with the gladius or the pilum. The spade, however, is a tool with which I excel, and there's not been a day since I joined the army when I wasn't digging something or other: ditches, foundations, drains, latrine pits, graves. You name it, I've dug it.

Today it was the ditch we were starting on, and, since I've never been one to shirk my duty, at least not when Vitalis was looking, I was the first to put spade to earth in Pinnata Castra. That's what we were calling it apparently, 'the fort on a wing and a prayer', this fort at the very edge of the empire. I, Lucius Valerius Silanus, Decanus of the Eighth Contubernium of the Third Century of the First Cohort, dug the first spadeful. So perhaps it was fitting that, in the end, the last spadeful was mine too.

In spite of the rain, we made decent enough progress that first day. You get to know earth in the army, and this was river silt, light and friable, easy to dig. The rest of the lads would be having a harder time of it, since they were further south on higher ground, beyond the marshy area, where they were building the usual temporary camp that was to be our home until the walls of the big bugger were finished. Our mules were over there together with our tents, latrines, cooking fires, and a decent palisade to keep out the natives. Did I mention the natives? Eventually, a trumpet rang out, marking the end of that day's shift, and I packed my spade away and clambered out of the ditch and up to the beginnings of the rampart. It wasn't as high as it was going to be since, for now, we were just marking the line, but it was high enough to make out a bit more of the countryside.

From that vantage point you could see it was a good place to have chosen. A river – the natives called it the Tava – ran around three sides of the plateau, headed east for a bit then took a turn south down to Fort Bertha, where the river turns tidal. Upstream, to the west, it ran out of a cleft in the hills. We'd driven the natives back into those hills after the battle. To the north and north-east there were more hills, with other rivers running out of them down narrow valleys. Smaller forts were being built at the mouths of the major valleys to control the natives. This was the frontier the last Governor, General Agricola, had planned, and the new Governor, whatshisname, was putting it in place. In time, however, we'd push beyond this frontier. We'd take over these northern lands as we'd taken over the rest of Brittania, and we'd turn the place Roman.

But, standing there on the rampart, I had that bad feeling again. There was something about the way the river coiled across the plain like a serpent, the way it flowed, silent and deep and sullen like the natives. Caledonians they were called. Barbarians. They painted themselves with animals – snakes and wolves and the like. Try to talk to them, and they'd ignore you. Even when you shouted they pretended they didn't understand. They'd come around in the end, however. We'd civilise them, whether they liked it or not.

But, as the days, then weeks, then months, went by, my bad feeling didn't go away. If anything, it got worse. There were portents, see. Now I'm no more superstitious than the next man, but there's no point in taking chances. There were Gods here – there are Gods everywhere – and they had to be placated. Mostly we worship our own Gods, those of the Legion and the Divine Emperor back in Rome who, judging from the face on the coins they were paying us with these days, was someone new. Domitian, I think his name was. But we also make offerings to the local Gods just to be on the safe side. They're the same as our own, but with different names; Vetiris is Mars, Taran is Jupiter. You get the idea. So the deal is that we make offerings to them, and they leave us alone. But here at the edge of empire I had the feeling they didn't want us to worship them, that these Gods, like their people, hated us.

Now this is how it's supposed to go. We march in and throw our weight about. They decide, eventually, to fight us in open battle. We beat them. Well, stands to reason. We're the best equipped, the best trained, the best disciplined, and there's a bloody lot of us. So, in a battle between us and a screaming lot of savages, who do you think wins? Right. Us. Up here, fighting the Caledonians, it had been embarrassingly easy. Agricola, who was the General at the battle, didn't even bother sending in the legions. He let the auxiliaries do the business – Batavians and Tungrians mostly, Germans and Gauls but decent enough lads once you get to know them. There were supposed to be thirty thousand in the Caledonian army, but it wasn't anything like that many. Still, it was a convincing enough defeat, lots of bodies lying around for us to clear up (more digging), and lots of chariots and horses and weapons abandoned. Most of the natives ran away though, disappeared into the hills and forests, but they'd have learned their lesson and would leave us alone from now on. That was what was supposed to happen.

We weren't here to fight, see. We were here to govern. What we do is find out who the local king is and we cut a deal. We offer them protection and the benefits of civilisation, and they're suitably grateful. They learn to speak Latin, and their sons get a proper education. Job done. Then we can trade. That's what it's all about. That was why we were there. To trade. Wheat, barley, skins, pelts, pearls, hunting dogs, woollen cloth, anything they've got that we want. And in return they get to pretend they're Roman. Seems a fair enough deal to me. It takes years, mind, would probably take as long as it was going to take us to build the fort; three years they reckoned if the whole legion pulled its weight. And then we'd have the place under control.

Didn't happen that way, though, did it? Bastards!

They never fought us in open battle again. They'd learned their lesson about that. But there were raids and ambushes. Patrols went out and never came back. Others got lost in the forest. Others disappeared in those cursed mountains. So we marched off to find their stronghold, thinking we'd teach them a lesson by burning it to the ground. But we never did find it. Never found a king neither. They didn't even have a *word* for a king. The locals called themselves Venicones but no-one could tell where one tribe ended and another began. All we knew was that they fought one another, and yet if we waded in to break up the fight they'd join together and turn on us. Bastards!

So by the time the fort was half finished I wasn't the only one with a bad feeling, wasn't the only one to jump at shadows, wasn't the only one complaining when the supply wagons didn't turn up because they'd been ambushed. No wine? Fuck that!

Vitalis, predictably, was more concerned about the building materials vanishing than the wine. They either got stolen on the way to the fort or disappeared at night from the site itself. Guard duty used to be a cushy option, but not any more.

'Bastards!' he started yelling one day. 'They've stolen the bloody nails!' Several chests of them had disappeared. Iron was valuable, and those nails would probably be melted down and turned into weapons. 'Two can play at that game . . .' Vitalis muttered. 'Silanus! Get your sorry arse over here!' He led me to one of the locked storage buildings where, piled in a corner, were all the weapons we'd collected after the battle. Beautiful, some of them. Long blades rippling with water patterns, their pommels set with smoky jewels, the hilts cast in swirling designs that flowed like snakes, like the river.

'What's wrong now? Got one of your bad feelings again? Well, tough. We need nails, so get this lot down to the smithy and get them melted down. You're in charge.' He smiled without humour at my expression. 'Aren't you always on about a promotion? Well, this is it.'

'But, Sir –'

He glared at me so I did what I do best; I obeyed as slowly as I could get away with and said nothing. But I did have a bad feeling. These weapons belonged to the Caledonians. They'd been forged with their spells, dedicated to their Gods, Gods that hated us. They were more than lumps of metal, even after they were melted down, even after they'd been turned into nails. Hammer one of those nails into a beam and the wood would split. Joints held in place with those nails would give way without warning. Three men died when a stable block collapsed. Eventually we stopped using them. Building work's dangerous enough without the bloody nails trying to kill you! We got a supply of good Roman nails a few weeks later, but even so the work was well behind, because if it wasn't the nails, it was something else. If it wasn't the constant attrition of troops and guards, it was the bloody weather. Did I mention the weather? Winters were frozen, springs wet, autumns stormy and summer only lasted a couple of weeks. And finally it was the weather that defeated us.

The end itself began quietly enough. We were well behind schedule and only half the place was finished. The barracks had all been built and most of the granaries, but the legate's praetorium and bath house hadn't even been started on. Then it began to rain. Nothing new there, you'll be thinking. But this time it didn't stop. It didn't let up even for an hour. The skies were dark, the clouds pressing down on us. Even the hills appeared to have been washed into the plain and it felt as if they were looming over the fort. The river rose and flooded. It was no longer a serpent, hissing and slinking around the ramparts, but a roaring monster that tore into the banks, creeping closer and closer as if it was trying to rip the fort away. One night was particularly bad, the rain battering the roofs, finding all the places that leaked, and the whole fort was a sea of mud. In the morning, however, it finally stopped raining. And that was when we saw what the river had done.

'Fuck,' Vitalis said, looking down from the rampart and speaking for us all. The day before the river had run north of the fort. Now it ran to the south. The river had changed its course in the night, cutting us off. We were still at the ends of empire, but we were on the wrong side of the frontier. It was, I suppose, the final straw.

Later they said the powers-that-be made the right decision. They said it was imperial policy to withdraw, and imperial policy can't be wrong. They said it was because the Dacians rebelled on the Danube frontier, that it made sense to send the Second to sort them out. And since that left Deva minus a legion, the logical step was to send the Twentieth to replace them. So leaving Pinnata Castra was nothing more than a temporary phased withdrawal, a carefully co-ordinated retrenchment and consolidation of pre-existing frontiers. That's what they called it. Not, absolutely not, a retreat. Call it a retreat and you'd be put on latrine duty for a week. Call it a defeat and it was a flogging offence. It wasn't a defeat. We were citizens of Rome, legionaries of the Twentieth Valeria Victrix, and defeat was as foreign to us as this bloody *bloody* country. So we said nothing as we painstakingly dismantled the fort we'd sweated blood to build, knowing that there was no sense in leaving it for the Caledonians to take possession of. Later, when we'd dealt with the Dacians, we'd come back. We'd build it again, and this time we'd mean business.

No-one really believed that, but no-one said anything. Best not. So my bad feelings were right once again, although Vitalis never acknowledged it. Indeed, he seemed to blame me for the whole sorry business. We were just packing up, tents on mules, spathae, pilae and spades on our shoulders, when he stopped me.

'Not so fast, Silanus. Haven't you forgotten something?'

He marched me across to the shell of a workshop. The roof had already been removed, but the walls still stood and, piled against the far wall, were the boxes of nails we'd tried to forget about. 'Can't let them fall into enemy hands, can we? So get your spade . . .'

And that's how I ended up in a hole in the ground in the rain.

'I think I'll leave you there, you useless bastard,' Vitalis said when the hole was deep enough. 'The Gauls sacrifice one of their men when they build a fort. Maybe we should have done that too. But it's not too late . . .'

He let me believe he was serious for a long, long moment. Then he laughed, reached down a hand, and pulled me out. 'Joke,' he said. *Well, there's a first*, I thought.

Between us, we tipped the boxes of nails into the hole, and I shovelled the earth back in and stamped it down. Then we set fire to the walls. They burned well in spite of the rain and sent a column of smoke up into the air, rising into the low grey clouds.

'We'll be back,' Vitalis said once we'd got to the other side of that bloody river, but I didn't think so. You can fight an enemy and turn him into an ally, but you can't fight the land. You can't fight hills and forests and the Gods of both. You can't fight a river. Pinnata Castra, the fort on the wing, lay beyond the edge of the empire now, and the land would take it back to grass and trees until it was forgotten. I had the distinct feeling that we wouldn't be back, that this was as far as we'd ever get, and that, as far as I was concerned, was a *good* feeling.

The Knowing

To begin with, there is only the wind and the rock and the sound the two make together, a grey sound in a grey place, a cold place in the wreathed grip of fog, wan in the half-light of a sun gone pallid with mist.

There is moisture in the air but none on the ground, not up here on the summit of the sacred mountain. There is neither pool nor stream. Only the sound, half-way down the mountain, of water running. From further away, below in the valley, comes the howl of a lone wolf. Nearer, invisible in the clinging shifting cloud, a raven quarks as it tumbles on the wind. Then silence once more. Just wind and rock and the sound the two make together. And from half-way down the mountain the sound of water running, agonisingly far away.

Agonisingly far away. That is a man's thought, thinks the boy. Only a man can take a sound and give it a shape it lacked before. He listens quite deliberately to the trickle of water and lets his thirst shape the sound to longing. He has not eaten since the fall of night on the previous day, and for a time hunger had stalked him. But it no longer does so. He has not drunk either, neither during the night's walk to the base of the mountain, nor the day's climb to its summit. He has crossed stream after stream, and each time the not drinking has been harder. His thirst is sharper now, but in time that too will go. And then will come the Knowing.

Sounds taking shape is part of it, he thinks, sounds being given shape. He waits for shape to shiver back into sound, for rock to blur and give voice – the grind of stone on stone – and wonders if light will quiver into music. He hears his own heart as the beat of a skin drum, the breath whistling in his throat like the song of a bone flute. But the light remains the same.

He had killed his first man only two days before, a man of the Taexali tribe, a spear thrust in the chest, a quick, clean kill. The priests marked his face with the man's blood, making the spirit marks of the oldest ones who'd pocked the sunstones with the same patterns. He had sat all that night beside the body, as was the custom, waiting for the sun to take the man's essence, and had seen it in the first rays of morning, a faint breath of spirit thinning into the wind. The man was not much older than himself but had been marked as a man with the bull sign of the Taexali. His flesh, by daylight, had been as flat and ashen as sun shining through thin cloud.

Afterwards, the priests sent him to the mountain so that he might find the Knowing and become a man. But first, they told him, he must cast loose the bindings of his boyhood flesh and swear neither to eat nor drink until he returns. It is a setting free, he understands, an emptying of his spirit to enable the Knowing to find its place. They warned him he would see things that were not truly there, that he would see things that were and not believe them. Only the Knowing will allow him to distinguish one from the other, the Knowing that is the gift of the God to man. When he returns from the mountain the priests will mark him as a man of the Venicone, the stag-tribe.

The boy walks on, the rocks tilting beneath his aching feet. He is colder now, naked to the wind. All protection had been taken from him: his leather kilt, his sheepskin vest, his twin spears and his charm of protection: the eagle feather tied with a thread of three colours. Up here on the God's mountain there is no protection except for the oath he has sworn, the three-fold oath that only a man may swear, or a boy sent to the mountain to find the Knowing.

May the sky fall on me, the earth gape and swallow me, the sea rise up and overwhelm me.

Up here, in the clouds, he feels the weight of the sky.

He's dizzy now, the mist swirling before his eyes. He sees a scatter of strangely shaped rocks, and it is some time before he recognises them as bones bleached by the sun and scattered by ravens. Further on, in the shadow of a boulder, lies a skull, still with shreds of dried skin and hair adhering to it, the blank sockets staring into the blind sun. There are those who seek the Knowing and do not return. He remembers a boy who had killed his man earlier that year in a spring raid on the Vacomagi, a boy who had failed to return from the mountain.

He finds his stone close by the scattered body, a pale stone the size of his fist, marked with a darker streak. Recognising his stone is the beginning, and thereafter omens start to cluster. The body of the boy who failed to return falls behind in the mist, but soon he finds the gold, a disk the size of his thumbnail, incised with the salmon mark. It is a good omen. Further on lies another and, further still, a group of discs that were once the necklace of a chieftain. The priests bring the bodies of the great ones to lie on the summit of the God's mountain as gifts for the ravens.

Perhaps his Knowing will take the form of a raven, for the God has many forms and the bird is one of them. The God has many names, and only the priests can speak them all, but the boy knows a few: Arddhu the dark one, Kernhe the horned one, Bran the raven. He has heard the raven cry, the wolf howl, but no stag bark. It would be good if the God was to take shape as the stag, his tribe's totem. But perhaps it will be the winter hare, who is sacred to the moon, or the bull who bears the sun between his horns. Even the serpent, although that would mark him as a priest rather than a warrior.

It is darker now, the sun dropping into deeper cloud, the day dimming. The raid had been unseasonably late in the year, long past the summer horse-fair, and in barely a moon's passing it will be Samhain, Feast of the Dead. He hopes his will not be one of the spirits made welcome at this year's feast. This unbidden thought is not a good one, a careless thought that lets fear take shape. Cold is forgotten, thirst a thing of the past, hunger almost unimagined. All he has now, naked on the God's mountain, is fear.

His feet falter, and the dead press close: the boy with his raven-emptied eyes, the gold-girt chieftain, the warriors who died in battle, the priests who see all things. The dead judge him, their spirits measuring his lack, and the weight of their judgement presses on him like the sky. He wishes the earth would gape and swallow his shame, the sea rise up and overwhelm his fear. He falls to his knees, and then his hands, and crawls the rest of the way, his belly to the ground, approaching the God as a serpent among the rocks. But still he keeps hold of the stone and the gold disc.

The way steepens through great slabs of stone split and shattered by the winter. They cut his hands and knees until his skin is slicked with blood, but he keeps going, onward and upward, until there is nowhere else to go. Ahead of him is the cairn of warriors, a mound of stones perched on the highest place. Beside it lies a pile of gold. He stares at the gold, his vision swimming, and it blinds him. The day, that had been darkening, now splits open, carved by a ray of sun, as the clouds part.

The boy gets to his knees and places his own stone on the cairn, his gold disc joining the others in the coruscating glimmer of unimagined wealth. He gets to his feet. Fear is gone, leaving behind a spirit wiped clean and ready for revelation. He walks past the cairn to the great prow of the hill. Vertigo takes him, and he is dizzy with distance. Far below he sees, as if his eyes are those of an eagle circling in the sky, the land of Circinn. His land lies spread out beneath him, layer upon layer, diminishing into the distance until it meets the hard flat glitter of the sea. Behind him, on the summit of the sacred mountain, will stand the God of his people, the one who holds up the sky with one hand and bears the Knowing in the other.

He turns slowly. A raven tumbles on the wind, crying as it does so, angling across the crest of the ridge. To one side a hare dips between rocks. Above him an eagle tilts and soars. None of them is the God, and yet he feels eyes on him, hears the wind breathe slow, a growl of gravel deep in its throat. He hears the slow, slow, thud of a heart beating out the seasons. His own heart beats light and fast, and his breath catches as he makes the final turn and sees . . .

He sees nothing. Only the cairn. Only the gold. Only the long ridge-back of grey stone, dark with remembered moisture. A shred of fog flees like a spirit on the wind. Perhaps it is his own.

But then he sees something else, a little thing he had not noticed before, a plane of rock, hollowed by wind and water to a smooth bowl. Within it, glinting and ruffling, lies a little pool of water.

Thirst spears him and floods the empty place inside him. There is nothing now but thirst. He crouches beside the pool on bloodied knees and stares into the basin of rainwater that holds nothing more than a handful of gravel. He has sworn the three-fold oath that he will not drink, and yet he knows that if he does not he will die here on the mountain. If he denies himself the water he will crouch beneath a rock, as had the dead-eyed boy, and, in the cold of the night, he will die.

This then is the Knowing, this then the choice. He leans forward and sees a reflection, but it is not the reflection of a boy who has come to find the Knowing. He smiles when he recognises it, and his bloodied hands break the surface to shatter the image of the smiling face. He slakes his thirst down to the very bottom of the pool, and it tastes better than anything he has ever tasted.

The sky sails steadily above him. The earth bulks beneath him and fails to open. The sea remains a rumour in the distance.

He gets to his feet, reclaims the gold disc, and sets off back along the ridge. Later, he will bind the disc to the first of his warrior braids beside his eagle's feather. The priests will mark him as a man of the tribe, prick out the symbols with their fine bone needles and the blue stain. There will be the salmon of knowledge for the disc, the stag for his tribe, and the caste marks of crescent and spear. For his warrior sept they will mark him with the creature whose form the God took in his Knowing. He will tell them it was a raven. But he knows now that the God takes no form, for the God who bears all names is all forms, even that of the creature who stared at him from the surface of a pool of water. Himself. And yet not himself.

This is the Knowing, worthy of the mountain, worthy of a man of the Venicones. That is a man's thought, thinks the man as he makes his way down the track, singing as he goes. That is a good thought.

Nechtansmere

A fterwards, you remember each thrust, each slash of the sword. You hear the wind on the blade's edge and your own voice screaming. Afterwards, you see the shape of the thing – the way the centre crumbled and how the edges of the line fell away under the rain of arrows from Ecgfrith's men. You hear it afterwards too, the roar that sounds like waves crashing on a shore. You smell the blood and the fear, your own rank in your nostrils. Later you will drink deep, for your mouth is dry with screaming, your throat raw with it. Your muscles will burn and your stomach rise up to meet your arid throat, but that is later. That is afterwards . . .

The opening credits have rolled, and the girl sitting opposite him has adjusted his microphone. To one side, on the edge of his vision, a green light begins to pulse. The girl fixes a smile on her face and turns to camera.

'Welcome to this week's edition of *Artlight*,' she says. 'Tonight, we have a very special guest: Jonathan Bullfield, sculptor and – some might say – famous recluse. Indeed, this is his first face-to-face interview in a long and, may I say, extremely distinguished career.'

She's dying to ask why, Jon thinks. But she won't; she'll be more subtle than that. They'll begin simply, talk about his retrospective, due to open shortly at the Royal Gallery, and then they'll touch on his background and influences, his methods of work. Only towards the end will she ask a few probing questions. But he's ready for those, even if he's still not sure if he'll speak out or not.

'Your work is clearly influenced by the art of the Picts,' the girl begins. 'Your methods are traditional, your pieces as enigmatic as the symbol stones whose patterns they seem not only to reflect but, in a very real way, develop. So I'm curious about the reasons for what I can only describe as a love affair with these mysterious people. Interestingly, your formative years weren't spent in Scotland, were they?'

She's in her twenties, young enough to be his daughter, he thinks, then revises that judgement with a troubling sense of his life slipping away. She's young enough to be his granddaughter.

'No,' he agrees. 'I was brought up in London and didn't move to Angus until I was fifteen. It was a culture shock, as you can probably imagine!'

'Get out from under my feet! And don't give me that face! We're here now, and we're staying, so you can damn well stop sulking about it!'

His mother had finally lost her temper. His father had given him one of those 'don't upset your mother' looks and jerked his head at the door. Jon had stormed out of the house, but there hadn't been anywhere to go. There was

nothing but fields and farms, hedges and woods, and a track that led no-
where. He hadn't wanted to leave London and come to Scotland, hadn't
wanted cleaner air, a better school and a healthier life. But no-one had asked
his opinion.

'And yet, in spite of your background, your work, even your early work, is
imbued with a sense of kinship, an impression of an oral tradition passed
down from one generation to the next, changing yet never losing its essential
essence...'

The interview goes well. He's urbane and, at moments, even witty, as befits
an elder statesman of sculpture. A recluse? Perhaps, but he has reasons for
that.

'... I'd like to come back, if I may, to the sense your work gives of a
personal link with the past. Those enigmatic images, the massive stones you
counterpoint with such delicate traceries, the way you use the landscape itself
to explore their meanings. You make them speak to us in a long-dead
language, almost as if you have some special connection that goes beyond
study or imagination. It's as if you *know* these people.'

This, he realises, is it – his opportunity to speak of what happened on the
twentieth of May all those years ago, the day when the veils had parted and
he'd almost, almost, stepped through...

❧

... but at the time, in the blood-washed beating heart of battle, there is only
the music and the dance. The music of the Gods swells inside you until it
deafens you, until it runs through your veins like fire and lightning, like the
wind that lifts you up on eagles' wings. For as long as the music lasts all that
matters is your arm rising and falling. Your horse is rearing and screaming
his own challenge, and you're sawing at the reins, jerking him around,
slashing down at an unprotected neck, hacking away a shield or blocking a
spear-thrust until your arm can rise no longer. For as long as the music lasts
you think you're immortal. But you're not. No-one is...

❧

He'd left the house and headed along a farm track that had petered out in
some rough grazing. A few sheep gazed incuriously at him from behind clumps
of thistles as he'd wandered aimlessly around the field in the half-dark of a
misty evening. Eventually, he'd come across an old weather-damaged sign that
declared that this was the site of some battle or other. He couldn't make it out
and didn't care. Why would anyone have fought here when there was nothing
to fight over? Even so, the thought of a battle stirred something inside him,
and when he came across the stick stuck into the ground he had the oddest
fancy that it might be a spear for it was long and straight, the shaft smooth and
polished, the head bound with a wisp of plaited grass in which were woven
three birds' feathers, barred like the wing-feathers of a hawk. It was an odd

129

thing to think, given that he knew little about hawks and even less about spears or battles. He ought to be getting back; his parents would be worrying about him. But he didn't leave. Instead he pulled the thing free and felt the heft of it in his hand, its perfect balance.

. . . and this time, in this battle, the blow falls, the one that will silence the music for ever, and all that is left is one note of the harp-string to mark your ending, for nothing remains now but the veil between the worlds. The mist is thinning and soon the pain will be gone, thirst too, and all that is left of a man, the part that will come again, over and over, will slip between the worlds and see such wonders . . .

He's yelling out some battle cry and brandishing the spear, cutting the mist into ribbons. He's already killed one clump of thistles, and now he draws back the spear to stab it into another.

'No!' The cry rips through the mist, and the clump of thistles resolves itself into a boy lying on the ground, a boy of his own age. At first Jon's surprised he hadn't noticed him before, then embarrassed when he realises the boy must have seen him dancing about like a little kid. But then he sees that the boy's hurt. Blood is flowing in a widening stain from a deep cut in his thigh.

'Jesus Christ!'

'Please!' the boy begs, his eyes on the spear in Jon's hand. Jon lets it fall to the ground as if it's red-hot.

'Are you one of them?' the boy asks. 'A Northumbrian?' His voice is strange, oddly accented.

'A Northumbrian?'

'You spoke the name of the God they worship.'

'You're hurt,' Jon says, wondering if the boy's quite right in the head. 'What happened? Listen, I'll get help.' He'll run home, tell his parents, get them to phone for an ambulance. But blood is still pouring from the boy's leg, and Jon knows he ought to do something about that first, so he pulls off his belt, wraps it around the boy's leg above the wound and pulls it tight. The flow slows to an ooze.

'What happened?' he asks again, but the boy just stares at Jon curiously. Jon stares back, noticing that the boy's hair is long and plaited at the sides, that his clothes are roughly sewn and he wears crude leather sandals on his feet. His bare arms are covered in tattoos of animals and birds, and he looks as if he's in a play or a film. Is that it? Has Jon stumbled on the set of a film? Is that blood, that wound, fake?

'Where's the rest of them?' he demands, feeling like some yokel who's never seen a film set before. *I'm from London!* he wants to shout. The other boy's grin seems to confirm Jon's suspicions.

'Your people?' the boy asks scathingly. 'Bridei's war-bands are hunting them north. We slaughtered Ecgfrith's men between the hill and the marsh. Didn't you know it was a trap? And now your king is defeated, and Bridei's bards will praise this day!' The boy's eyes are bright with triumph, but after a moment his expression sobers. 'You should go before my brother-warriors find you. Flee while you can, but take this –' He pulls something from around his neck, a pendant on a leather thong. 'Show them this if they catch you. Tell them Gartnait of Circinn, of the stag-tribe, owes you a debt of life. Quickly now! Listen! They're coming!'

At first Jon hears nothing, but after a moment, faintly, he can make out the sound of men shouting and horses neighing and whickering. He hears music also, but it seems to come from inside him, and he doesn't want to run as the boy has urged. He wants to stay, to snatch up the spear, to meet those who're coming and let the music sweep him away. Almost, almost, he steps through. *It's as if you* know *these people.*

He does. He knows them as no-one else does, or ever will, and part of him wants to tell the girl, to tell everyone. He wants to repeat their poems and sing their songs, to describe a life lived as close to the edge as Garnait's, as vivid and as brightly coloured. He wants to make them live again as fiercely as once they lived. Even now he wonders if that's his purpose, if coming here and speaking out for the first time in fifty years is intended to be the climax of his existence. But the question that's dominated his life since that day in May all those years before still remains unanswered. What do you do when you clasp hands with a world that's more than a thousand years old? Do you speak? Or do you keep your silence?

He still has the pendant, a roughly pierced disc of stone with the image of a stag scratched on its surface. It was all he had to show for that day, other than the loss of his belt and that faint sense of otherness that has never left him. He'd run from the field, his heart pounding with fear and – yes – regret. Only when he'd left that strange mist behind had he wondered what he was doing running away. *That boy's hurt!* he'd told himself sternly and had turned back. But although he'd searched and searched, he could find neither boy nor spear. And although he listened, he could hear neither the sound of horses and men, nor the music inside him, except in memory.

'That battle, the one near here – what was that all about?' he'd asked his father later that evening. The pendant hung around his neck beneath his tee-shirt, cold against his bare skin.

'Nechtansmere?' his father asked in surprise. 'It was in the seventh century. The Picts defeated the Northumbrians.' He got out and flicked through a reference book. '685, on the twentieth of May. Goodness, that's today!' Jon wasn't surprised about that. 'There's a Pictish stone at Aberlemno that's supposed to tell the story of the battle,' he went on, still reading from the book.

'Can we go and see it?'

His parents exchanged a look and a half-smile of relief. Had he really been that much of a pain?

'Yes, of course,' his father said. 'But why the sudden interest?'

He shrugged and said nothing. Even then he'd begun to ask himself that still unanswered question. *Do you speak?* Even then he was beginning to shape a response, or beginning to be shaped.

A year later, on the twentieth of May, he'd taken the little track once more. Gartnait had been there, still limping from the leg wound that was to plague him for the rest of his long and eventful life. They'd talked and talked until the light had faded, and Jon realised he was talking to himself. But he'd gone back the following year, and the year after that, and now he knows everything there is to know about Gartnait's people. He knows what matters to them, what they believe in, how they fight and what they feel.

In all those years he hasn't spoken, although at times the temptation's been strong. He could have become an historian, since he alone knows the story of their years, or a linguist, for he alone can speak their language. But he'd been aware of the dangers of seeming to know too much. Art, however, had been a different matter, since it was their art that had survived. What was it the girl had said? That he'd not merely copied their works but developed them? Yes, that was what he'd tried to do. He'd shone a light on them that wasn't the searchlight of history but the dim, half-imagined light that lies beyond the veil. They were an enigma called to mind but never explained. *It's as if you* know *these people,* the girl had remarked.

He smiles one of his urbane, opaque smiles. 'Do I know them? I'd like to, but of course I don't. I have no special connection, nothing that goes beyond study and imagination.'

The girl is disappointed but smiles brightly and finishes up with some bland compliments. The title music begins again, and in the background to the credits there's a series of photographs of his better known works: a salmon carved into a forest, a goose into the face of a dune, a serpent with its broken spear inlaid in gold on the wall of a government building. Each symbol follows the next, enigmatic and compelling, his homage to the past, a debt of memory that finally, at the end, has proved to be enough. He understands now that he's already spoken in the only way he knows how.

The pendant hangs, warmer now, beneath his shirt, close to the faltering organ that beats so painfully these days, as close as the secret he's kept for fifty years. That interview had been his final test he thinks as he tramps along the road, carrying his bag, having left his car parked in a layby. Or perhaps it had simply been a farewell.

It's the twentieth of May, and Gartnait is there as usual, looking older than his years, a scrawny grey-haired man held together more by will than bones and muscles. But his eyes still glitter as they had all those years before when he'd been a seasoned warrior in Bridei's war-band, when he'd fought and fallen at Linn Garan, the Pool of the Herons. At Nechtansmere.

'You look tired, my friend,' Gartnait says, leaning on his spear. 'You should come and rest in my Hall.' He smiles because he's made the offer before and been refused on each occasion.

'Perhaps I will,' Jon replies as usual, with an answering smile. They don't need to talk any more. Everything has been said. The flood of questions has long since slowed to a trickle, the disbelief and the arguments have mellowed into a comfortable silence in which small things can be asked: about the health of a grandchild, the building of a new hut, the birth of a litter of wolf-hounds. Of Jon's world nothing has been said. To Gartnait it's the other world, the place he'll go to when he dies, a world of wonders and terrors, of joy and sadness, of shadows and of light. He's not that wrong, Jon thinks.

'What of the stone?' Jon asks. 'Has the carving begun?'

'The sculptor died,' Gartnait says with a shrug. Death is a frequent guest at Gartnait's table. 'So I must find another.'

'I think you need not look very far,' Jon says and picks up his bag of tools. Already he knows how he'll begin. He's seen the stone so many times. Every year he goes to look at it, and now each grain of the sandstone is fixed in his mind, each stroke of the chisel. It will take him six months, he reckons. If his cardiologist is right, he should just about make it.

. . . *he hears the sandpiper trilling of the bone flutes and the stag-roar of the horns, and his heart begins to drum in time to the notes of the harp-strings. Everything of what he was has been put aside, and nothing remains but the veil between the worlds. The mist is thinning now, and soon all pain will be gone, and all that is left of a man, the part that will come again, over and over, will slip between the worlds and see such wonders . . .*

A Bohemian Christmas

'Think he'll come?' Paige asked for the fifth time that day – King had been counting. The nasal twang of the east-coast States grated on King's ears, although he was hardly in a position to criticise; his own English betrayed his Czech origins all too clearly.

King controlled his growing irritation and said nothing. Instead he scrubbed at the windscreen with the back of a gloved hand, wiping away the condensation, and peered out at the town square.

'You see him?' Paige asked, craning forward to see for himself. But the square was empty, the windows of the buildings shuttered, the snow lying like a shroud over the bushes and parked cars. King shivered. The sun had been shining earlier, giving a little warmth, but now it was setting behind the hills, and the temperature was plummeting. The night would be a bitter one, cruel with frost.

'He's not coming, is he?' Paige concluded. 'Why should he? Tonight of all nights! A man should be with his kids on Christmas Eve.'

'He hasn't got any kids.'

'I meant me. I should be with my kids. What about you? Got any kids?'

King shook his head. He didn't have anyone. Not since Marissa had died a few months before, making her final unequivocal escape from the West. She'd never liked their life in Vienna, although since the end of the Cold War she'd seemed more reconciled. He'd always intended to take her back to Czechoslovakia one day, the Czech Republic as it was now, but, for one reason or another, he hadn't. He'd certainly never imagined returning without her, or that when he did so it would be to spend a day in a cold car in a little town in what had once been Bohemia with only Paige for company, waiting for a man from his past, a man who hadn't come.

He scrubbed at the window once more and looked out across the square. The streetlights washed the snow to a lurid unseasonal shade of amber. An ancient farm truck had pulled up at the nearby petrol station, and an old man, his bent figure swathed in a ragged overcoat, was filling some rusting cans with fuel. He slung them awkwardly into the back of the truck before turning briefly to look across at the parked car in which King and Paige sat. Then he hauled himself into the driver's seat and drove the asthmatic vehicle back into the gathering dusk.

'Do you seriously expect me to recognise Vaclav after twenty years?' King had complained. It was the reason they'd asked him, of course, for he'd once known the man for whom they were waiting. But twenty years could make a difference. He'd pointed this out to the Americans, but they'd dismissed his objections.

Just talk to him, they'd urged. *All we want to do is close the file on the Network. He's reappeared after all these years and says he wants to talk – but only to you.* They'd given him a location, a date, and Paige for company.

'People don't change,' Paige had said.

'No?' King had asked sourly. What did Paige know about people? The American was less than half his age and could only have been a child twenty years before when the Network had been blown wide open, when they'd all fled – or tried to flee. Only King had made it to the West, taking Marissa with him. To Paige, it was a barely believable tale from the old days of the Cold War, when the Americans and the British between them had run a Network of informants in Czechoslovakia, until it had been betrayed. An inside job, they'd concluded. Years later, it was of academic interest only, at least to Paige, but King remembered all too vividly the day he'd crossed the border with Marissa, expecting shots to ring out at any moment, yet not sure from which direction they'd come. Fear had dried up his throat as he'd forced himself to go slowly, to wait patiently for their forged documents to be checked, to joke with the border guards. Most of the others were already dead, Igor and Eva and little Sasha, and he'd assumed that Vaclav was dead too, laughing clever Vaclav. They'd done everything together, him and Vaclav. Until the day King had escaped and his friend hadn't. But it seemed Vaclav was still alive and wanted to talk. What about? Why now, after all these years? *Had* he changed?

'No,' he said softly to himself and switched on the engine.

'What are you doing?' Paige asked in surprise. 'Are we leaving?'

'Not leaving – following,' King said shortly. 'He wants us to follow him.'

'That was him?' Paige said incredulously. 'That old man? That was the one who sold out the Network?'

King wasn't surprised Paige had reached this conclusion. The Americans liked obvious solutions, and now all they wanted to do was write the history and forget it. So they'd asked for King, and the British had insisted he help the Americans. There had been a debt to pay, he'd been reminded, not only for twenty years' employment but his new identity and the name he'd chosen to go with it: King, his old Network name. They'd never been able to pronounce his real name correctly.

The truck had disappeared, but its tracks were still visible in the otherwise unmarked snow on the street leading north out of the town. The road was treacherous, and King drove carefully. Outside the town, away from the streetlights, the landscape was white beneath a moon that blinked in and out of the gathering clouds. The fields gleamed as if phosphorescent, and, in the distance, the forest in the foothills was a black splash of ink. As the road began to climb it started to snow, lightly at first, just flurries on the wind to begin with, then becoming heavier. The moon vanished behind the clouds. King peered into the thickening night and slowed to a crawl.

'He turned off there!' Paige announced as they approached a gateway by the side of the road. There was a sign obscured by snow and a rusting metal gate that hung open. The tracks of the truck, fainter now they were filling with fresh snow, turned into the gateway. King braked carefully, but the car slewed sideways on a patch of ice, crabbed into a shallow ditch, and stalled. King swore.

'Come on, we'll have to walk. It's not far to the farm. I'll go first and break a trail.'

In the distance, he could make out a group of buildings, pale against the forest, and one wan light from a window. They got out of the car, their breath pluming on the cold air, and King waded through the snow, thrusting with his thighs until they ached, while Paige followed behind, stumbling in the drifts and complaining bitterly. It seemed to be miles before they reached the outbuildings of the farm, but in truth it was probably only a kilometre. They made their way towards the light that spilled from around an ill-fitting door. King pushed his way into the house, into the main room of the farm, a draughty kitchen that stank of paraffin. An oil-lamp threw wavering shadows into the corners of the room but shone full on the face of the man who sat on the other side of a table. The face had changed in twenty years, but King recognised it as well as his own.

'Hello, Vaclav.'

The two men looked at each other over the waste of years. They were the same age, but Vaclav looked older now. His skin was a dirty grey, his clothes thin and frayed, his hands gnarled and swollen. He was no longer the laughing man King remembered from the days of the Network, but he smiled his old smile as King reached into his overcoat. Paige, close behind King, reached into his own coat, pulled out his gun and levelled it nervously at Vaclav.

'Put it away, boy,' King said irritably, placing the half-bottle of brandy and length of sausage he'd brought with him on the table. The American put his gun away in some embarrassment, muttering an apology, but Vaclav ignored him, reached for the brandy, unscrewed the top, took a long swallow, and handed it back to King.

'Remember how we used to spend Christmas together?' Vaclav said, cutting the sausage with a penknife. 'The three of us? You, me and Marissa?'

'Marissa's dead.' Strange how the words still hurt no matter how many times he said them.

'I know,' Vaclav said softly. 'Did you imagine I didn't?' He frowned. 'Do you think I didn't keep in touch, in spite of everything?'

'You've been to Vienna?' King asked in surprise.

'Many times,' Vaclav nodded, reaching for the brandy once more. 'Many, many times.'

A spurt of fear burned through King's guts. 'Why?'

Vaclav smiled once more. It wasn't a smile King remembered, or liked. 'Not to see you, obviously. Or your employers. But I'm glad you've come to see me instead.' He nodded politely at Paige. 'Both of you. It gives me a chance to set the record straight.'

King reached into his overcoat once more, glancing a faint ironic warning at Paige as he did so. The American, still feeling foolish, flushed and looked away as the shot rang out. Perhaps Paige was aware of the sound, perhaps not. Perhaps he only realised what was happening when King's bullet drilled a neat hole in his temple and erupted in a fan of blood and bone and brains from the other side of his skull. He slid sideways, crashed to the ground, and blood pooled behind his head.

Vaclav tutted mildly, although whether this was at the loss of life, or the ruin of his threadbare carpet, was impossible to say. King made a gesture with his hands, wholly European, of acceptance, resignation, and regret.

'He was getting on my nerves,' he excused himself.

'And I never got on your nerves?'

King shook his head. Never that. Laughing, clever Vaclav. They'd all loved him. Even Marissa. There had been only one solution, and King had snatched at it. Did it matter now who'd betrayed the Network? It only mattered to those who'd write the history and close the file. But he was going to have a say in how it closed, especially now he was free to write the ending himself.

He thought about how it might go; that Vaclav had shot the American, then tried to shoot King, the friend he'd betrayed twenty years before. But, before he did, he'd wanted to make his confession, to set the record straight. Perhaps after he'd done so he'd shoot himself, or maybe King would be forced to kill him in self-defence. Pity about the American, but there it was. He'd tried to stop Vaclav, but . . . History re-wrote itself in his head.

'You don't look well,' King remarked idly, as he thought through the complexities of trajectory and fingerprints.

Vaclav shrugged. 'I'm not.'

'You should come to Vienna. Get better treatment.'

'I've seen your hospitals in Vienna. And your hospices. I don't want to see them again.'

King's throat dried as it had done twenty years before, but with a different fear this time.

Vaclav smiled, still that unpleasant little smile. 'I only went to Vienna to see Marissa.' He raised a hand at King's instinctive protest. 'Oh, yes. I saw Marissa. I saw her many times, when she was dying, when she was ill, and before that. I was on the run for a long time, in hiding in this god-forsaken farm for longer. But when the borders opened I went to see her again. Secretly, of course. Marissa liked secrets. She liked me too.' Vaclav's smile softened with memory. 'She always liked me best of all.'

Twenty years before King had crossed the border, his skin and muscles tensing. Now he felt the hammer-blow of the shot. Marissa and Vaclav? For all those years? The irony of that betrayal didn't escape him. He raised the gun again, a red mist flaring at the edges of his vision.

'Why are you telling me this?' he demanded. 'Why now, after all this time?'

'I'm ill,' said Vaclav, ignoring the gun. 'Like Marissa. I'm dying of something painful and unpleasant. I can afford this luxury.' He glanced around the room in some amusement, at the scarred furniture, the ill-fitting windows, the empty grate. 'I didn't want you thinking you'd got away with it. Marissa never could make up her mind, could she? So you made certain there wasn't anyone else to choose. Except I wasn't shot in a basement like the others. I ran and kept running. But there was always a price to pay, my friend, and I took payment. I just wanted you to know before the end.'

King tightened his finger on the trigger, squeezed and shot Vaclav through the chest. His friend slammed against the back of the chair then slumped forward, one hand outstretched in . . . what? Appeal? Contrition? Gratitude? King took the hand and was surprised by the strength of the grip.

'Vaclav . . .' he began, not knowing what he wanted to say, but Vaclav pulled himself forward, looked up into his friend's face and smiled once more, the old affectionate smile King remembered.

'I told them, you know.' The words were just a breath of sound, bubbling with blood. 'They gave you just enough rope . . . You always were a fool, Wenceslas.'

King raised the gun again, took careful aim, and fired once more. Vaclav's head jerked back, and he toppled over and lay still, sprawled across the table. The red mist had gone, and King was cold now. He tossed the gun away and walked out into the snow.

They'd come after him, of course, the Czechs, the Americans, the British. They'd find him in the end. He wouldn't be able to run for long; he was too old, too tired. But he didn't start running just yet. It had stopped snowing and the wind had dropped. It was peaceful there in the moonlight. He paused, savouring the silence and the beauty of this Bohemian Christmas Eve, the Feast of Stephen. Then he squared his shoulders and walked into the night, into the snow. It lay all about, deep, and crisp, and even.

The Orb-weaver and the King

Hey, watch it you! Now look what you've done! You've just gone and bloody ruined it! All morning it took me to weave this web, and you walked through it like it wasn't there!

That's right, take your ease in *my* cave. At least you've not invited all your men to join you. You sent them back down the track to fetch the horses, poor buggers, but they went willingly enough. They even called you 'Sire'. But then, I was forgetting. You're a king, aren't you?

Not that you look like a king. Where's the crown, the gold, the ermine? All you have is a sodden cloak, a sword that's seen better days, and the impression of a hunted man. Poor king. Aye, I know all about you. Do you think we spiders do nothing but sift midges from the air? The winds blow other things into the cracks and crevices of the world; our webs are fine enough to trap even the faintest whisper of history. We spiders know what's going on, and I know all about you, even the things you'd rather I didn't.

You're on the run, fleeing into the west. At least you were until the rain came on and drove you into my cave. Now you're sitting there watching me hang from my thread. Watch if you like, king, but I've got work to do. I've to get on with my web. Unlike you, I've no time for hanging about.

Hanging. It has a different meaning for your sort, doesn't it? You shudder, knowing how easily it can be followed by drawing and quartering. I expect you're remembering Wallace, the little man from Elderslie. Not the nobility of course, but good enough to be sent South to die like a traitor, while you stayed behind and wondered which way to jump. But now you've jumped, and I hear Edward's threatened you with the same death, that he's just been waiting for you to make a mistake before heading North and squashing you like . . . well, like a spider. Maybe you're beginning to suspect that murder in Dumfries might have been a mistake, satisfying though it must have been at the time. Maybe you're watching me hanging from my thread, and you're feeling the rope around your neck.

Unlike you, however, I'm in no danger. I can scuttle back up my rope any time I like. I'm just hanging here to test the air, to taste the wind and make my plans. The wind has dropped with the rain, but there's a faint air blowing into the cave. It's a good place for a web, and I've got the plan in my head. It's the design I always use, but it works so why change it? I'll just run a dragline to that twig, a loose elastic thread to bridge the entrance, then a few radii down to that leaf, that rocky projection, that stem of ivy. Only when I'm happy with the structure will I start on the frame.

Are you still watching? Are you learning something? Are you beginning to understand the importance of a strong framework? Get it wrong, my king, and, not to put too fine a point on it, you're buggered. Excuse my French. But then, you are, aren't you? French, that is. Robert de Brus, Norman claimant to the throne of a people who've been conquered often enough by other folk speaking different tongues: Picts, Gaels, Scots, Angles, Vikings. So I suppose there's a precedent for it, but I wouldn't, myself, have called it a strong thread in the web you're trying to weave.

Yes, yes, I know what you're going to say. That you're descended from a King of Scotland, but it's a bit tenuous, isn't it? Through the daughter of a cousin. Not that I've got anything against descent through the female line. We spiders have a history of it. And, just to make sure, some of us eat our mates. But that will be one lesson you won't learn from me today. Poor male. What use are you once you've passed on your seed? About as much use as an outlawed king with his ever-so-flexible adherence to the principle of primogeniture.

You'd do better to study the spiders. Or, failing that, the Picts. Their method worked well enough for generations, nephew ruling after uncle in their crooked line of kings. And you're blessed with brothers, if not with sons, so you must be prey to a certain wistful longing for the old traditions. Except you can't admit it, can you? For then you'd have to concede that your enemy, the Earl of Badenoch, Red John Comyn, had, by Pictish calculations, a slightly better claim to the throne than you. So maybe that's why you killed him.

Well, there it is. Two of the strands on which you hope to weave your kingdom are a dubious inheritance and a sacrilegious murder in a church. But, knowing their weakness, you've woven in another, stronger, strand. Your one chance to save your skin was to claim the throne, to speak of ancient rights, of independence, and that headiest of words – freedom. Funny, but I thought I'd heard those words on someone else's tongue. A coarser tongue, a coarser accent, but what can you expect from a peasant? Wallace wasn't even a Norman! A Strathclyde Briton, a little man with a little land and no claim to the throne at all. So you stood by and let him fight your battles and, more importantly, suffer your defeats. You stood by and let his coarse tongue be torn from his throat. One less rival. One more strand in your web – but a borrowed one.

Maybe I'm being too hard on you, you poor human. How can you hope to compete with me, with my innate skills, my silk glands, my spinnerets, my eight eyes that so easily judge angle and incidence, my eight legs with their combs and bristles, my millennia of breeding? We spiders are perfect for the niche in which we find ourselves. Did you know that I can spin seven different sorts of silk? Not that I'll be using them all for my web, of course. But what do you have with which to weave your royal dreams except the six peoples of Scotland? Some of them are fragile, some too strong to be bent, all of them elastic in their loyalty to you, all of them at one another's throats, but they all have their uses, just like my silk. The difference between us is that I know what I'm doing. I've been weaving this web all my life while you've only just begun. So watch, my king, and learn.

Lines span the space now, radiating from the hub. My web's rigid right now, but it's too rigid. It has to stretch with the wind and flex to each current of air. It must bend but not break. So now I build a frame, beginning with the bridge thread that spans the top of the web. That's the important one. What will yours be? The Gaels? Can you trust them, those sea-wolves of the West, the Lords of the Isles with their Viking blood, their love of independence, their predilection for treachery? Take care in the sea-lochs and skerries, for the Gaels are a strong but unreliable thread. They'll stand in a storm then snap in a zephyr. Yet you've little choice but to depend on them, for no-where is safe at the moment, even here in the rocky wilds of Kintyre, for all that they're Donald lands. And the only reason Angus Og of Islay will aid you is that you made enemies of his enemies, the men of Lorn. But perhaps you do well to base your bridging strand on old enmities rather than new friendships.

Watch me build the framework, dragging lines around the periphery, connecting each radius to the next. Do you see how each strand strengthens the one beside it? Perhaps you're beginning to understand the importance of flexibility. This land isn't a place for fixed positions, or for standing alone in the gale from the South that is Edward of England's ambition. But you're alone now, your followers scattered, your enemies hunting you, their net cast wide. It's just as well they lack the spider's skill in the weaving of nets and have made it too coarse to stop you slipping through. But others didn't make it, and they've been dragged back to Edward's lairs in Berwick and Roxburgh to be imprisoned. It's a high price they've paid for their loyalty to you, or to what they saw as their self-interest. Edward's capacity for retribution grows with his years.

Now there's a strand of hope. His years. His illness. That son who's an argument against primogeniture if ever there was one! Not that the son is likely to have sons of his own, not if the rumours about him and that Gascon favourite of his are true. So maybe you'll just have to wait. I can see you considering it as you watch how patiently I remake the web you destroyed. You're considering the benefits of patience.

I'm spinning the radii now, the ones that run from the hub to the framing strands, each one equidistant from the next, each one tensioning the whole construction, each one balancing the others. Balance – that's the thing. What you need to do is judge the balance of opportunities. Should you hide and wait, or strike before your support slips away? You're tempted to give up, to head for the sea and make your escape to France. But you're also tempted to burst out of these hills, with those screaming Gaels behind you, and head for your own country with its twisting valleys, its steep-sided rivers, its moorlands and cloud-wracked wastes. Border country, bandit country, where you can wage your guerrilla war, while Edward, with his failing strength, draws his net ever tighter around you. Which is it to be? Caution or boldness?

You're fascinated now, watching me build my auxiliary spiral, the structural threads that cross the radii, each strand woven into the next, each line longer than the last, each step greater than the one that went before it. Maybe you wish your life had that sort of simplicity rather than all that endless backtracking, the oaths made and broken, the rebellions, defeats, and submissions. But in Dumfries you took the first step in the spiral, and you can't, for once, retreat. It brought you here to my cave, and perhaps it will spin you onwards into oblivion. Who knows? Only the man who writes the history.

Perhaps you'll be that man. It all depends on the choices you make here in this cave. But it doesn't look good.

It was going so well to begin with, your one powerful rival dying at your hands, the liberty of Scotland becoming *your* liberty. This time it was personal! Your men seized Dumfries Castle then headed north for the other strongholds, while you made for Glasgow in a bid for the next strand in your kingship – absolution for your sacrilegious murder from a man as cunning and devious as yourself: Bishop Wishart. You took a chance there, didn't you? One step across the abyss, your life and liberty hanging by a thread. But he held firm to his self-interest, if not his principles, and five weeks later you were crowned. Heady days! They must seem a long time ago now.

Of course, you always knew Edward would come, his levies sweeping over the Border like a great cloud of midges: archers, spearmen, mounted warriors. They scattered your supporters like chaff on the wind, slaughtered two of your brothers, imprisoned your women, took your lands and gave them to your enemies. And now your great plan is in abeyance – the support you planned to claim or buy: the Pictish Earls of the North, the crafty Angle barons, the wild Gaels with their Viking fierceness, the sullen hardy Scots, the dreaming Britons – the disparate warring strands of the peoples from whom you planned to weave a nation.

I pause, and you hold your breath. You think I might abandon my web, that I might scuttle off into the darkness of the cave, leaving it incomplete, the strands too wide, a poor ineffective thing, not unlike your dreams. You think I weave omens for you, here in my cave. But I pause only to spin a different sort of silk, a sticky fragile thread that I draw behind me, as fine as gossamer. You nod. You understand. I am a sign, a message, a lesson you needed to learn. Like me, you'll not abandon what you've begun.

There's a shout from outside the cave. The rain has eased, and horses snort and jingle on the little path that leads over these hills and down to the sea, to safety and exile – the way of a patient man, of a cautious man.

'Robert? Sire?'

Black James Douglas crawls into the cave, missing my web, and crouches beside you. 'The rain is off. Do we ride, Sire?'

'Aye, Jamie,' you say to your captain. 'We ride. But first I want to show you something.' You gesture at my web. 'You can learn a lot from a spider.'

Jamie Douglas looks confused. He barely sees my web, far less its symmetry, its strength, its example. Jamie Douglas like simple things like revenge and slaughter. 'What?' he asks.

You point at my web with your dagger. 'Edward has set a trap for me and I was about to fall into it. But now I see that his trap is based on only a few strands – those bastards Comyn and Buchan, those traitors, the McDougalls of Lorn, and his poxed Border earls.'

You reach out and break the strands that bind my web to the cave! Now look what you've done! Bloody ruined it again! Unsupported, it flutters free, coils up on itself and collapses, and I scuttle out of reach.

Jamie Douglas grins. 'So we head north?'

'We head north, then back to Annandale. Then we'll break them one by one, one strand at a time.'

'And then?'

You smile. You've learned a lesson here. It isn't the one I was trying to teach you, but there's no teaching a king.

'Then we'll build us a kingdom.' You peer into the darkness of the cave where I've hidden myself. I'm waiting for you to leave so I can begin all over again.

A spider is patient. A spider is persistent. A king must be both.

The Washer at the Ford

J eannie Campbell had never had a man. Not as such. There was the telling of a stillborn bairn buried up by the ruined shieling on the track that led down to Strath Beag, but Eilidh McFarlane, being sixteen, going on seventeen, and thus grown wise, wasn't so sure of the truth of this. She knew how easily the talk around the fire wandered in and out of the old tales, taking the folk of the here and now with it, until they were changed and grown unfamiliar. And so, being a sensible girl, she also discounted the story of how her Uncle Iain had once taken a fancy to Jeannie Campbell, her having been a woman of great and abiding beauty.

'And a queen, forby,' added Eilidh.

'Don't be daft, lass,' said her grandmother sternly as Eilidh smiled at the thought of dour old Uncle Iain, who was sixty if he was a day and plagued with pains in his joints, ever having been in love with Jeannie Campbell who, being even older, had little to show of any beauty she might once have possessed.

But whatever the truth or otherwise of this tale or the other, there was no denying the fact that it was a terrible thing for a woman with a croft of her own not to have a man to help her farm it. Yet Jeannie Campbell, having neither a man to fish for herring when they ran into the bay, nor a son to dig the peats at the year end, got by without them. She ploughed her rigs for barley, herded her wild-eyes stirks and the little flock of dun-coloured sheep up to the moor on May Day, and lived alone with her ragged-eared cat, her patient collie and the cluster of hens that pecked in and out of the old byre at the back of the yard.

When times were hard – and that was often enough – she'd wring the neck of one of her hens and come down to Eilidh's grandmother's croft to exchange it for a cartload of fodder, or a wheel of the new cheese. And stringy fowls they'd been too, Eilidh remembered, scarce fit to eat, but her grandmother had told Jeannie Campbell otherwise.

'It seemed a kindness,' she explained later, and Eilidh nodded, for such was the way of things in the little village that huddled around the bay at the western end of the sea loch. Pride was as carefully nurtured as were the beasts and the grain, and it would have been as unlikely for Jeannie Campbell to accept charity as it would have been for anyone to offer it.

But maybe, thought Eilidh, with the wisdom of her years, it was from an impulse of charity that Lady Sarah from the big house had hired Jeannie Campbell to do her laundry, for surely as fine a lady as Sarah Mackenzie of Carnach would have her own laundry maids?

'Maybe. Maybe not,' said her grandmother. 'Things haven't been the same up at the big house since young Mr Malcolm was killed in that foreign war.'

She made a sign with her left hand that would have distressed Mr McLeod, the Minister, then tutted in sympathy. 'Poor lad. And his poor mother. They said she took to her bed when Jeannie Campbell told her.'

'But how did Jeannie Campbell know?' Eilidh asked, but her grandmother looked up sharply and shook her head in swift denial.

'Know? Of course she didn't know! She was just there when the word came, up at the big house, seeing about the laundry. No matter what anyone says about her, there's no denying she's got a knack with the washing.'

That at least was true. Perhaps it was the softness of the water in the stream that ran close by her house and in which she washed the linen, or the freshness of the air from the sea down by the shore where she hung everything to dry, or the scents, in season, of broom or heather or sweet wild gale that filled the blowing sheets and lacy tablecloths, but when she took them back, folded and prim, they were as white and soft and sweet-smelling as if they were new. So maybe it wasn't charity after all. Or maybe it was because when you thought of sheets at all you couldn't help but think of Jeannie Campbell, since there was another thing for which she was known in the village and up at the big house.

She laid out the dead.

'Someone has to do it,' her grandmother pointed out when Eilidh expressed her distaste for the whole business, the washing of the body, the wrapping in the shroud. 'And it will be Jeannie Campbell who lays me out when my time comes.'

Her grandmother tilted her head to one side. Outside, high and clear, came the sound of geese, skeining the evening sky.

'Do you hear that, lass?' she whispered, on a shiver of breath. 'I'm thinking one of them has just flown over my grave.'

It was an old woman's fancy, thought Eilidh, but there's a truth in such sayings, and within a month her grandmother was gone. Eilidh found her one morning sitting in her usual chair by the glowing peats of the fire, as cold as a stone. There was an expression on her face in which surprise was mixed with annoyance that she'd been taken before she was ready, for she still had the cow to milk, the herrings to salt, the bracken to cut and, oh, a hundred things to do.

'But it was a good death,' said Jeannie Campbell who, true to her grandmother's prediction, had come to lay her out in the back bedroom. 'A good death,' she repeated with heavy emphasis, as if she'd seen deaths that weren't so good. But she wasn't one to talk of such things, and Eilidh didn't have the courage to ask her, so she left her alone to lay out her grandmother's body. Afterwards, Eilidh pressed her to stay for the wake, but Jeannie Campbell shook her head.

'No, lass. I've to get back. I'm expecting a visitor.' Of all the excuses she might have given this was the strangest, for she wasn't known to have visitors. But there was no persuading her to stay. She wasn't much missed, however, for the house was full during the three days of the wake, as all who could came to pay their respects to Eilidh's grandmother who lay in the back bedroom, a silent but ever-present guest of honour at a celebration she would have enjoyed just as much as any of them.

The villagers came, as they always did at such times, to talk and tell stories. The firelight ran like water, and there was song and whisky and much remembering of things already half-forgotten. Some even came from outside the village: Eilidh's Aunty Mairead from down Rireavach way, Peggie Drummond, her grandmother's best friend and rival, who'd moved to Scoraig, Shona McNichol who was housekeeper up at Dundonnell, and Angus McFarlane, a cousin of some sort from Badrallach, who brought with him a battered fiddle and a fund of stories. Even Elsie Matheson came, a slattern of a woman her grandmother had disapproved of, another woman without a man to call her own and yet who had a flock of bairns notwithstanding. She seemed friendly with Eilidh's Uncle Iain, a fact that was pointedly ignored by the Minister from the Manse, Mr McLeod.

The Minister was a broad-shouldered good-natured man as fond of a dram and a tale as the rest of them, and he brought with him his son, Donald, new back to the village after being away at the University. When the wake was over, three days hence, Mr McLeod would solemnly consign her grandmother's body to the kirkyard where five of her sons, two daughters and numerous grandchildren were already buried. In the meantime, however, he was as determined as everyone else to enjoy himself.

Eilidh liked a wake too, but she felt guilty enjoying her own grandmother's. However, Jeannie Campbell's parting words consoled her. Her grandmother had been old, right enough, and had died a 'good death'. There were few enough causes for celebration, not when you thought of all that was wrong with the world, the famines and the wars and the terrible goings on in Africa where the traitors in the Cape had taken it into their heads to join the Boers and rise up against the rightful British Government. Or so said Mr McLeod.

'It's not that simple, father,' said young Donald. 'It's all to do with the gold in the Transvaal.'

Eilidh hadn't heard of the Boers, or of the Transvaal, and she knew nothing about gold at all, but even if she had she wouldn't have dreamt of answering the Minister back, and she stared at young Donald McLeod in astonishment.

She'd barely noticed him before, but now she looked at him more closely. He was a thin young man who'd grown tall but who hadn't yet grown into his height, and he was nothing to look at – too bony, too pale, too awkward – and, apart from that startling comment, he'd little to say for himself. He'd no tales to tell or songs to sing, but perhaps that was to the good for his voice was not the sweetest she'd ever heard. And yet she found herself listening for it. She watched him too and wondered why she did so. When he left with his father at the end of the evening he took her hand and said, as everyone else had said, that he was sorry for her loss. Eilidh felt a strange and fearful pressure in her chest, something that took the breath from her throat, and, when he'd gone, there seemed to be a place within her that had turned hollow, an emptiness she put down to missing her grandmother.

But, before long, she didn't think so often of her grandmother and she forgot about Jeannie Campbell completely. It was Donald McLeod who occupied her waking thoughts as she milked the kye and hoed the kale. It was Donald McLeod of whom she dreamed at night, disturbing shameful dreams she half-regretted waking up from. It was Donald McLeod's tall form she looked for when she made her way back from the moors where the cattle and sheep foraged in the long summer evenings. If they met by chance she'd walk with him along the high track that led towards Ben Ghobhlach, in the June light that lingered by the mossy hollows and reed-fringed tarns where the golden plovers piped their lilting mournful calls.

It was Donald McLeod who told her about the war in the Transvaal, but it seemed so far away she barely listened. It was Donald McLeod who laughed at her stories about the people in the village: of Elsie Matheson who was no better than she should be, old Jock Stewart who'd once been to Glasgow, and Jeannie Campbell who'd never had a man of her own.

'Do you believe that?' he asked.

'No,' said Eilidh who, being seventeen now and having once been kissed by Dougal McRae, knew the ways of the world. 'For there have been times when I've seen a man going along the road to her door, always of an evening. And –' She lowered her voice to a whisper. '– I've not seen him leave!'

'My father said she once walked out with a man who was fee'd to the big house at Carnach. But he joined the regiment and was killed at the siege of Sevastopol.' He began to tell her about that but she stopped listening. She was thinking about when she'd been kissed by Dougal McRae and how she'd wondered what all the fuss was about. But now she thought she might like to try it again, just to see . . .

When she told him this the blood rushed into his pale face, but he'd kissed her anyway, and it was quite, quite different . . . She forgot about Jeannie Campbell again, forgot all about the man going to her door and not coming back, and how she'd seen Jeannie the next morning down by the ford where she usually washed the sheets. She forgot it had been a man's jacket and hose Jeannie Campbell had been washing, and how she'd knelt in the water and cried as if her heart would break.

Eilidh McFarlane didn't believe a heart could break. Like so many things, it was just something they said in the old stories. But when Donald McLeod told her he was joining the regiment and going to the Transvaal to fight the Boers, she began to think the old tales might have the right of it.

'But you aren't a soldier!'

'No, perhaps not,' he said, flushing then blanching pale again and turning away so she wouldn't see how afraid he was that she might ask him to stay, and how close he was to weakening. But she saw right enough, and so said nothing. Indeed, she didn't think she could speak at all, for there was a pain in her chest, and her breathing had gone from her throat, just like on the night of her grandmother's wake, and it left her with that same hollowness. But it wasn't the same at all. Even when he promised to come back. Promised on all the things that were dear to him. 'No matter what,' he said.

High above, the geese flew inland, calling to one another, and she shivered as once her grandmother had shivered.

She looked for him all the next summer and when the geese began to wing their way south. His father grew drawn and ceased to preach about the supremacy of the British Empire and the nobility of sacrifice. He even lost his fondness for a dram, and she knew he feared for Donald almost as much as her. Then one evening, as October drew to a close, there was a knock at the door, and when she opened it Jeannie Campbell stood there, clutching a shawl around her shoulders against the chill of the night, with a strange wild look in her face.

'I've come to tell you, lass. He's coming home, that lad of yours. See you've a welcome for him.'

Then she was gone, muttering that she'd things to see to. She was expecting a visitor.

Eilidh waited, a breathless expectation fluttering in her throat, and when the light was almost gone from the sky she walked out of the house. High above there came a cry that was echoed by another and then another and, looking up, she saw the wild geese flighting, the last of the sunset flooding their pale bodies to gold against the slate of rainclouds. She followed the beating veins of their flight far up the sea-loch, and only when they vanished into the shadows beneath the hills did she look down the track. He was trudging slowly towards her, a heavy pack hanging from one shoulder, his uniform torn and filthy.

'I promised I'd come back,' he said. 'No matter what.'

She drew him in to the heat of the fire, stilled his shivering with the warmth of her body, and held him all that night as the wild geese flew overhead, crying their strange unearthly cries, and the wind moaned in the eaves before dying away with the dawn. She left him sleeping, pale and thin in the wan light, dressed herself quickly and took his clothes down to the stream, thinking to wash them and dry them in front of the fire before he awoke.

Jeannie Campbell was already there, kneeling in the water, her skirts tucked into her kirtle, washing some clothes that to Eilidh's eyes seemed hardly worth the washing, so torn and ragged were they. Jeannie nodded to her but said nothing, and together the two women scrubbed at the clothes, trying not to tear the fabric more than it was already, trying to wash the blood from the uniforms. But it was no use. Eilidh MacFarlane began to cry, and you'd think, hearing her, that her heart had broken.

Later that week Mr McLeod showed her a stained and crumpled letter he'd been sent by Donald's commanding officer. She couldn't read the English, but he told her what it said.

'A clean shot in the heart. He didn't suffer. He died with courage and honour. That's what it says here.' He looked up from the letter, his old eyes red and fierce. 'It was a good death, Eilidh, a good death! What more can we ask God to grant us? What more!?'

He raised both arms and shook his fists at the God who'd given him such a gift. She didn't think he wanted her to answer, so she said nothing. A clean shot to the heart, he'd said. But she'd seen the deep rent in the belly of the jacket, the slashes in the back, the way the blood had seeped into fabric that was caked with dust and grit from a land on the far side of the world.

She left the manse and went slowly back along the track he'd walked down in his filthy uniform, and down which he would walk again, coming to her door one evening as the light left the sky, one evening when the wild geese were flighting. No-one would see him leave, and in the morning she'd go down to the ford to wash the blood from his clothes.

The Sparrow

Elsie doesn't know if she'll marry Joe McBride when he asks her, but she knows he'll ask. He won't be the first, and, if she turns him down, he won't be the last.

'You want to watch out, my girl,' her mother warns her. 'One of these days you'll run out of lads falling at your feet. Daft creatures, the lot of them.'

Elsie isn't beautiful. Her mirror tells her that. She's too tall, too thin, her hair too straight, too mousy. Her eyes are too grey, her mouth too wide. But sometimes Elsie catches sight of herself in less reliable reflections – a puddle in the street or a pane of glass in a window as it swings shut – and sees the Elsie the lads see, the one who moves and breathes and laughs, a quicksilver being who flows through the fingers like a wave on the shore. In these moments she sees the person who lies beneath, a creature of bone and spirit, a swift flame that burns strong and steady and draws, like moths to a lamp, the Joe McBrides of her world.

'Although what you see in him I don't know, big lump that he is!' her mother says angrily since she still regrets the loss of Freddy Simpson, the pit-manager's son, the son-in-law she'd longed for, the small man with the big ideas.

'Too big for his boots, that one,' her father, a man of few words, announces after Freddy Simpson passes, with flying colours, the ordeal of afternoon tea, the one all prospective son-in-laws are subjected to.

'A little milk, Frederick?' her mother coos.

'No, thank you, Mrs Armitage, just a slice of lemon if you will.'

Elsie's mother is both mortified and thrilled in equal measure. She doesn't have a lemon, of course, but for Freddy to consider her the sort of woman who might . . . He graciously accepts a cup of tea with a splash of milk and an iced fancy – proper shop-bought – and Elsie watches, fascinated, as he picks up the delicate dish of porcelain with its equally delicate tea, lifting it between two fingers that have worked with nothing more manly than a pen, and tilting the remaining fingers into the air. Perhaps the way he holds the cup is the reason she turns him down.

Joe, subjected to the same ordeal once they start walking out, fails miserably.

'Lemon or milk, Joe?' her mother asks as Joe stares in horror at the fragile cup with its piss-coloured liquid. Her mother's voice is as tart as the lemon she hasn't bothered buying since she already knows – as she tells Elsie later – what the answer will be. 'Didn't even drink the tea,' she complains, for Joe just looks at the cup, then at his hands, big hands, scarred and dented from his work in McEwan's the Cabinet Maker's, then smiles apologetically. 'I'm not one for tea, Mrs Armitage,' he says.

'As bare-faced a lie as ever I've heard!' her mother complains later. 'And did he not eat three of my iced fancies? *Three!* Wolfed them down like an animal. Yes, just like an animal. And all the time he was staring at you, Elsie, with those big soulful eyes. Just like that damned dog.'

'Jess was a good dog,' her father says quietly, lifting his newspaper and disappearing behind it. Later, when he lowers it, Elsie can see that his eyes are redder than usual, and when he drops his hand to lay it on his knee his hand rests briefly on the air as it had once rested on the head of the dog who'd spent so much time with him, her flank warm against his legs, her chin on his thigh, her eyes on his face. Poor Jess. A sheepdog who'd been afraid of sheep but who'd loved to herd the chickens in the yard, guiding them from one corner to the next until she was seen off by the cockerel. Jess, who'd chased the little chicks about, wagging her tail and picking up any that strayed in her jaws, then setting them down again by their clucking mothers, damp but unharmed. Until the day she'd strayed herself and hadn't returned.

It was Elsie who'd found her up by the grounds to the big house. They'd said she was chasing pheasants. After they'd shot her, they'd hung her body from a wire fence as a warning to others. Elsie had carried her back herself, the blood staining the bodice of her dress until it looked as if her heart had burst open, as if it had been torn apart by some fierce and implacable part of herself she didn't know and didn't like. They'd buried Jess in the kale-yard.

'She was a good dog,' her father had said, but thereafter he'd sunk into himself, and it seemed to Elsie that the lung disease that had robbed him of breath and work surged forward from that day onwards, like a tide flooding to the peak, drowning his lungs and his spirit. Poor Jess. Poor father, more conscious now of that absent head on his thigh than of all the life going on around him.

Sometimes, when her father has wheezed his way out to the yard, Elsie looks at the empty chair by the fire, at the newspaper lying on the floor, screaming its headlines, and feels the shape of his coming absence like a wound, like her heart bursting. Sometimes she tries to shape the same absence out of the young men, but none take form with the same painful clarity. Perhaps that's why she turns them down.

Elsie works in the grocers on the high street, weighing out tea and flour and sugar, slicing bacon on the big rocking slicer, and cutting through rounds of cheese or slabs of butter with a cheese-wire. McEwan's is on the next street, a big barn of a place full of men who, when they're not working, laugh and curse and drink tea so strong you could stand your spoon up in it. Joe likes that sort of tea. Sometimes Elsie stops there on her way home as the men leave for the day, and when she does it's not uncommon for Joe to stay on. He doesn't like to leave work unfinished, he tells her, and when they're alone she might watch him turn a chair leg on the lathe, his big hands sure and dextrous, his fingertips brushing the wood as if he can feel the grain and sense its strengths and weaknesses. Once he'd shown her a bowl someone had shaped from a block of sycamore. It was smoothed and polished until the grain stood out, rippling and iridescent like lines of sand after the waves have beaten it into shape. The lines of the grain make her think of her own hands, small but strong and lined with her future, her loves and life and fortune. The lines in the wood come from the past, Joe explains. They mark times of plenty, of drought, of good years and bad.

'I'll make you a bowl like this one day,' he says, looking at her as Jess had looked at her father.

Is that love? she wonders. She's never been in love herself, or never been certain of it.

'If you're not certain, you're not,' her father says. He glances at his wife for a moment. It's just a moment, but it's long enough for Elsie to understand something she hadn't realised until then.

'When you find a man who can look after you for the whole of your life, *that's* when you know,' her mother says, looking at her husband with his wheeze and his newspaper, and what Elsie sees this time is a hurt and resentful betrayal, as if the man her mother loved has left her, leaving nothing behind but a living absence. 'Someone like Freddy Simpson,' she adds, although by then Freddy Simpson is long gone.

Elsie's late leaving work that day, and by the time she gets to McEwan's the place is silent. But the door's still open, and she pauses in the doorway to breathe in the mixed scents of oak and pine, new wood-shavings and old sawdust, wax and resin and the cold metallic stench of oiled chisels and planes. She can smell male sweat too and stewed tea. Joe must have left already, she thinks, but still she stands there, thinking of the big man with the scarred hands, a man who's neither handsome nor articulate. Before she can shape him fully, he appears, moving quietly from the back yard, carrying a length of timber. A draught blows down the workshop as both doors open, lifting the dust into a swirling cloud of sun-shot spears of light, a confusing tracery of sunbeams. Something flies past her, brushing her face, a bird, escaping a hawk perhaps, a sparrow, passing from light to dark, seeking light beyond. But when the door to the yard bangs shut, it flies about in panic, crashes into one of the windows and falls with a soft thud.

Joe cries out. He hasn't seen Elsie standing by the doorway. She watches him pick up the bird and hold it cupped in his huge hands, one finger stroking a head that's smaller than the end of his thumb. Elsie creeps closer, feet soft on the sawdust. She watches as Joe lifts one wing and then the other, stretching each gently to see if anything's broken. The bird's eyes are open and it's looking at Joe with Jess's expression, hopeful and trusting of his good intentions. Elsie wonders if Jess had wagged her tail as the barrels were aimed at her, as the trigger was squeezed.

'Is it all right?' He should have been startled, but he doesn't react. It's as if he knows she's there, as if he'll always know where she is, as if he can sense the whole of her as he senses the grain in the wood. He's still holding the bird cupped in his palms, and she can see its heart beating. She can feel her own heart beating as if it might burst through her chest. She wants to be held like the bird, as if she too is small and fragile, although she's neither. She wants to be picked up by something that could crush and bite and yet be laid down safely. She wants to hold and be held in just that way. Something turns to liquid inside her, shot through with sun like the crest of a wave that's about to break on a sandy shore and write its future in rippled lines of grain. It's as if she's in the wave and is the wave itself all at the same time.

'It's just stunned itself,' Joe says quietly. 'I think it's going to be all right.'

He lays it down in a box in a nest of wood-shavings and places it near the door where it can see the sun. Then Joe looks at Elsie, flushing, and clears his throat.

'Elsie, I've been meaning to . . . That is, I was wondering . . . I know I'm not much to look at like, but maybe you, that is, we, could –'

'Yes, Joe,' she says.

'You don't know what I was going to ask!'

'I do. I know. And the answer's yes.'

She puts her hand out, lets him take it in his, feels her hand nestle there like a bird, feels her own strength as the wave begins to crash and tumble. She's inside the wave and she's safe and she's fierce and this is love. This is life and it's just begun. It's summer. It's July. It's 1914. And everything's going to be all right.

Love and Loss

Introduction

T he stories in this collection are all concerned, in one way or another, with coming to terms with loss, whether this be of love, independence or faith, and it is in this section that this theme is most evident.

In *What She Would Have Wanted*, a man and his grandchild find common ground when they go to scatter the grandmother's ashes. *Stolen Away* follows a man as he grasps an opportunity to remake his lost past. *Like the Tide* is about infidelity and a woman's response to it. In *Evidence of Ice*, however, the infidelity turns out to be of a rather different nature. *The Bogeyman* is about the loss of innocence and the fatal consequences of prejudice. Growing apart is the theme in *Looking for the Leonids,* as a man looks to the stars and tries to make sense of his failing marriage. In *Fogbound* a man confronts the darkness in his own soul, while in *The Mushroom Pickers* a man wonders how to reach out to his increasingly distant wife. *Appointment on Valentine's Day* follows a clergyman as he wrestles with his own mortality and his belief in God, while in *Theophany*, set in the future, a couple's faith in the rational is tested. *Moving On* and *The Butterfly Effect* are also set in the future and were stories I wrote in response to climate change. In *Moving On* a paraplegic man is forced to test the extent of his abilities when a flood sweeps through the Fens. In *The Butterfly Effect*, set in a post-apocalyptic future, a man deals with guilt in the wake of a catastrophic sea-level rise coupled with a devastating pandemic.

There is further information about each of these stories in the Appendix.

What She Would Have Wanted

'**W**ill there be fingernails, Grandad?'

Walter frowns down at the boy in what he hopes is a repressive manner.

'Or teeth?' the boy asks.

'There won't be anything like that,' Walter repeats, since he's been asked something similar several times already. It had been a bit of a theme on the drive to the carpark at Braedownie. 'I told you; there's nothing left after a cremation except for dust.'

'Dust?' The boy brightens. 'Like in the Golden Compass?'

Walter is vaguely aware that this is a children's book, but he hasn't read it. 'Something like that,' he says, hazarding a guess.

'Cool,' says the boy, the first sign of animation he's shown so far.

They're walking through the forest by now. The farm and the old lodge are behind them, and there's nothing ahead of them but the track. It isn't a brilliant day. A layer of cloud is lipping the hills, and there's a chill little wind and the threat of rain to come in the colour of the sky to the north. Walter glances at the boy's new walking boots and hopes Sheila has had the sense to buy him waterproof ones. The rest of his gear, bought by Sheila especially for this trip, is, in contrast to Walter's own, new and of dubious quality. It had, of course, been her idea for him to take the boy along with him.

'You can't go on your own, Dad. All that way, at your age.'

Walter hadn't been sure which statement he should take umbrage at first, so he'd decided to address them chronologically.

'I've been walking those hills on my own for more years than I care to remember. It's not far, only ten miles or so. And I might be sixty-five, but I'm a darn sight fitter than you, young lady.'

The young lady in question, his and Mairi's only daughter, an overweight matron in her forties, had grinned ruefully. 'You wouldn't get me up there, even if I could walk that far. When I'm dead I want to be dead and buried, not scattered to the winds in the middle of nowhere.'

'It's what your mother would have wanted,' he'd said sternly.

'How do you know? She didn't say anything about it to me.'

'We talked about it years ago. It's where she'd want her ashes scattered: in the glen with her family.'

Sheila had snorted in disbelief. 'I still don't like the idea of you going up there on your own. Why don't you take Sean with you?' She'd nudged the boy sprawled next to her on the sofa, immersed in some game on his phone. 'Do you want to go up a mountain with your Grandad?'

Walter had winced at the word 'Grandad', wishing there was some other word to describe his relationship to young Sean, the twelve-year old son of

Sheila's current partner, Wayne, a taciturn wastrel from London from whom Sean had evidently inherited his monosyllabic style of conversation.

'S'pose,' he'd said, not looking up from his game for an instant.

'I don't think –' Walter had begun.

'Mum would have wanted you to take him,' Sheila had said firmly, and that had settled the matter.

Now, taking the right fork where Jock's Road peels off from the forestry track, Walter wonders if Sheila had been right. Would Mairi have wanted him to bring Sean along to help him scatter her ashes? It had been odd that she'd failed to make her wishes about her remains clear when she'd been so firm about all the other details of the funeral and everything that went with it. By the time he'd thought to ask it was already too late. What would she think about him bringing along a boy who isn't really family?

Mairi had been strong on family. They both had been. That's why they'd liked the glen so much, the high moorlands overlooked only by clouds and the occasional deer, this empty place. But to him and Mairi it had never been empty, because it was filled with the ghosts of their past. Their own families had come from these parts – old Lindsay clan lands – and she'd often tell people, only half in jest, that he, Walter Lindsay, would never have married her if she hadn't turned out to be a Lindsay on her mother's side. Walter sometimes feels as if the memories run in his blood, that he can look around and see what his ancestors had seen: the summer shielings, the cattle grazing on the slopes, the stirks winding their way down this very track on their way to the big cattle tryst at Crieff. He can recite the names of the old farms and settlements, the hills and streams, as if they are old but familiar friends. They both could, so surely it's here Mairi would have wanted her ashes to be scattered?

'Won't there be any bones then?' Sean asks, the prospect of dust losing its appeal.

'No,' Walter says shortly. 'There won't be any bones.'

She'd been so light at the end, just skin and the bones Sean is so ghoulishly imagining. Bird-boned, he'd thought of her when she'd been lying there in the bed at the hospice, and, in a moment of fancy, he'd imagined her taking flight, soaring on the breeze and winging her way north to the place they'd both loved so much. Now he's bringing what's left of her by a more pedestrian method, and he adjusts the straps on his rucksack which are digging into his shoulders. The urn and its contents are surprisingly heavy. *Ashes and dust*, he thinks, wondering if anything is left of the Mairi he remembers, anything that is travelling with him, watching over him, and nodding in approval when she sees where he's taking her. He's not religious, wasn't sure if she was. They hadn't talked about it, even towards the end. But she'd believed in family and the past, he knew that much.

'Your grandma's people came from here,' he tells the boy. 'They were Lindsays. They farmed the land around here.'

They boy looks disbelievingly at the sour heather that fills the valley, the dense forest behind them and at the narrow track that rises across the face of the eastern slope, heading for a notch in the hills.

'When can we eat our sandwiches?'

Walter sighs. 'Not yet,' he says. 'Not till we get there.'

'Get where?'

'The top.'

'I can't see no top.'

'Well, it's up there. Look, here on the map. This is where we are, and this is where we're going.' He tries to interest the boy in the route, pointing out the carpark at Braedownie, the place the track had divided, the name, Jock's Road, written on the very section they're climbing. 'How long do you think it will take to get there?' he asks, trying to make an educational point of the exercise.

'Dunno,' says the boy, and Walter sighs again as he puts away the map. He's lost the knack – if he ever had it – of relating to children. Sheila had been born so long ago and has never had children of her own, a cause of grief to himself and Mairi. In his darker moments he's sometimes felt as if they were a withered twig on their extensive family tree. Mairi had liked children, and if she'd been with them today she would have been pointing out this crag or that stream and explaining how they got their names. She'd be telling Sean the stories of this clan-chief or that bonnie maiden, of the water-horses that infest each and every loch, and of the great grey man who stalks the hills when the mist comes down. She'd be telling him about their past and making it his. Except it isn't Sean's past and never will be. Bones and blood, that's the inheritance of the lives that have gone before, and Sean shares neither.

'Come on,' he says, picking up the pace. 'Get a move on or we'll never get there.'

The valley narrows around them and the track begins to steepen and curve around little mossy hollows, and Walter finds himself puffing along in the boy's wake.

'We'll stop here for a moment,' he says when they reach the old howff at Cairn Lunkard. 'We'll have our elevenses.'

Normally he would have packed his own food, but he'd let Sheila do it this time since she knows what boys eat, and Walter isn't all that fussy. But when he opens the plastic box and sees the iced buns he realises she's packed left-overs from Mairi's funeral tea, and the sight and smell of the cake brings it all back: the car to the crematorium and the people falling silent as he walks into the place with Sheila holding his arm and sniffing into a hanky. He sees their dark unfamiliar clothing, hears their muted whispers and the formal words, feels their hands shaking his, smells the rising damp in the church hall back in the village, and tastes the food laid out on the trestle tables. He remembers how family member had greeted relatives they hadn't seen since the last funeral, how they'd all said what a sad day it was, and how they'd all looked as if they were enjoying themselves, all except for Wayne and Sean who, after all, didn't really belong.

But it was what Mairi would have wanted. He'd lost count of the number of people who'd told him so, and, although he'd never admit it to a soul, he'd been pleased by how well the funeral had gone. He supposes now that making all the arrangements had been his way of coping, but somehow the masterminding of the whole affair had been balm to his grieving spirit, as had the gathering together of the scattered Lindsay clan, the drawing back into the present of the ghosts time and circumstance had been dragging away into the past. He'd pulled them together from all corners of the country to celebrate Mairi's life in the only way he'd known how: with the quiet munching of bridge rolls and iced pastries, the drinking of tea and whisky and the telling of old family stories and scandals in the company of others who, in one way or another, shared her blood and bones. Now he's bringing what's left of those bones to join the more ancient ghosts who'd walked these hills in their bare feet with their possessions on their backs, driving their stirks to market, singing as they went. It was all about family, one way or another. All about roots.

'Not far now,' he tells the boy when they set off once more. The track turns muddy as it approaches the plateau, then loses itself completely in the grass. It spite of its name, Jock's Road is very far from being a road at this point. 'Up there,' he says, pointing to a rocky knoll in the distance that's coming and going through the cloud, Crow Craigies, where he's decided to scatter Mairi's ashes.

It's about a mile away, but the going's good, and it's not long before they're climbing the last little bit, through the rocky outcrops and up to the summit. After a while the clouds lift, but he's been here many times before, and today he's not here for the view. He unshoulders his rucksack, pulls out the urn and judges the direction of the wind. The boy's standing downwind.

'Come on, Sean, get out of the way.'

But Sean doesn't move, doesn't even seem to hear him. He's staring all around, at the mountains to the northwest breaking through the clouds, the distant Cairngorms still capped with snow on this late spring day. He's staring at the Tolmount that lies just to the west, looming over the deep-cut glen of Loch Callater and, just behind it, the domed swell of Tom Buidhe. He's peering north to the outlying peaks of Lochnagar and north-east, behind the stony summit of Broad Cairn, to Lochnagar itself, a massive brute of a hill, still clinging on to winter. To the south, across a dull rolling plateau, are Mayar and Driesh, and behind them the Braes of Angus, dipping in layers, grey on grey, away into the distance.

'Wow!' the boy whispers. Not 'Cool' or 'Dunno' or 'S'pose', but 'Wow', the word not yelled, not truly intended to be heard, but whispered to himself alone, a word from the heart uttered by a boy who knows nothing of history or family, who doesn't belong to this place, but who, with that one whispered word, has claimed the right to be there, the right to belong. Walter puts the urn down and steps up beside him then crouches down to his level and points out each and every peak. As he does so he knows that for this boy they lie in the years to come, and he understands that roots aren't about ghosts or an imagined past but are something that nourishes the future. He understands that family has little to do with blood and bones, or dust and ashes, and that Mairi had known it all along.

'Come on, son,' he says. 'Let's head back for today.' Another time they'll go further or take a different route. Another time he'll tell him one of Mairi's stories, one of the family stories, because, in a funny sort of way, in the only way that matters, Sean is family now.

'What about Grandma's dust?' the boy wants to know.

'Oh, I think we'll take her home,' Walter says, packing the urn back into his rucksack. He knows just the place in the garden, and he'll plant a rose bush there. He'd seen one in a garden centre not that long ago. 'Mary-Ann', it was called, a hybrid tea with mauve flowers. Mairi had always liked mauve. She would have wanted to nourish the roots of something growing into the future, not the past. He puts his hand on the boy's shoulder as they walk back down the track. Yes, it's what she would have wanted.

Stolen Away

I t comes to him, as ever, in a dream, a low rumbling that seems to shake the house, then a strange rhythmic creaking. There's a smell too, of diesel fumes and axle grease, of burnt sugar and fried onions. Then, in the way of dreams, it's gone, leaving nothing but a shape at the back of his mind, a gasp of memory, and the conviction that something has been lost.

When Peter wakes up it's four o'clock, and the house is silent, save for the ticking of a clock and Sandra snoring gently on the other side of the room. All he can smell is talc and pot pourri. He huddles down beneath the duvet and tries to get back to sleep, to catch hold of the dream. But it slips ahead of him like an eel, diving deeper and deeper . . . *It's July*, is his last conscious thought. *Of course!*

'I see the Fair's arrived,' Sandra observes over their high-fibre, low-cholesterol, breakfast.

'Really?' he says and briefly considers adding *Maybe we could go and take a look*. But life has taught him the wisdom of thinking carefully before he speaks, and Sandra beats him to it.

'I don't know why the Council allows it! Those people must be breaking all sorts of regulations.' She ticks them off on her fingers. Hygiene, or lack of it, is at the top of the list, closely followed by planning regulations and noise pollution. '– and how Arthur is going to manage, I don't know, since his house is so close to the Common. That Poor Man won't get a wink of sleep!'

Peter had been wondering when Poor Arthur would come into it.

It's funny, he thinks, how time is structured, how it tends to fall into two unequal parts, divided by some significant event. For Sandra, life consists of the time before they'd got to know Cynthia and Arthur, and the greatly improved time of 'after'. But Cynthia's dead now, and Arthur has been transformed into 'Poor Arthur', so now it's 'when Cynthia was still alive' and 'since Cynthia died'. Peter, however, sees things differently. Life for him is divided into when he worked, and the less desirable 'since he retired'. He doesn't seem to be cut out for retirement, even if 'he jolly well deserved it' as Sandra keeps pointing out. But of course his early retirement enabled them to take all the little holidays Sandra's so fond of, the ones they take, or used to take, with Cynthia and Arthur.

'I'm just popping over to Arthur's,' Sandra announces later that morning before slamming the door behind her. She click-clacks down the path carrying a number of plastic boxes. That will be Arthur's lunch, Peter thinks sourly. *Poor Arthur depended on Cynthia for everything,* Sandra had whispered at the funeral. *However is he going to manage?*

Peter thinks Arthur's managing rather well in the circumstances. He, on the other hand, will be expected to find his own lunch and run the risk of eating something destined for Arthur's supper and thus incurring Sandra's wrath. It's safer, he decides, to go down to the corner shop for a tin of soup, and maybe he'll walk past the Common on the way back. Sandra's always saying he should take more exercise.

The Fair arrives in the last week of July. Normally he misses it since he and Sandra are away at the end of July; they have a time-share on the Algarve with Cynthia and Arthur. This year, however, they haven't gone to Portugal, much to Sandra's private regret. 'Of course, we wouldn't *dream* of going, in the circumstances. Poor Arthur.' But she'd perked up at the thought of the other holiday they always take in September, to the Canaries, because surely Poor Arthur will be feeling more like it by then?

Actually, Peter has never liked going on holiday with Cynthia and Arthur. He doesn't like the heat, the foreign food, the flies, the travelling by air, the having to wear silly shorts and silly hats, and he doesn't like Cynthia and Arthur. What he'd really like to do is pack a rucksack, get out his old walking boots, and just set off, to go on the tramp like he used to do. He'd like to see Britain in the old way, to stroll down shaded lanes and towpaths, sit at village pubs of an evening, cool his feet in streams, eat pork-pies and pass the time of day with farmers. He wants to recover his past, the self he'd imagined once, before that day all those years ago. The day at the Fair.

It's an old tradition, centuries, even millennia, old: the summer fair, Lughnasadh, festival of the sun, a time for the buying and selling of stock, the settling of old debts and incurring of new ones, the hiring and firing of labour and the plighting of troths. Lammas, they call it now, although all that remains of the mediaeval fair are the painted horses that ride endlessly around the carousel.

Peter walks past the Common on the way back from the shop, but the Fair's still being set up. Painted panels are being knocked together and stubby dodgems unloaded from lorries. A generator is pulsing throatily – *how is Poor Arthur going to sleep?* – and there are shouts and the protest of metal grinding on metal. It looks, even to his eyes, a bit tired and tawdry, the paint faded and flaked, but the smell, that uneasy amalgam of diesel fumes and caramel, reminds him of his dream. Unsettled, he hurries on past, averting his eyes, and bumps into Sandra who's on her way home, boxless now.

'How's Arthur?' he asks, but she misses the sarcasm in his voice.

'Oh, bearing up,' she replies, a steely glint in her eye. 'That Margaret Spicer was there, dropping off some of those rocks she calls scones. That was her excuse anyway, and Poor Arthur's too much of a gentleman not to invite her in. Although it's not as if he and Cynthia were ever friendly with Margaret and Tom.'

Peter says nothing. When Sandra's put out it's best to keep a low profile, and, to his relief, she finds another target for her irritation.

'Disgusting, I call it,' she snaps with a jerk of her head at the Fair. 'Just look at that child, doing its business in the bushes! Filthy people!'

Peter catches sight of a boy, now running back to the wagons, untidy hair flying, a grin splitting a distinctly dirty face as he catches Peter looking at him. Peter meets the boy's eyes, and, abruptly, he's lost, transported back to that day at the Fair all those years before.

Filthy people! His grandmother had refused to let him go to the Fair. She'd had a horror of strangers, believing they carried some infection of the body or the mind. Once, he remembered, one of them had come to the door, selling pegs or the like, and she'd slammed the door in the woman's face then cleaned the doorknocker with carbolic soap. *Thieving gypsies!* she'd muttered.

Peter had read about gypsies in fairy-tales. They stole children, didn't they? They lured them with sweets and took them from their beds in the dead of night. By morning, the gypsies would be gone, leaving nothing behind but the ashes of a smoored fire. The stolen children had vanished. They'd be riding the coloured wagons down the leafy lanes of Britain, lost to their homes and families, becoming gypsies themselves, forever travelling, forever on the move.

Sandra spends the afternoon on the phone, rallying the troops. She has a coterie of friends, members of the same hard-line organisations: the Church Social Committee and the Old Folks' Outing Organisers. Useful women, no-nonsense women, *plain* women, whom Sandra quickly organises into a rota to 'look after Poor Arthur'. Eventually, she lays down the phone with a metaphorical dusting of the hands, and Peter understands that the Margaret Spicers of this world have been routed. It appears, however, that a watching brief is still required.

'I've defrosted that left-over casserole for you, the one we had at Easter. It needs using. I'll take Arthur something from the Indian. He just *adores* curries, but I don't have time to make one since I'm going to help him go through Cynthia's things. All those little reminders! It must be quite dreadful for the Poor Man!' Cynthia is to be expunged, Peter understands, and then there will just be the three of them, Arthur, Sandra, and Peter.

He'd defied his grandmother and escaped that day, all those years ago. How, he can't quite remember now, some deception no doubt, and he'd made his way down to the Fair. He'd no money of course, but he could watch. He could breathe in the smells. He could listen to the tinny music and touch the gilded horses.

'Oi! You there! You paying for a ride or what?!'

He'd backed away, straight into the arms of the woman.

'Nearly knocked me for six, you did! You going on the ride? No? Run out of money, have you? Tell you what, son. You nip up to the shop for me, get me a pint of milk, and I'll see you get a ride.'

She'd crossed his palm with silver. They did that, according to his story books. It was a sort of spell. Willingly, he'd let himself be enchanted. He'd run this errand, then maybe there would be others. Maybe they'd let him help on one of the rides, or in a booth. Maybe he'd be so useful they'd steal him away, leaving nothing behind but a smoor of warm ash.

He'd run, afraid the shop might shut early or that they'd have run out of milk. He'd run so fast he'd tripped in a patch of gravel, and the silver coin had gone flying. Frantically, he'd searched but couldn't find it. He'd gone on searching long after the shop had run out of milk, long after it had closed its doors. Down on the Common the music played, and he'd imagined the woman waiting for him to return with the milk or her money. But he'd gone home, and there, on the kitchen table, he'd seen his grandmother's purse.

Thieving gypsies!

Peter offers to go with Sandra that evening. They could all have a take-away from the Indian, he suggests, and then he could help Arthur sort through Cynthia's things. But his offer is rejected. 'I've already defrosted the casserole, and I don't want it to go to waste. Anyway, you'd be useless. You know how you are.'

How is he? he wonders. How was he then, all those years ago? Was he a thief?

That evening, after shoving the casserole to the back of the fridge, he goes down to the Fair. He has money now, but he's too old for the chair-a-planes or the dodgems. He can still watch, though. He can still breathe in the foreign smells and touch the flaking fake-gold horses. He can eat a hamburger full of BSE and a huge mound of sickly-sweet pink candyfloss handed to him by a distinctly grubby hand. The boy he'd wanted to be all those years ago grins at him.

'FORTUNES!' the sign announces. 'READ BY MADAME STELLA.'

She's an old woman. Well, she would be after all these years, and she looks at him without recognition, puzzled. She's used to breathless young girls wanting to know what lies in store for them, not retired old men.

'You want me to tell your future?' she asks, eyeing him uncertainly as he crosses her palm with silver, rather a lot actually.

'Not exactly,' he says. They talk for a long time. Outside the wagon a queue builds up, but he's paid well. He's no thief.

That had been it, of course. The choice. The deciding what he was and what he wasn't. He'd looked at his grandmother's purse. He'd even opened it. There had been a silver coin there, just like the one he'd lost. But he'd closed the purse and gone to his room. He wasn't a thieving gypsy. He wasn't a gypsy at all. He'd been tested and found wanting. Nevertheless, all that night he'd waited, awake and fully dressed, ready to leave, ready to be stolen away. He'd heard the music stop, then a distant banging as the Fair was dismantled. Boards and horses were packed away in wagons, and the travelling people swung themselves up into lorries and trailers. There was a low rumbling and a strange rhythmic creaking as the Fair moved up the lane and onto the main road, heading for its next destination, leaving nothing behind but litter on the Common and a lingering smell of diesel and caramel.

And him.

He'd always reckoned his childhood had ended the night he hadn't been stolen away. The one important discontinuity.

He's back before Sandra. 'Arthur enjoy his curry?' he asks. 'The casserole was nice.'

Lying is easier than he'd expected. He goes to bed and sleeps dreamlessly in the pot pourri-scented bedroom. For the next few days he does as he always does. He goes to the library, watches television, reads the newspaper, and nods in ironic understanding as Sandra describes Arthur's helplessness and his understandable and complete dependence on her. On Friday he stays up late, listening to the banging from the Common as the travellers dismantle the Fair. Later the rumbling begins, and he goes out into the lane.

'All right?' The woman stops her lorry, leans out of the window, and jerks her head. Peter walks round to the other side and climbs in. His old boots are uncomfortable, and the rucksack is digging into his shoulders, but he'll get used to it. The boy grins and shifts along to make space. By the time the sun rises he's gone. He's travelling now, from place to place, horizon to horizon, country to country. He's vanished, leaving Sandra to Arthur and Arthur to Sandra. Behind him there's only the festering remains of a once-frozen casserole, and a strangely empty bank account.

He's a gypsy now, and he's stolen himself away.

Like the Tide

I still have the grey silk dress. It hangs at the back of the wardrobe between my winter coat and the dark red suit that doesn't fit me now. I loved it once, its sheen and slide that made me think of a river running slow beneath a winter's sky. The fabric caught the light and the eye; on its surface was a damasked pattern of flowers and leaves, and you touched it carefully in case they crumbled into dust. It's silent now, where once it slid and rustled, silk on silk, skin on skin, but its scent still hangs in the shadows, a dusty perfume and the tang of sweat, the salt smell of a summer evening's fog. One day I'll look for it and find it gone, the ghost of a foolish dream, slipping away on the tide.

——

'I still have it, you know,' I say out loud. 'The grey silk dress.'

Your mind is racing behind the blank wall of your eyes. *Who? When? How? Why?* Reluctantly, you tear yourself away from that inner search and look at me. A spasm of irritation flickers across your face.

'What on earth are you talking about?'

Why talk at all? you want to say. *Why now? Don't you realise? Can't you hear the clamour?* The phone is ringing, and there's shouting from the press who've camped outside the house, but you've stopped hearing these things. Instead, you're listening to the silence from your private phone, the one whose number only the Prime Minister knows. The silence is deafening, and to drown it out you return to your desperate futile questionings. *Who? When? How? Why?*

'The grey silk dress, Marcus,' I repeat patiently, as if I'm talking to a child. 'The one I wore to the Bracknells' reception. Goodness! It must be all of fifteen years ago now! But I still have it. I kept it, you see.'

Why? But you don't ask the question. You're thinking back to fifteen years ago, to the night you were on display as a possible candidate for the by-election. Eleanor, Lady Bracknell, your oldest and dearest friend, had arranged it for you, helping you with that first step on your way, and after that night there was no looking back. Now, fifteen years later, you'd intended to stand for the leadership, and everyone expected you would win. What irony, you wonder, compels me to remind you of the night that set you on your way? Why now when everything is falling to pieces all around you?

'I'll stand by you, of course,' I reassure you. 'I think you can rely on me for that.' Should I have said it earlier? Should you, perhaps, have asked? But it didn't occur to you, did it? I'm your wife, so naturally I'll stand by you. 'Because I know it's all lies,' I add.

But I know nothing of the sort. I watched you read the newspapers. I watched the blood drain from your face. I watched you feel your carefully constructed world tilt and topple and begin to crumble. *Who? When? How? Why?*

Are you beginning to understand that it all began with the grey silk dress . . ?

'You'd better get something new,' you'd said after telling me about the reception and what it might mean. 'Something elegant and understated. Blue would be best, of course. Get Eleanor to go with you.'

Tactless, Marcus! I wasn't a child. I might only have been nineteen, a child to a man of thirty-two, but I was quite capable of choosing an evening dress that wouldn't disgrace you. So why did Eleanor have to go with me? Being your oldest friend didn't make her mine. But you didn't trust me, did you? You thought me too young, too inexperienced. You thought me a bore. Admit it. If it wasn't for my money you would never have married me. But a man with political ambitions needed money. Isn't that what Eleanor always told you? And she should know since she'd married money herself. Dear, dear Eleanor!

'Yes, of course,' I said, deliberately vague about exactly which of your edicts I intended to obey. You hated that, didn't you, my vagueness? I cultivated it at times just to annoy you.

I did look for a dress, as you'd commanded. I even looked for one in blue. But your tactless words stirred me to rebellion, and I found that nothing that matched your exacting requirements was quite to my taste. And so, in the end, knowing perfectly well you would disapprove, I decided to make my own dress. I made my way to the haberdashery section of the store, an Aladdin's cave of fabrics: figured velvets, rich damasks, chiffons, and silks. I looked for something in blue to begin with, intending to obey you in this, if nothing else, but then I saw it, pale and aloof against the fuchsias and cobalts of the bolder fabrics. A bolt of pure grey silk.

I told myself that grey was elegant and understated. I convinced myself that in a certain light it had a hint of blue. That was its charm, you see, a chameleon-like ability to pick up colour, like the pearl within a mussel's shell. The feel of it enchanted me, the dull weight that made me think of rainclouds, and it slipped through my fingers like mist on the edge of the sea. It was subtle and mysterious and made me dream a little. Perhaps too much.

I didn't tell you, of course, and you didn't ask. I intended to surprise you, forgetting how much you hate surprises. I was too intrigued by the possibilities of the fabric, the way it shimmered by day like sun on the river or gleamed by night as if moonlight was falling on fresh snow. It was warm to the touch, as soft as the breast-feathers of a dove, and felt almost like skin itself, growing beneath my fingers as I pinned and hemmed the fabric into an evening dress, into a second skin that didn't so much conceal my own but reveal it. That was what I wanted, Marcus – to reveal myself to you, clothed in the colours of the sea and sky, and make you see that I wasn't a child but someone who could match you in your ambitions, someone on whom you could rely. Was that so very much to ask?

I was pleased with what I created. The fabric fell from the shoulders almost to the base of my spine. The skirt was tucked discretely and cut on the bias so that it moulded itself to my legs and hips and fell full and heavy to the floor. It was unusual, the style no longer in fashion, but it was elegant, as you'd required. Understated? Perhaps. Not blue, of course, but I thought you might forgive that.

'Is this some sort of joke?' you asked.

'Joke?'

'What on earth are you wearing? It looks . . .'

You hesitated, and I thought you saw it then. I thought you realised it wasn't mere fabric but a distillation of air and sea, a distillation of myself, that it made me into a woman whom perhaps you didn't want but whom you might come to understand you needed. I had a breathless certainty of life poised on the turn, like the tide beginning to flood into the river.

'It looks drab,' you said. 'Where on earth did you buy it?'

'Liberty's', I told you, feeling my life pause, hang on its turning point, not yet beginning to flow. But it would; I was confident of that. All I had to do was wait for you to see me through the eyes of others less blinded by habit than you.

'Charming,' said the retiring MP, peering over his half-moon glasses to look at me. Looking, then looking again, seeing me as you hadn't. 'Charming,' he repeated in a quite different tone. You winced and made some bland remark.

'What an interesting dress!' observed an older woman in aquamarine crepe and too many diamonds. 'So nice to see something original!' she added to her husband, whom I knew to be from the Whips' Office. He smiled his assent but looked speculatively at you, wondering whether originality in your wife might have its source in a dangerous originality in your thinking.

I excused myself and circulated. You watched me cautiously, not quite trusting me, not yet seeing me for what I could be. And yet I made myself agreeable, propounded views I knew you held, was pleasant to people I privately despised. I flowed, smooth as the river I resembled, among the rocks and shoals of the political world, my confidence flooding once more, my beautiful dress swirling around me like quicksilver in the candlelight, drawing every eye.

But not yours, Marcus, because you were whispering with Eleanor. She was dressed in blue, of course, a turquoise blue that matched her eyes, and her dress was very much in the style of the day, fitting close around the waist and falling in a deep V from narrow shoulder straps.

'My dear! What a beautiful gown! So unconventional!' We kissed the air beside each other's cheeks.

'I made it myself,' I told her and saw your mouth thin in irritation.

'Well, one would hardly know,' she said, reassuring you rather than me. 'The colour reminds me of dear John Major. What a pity we've not to speak of him these days!'

She exchanged a smile with you, Marcus, the very private smile of two people who've known each other for ages, two people with the same ambitions, the same drives, both of whom had married for money. You shared backgrounds and circumstances, an understanding of what and who mattered, and how best to get what one wanted out of life.

Who shared, I now realised, rather more than that.

How long had you been lovers? Since we'd been married? Since before that? Did you never think to tell me? I wouldn't have minded. I might even have understood. You could have *shared* this with me! But you didn't need to, did you? You didn't need to share anything with me. And you never would.

I stood very still, absorbing this knowledge through my skin, feeling a chill as if my silver dress had turned to pewter. I didn't say anything. I wasn't going to make a scene. You could rely on me for that at least. So, smiling at your mistress, I took a glass of champagne from a passing waiter, while you took two glasses of red wine and handed one to Eleanor, still with that private smile in your eyes, that shared understanding of what had to be done.

She stepped forward, tripped on the hem of her gown, and shrieked discretely. The glass toppled from her hand and the wine, deepest red, spilled down the front of my silver dress.

She apologised of course and patted ineffectually at the stain that bled its way from my heart. I tried to tell her that it was just a flesh wound, although I knew differently. I waited with surprising calm for the air to reach the wound and the pain to begin. But she, more concerned with your interests than mine, whisked me upstairs to find me something else to wear, something in blue, naturally, much like her own dress. Much like the dress of every other woman in the room.

'This is such an important night for Marcus,' she told me gently as if I might not have understood. 'He has a great future ahead of him, but these early stages are so . . . delicate.'

I smiled at her to let her know I knew, that I wouldn't make a fuss, that I might even be grateful for her willingness to share you with me. She was more generous than you ever were, Marcus.

I still have the dress that you've forgotten, the ghost of a foolish dream, and the stain has faded to a dull mark. I'm still friends with Eleanor, and with all the others who succeeded her, those discrete women who wouldn't jeopardise your career. All your life you've relied upon the discretion of unfaithful women, never on me. And for that betrayal I still wear my secret skin. It was warm once, hopeful moonlight on the flooding tide, but now it has the chill of snow melt under the stars, frozen to a sheet of steel, dull as slate. Like ice, it is transparent and you fail to see it, Marcus, just as you failed to see all those years ago what I could have been to you, just as you now fail to see who it is who has betrayed you – the one woman on whom you could not rely. Your wife.

I let you rise almost to the pinnacle of your career before I judged the time was right to bring you down. All it took was a whispered word in the right ear to undermine the edifice you'd built. I'll stand by you, of course, as a good wife should. I'll stand by and watch you fall, just as I stood all those years ago, letting my beautiful dress, my secret self, slide to the floor to pool around my feet, the silk flowing through my fingers like the river.

Like the tide, ebbing.

Evidence of Ice

*A*s she drives North, Olivia begins to think of ice. Not that it grows colder – quite the reverse in fact – and it's not as if she's thinking of ice as such. No, it's evidence of ice she begins to see, then to look for and, finally, to find.

ᘓ─ᕲ

I'm leaving you, Alex.

For a brief, horrifying moment, Olivia believes she's spoken aloud. Now isn't the time, and this isn't the place, but nevertheless the words beat at the back of her throat. He's left her often enough in the past, she might say. And now he's left her again, although it's different this time.

'I'm leaving now, Alex.' That's what she actually says. Her voice is careful and controlled, but, even so, it rises a little in a sort of half-question, an invitation for him to object or at least reply. She isn't sure if he hears the invitation that's barely audible, even to her, but his response is unequivocal.

'I'm with Rosie, now.'

Rosie – is that the girl's name? – smiles in embarrassment, too inexperienced to deal with this easily. She's too naive for Alex, Olivia thinks, not his usual type. But the girl puts her hand on his shoulder, and he lets it lie there. Olivia wonders if he's being passive or complicit. He's been both in the past.

'I'm with Rosie, now,' he repeats, his eyes sliding away from Olivia's. Complicit then, she decides.

'We'll be fine,' the girl says firmly and Olivia bristles at the casual assumption of ownership. The words *'Take your hands off my husband!'* echo in the empty spaces of her head but she doesn't say anything so shamelessly melodramatic. Instead she nods.

'I'm sure you will.' Who she means by 'you' is left deliberately ambivalent. Alex, or the girl, or both. Not herself, of course. She won't be fine, but she's already accepted that.

The girl is clearly impatient for Olivia to be gone, to be left alone with Alex. Olivia is surprised, and then not, that he still retains his ability to affect women that way. He's always liked them young, ready to be impressed, like soft wax, to be infected by his lazy intelligent charm, an infection from which few recover. Olivia wonders if she ought to warn the girl about that. The girl smiles at Alex, a complicit little smile, and Olivia imagines she sees something warmer than passivity stir in his eyes.

So, driving north, leaving her husband with another woman, and not for the first time, Olivia begins to think of ice. Not that it grows colder – quite the reverse in fact, for the sun is white and clear and makes the April landscape shimmer uneasily. The traffic is heavy, the motorway hazy with fumes, but beyond the suburbs the fields are winter black. Snow lingers by walls and hedges in shadowed crescents.

She wonders if she's being too civilised about the whole thing. The girl had walked her to the door, chatting determinedly about this and that, trying to make things as painless as possible for everyone. But Olivia hadn't been listening. She'd been imagining Alex's voice, warm and amused. *It won't last, Olivia. It never has before. It's always you I come back to. Always you. They mean nothing to me,* he's whispered, his mouth close to hers. *One day,* he's promised, *there will just be the two of us. One day . . .* Has she been too willing to put aside the moment for this possible, less tangible, future? But 'one day' – the future she now inhabits – is a landscape changed beyond all recognition. Perhaps that's why she begins to think of ice

She's well past the Midlands, and the land is rising. There's an escarpment on the left, a low mound on the right, clouds gathering on the high ground, a cool grey edge to the earth colours and sullen greens of lowland forests. Up, up, the car climbing into cloud-shadows, long curves of road, dark from an earlier shower. In a water-worn gully she sees the white gleam of a fall and then, coming into view on a bend, a wide sweep of valley with steep sides and a ribbon of river coiling lazily between fields.

She stops, pulls into a lay-by, and gets out. It's colder here, a wind blowing from higher ground, laced with frost. These hills, she remembers, once lay under a sheet of ice, and this valley was hollowed out by a glacier tongue. For some reason, her eye is attuned to this not-quite-forgotten knowledge, and, when she returns to the car and continues her drive north, she begins to look for evidence of ice. She imagines glaciers and high, ice-locked lakes and sees lines in the land, terraces that were once the shores of a sea.

She understands that this is a form of escape, but nevertheless she continues heading north, following the route of glacial retreat, with the possibility glimmering on the horizon that this time she might not go back. *I'm leaving you, Alex.* But she hadn't said those words. He's never lied to her, although there have been times when she would have preferred him to, so she must offer him the same grace. Of course she'll go back. She'll spend the week as she'd planned, doing some walking in the North and thinking about herself and Alex, trying to come to terms with what has happened to them. Not thinking about ice at all.

The land has fallen away now. She's skirted the Lakeland fells and is heading for the Borders: a long slow fall and then a line of smooth rounded hills. Once, they'd lain, dreaming, on an ocean floor. Now they lie, still dreaming, in clear spring sunshine, careless of their past. Gradually, they too fall behind her, and she drops down into the central belt, that great rift in the earth. She doesn't see the towns and fields, the factories and retail parks. An odd clarity of vision lets her see what lies beneath, what lies in the past.

There's a moment, in a petrol station near Glasgow, when she thinks of going back, of heading south and taking him away from the girl. It should be easy. She's had half a lifetime's experience after all. There have been others in the past who were more of a threat than a girl with nothing to recommend her but soft white hands and a soothing voice. If there's to be a final woman in Alex's life, Olivia wants it to be herself. She wants things to be the way he promised, just the two of them together at the end. He's never lied to her before.

But the moment passes, and, when she leaves the petrol station, it's to continue her journey. She drives on, weaving her way through the complexities of motorways and flyovers, leaving the city behind and following the shores of a loch. Here the land has cracked open and water has gathered in the fissure, scoured by ice at its northern end, land-locked by moraines in the south.

She's tried to change him, of course, but without success. Instead, it's she who's been changed, moulded by compromise and accommodations and promises she doesn't entirely believe. She sees that now, here in the clear northern light, in the bronze angled rays of a spring evening. She looks into the shadows of a landscape sculpted by ice and knows herself to be similarly carved. She's just one of the many possible women she might have become.

She stays somewhere, a farmhouse, clean sheets in an unfamiliar room, a larger breakfast than she's used to, an awkward exchange of cash, then she's heading north once more, with a little easting. It rains briefly, a greying blur on snow-streaked slopes, a shower-slant along a reservoir, a patch of mist in a fringe of pines. To one side, hills rise into cloud. The rain clears and she catches sight of a high corrie she knows will hold, cupped in a scoop of rock, a cold clear lochan.

She's heading north-east now, crossing moors with grey hills to the left, a jumble of low mounds, a wide pass. She's in the heart of it now, the glacial outwash plain, a broad valley, beds of gravel, a high wintry plateau. A little road weaves into the hills and ends in a circle of grass. She parks, pulls on her boots and shoulders a rucksack packed days before. Close-up, the shape of the land is less obvious. The minutiae of heather and rock obscure the tilt of the ground, just as the minutiae of life obscure the shape of a marriage. But once she reaches the plateau, a patchwork of white drifts and rolling mounds of dark heather beneath a sky that still holds the glint of ancient reflections, things seem clearer.

She walks across a moorland that once lay beneath a mile of ice. She can barely imagine the weight of it, since all she can see are the scoops and drifts of a single season's snow melting beneath the beat of the sun. The ice is long since gone, and yet she feels the ground rising beneath her feet, easing itself upwards, stretching and tilting. The land, crushed and carved by ice, survives. It's still alive, still changing. She feels light, as if something in her has expanded too. Perhaps it's her heart. She walks easily now, the weight of Alex's casual infidelities sliding from her. They mean nothing to her any more, but still she feels scarred and landscaped, smoothed and hollowed. She's ready now for what comes after, and she no longer thinks of ice but of melt water, of rivers rushing, salts dissolving, of winds blowing from the south, bearing dust and seeds. She thinks of seas rising, lands subsumed.

The week passes, and she goes back to him, as she'd known she would. She's driven over a thousand miles and travelled much further. But Alex hasn't moved at all. He's sitting in the same chair, his face turned to an open window that looks out on carefully tended lawns and mature trees. There's the sound of birdsong and the distant clank of a trolley.

'Has he spoken of me at all?' she asks the girl, Rachel or Rhona, or something like that.

The girl shakes her head and makes a helpless gesture of apology. Olivia touches her shoulder briefly in acknowledgement of something shared and lost. 'It's all right,' she says, although it isn't. 'It's all right.'

Olivia puts her hand on Alex' shoulder, just as the girl had done, and lets it lie there for a moment, feeling bones beneath his skin, the absence of him.

'I'm with Rosie now,' he says.

The girl unpins the badge on her uniform and hands it to him.

'Ruby, Alex. Look, there's my name on the badge. And this is Olivia. You remember Olivia?'

'Olivia.' He fingers the badge, running his fingers over its embossed surface. He doesn't look at her, and Olivia isn't sure if it's a statement or a question. She looks down at him, a man who's loved her, deceived her, and drawn her back, time after time, after each betrayal. Even now. Even this time. But he looks past her, his eyes empty of passivity, of memory, of her own name.

Olivia thinks of a land, freed from the weight of ice, rising imperceptibly. She thinks of deeply scored valleys and cold pools rimed with frost, of spores and ferns unfolding in flat white sunshine. She thinks of the man whose life collided with her own, moulding her into the strange geographies she's only just begun to explore.

The Bogeyman

'**H**e touched you, didn't he?'

The lady police officer was an easy-natured motherly type, but the tone of her voice was far from easy-natured, and the little girl promptly burst into tears.

The lady police officer knew she shouldn't have asked that question, but she'd been overcome by the magnitude of her own outrage. She knew, of course, that such things happened in other places to other children: faceless children living in conditions – a city tenement perhaps – where such things might be considered commonplace. But not here. Not in a little village where crimes, when they happened at all, were crimes of property: a little shoplifting, some gentle petty larceny, the disturbing of the peace on a Friday night, a peace so deeply ingrained into the place she'd sometimes felt it was just asking to be disturbed.

But not by this. Not by that sort of thing. For all her training, her reading of newspapers and watching of documentaries, she could persuade neither her mind nor her tongue to give this particular crime a name. But she'd understood from the girl's mother's inability to give it a name either what must have happened.

The child, a girl of seven with untidy dark hair and pansy-coloured eyes, looked at her gravely, neither confirming nor, more to the point, denying the accusation. The policewoman knew her of course, as she knew most of the children in the village. Indeed, the girl was one of a class of infants to whom she'd recently given the annual lecture on the importance of not accepting sweets from strangers, of not being tempted by a man – and it would usually be a man – to get into his car on the promise of baskets of puppies or kittens or the like. These routine warnings were delivered with rather less urgency – since the risk was felt to be smaller – than the injunction to look both ways before crossing the road, or to clean your teeth before bedtime. Because, in a village where everyone knew everyone else, who was a stranger? Who was strange?

One man.

'That man!' announced the policewoman, outrage making her head throb and her plump hands curve into talons. 'You went into his garden, didn't you?'

The girl nodded. She'd been seen opening the gate and going into the man's garden. But, because he'd lived there for years, and although he was strange he'd never been considered dangerous, no-one had thought to watch what happened next. However, they'd all heard and seen the girl as she'd run away sobbing. Yet all her mother could get out of her was that her distress was due to the Bogeyman.

He was a Pole, with a name no-one could pronounce so everyone avoided calling him by any name at all. He was just 'The Pole', a refugee from the war who'd married a local woman. Men had been scarce after the war and women desperate. His wife, some years before, had died of some lingering disease and, instead of returning to wherever it was he'd come from, he'd remained, in her village, in her house, tending her garden in which he grew strange and possibly, for all one knew, poisonous plants, and chased the cats who fouled his lawns with such ferocity that when any cat went missing in the neighbourhood he was regarded with even more suspicion than usual. He kept himself to himself and made as little effort to learn to speak English properly as his neighbours made to pronounce his name. Although how his English could be expected to improve when no-one spoke to him was something they didn't choose to go into. The children called him 'The Bogeyman' just as their parents called him 'The Pole'. A solitary foreign-looking man with an expression which had soured with the years. An outsider. A stranger.

'It was The Bogeyman,' the girl said, tears welling from her pansy eyes and with an expression on her face that was neither fear nor disgust but something more profound. It made the motherly policewoman feel murderous and dangerous, but she forced herself to be gentle when she asked her next question.

'So, after you went into his garden, what happened to make you cry?'

The girl began to cry all the harder.

'He told me a bad thing,' she said between sobs.

The policewoman delivered her back to her anxious mother and immediately wrote her report in language not as cool and official as it might have been had she waited an hour or a day. Then she handed it to her Sergeant who, since he had a little girl of his own, reacted in much the same way as his colleague. Without waiting for an hour or a day, he got into his car and went to see the man.

His language was official but his expression wasn't. The man was defensive and sullen and denied he'd done anything wrong. He agreed he'd spoken to the girl but couldn't imagine what might have made her cry. What had he said? the Sergeant demanded.

'I just tell her a story,' said the Pole, unwilling, it seemed, to meet the Sergeant's eyes.

'What sort of story?'

'A fairy tale.' The man shrugged in that foreign way he had. The Sergeant thought he was probably Jewish. They had a funny diet, he remembered, wondering about the cats. Funny ways too, no doubt. He certainly dressed strangely and smelled odd. The Sergeant sniffed in disgust.

'Keep a cat do you, sir?' he asked, sniffing again.

'A stray. I feed her time to time,' the man muttered, his eyes on the floor.

The Sergeant, being fond of cats himself, didn't believe him, but there it was left, with a warning about further enquiries. Yet when these were made, they bore out the man's claim. A passer-by had seen the girl listening to the man in the garden then running away. She hadn't gone into the house. And when it occurred to the Sergeant to ask the girl if she'd stayed in the garden she'd nodded but still wouldn't say what the man had told her, whether it was a fairy tale (a likely story!) or some piece of filth.

Charges weren't pressed, but everyone knew and came to their own conclusions. He'd been tolerated. Now he was despised. From being a vague presence in the village he became a concrete invisibility. He used to shop in the grocer's just across the road, but now everyone seemed to jump the queue, and he was forced to go to the less particular newsagent in the housing estate. He stopped going to the pub on a Friday night for his solitary glass of beer and began to tend his garden early in the morning or late at night when no-one was around.

Gradually he faded and became, even in the minds of the adults, the shadowy figure the children all believed him to be, The Bogeyman of myth and legend. Not a threat. No, eventually they all travelled beyond their first suspicion and might have forgotten it in time. But still the taste of it remained, the shadow of something atavistic that they might forget, but couldn't forgive. And so he faded until he was gone. Not suddenly, in the way of ogres, no defeat of evil at the hands of good, but the slow slipping away of a dark presence, much as night fades. Or childhood.

It was the Postman who noticed. Had the deliveries of earlier days continued, it might have been the Milkman or the Newsagent who would have reported his absence, but the man had few correspondents and it took a while for sufficient mail to pile up before anyone noticed.

He was wearing his uniform, that of a captain in a Polish regiment that had been much respected during the war. He was wearing his medals. Oh, yes, there were medals. Rather a lot, it was felt, for a refugee. And his service revolver was well cared for and polished. Not clean, of course, in the circumstances, but one imagined that if he'd missed his target – unlikely in view of all those medals – his first reaction wouldn't have been to preserve a life that had become wearisome but to clean the revolver that reminded him of a life of respect and comradeship, a life long since gone.

The reasons? None were given officially. Shame was suggested, the face-saving explanation of people who were themselves ashamed. *Good riddance*, said some. *Best forgotten*, said others more charitably. Easier said than done.

And the little girl? Ah, yes. The little girl.

The house remained empty while lawyers squabbled desultorily over the remains. The little girl walked past the house with her mother, paused and looked down the garden path. At the door a cat, scrawny and mottled with mange, clawed at the door and cried. The little girl began to cry too.

'It's all right, love. He's gone away. The Bogeyman's gone away for good.'

'Is he dead?'

'Yes, he's dead,' said the mother, but the little girl cried all the harder, as if she'd lost something that could never be recovered.

Twenty years later, in another little village, the little girl, now grown up and with a little girl of her own, watched an old man limp up the road. He wore a turban and a long yellow-stained tunic over baggy trousers.

'I don't like that man,' her daughter announced. 'He talks funny and he smells.'

So she'd thought twenty years before.

'Are you a Bogeyman?' she'd asked. Greatly daring, she'd marched up his garden path to where he was weeding a flowerbed. 'You are a Bogeyman,' she'd said. 'A woodcutter will chop off your head.' She'd been so certain, so confident.

'Why?' he'd asked.

'Because you're a bad man,' she'd said.

'Why? What I do?' He'd smiled. He shouldn't have smiled. She knew what he was, and she'd heard the whispers about the cats and had come to her own conclusion.

'You eat pussycats!' she'd accused him.

He'd said nothing but looked towards the door. On the step were two small bowls, one of food and one of water. And there, in the shade of a shrub, was a little grey cat with big eyes.

'And if woodcutter chop off my head, who feed my little Sophie? Who chase away the big cats that frighten her? Where she go on cold nights?'

She'd had no answer.

'Sophie has no-one else to take care of her. Just an old man whose head will be chopped off. What then, little girl, when my head is chopped off? I'll be dead. Not coming back. Do you know what dead is? I do.'

He'd looked angry then and turned away. She'd looked at the little cat and thought about it being all alone and cold and hungry. And she'd realised that even a bogeyman might have someone who'd care if he went away, who'd care if he was dead.

That was what made her cry, that two-edged realisation. If a Bogeyman could be good what about the good people – the teachers, the policemen, the firemen, even the parents? Could they be bad? Suddenly, the world was a threatening place. She was no longer certain of being a princess. The possibility of being a beggar girl overwhelmed her.

Only later did she realise something else; he'd been punished for a crime he hadn't committed. And it was her fault.

But maybe not. He was a stranger, after all, someone it wasn't possible to trust, someone on whom suspicion, for whatever reason, would duly fall. The one who left the circle of the fire, stoned, perhaps, starved certainly, who took the sins of the village upon himself, willingly or unwillingly. Who atoned for loss of innocence. Who knowingly, or unknowingly, told the truth.

He was The Scapegoat.

He was The Bogeyman.

Looking for the Leonids

T he garden is strange by night. Bushes bulk into shadow, and frost-blackened irises form a jagged mass beside a lawn of odd dips and hollows. He has the sense of moving into unfamiliar territory as he walks down the path through the gap in the yew hedge and into the rough meadow that lies between the garden and the open fields. The hedge shields the ground beyond from the faint light of the house, and he moves gratefully into darkness.

It's cold but he'd expected that. The sun had set in a clear sky that was the colour of tarnished brass. A few clouds had barred the sun behind a network of pewter, but they've long since vanished, contracting down from chilling vapours to steely fragments of ice that might have ringed the moon had there been a moon that night. But there isn't, and he'd expected that too. Had anyone asked, he would have predicted this cold and moonless night.

I'm leaving you.

He hadn't predicted that.

Surely you've seen it coming?

No, actually. He hadn't.

This happens to lots of couples, Martin. One partner moves on, matures. The other remains behind. That's all there is to it. It's nobody's fault.

He wants the release of tears, the warmth of moisture on his skin, but now he's reached the concealment of darkness he finds he's too cold for crying, although the pressure of unshed tears makes his sinuses ache. He flings back his head and squeezes his eyes shut as if he might press the tears back into the glands from which they've seeped. But when he opens his eyes again, all thoughts of tears have gone, and he stares at the sky in astonishment, a sky luminous with stars. Amazingly, he'd forgotten about stars. Now, there's irony for you!

'You're Pisces,' she'd announced when he'd told her his birthday. 'And I'm Leo.' She'd looked concerned.

'So?' he'd asked. She had auburn hair, a way of flaring up into laughter as a fire flares into light.

'So . . .' She'd giggled. 'So we're totally incompatible!'

'Want a bet?' He'd been full of himself in those days, had wanted to prove her wrong almost more than he'd wanted her.

Surely you've seen it coming? Should he have done? Was it then? The prediction he'd not believed?

He looks up at the sky, searching out the brightest stars, and tries to trace their patterns. There's the Plough, Ursa Major, there the belted warrior, Orion, and, high above him, the jagged angles of Cassiopeia. He lets his eyes wander, and gradually, as if he's a traveller returning to an almost forgotten landscape, the names come back to him: Aldebaran, Sirius, the cluster of the Pleiades and there, lower in the east, one bright star he remembers as Regulus. It's in the constellation of Leo, her sign.

He'd never been a great believer in astrology, but, when it turned out to be profitable, he'd changed his mind. She'd had a flair for it and in time had become *Seren, Lady of the Stars*, with her own TV programme, a column in one of the better tabloids, and a series of books, the latest of which, *Your Stars: Your Future* has just gone on sale in time for Christmas. He's her manager, her husband, and her lover – in that order. She's offered to keep him on in the first of those roles. His gratitude had sickened him.

But we'll still be friends, of course. Had they ever been friends? He hadn't realised.

He stares up at a sky that's full of symbols. There's Leo, the lion, with its bright star of Regulus, there the coruscating pair of Castor and Pollux in Gemini, the twins. Close by is the faint constellation of Cancer, the crab, and, in the distance, sinking vaguely into the horizon, his own sign of Pisces, the fish, a water sign. Naturally, that had come into it.

'I suppose this new man of yours is more compatible!' he'd said, surprise and humiliation making him petty. 'What is he then? Taurus? A bull, is he?'

She'd turned flint-eyed. 'Actually, Sebastian is a Libra. But it hasn't got anything to do with him. Sebastian's just a symptom of everything that's gone wrong between us. Surely you can see that? Let's not descend to personalities, Martin.'

But he hadn't been able to resist the temptation. He'd called her a mad self-serving bitch, a statement he would have apologised for later, had she not then accused him of being a mercenary cold-blooded parasite.

'– and I'm someone who needs warmth, Martin! I need fire and heat and someone to believe in me, but you're such an emotionless fish!'

He'd turned on his heel with icy precision – because why not conform to the stereotype? – and had gone out into the black frosty night so she wouldn't see him cry. There, in darkness, standing beneath a sky that pulses with its own elusive patterns, he tries to find his own meaning in the stars. He doesn't have her skills, but perhaps, if he looks hard enough, he'll be able to see patterns not only in the past, but in the future.

He shivers and thrusts his hands deeper into his pockets. It's the bottom of the night. In the distance, across the fields, the clock on the village steeple chimes a cracked discordant four o'clock. There's no wind to stir the bushes, nor, at that time of night, the hum of traffic from the bypass on the far side of the hill. Nothing moves, no cat prowling by the hedge, no field-mouse skittering beneath the stacked logs. The silence presses on his ears until he begins to imagine sounds: blood flowing in his veins, the distant thud of his heart, and the faint sound of the world turning through space, that rasp of atmosphere on vacuum. Then even those sounds fall away to nothing, and he feels as if he's come to a standstill, as if he's poised between the past – which has a pattern – and the future which, as yet, does not.

Yet he knows that the world turns. He knows that if he stands there long enough he'll see the western stars set and new stars lift from the eastern horizon. He knows that the heavens, with their faint illusory signals, will turn through the night. Stars will fade into daylight, and the sun will leap from the east in a fanfare of silver. That's the pattern, one of circles returning to the place where each began. That's his belief. Eventually, she'll come back to him. He's not sure if that's what he wants, but the possibility exists in the structure of the sky.

He stares at the stars, searching for proof, trying to detect their movement, that faint shift of arc. They glitter fixedly at him then blur and tremble. It's then that he sees it, a flash of light, one star striking across the sky in a pure diagonal of light. Then it's gone, leaving only a trace of fire on his retina and the conviction that the world has changed. A star has gone from the sky, a gap that won't be filled no matter how often the earth turns on its axis.

He knows what it is of course, a shooting star, a meteor, a frozen lump of rock that has come too close to the earth, been trapped by gravity, and begun to fall. As it falls it's warmed by friction until it glows, a transient star that streaks across the sky before falling into the east to be quenched by the sea.

He nods, having found a pattern he hadn't expected, and, as he struggles to understand, to see the shape of it, there's another and then another, arrowing flights of light radiating from Leo, her sign, stones of ice flaring brilliant before falling into water. A name surfaces from the far reaches of his memory. *The Leonids.*

'Are you going to stay out here all night?' she asks from behind him. She's standing on the path, a heavy coat over her nightdress. Her hair, that once gleamed chestnut, is a disordered mass, bleached by starlight to a dull silver.

He wants to say, 'Why should you care?' but stops himself and shrugs instead. 'I'm looking for the Leonids,' he says.

'The what?' She sounds irritated.

'The Leonids. Shooting stars.' Details come back to him. 'It's a meteor shower originating from the sector of the sky your lot call Leo.'

'My lot?'

'Astrologers.' He hesitates. The word he's about to say will change the future, no matter what pattern either of them might find in the stars. 'Charlatans. Self-deluded charlatans.'

He turns away from her, ignoring her gasp, and looks back at the sky. He feels the streaks of light fall on the back of his eyes. They're warm, somehow, like tears. He watches the meteors fall towards the distant sea and sees them in his mind's eye, flashing from darkness towards the frosted, tilting surface of the water. He sees them strike in a puff of steam, their light quenching, cooling as they fall down through the fathoms. He no longer believes in astrology and knows now that he never has. He had, deliberately in his case, deluded himself too. But in these at least he can believe: gravity, temperature, meteors, and the immensities of space.

She's correct in one thing at least; this happens to lots of couples. One partner moves on, matures, and the other remains behind. That's how it will be, he decides. He'll leave her standing there beneath her stars, in the dark unfamiliar garden. He'll follow the Leonids, search out their fading warmth: a cold-blooded fish swimming into darkness.

Fogbound

'Christ!! We'll never get there at this rate!' the girl complains, as if it's his fault the motorway traffic has slowed to a crawl. Ahead of them, a snail-trail of fog-lights bleeds a runnel of red into the near distance before being swallowed up by the loom of sodium.

He's already forgotten her name and where she's going, but, with an effort, the place comes back to him – Skipton – and then the name. Sharon, that's it. Sharon going to Skipton. It sounds like the title of a song, and he begins to hum, tapping his fingers on the steering wheel to mark the time. But then he stops. Why is *he* going to Skipton?

Beside him, the girl tuts and fusses, her short skirt riding up. Fat thighs, he notices.

'Haven't you got a music player?'

He wonders why he'd given in to the impulse: the girl standing by the slip-road from the service station, her thumb out, the traffic backed up, the fog thickening. The Fog. Yes, it had probably been the fog.

'There!' She grabs him by the arm. Ahead, in an aureole of light, a sign slides slowly into view then falls away into the rear-view mirror. An exit, a mile away, going to a place he doesn't know. In the fog names distort, lose their meanings and acquire new ones. He imagines the road plunging into the countryside, a matte-grey ribbon between blurred black hedges, fields mysterious with the bulking shapes of cattle, trees still holding the bleached remnants of daylight in the smoke of their branches. He imagines the road snaking across country, plunging down into river valleys and up over hard ribs of land.

'All right,' he says, veering the car onto the slip-road, away from the motorway with its wound of brake-lights. Soon it's left behind, and the day draws in, the fog thickening and closing in, clasping their bubble of glass and steel in its cold moist hand. He switches off the headlights, and the day opens out a little as a tinge of sun catches the droplets of moisture, lending the fog a strange luminosity.

'What are you doing? Are you mad?'

'The fog lights don't help,' he says. 'I can see better without them.' Indeed, now that the headlights are no longer punching their way into the fog, it seems to weaken, sliding apart and letting them through as it draws back one milky veil after another.

'But if a car comes the other way it won't see us. We're invisible!'

He smiles. That's part of it. Being invisible. Being a ghost. Being at one with the fog.

'No-one else is on this road,' he says. 'At least we're moving.'

He's driving fast now, down the white line. The fog parts ahead, then closes in behind them like a wet mouth. He's skimming around corners, spattering mud, sheeting through puddles with the hiss and thump of spray. The girl clutches her seatbelt, pulls down her skirt, grows silent.

'Look,' she says after some time. 'We could stop, couldn't we? Find a pub somewhere. We could sit it out. A nice pub with a coal fire, eh? We could have a drink or two . . .' She glances sidewards at him, her face as pallid as her thighs. 'I'm not in a hurry. Not really. Let's just have a nice drink, eh?'

He can tell what she's thinking. He can see it: the lights pushing back the fog, a neon sign, the pulse of music, the voices of other people. He knows what she wants. Light, clarity, escape. She wants it so badly he can smell it. But he wants something quite different.

He ignores her and loses himself in the swirl and sweep of the fog as he drives into nothingness. Possibilities form and vanish as he approaches them. The road begins to climb, and the hedges thin and falter, become bushes clouded with grass that's dull with autumn, the seed-heads hanging in damp arcs. The sky is smoked glass, pressing down, squeezing the fog into the moor until it's puddled with pools of water. At the crest, he pulls off the road into a gravely lay-by and switches off the engine. He smells her fear, sour and acrid.

'Going to take a leak,' he says, getting out of the car. He goes a little way down the road until the car and the girl have vanished behind him. He's alone in the fog, as insubstantial as the air, as invisible as the wind, as powerful as all the possibilities that lurk in the half-light, in his dreams of dark places and uncertain shapes. He's ready to be reborn.

He returns, pumps the accelerator and floods the carburettor. The engine turns but refuses to catch.

'Jesus!' she breathes, her smell so rank now he almost gags at it.

'Spark plugs. Moisture's got to them,' he says. 'It's all right. I'll walk back. There was a garage a couple of miles down the road. Want to come?'

She shakes her head.

'Suit yourself. I'll be an hour, I reckon. There's a farm down that track.' He nods at a rusting sign on the other side of the road. 'Try that if you get bored.'

He doesn't go far. He hears the car-door bang, heels clack down the tarmac, a hesitation at the sign, a muttered profanity. She's easy to follow, her breathing loud and ragged, her smell still strong. Once, in a thinning, he sees her stumbling in the leaden light, those pale thighs thrusting through the fog.

Ruined buildings loom, a rusting barbed wire fence, a rotting bale of straw, the abandoned innards of a tractor. She calls out. Her voice echoes and falls away, the fog absorbing all sound except for her harsh erratic breathing.

'It's all right, Sharon,' he says. 'I'm here. I'm right behind you.'

He's the thing that rushes out of the night. In this dark place he's the shape of everything.

The fog absorbs all sound. Eventually, once time and space have come and gone, there's only the harsh erratic breathing. Now it's his own. Gradually it stills and slows to a languid inhalation as he walks back to the car.

It fires at the first turn of the key, and soon he's descending from the moor, carefully now since the fog is thick. As he descends, the air brightens. The fog thins to pale opalescent streamings, and the sun, low on the horizon, is a cold white hole in a nebulous sky. Hedges form and mark the margins of the road.

Trees stand sentinel at crossroads, rooks swirling in their branches like charred scraps of paper. The world opens out. This is the road to Skipton, isn't it? Why is he going there? Oh, yes. A sales conference. He'll be late now. He shouldn't have taken the back road. Should have stuck to the motorway, sat it out in a service station. There had been a girl at the last one, hitching a lift somewhere. Good luck to her. He never picks up hikers.

Ahead the road curves and twists through an achromatic landscape. He drives onwards into a future of uncertain shape, where banks of fog lie waiting, ready to rush out of the dark. He drives without will, without apprehension, as if he's been reborn.

The Mushroom Pickers

'Y ou need to get your eye in,' she tells him after comparing the contents of his basket with her own.

She's done rather well; already her basket is half-full of bay boletes, the brown-capped edible fungi that grow in such profusion – or so she claims – in this clearing in the forest. But to his eye they're indistinguishable from the scales of pine bark that litter the forest floor, and, as a result, his basket is virtually empty. He has, however, found one rather fine specimen of another species entirely, a bright-yellow gilled fungus that had been growing beneath a birch.

'What do you think that is?' she asks, eyeing it suspiciously.

'A chanterelle,' he says, but she shakes her head.

'That's a false chanterelle, *Cantharellus aurantiacus*.' She still knows all their Latin names.

'Aren't they edible?'

'Some books say they are,' she says with a shrug. 'But they're supposed to be hallucinogenic.'

They're too these days old for mind-altering substances, but nevertheless he peers with interest at the rejected fungus. It still looks like a proper chanterelle to him: the frilled cap, the curved gills, that egg-yolk colour.

'How do you know it's not a real chanterelle?' he asks. She hesitates, as if considering whether or not she can be bothered to explain, then shakes her head, her eyes sliding away.

'You just know.' Some things, she implies, are instinctive.

He watches her walk away through the trees, her eyes on the ground, moving ponderously. She's put on weight recently, but he minds less than she does; he's always thought her too thin. Not that he's said so. She pauses and bends down, her hips straining cord trousers that are the same texture and shade as the caps of the boletes. Her shirt is the same creamy beige as their paler spongy undersides. Later, at home, they'll slice the fungi for drying, and their caps will flush a fleshy blue, the same colour as the veins that run along the inside of her thighs.

'Let's go and pick mushrooms,' she'd said that morning just after breakfast. 'Like we used to.'

He hadn't been that keen, but, after casting a lingering glance at the Sunday papers, he'd agreed. She'd been looking off-colour recently. Perhaps the fresh air would do her good. He'd needed the exercise too, and, to be honest, he'd quite enjoyed the brisk walk through the village and along the country lanes to the forest. The air was cool and blowy and smelled of autumn, but when they'd reached the trees and wandered into the wood he'd found the slower pace frustrating, the autumnal smell heavier, dense with spores and rotting vegetation. The light, filtered through branch and web, hazy with insects, had been unsettling. The wood unnerves him as it hadn't in the old days.

He tries to ignore his unease and concentrates on the mossy floor beneath the tall pines where tumbled rotting branches are half-covered with heather and bilberry and tufts of reedy grass. Many fungi flourish in the moist autumn that has followed a cool wet summer, but most are inedible, if not downright poisonous. He's searching for the elusive bay boletes, but his eye is seduced by the brighter colours of the other species: the burgundy and claret russulas, the lime-yellow sulphur tufts, and the pale little parasol mushrooms whose name he's forgotten. Fly agaric wink slyly at him, their flat crimson plates scattered with white warty fragments of veil. That red is too red, he thinks, too unnatural. Recently, she's taken to wearing lipstick in just that colour. He doesn't like it, although he wouldn't dream of saying so. He thinks it too bright for a woman of her years, but now he understands his dislike of the shade. On her too it seems to be a warning colour.

'For God's sake, let's just do *something!*' she'd said that morning.

She's been in a strange mood in the last few months, jumping from one thing to the next, up in the air one minute then down. This nostalgic whim for picking mushrooms seems part of that mood, but he understands that women have strange fancies at her time of life, and he tries to make allowances.

He turns his attention to the ground beneath his feet, deliberately closing his eyes to the blandishments of the brighter fungi, and eventually he finds a bay bolete. He crouches and tugs it free of the moss, but her doubt about the chanterelle makes him wonder if it really is a bay bolete. He knows there are poisonous boletes, although they're rare, and he can't recall what they look like.

How do you know that's not a Satan's bolete? he can imagine her asking.

'They don't grow this far north,' he might say. But she'll make no response other than a raised eyebrow to invite him to think of global warming: the continental butterflies that overwinter in Kent nowadays, the fears of malaria on the south coast – and the possible spread of *Boletus satanus* as far north as their wood. But then she'll smile to let him know she's teasing. Of course it isn't a Satan's bolete! He's rationalised. But she *knows*.

That's the difference between them he supposes, as he puts the putative bay bolete into his basket. One of the differences, he thinks, watching her pause then bend down to the ground, straighten, walk a few steps on then bend again. She's moving further and further away. Before long, if he calls out, she might not hear him. He looks back the way they've come to see if he can still see the track, but it isn't far away. Instinctively, he's moved parallel to the safety of the main path, as if he's afraid of getting lost. Which of course he isn't. Or at least he didn't used to be.

And that's another difference.

'Oh, are we lost?' she might say with little concern, then look around, measure a gradient that has nothing to do with the direction of the sun or the pressure of the wind and find her way by some grassy path beneath dark stands of beech, a path that bends and twists and smells of fox or badger. Not the rigid north-south or east-west grids of the forestry tracks with which he feels more comfortable.

'There,' she might say when they reach familiar territory. 'We weren't lost after all.' But they had been.

He moves closer to the main path. If asked, he'll say he's looking for ceps, the prized *Boletus edulis* that prefer the drier conditions of the track's sandy margins. It's late in the season for ceps, but if he finds one it will go some way to make up for the paucity of his collection so far. One cep, he reckons, is worth ten or twenty bay boletes.

'It isn't a competition!' she used to say. But of course it always has been: a competition to see who can find the most or the best specimens, or the greater number of edible species. It was a game of sorts, one she usually won. They're too old for games now, but, strangely, he still feels as if it's a competition, although he can no longer say for certain with whom he thinks he's competing, or what the prize might be. But his gamble of finding the rare and elusive cep, the valuable cep, doesn't pay off, his eye not being attuned to find them, and he wanders back into the wood. Only to discover that she's vanished.

Her jacket is a dull green; her hair, in spite of her years, is still the foxy shade of autumn bracken. She's clothed herself in woodland colours, he realises, and remembers that today she isn't wearing the red lipstick that so disturbs him. He wonders uneasily if her camouflage is deliberate, if she's come to the wood with the intention of slipping into its silences. And leaving him alone.

He discards that particular thought. She's just paused, or crouched down, or stepped into a hollow he can't make out among the dense green undergrowth. If he calls out she'll hear him. But he doesn't call. Instead, moving into the wood, he follows the faint traces of her passage. He has an eye for these, he finds, and marks a crushed tuft of grass, a broken twig, the discarded stalk of some fungus. It's a male thing, he decides, this ability to track. It's a rational interpretation of clues, nothing instinctive. And so his pleasure when he finds her is surely due to satisfaction in his own abilities and nothing to do with relief at finding her at all.

She's sitting on a fallen trunk, her basket abandoned at her feet. She's given up her search for mushrooms but still gives the impression of someone harvesting. Not fungi now but the wood itself, its silences and its sounds: the wind in the pines, the chink of wrens in the undergrowth, the chittering of a squirrel. She breathes deeply, absorbing the smell of the wood that so disturbs him, the smell of decomposition and the cycle of the years. She sits on the trunk, her shoulders slumped, taking the forest in to herself as if it's balm to a grief he hasn't noticed, his eye not being attuned to it.

But standing there, stilled by the shock of finding a stranger, he sees what he's failed to see until now: the spore print of a disappointment that's rooted in the years, something that's grown and burst, like the puff-balls that grow all around, leaving nothing but dust on the wind. Once she'd taken strange foxy paths and found her way home. Now, perhaps, one of those paths has led instead to a waste of thorns and nettles. Whatever has happened to her – to them? – he refuses to give a name to. She's the one who's good with names, not him, but he recognises the distinguishing marks – the warning colour, the gaiety that might be false – as he might recognise this fungus or that. The name is unimportant. Is it poisonous or not? That's all that matters.

He steps on a twig, and it breaks beneath his foot with a sound like a gunshot. She looks up quickly, then away, fusses with her basket, wipes a hand across her face as if an insect has got in her eye.

'Hello,' she says with her old unconcern. 'I thought you were lost.'

He shrugs. 'If I am, we're both lost.' He holds up his basket. 'I've not done awfully well, I'm afraid, but between us we've probably got enough.'

It isn't a competition, or so she's always said. He still isn't certain with what, or who, he's competing, but he knows what the prize is now.

She smiles uncertainly. Her lips are the flushed pink of a field mushroom's gills.

'Let's go home,' he suggests. She nods, gets up and heads towards the track, but he reaches out, touches her on the arm, and nods in the other direction.

'Let's see where that goes.' He turns towards a small path on the other side of the clearing, a path dark with bracken and the grey boles of beech, a path he's sure will smell of fox or badger. He senses a gradient that has nothing to do with the wind or the sun.

He's got his eye in now.

Theophany

I t's dusk when Ianthe first sees The Garden. And so, to begin with, she thinks it must be a trick of the light. Dusk is an ambivalent time, and it has always seemed to her that the change of light brings with it other changes, not least in herself.

She doesn't say anything to Jord. At another time of day she might have done so. 'I've seen a garden,' she might say. 'Nonsense,' he'd reply, and they'd go on as before. But the self that emerges each day, in the moments that lie between day and night, finds other reasons to conceal her vision, for such it must be. She holds it in her mind and memory for what it is: a distant glimpse of green in an otherwise grey city, the curves and spheres of moving trees and shrubs amongst the static grids and angles of the buildings. An impossibility.

Dusk is brief, a time when daylight leaves the sky and is replaced by the equivalent light of the City. Night, as an absence of light, no longer exists. Darkness was an inconvenience and so has been dispensed with. But between the lights, different in quality if the same in intensity, things change. Moods alter, melancholy stirs, and visions are longed for enough to be seen. But then the lights of the City wax and things disappear once more. So Ianthe watches The Garden, perched on the top of a building, transfigure itself to nothing.

But it's there again the next time she looks out of the window at dusk: a green flash from between the buildings, the wink of a green eye, and she knows this is more than vision.

'There's a Garden out there. On the Austler Building,' she tells Jord, her voice light, self-mocking. She likes to play this game with him, the tone of her voice at odds with its content. She likes the ambiguity, the keeping of one facet of a secret, the revealing of another.

'Nonsense,' he says, too quickly. She wonders if he plays his own games with her. It's as if he tries to catch her thoughts before she speaks them, to prove that his powers of analysis are greater than hers. Even now, his hands are moving over the data-entry zone, his eyes on the screens, scanning the myriad images of the City from viewpoints high on the buildings. One image slides onto the screen, centres and focuses. It's the top of the Austler Building, and it's gardenless. 'Nonsense,' he repeats, with nothing in his voice to tell her that he might, for a moment, have wanted to believe her.

She goes over and puts a hand on his shoulder. 'Of course,' she agrees, feeling the shape of his collarbone beneath her fingers. Then she lifts her hand, still holding the shape and texture of his body, and feels the warmth leave her fingers as absence fills the cooling space in her palm. He doesn't move. Perhaps he's sensing the same withdrawal and, like her, is exploring the sensation, the possibility.

They've been together for six months now, longer than most. It's long enough that she's forgotten how they met, to which precise interest-group they both belonged, what attracted her to him in particular, above all the similar others. She looks around the apartment in which they live and work and sees evidence of a merging of their tastes in the moving images that decorate the walls, the discordant plangent chords that fill the space between them. *Time to move on,* she thinks. *Time to move apart.* The tests and games are part of it, a drawing out of the threads of a conjoined existence, like the cytoplasm of some unicellular organism that is ready to divide. She wonders, with the less than rational side of her dusk self, if The Garden is a portent, somehow, of this organic process.

The following evening she looks out of the window once more. 'There it is again,' she says.

Jord doesn't like the window. He thinks it an anachronism. Why do they need a window to see the City? Why look at a static image hazed with distance when the screens and data streams reveal it so much more clearly? But he comes over to stand beside her, looks out of the window, then turns away. She catches a glimpse of his face as he moves, and thinks she sees a flash of green in his eyes. Then he blinks and his eyes are grey once more as the City brightens. He says nothing, and the silence crystallises into something other than disbelief.

'It was just a trick of the light,' he says later, apropos of nothing, his voice light, self-mocking.

I have been here, she thinks. *I was here two days ago. I am two days ahead of him!*

The thought frightens her for a moment. If she's ahead of him doesn't that mean she has a direction? A destination?

She talks of other things, gets on with her work, makes contact with friends and acquaintances, and watches him do the same. She lets the silence grow between them until she recognises it for what it is. Conspiracy.

'We could go there,' she suggests several days later when she's certain, when she's seen him walk past the window at dusk, glance and look away. Green flares briefly, half-imagined. 'We could see for ourselves. Prove that it's there.'

'Or isn't,' he says, perhaps having a different destination in mind. But, destination or not, the rational part of each of them that requires proof gives them direction, a brief purpose, a drawing in of those strands of cytoplasm. They discuss when and how but not why. Not yet.

To do as she suggests is no minor matter, for people don't often leave the vast work-units in which they live their lives. Such friends as they have live in the same complex, in apartments much like their own. They don't discuss The Garden with any of the friends, and their failure to do so draws them briefly together, although not so close that they can begin to discuss The Garden with one another.

They set off at an hour they've calculated will bring them to the Austler Building in time to reach the top at dusk. The Outside surprises them a little, for although they know it as much as any city dweller can, having explored it on their screens, mapped their route and viewed its ways, the air of Outside is different from Inside, being warmer than they expect, moister and full of movement. The streets, the thoroughfares of the old days, are empty, blocked in places with the outfall of the buildings, and yet, like the air, there's movement here too in the swirling billows of refuse, the skitter of dark-skinned animals, a suspicion of eyes in the daylight shadows. It's not yet dusk, but Ianthe has the same sense of transition, of things changing, not least herself, and she thinks back in astonishment to her casual suggestion. *We could go there,* she'd said. *An experiment,* Jord had concluded, as if it would be a simple test of their faith in logic, in the evidence of their senses. *To find out, one way or the other,* they'd agreed. But now she's aware that something else is being tested here, that there's more at stake than she'd planned. She decides that, one way or the other, she will leave Jord, or let him leave. Or neither. It all depends.

It takes longer than they've calculated, or so it seems. Perhaps they've lingered too long in the valley of shadows and made unnecessary detours through alleyways and underpasses. Maybe time, like the air, is different on the Outside and moves with the same uneasy swirls and billows. Or perhaps they're afraid, in spite of there being no reason for fear. Yet when they reach the Austler Building and pass Inside again to the cool still certainties of a place much like their own, she's aware of her heart thudding. Jord's breathing is light and shallow as they watch the elevator blink through the levels. The door hisses open, inviting them to enter an area of doored units and coloured partitions, of space apportioned to and occupied by people much like themselves – except those others aren't troubled by the possibility of Gardens and may have no knowledge of the one green door on the upper floor that stands ajar. Ianthe and Jord hesitate, but he takes her hand, or she takes his, and they step through the door onto the roof.

They see grey walls and straight lines, long vistas of building and a city hazed with distance. Dust sifts and moves. Epiphany hangs in the air like a cloud.

Dusk falls. The light changes, mutes for a moment, and drops a register. There's a scent borne on a waft of moisture; it's a breath only, but it catches in her throat. *It's beginning!* she thinks and feels her heart race as she watches the angles and planes shift within their grid of walls and walkways and shiver a little in a movement of moist air, in a trick of the light. But then they settle once more into what they are, into what they've always been. Moisture condenses on her cheeks and slides down her face. Her palms are empty, her fingers cold, and her heart grows sluggish. Jord glances at her then looks away, failing to find a glimpse of green in her eyes to fill the absence in his own. His breathing slows.

'So, now we know,' Jord says, his voice flat. Somehow, she'd expected an echo.

'One way or the other,' she agrees.

He's gone the next day. She's not sure if he's left or if she's let him go, but she feels his absence with all the planes of her body. The plangent chords echo in the spaces of the apartment. She looks out of the window at dusk, her mood of melancholy deeper than usual, her need for vision heightened. But there is nothing. It was too fragile, she concludes, to be tested. As was whatever lay between herself and Jord.

Behind her she hears a door closing and is briefly aware of a breath of perfume. But she no longer trusts the evidence of her senses.

'I brought something to remind us,' Jord says. She turns to see him holding in his hand a stem of glass from which pale bells hang, a fragile thing, furled in a wisp of glassy green leaves.

'Lily of the valley,' he says. 'I could smell it up there on the roof.'

'You imagined it,' she says coldly, turning her eyes from the unambivalent sight of green, but he lays the ornament in her hand. It's cold against her fingers and the glass bells tinkle faintly with a shiver of sound that reminds her of the muting of the light.

'Yes, I imagined it,' he agrees. 'We both imagined everything.' He pauses. 'I didn't know how much it was possible to imagine.'

He's ahead of her now. A leap of faith ahead.

'It was a trick of the light,' she insists, frightened by the prospect of falling. She closes her fingers on his fragile gift, but it doesn't break. Instead, warmed within her hand, the chill of glass evaporates, and her palm is filled with the scent of lilies.

He smiles and walks over to the window where dusk is changing the sky. He turns and holds out his hand.

Behind him, in the numinous changeable light, The Garden glows from the top of the Austler Building. Behind him, all over the City, Gardens bloom.

Appointment on Valentine's Day

*I*mmortal, invisible, God only wise . . .
The words of the hymn run through my head as I stand in the hospital concourse letting the crowds wash past me. My disguise is more effective than I'd expected, and I'm not only unrecognisable but invisible. Immortal? Well, that's another story.

The security guard, who usually nods, lets his gaze drift past me, and the woman in the flower booth ignores me, although I go there almost every day and we have a bit of a routine going.

'Flowers?' she'll say, archly.

'For one of my flock,' I'll reply.

'Go on!' she'll say. 'Bet they're for the missus. Bet you're a closet romantic, Reverend!'

Nothing could be further from the truth, but I smile coyly and leave her with her illusions. It's my job, after all, the fostering of illusions.

Today, however, I merely glance at the flower booth window to check my disguise, because today I'm pretending to be a normal man. I'm wearing a tweed jacket and an open necked shirt, but I'm so used to my tight clerical collar that the open neck gives me a strange sense of exposure, and I fiddle nervously with it as I peer at my reflection.

It's then that I see them. Hearts. Hundreds of them: big red ones, little pink ones, hearts in the paws of fluffy teddy bears, hearts on spikes and hearts blown up into balloons. It's Valentine's day, apparently.

Nice one, God!

Oh yes, I still speak to God. I still believe in his existence, although I've also come to believe in his profound indifference, in spite of those occasional flashes of irony. But I excuse his indifference with the same excuse I use for Rebecca – that God, like my good wife, is just too busy.

'And how is Mrs Yardley?' ask my parishioners, unable to resist the opportunity of contrasting their devotion to the church with Rebecca's disregard. 'We all missed her on Sunday.'

'Oh, she's very well,' I say, assuming that anyone who was in Church to notice she wasn't there couldn't also have been at the Golf Club to see that she was taking yet another lesson with Sandy Patterson, the Golf Professional. 'Busy of course, very busy.'

'Dear Rebecca! Such a lot of interests! I don't know where she gets the energy!'

Not from me. And she doesn't get her interests from me either, not any more. Her interests are inclined to ephemeracy. Once, twenty years ago, her interest in me, or my conviction of it, lasted long enough for us to get married. Then organic gardening took over, watercolours, a brief fling with Buddhism, a rather longer fling with the aroma therapist on the High Street. And so on, and so on.

'And how is your dear wife, Mr Yardley?'

'Very well,' I might say, confident that since no-one cares no-one will listen. 'She's having an affair with Tommy Protheroe, the Chairman of the Donkey Rescue Association, so she's busy of course, very busy.'

'Dear Rebecca! So involved with all her charities! I don't know where she gets the energy!'

Actually, it was Rebecca's energy that got me here in the first place. Or rather my own lack of energy, since it's always seemed easier to avoid confrontation or argument by filling my hours as frantically as her. But I couldn't keep it up, and eventually I developed some alarming symptoms. So now I'm visiting the hospital to present myself at the outpatients' clinic of Dr Bolton, a specialist in cardiac medicine, who'll tell me just how ill I am.

Thanks, God!

There's that irony again. It's Rebecca who should have heart disease, not me. Surely her heart, with its constant ricocheting from one unsuitable love-affair to the next, ought to be feeling the strain? So how unfair that I should have disease in an organ I've not used in years. Atrophy, certainly, but one never hears of specialists in that. Not in the National Health Service.

I make my way down through unfamiliar levels, following increasingly alarming signs – Renal Emergencies, Hypoxic Shock Unit – until, finally, I reach Coronary Care. They could at least call it Coronary Treatment. The word 'care' makes me think of sad-eyed individuals, dressed in clerical greys and wearing benign expressions of belief in the love of God on their faces, standing by my bed saying, 'Never mind. There's always the after-life . . .'

I hand over my card, slide into place beside the others who're sitting in the waiting room – all men I notice – and pretend to be one of them. I'm surrounded by other normal men, and yet I have such an anguished sense of exposure I daren't look at the others for fear of being denounced. Instead, I look at the posters on the walls, and there they are again. Hearts, red mostly, but now they've nothing to do with St Valentine. *Heart disease!* the posters scream at me, as if I needed reminding, since the appointment card's been burning such a metaphorical hole in the pocket of my jacket I'd begun to fear it carried its own self-fulfilling prophecy.

Fear. Yes, I admit it. That's what I'm trying to hide beneath this pathetically transparent disguise. I thrust my hands deep into the pockets of my trousers in case they betray my nervousness and wonder how the others can sit so patiently. Then it occurs to me that soon I shall be a patient too. At some point in the next hour, some personal epiphany of medicine and administration will take place, and I will cease to be a well man with certain alarming symptoms and turn into an ill man who must be patient. I sigh, both longing for and fearing this transformation.

'It's always like this,' the man next to me says, hearing me sigh. I glance at him curiously. 'Always' has a hopeful ring to it. Once, like me, he came here for the first time, so long ago that 'always' has intervened. How long has his 'always' been? How long might mine be? I'm so used to regarding eternity as something lying on the other side of death I've failed to consider that it might have some validity on this side. The thought is both terrifying and comforting at the same time.

'God must be a comfort to you,' one of my parishioners once said in a moment of weakness then, embarrassed by mentioning God at all, quickly changed the subject. Fortunately, her embarrassment was such that she didn't notice my shocked expression. God a *comfort*? The concept had never occurred to me, but it comes back to me now. I look around at the other men and wonder how they'd regard me if I wasn't pretending to be one of them. Would they see a man in a clerical collar and think that, whatever the seriousness of my condition, God must be a comfort to me? And of course that's the reason for my disguise. I'm pretending to be normal so that if I show fear that will be considered normal too. A clergyman, with God busy being a comfort to him, has no right to be afraid.

A name is called. It's not mine, but I look up anyway. Opposite me sits an elderly man who looks like what I imagine a 'heart case' to look like; he's highly coloured, his breathing's bad, and he's in his eighties at least. Whereas when I'd looked in the mirror that morning to check my disguise, I'd seen a man in his late forties who's thin in spite of, or perhaps because of, Rebecca's erratic approach to nutrition, and who's pale to the point of greyness, a grey man in a grey uniform, terrified of his own mortality.

It's not that I don't believe in the afterlife. It's just that my faith, like my person, has faded with the years. It's gone out of focus as if it's moving slowly into the distance, and I no longer have the energy to catch it up. It's taken my vision of the afterlife with it, so now it bears a marked resemblance to my present life, the only difference being that it lasts forever. Which is hardly a happy prospect. An eternity of *this*? Now, there's irony for you!

Not that the Bishop would approve of these sentiments, and – if I was weak enough to articulate them – he would simply urge me to pray. There seems little point in telling him that nowadays God as a concept seems a little too remote for everyday use. He might very well be the great designer of all we survey, but, being so very busy with whatever it is he does, he's left us to fill in the details, like a colouring book for children. 'Just get on with it yourselves. I'm really very busy so don't expect divine intervention.' But I keep these thoughts to myself and urge my flagging congregation to the prayer I don't believe in.

Let us pray.

For what should I pray at this precise moment? To be someone like Rebecca whose life is filled with such desperate hope she barely notices the inevitable disappointments? To be someone other than a man so disillusioned he no longer believes in hope at all? To have a heart that's strong enough to stir without the possibility that such unlikely stirrings might well prove fatal? For the next name to be called to be mine?

But it isn't, and the old man struggles to his feet with the help of a nurse. 'All right, George?' she asks. 'How are you today?'

'Never better,' he wheezes and limps off on her arm.

I hope they don't call me by my Christian name. I hope they don't ask me how I am. I hope I can stop myself from saying 'never better' in a pathetic attempt to deny that I'm far from well at all.

'It's the Prof,' the man next to me says. 'He's running late as usual.'

'The Prof?'

'You're seeing the Prof, ain't you? That's why we're at the end of the list.'

'I thought I was seeing Dr Bolton.'

'Professor Sir William Bolton to you and me, pal,' he says with a grin. 'He always sees the interesting cases!'

The comfort of 'always' has been expunged. *Interesting?* How interesting? Interestingly terminal? Or interesting in that there's now a new cure for certain fortunate individuals? I feel an intense longing to believe in divine intervention and an overwhelming urge to pray. I'd like to ask my neighbour what's so interesting about him, but his name is called and he goes off with the nurse, chatting away to her as if he isn't interesting at all.

Eventually I'm on my own and have no more need to pretend. I finger the collar of my shirt, still with that sense of imminent exposure. I suppose I'd better get used to it. There will be medical notes, no doubt, that detail my history, my childhood illnesses, my insomnia, my weak digestion, the rather embarrassing infection I get from time to time. I'll be exposed in so many ways I begin to number them for myself and don't hear the name for which I've been waiting so anxiously for the last hour.

'Geoffrey?' I look up and see a nurse with a clipboard. She's half my age, a pert thing with a uniform surely too tight for the good of men with heart conditions. The words *Reverend Yardley to you, Miss!* rise in my throat and stick there – because it isn't the nurse who's spoken.

'Geoffrey?' Rebecca's voice is uncertain, and in some remote way I'm pleased my disguise is so effective.

'What are you doing here?' I ask.

'I saw the appointment card. I know you don't want me here, but I was so worried I came anyway.' She flops into the seat next to me. 'Why didn't you tell me?'

'Why didn't you tell me about Tommy Protheroe?'

I look around, wondering who's spoken and, to my astonishment, conclude it's myself.

'Oh, that doesn't matter, Geoffrey! This does.'

I look closely at her and see a middle-aged woman, a little frazzled around the edges, a woman who might once have been attractive and might still be if she hadn't been crying.

'There's nothing to worry about,' I say and hope God isn't listening.

'But I *am* worried. Aren't you? I would be. I'd want someone to hold my hand.'

It's all right, I consider saying. *God will be a comfort to me.* Then it occurs to me that, oddly, God is. Not directly, of course. He's far too busy for that. So he's sent this frazzled, middle-aged woman to be a comfort to me instead. God puts my wife's hand in mine, and I find myself gripping it tightly.

'You'll be all right,' she says, comfortingly. 'You'll probably just have to take things easy for a bit. You've been so busy. We've both been too busy.'

Just like God, I think. Busy, but not ineffective. Busy, but not unperceptive. God has seen through my disguise just as he sees through my normal garb: the austere clerical greys and my expression of benign belief in his goodness and love. He understands that the man who lies beneath has ceased to believe in such things. He even understands why. Ironically, I realise I've felt exposed all day, not because I'm in disguise but because, for the first time in years, I'm not. And yet I don't meet the derision I expect but the considered gaze of a woman who sees into my heart as clearly as do the doctors with their scanners and computer software, as clearly as God. My heart, thus exposed, begins to beat strangely, falteringly, as if it's lain unmoved for years.

'Mr Yardley?' asks the nurse with the tight uniform and the clipboard. 'And how are you today?'

'Fine,' I say, a foul nervous taste on my tongue.

'Good! That's what we like to hear! Well, if you'll just go through that door, Dr Bolton will see you now.'

The door opens and a man looks out. He's short and fat and bald and has an ill-tempered expression on his face.

'Come along then,' he snaps at me, but, once in his room, he's kindness itself. He has no interest in me, I find, only in the organ that's begun to beat uncertainly within my chest. I have no sense of exposure now, no need for disguise, nor even, although the prognosis isn't good, any further sense of fear. It's an epiphany of a sort, not of medicine and administration, but of the blind hand of fate, in which I don't believe. It's the answer to a prayer I haven't spoken, since I don't believe in those either. It's divine intervention from a God who might be busy, whose interests, like Rebecca's, might wax and wane, but who's never, by any stretch of the imagination, indifferent.

'. . . lots of tests, I'm afraid, and regular visits to the clinic to see how you're getting on,' Dr Bolton concludes, scribbling some notes on a slip of paper which he hands to me. 'But that won't be too much of a bind, will it? You chaps only work on Sundays after all!'

He laughs at his little joke and thinks I'm smiling in agreement as he ushers me back to the waiting room. Rebecca's still there, waiting patiently.

The nurses at the desk stare at me as I hand over the slip. They're not used to it, I suppose, seeing a man who's just been told how poor his chances of survival are smiling as I'm smiling. As if my heart might burst.

'Happy Valentine's day!' I say and they all smile too. I love them all. I love Rebecca. I love all humanity. I even love God, ironic, capricious God, and, for the first time in years, I believe my love might not be unrequited.

Moving On

To begin with, Joel didn't pay much attention to the rain. It wasn't as if he could go outside, and anyway rain suited his mood. He wasn't sleeping well, and the hiss on the roof, the rattle of showers against the window-panes and the rush of water in the drain that ran alongside the track, were soothing sounds that kept the dreams at a distance.

His dreams had been bad since the accident, especially the ones where he watched his ice-axe bite into a spongy layer of ice gone rotten in an unseasonably mild winter, then felt himself falling. Usually he woke up before the impact, but sometimes, in his dream, the rock smashed into his spine, and he'd wake up confused, not knowing where he was, or what.

Every day that summer, his first in the Mill House, it had rained in one way or another. Sometimes the rain would arrive out of an empty sky, without sound or shape, a blurring of the light that thickened imperceptibly, so it wasn't until Joel heard a hiss like static that he'd realise it was raining. At other times it was a thunderous deluge out of a slate-coloured sky, or a weeping mizzle that shrouded the house in ashen gloom. But, whatever its form, it was always grey.

His friends and family thought he was mad, moving to the Fens. 'It's miles from anywhere!' By which they meant miles from them, but to Joel that was the whole point of leaving London as soon as his rehabilitation was deemed to be complete.

'How are you going to manage on your own?' they'd wanted to know. *The way you are now.* They hadn't said it though. Joel had learned to be grateful for certain silences.

'Technology,' he'd replied, a little too brightly. 'I'll have the internet, and phones do actually work there you know.' He'd order everything he needed on-line and get it delivered. He'd promised to keep in touch by Skype and Facebook but hadn't. He'd become too familiar with all the forms of pity: the friends who, not knowing what to say, said nothing at all, and, worse, the ones who, with hopeless optimism, declared that he'd soon be back on his feet, although everyone knew he wouldn't be. He'd even found Jennifer's steadfast practicality to be unbearable.

'You have to accept your limitations, Joel, and move on.' Which he'd felt to be an insensitive choice of words.

'I can't move anywhere. In case you hadn't noticed, I'm a . . .' He'd faltered at this, the most minor of hurdles.

'Say it,' she'd insisted, and so, with an effort that made him want to weep, he had.

I'm a paraplegic, a fucking cripple! I can't go anywhere or do anything!'

'You can if you try. I'm here Joel. But you'll have to walk towards me.'

He'd sworn at her with uncharacteristic savagery, pouring out all his frustrations in a torrent of vitriol.

'I'm still here,' she'd said quietly when it was over, before turning on her heel and walking away. He'd never forgive her for that – not for walking away, since it was the best thing she could have done for herself – but for having the power to walk away when he had no power at all.

So it was hardly surprising that he'd fled – in as much as a man who's lost the use of his legs can flee – to the house he'd bought in the Fens with the insurance money, a house he'd never even seen. All he'd wanted was a refuge from the past he longed for and the future he couldn't face. The landscape of the Fens was part of his flight, its flat distances and vast skies so utterly different from the mountains he'd loved. He'd chosen the house for its outlook to a relentless horizon where water and sky merged, each reflecting the other. The Fens were permeated with marshes and meres, streams and rivers, a reclaimed land whose dikes and culverts barely contained all that moisture. The house itself had once been part of the land's battle with the water, but the mill was long gone, leaving behind only its name and the pond at the far end of the garden.

It was a place unlike any he'd ever known, a place where he believed he could write. Black Diamond had sent him a couple of ice-axes to review, which he considered tactless, but maybe they didn't know what had happened. The axes lay on a sofa in the living room; he couldn't even bear to touch them. Rock and Ice had asked him to write an article about ice-climbs in the Rjukan Valley. Since that was where he'd fallen, he thought that tactless too. Worst of all, Harper Collins wanted him to write his memoirs. He was only thirty-two. Surely you don't write your memoirs until your life's almost over? But of course it was.

He needed the money though, so he'd accepted, but he'd done no work at all since coming to the Fens and had just wheeled himself from room to room and stared out of the windows, watching the rain fall and the water rise. He could almost feel the land grow spongy, the leaden sky squeezing the moisture back out of the ground until the fields were pocked with pools. The millpond swelled and overflowed, and the drain beside the track to the house turned into a stream. He supposed this happened often and wasn't alarmed, but the man who delivered his groceries took a more pessimistic view.

'It's that there global warming,' he said dolefully. 'Wasn't like this when I were a boy, and I've lived here all my life. Seen it coming, I have, wetter summers and the floods worse year on year. Get your house cheap did you? I'm not surprised. Folks around here are all moving away. Talk about a ghost town ... This is a ghost county.' He jerked his head at the road that led towards the etched blur of the nearest town. 'See that road? It'll be under water before long, you mark my words. Best move out while you can. This is no place for a –' He stopped abruptly, his face reddening.

'Quite,' Joel said dryly, but he didn't take the man's advice. There was no way he was crawling back to London, literally or otherwise. But it kept on raining, and, true to the man's prediction, the road did indeed flood, but Joel still wasn't concerned. He'd stocked up with food and fuel, enough to see him through until the water went down again and the road opened. He even felt a reluctant admiration for the rain that was causing all this flooding. Until then he'd considered rain to be quixotic and ephemeral, but now it had changed its character, changed the rules. It was as if rain had declared war on the land and allied itself with the rivers and streams, all of them marching inland like some vast invading army whose onslaught nothing and no one could withstand. There was a magnificent inevitability about it all.

It wasn't until the electricity went off that he realised things were serious, that he was too dependent on technology, too dependent on power. He still had batteries for essential equipment – his laptop, radio, torches, the motor on his chair – but, as the rain kept falling and the water went on rising, the electricity remained off, and, one by one, his batteries gave up the ghost. Even the radio's increasingly alarming weather reports eventually gave way to a dull hiss barely distinguishable from the hiss of the rain outside.

His phone still had power, however, and, after several attempts, he got through to a harassed woman at the Environment Agency who assured him that rescue was on its way. 'Just stay in the house,' she recommended, a piece of advice that made him smile wryly. As if he had any choice.

By now he knew he should never have come to the Fens, that everyone had been right. He'd done no research, hadn't appreciated the risks. He should have understood how marginal his life was and never come to a place that was equally marginal. The world was changing. He'd seen that to his cost. The climate was taking the land back, taking livelihoods with it, and no-one had the power to stop it. He found it oddly comforting to know he wasn't alone in being powerless.

It was the next day, around dawn, when the rain came in for the kill. He heard a growl of triumph, as if a besieging army had broken through the defences of a citadel. He wheeled himself to the French windows in time to see a wave of water, shot through with fence posts, come charging towards him. Some dike must have breached, he understood vaguely as the water burst through the French doors. He grabbed a radiator as the water surged into the room, swung his wheelchair to one side and swirled about the room in a grey slurry of silt and branches that rose first to his ankles, then to his knees. It wasn't until it reached his waist that he remembered the phone in his top pocket and, still clinging to the radiator, dialled 999.

'Can you get upstairs?' a woman asked. She sounded just as harassed as the one from the Environment Agency when he explained that he didn't have an upstairs. 'Then can you manage to get onto the roof?'

For a moment he wanted to laugh. The roof, a mere ten feet above him, was as remote as the moon.

'I'm –' he began.

Say it. He seemed to hear Jennifer's voice even above the clamour of the water. *Say it!*

'I'm sure I'll manage . . .'

You idiot! he thought. Why couldn't he have said he was in a wheelchair, that he was a paraplegic, that he needed help, that the water was still rising and he was powerless to stop it? *You have to accept your limitations, Jennifer* had said. *Accept them and die,* he thought, imagining the headline. *Crippled Rock-Jock drowned in Fens Floods.*

Accept your limitations, Joel. Accept what he could no longer do. Why was it necessary for him to be clinging to a radiator in imminent danger of drowning before he could understand what she'd really meant: that he needed to find out not what he couldn't do, but what he could.

So he let go of the radiator.

The force of the water swung him sideways, toppling his chair and dragging him under the surface. He tried to kick up with his legs and when, inevitably, he failed, flailed out with his arms instead and grabbed the sofa to haul himself up. The Black Diamond ice axes were still there, and he gripped one of them, slammed it into the back of the sofa to stop himself from sliding back into the water, then hooked the other around the sofa's arm. Slowly, using the axes to seize hold of anything he could reach, he pulled himself and his useless legs towards the shattered door and out into the swirling waters.

The house had been built in the mid-eighteen hundreds and hadn't been looked after. The estate agent had recommended repointing, but Joel had never got around to arranging it, an oversight that might just be about to save his life. The force of the water slammed him against the kitchen wall, and he hooked one ice axe onto the windowsill to hold himself in place. Looking up, he could see that the uneven crumbling wall was less than a pitch in height, not anything like as far as the moon. He slammed his right-hand axe up into the wall, felt it dig into the mortar and hook on brick. Then he pulled up and drove the tip of the left-hand axe higher up the wall. And again and again until he was free of the water. Only then did he look down and, conscious of the weight of his legs dragging at his body, feel a moment of doubt. But hadn't he conquered the overhanging section of the Helmcken Falls, hanging at times from one hand?

He looked back up the wall and began to think like a climber, planning each move, searching out the tiny ledges that would give him purchase, assessing the weakness of the guttering and, hanging from one axe, smashing it with the other until he could get a grip on the tarred and felted flat roof of the kitchen. Getting over the edge was the crux of this particular climb, but, with an effort that made him scream, he pulled himself up and over until he was safe, spread-eagled on the roof. Eventually he eased himself up onto one elbow to take stock of his situation.

He was on an island a few feet above a swirling tide of glinting grey water. In the distance, on the horizon, he could make out a church tower. But where there had once been fields there was nothing now but a huge lake, punctuated by the scribbled outlines of trees and, here and there, the roofs of farm buildings. The sun, still rising, slid between two bars of pewter cloud and spread itself across the water like mercury, turning the matte grey flood into a shivering sheet of silver and steel. Now he could truly appreciate the extent of the flooding and the power of the water and realise how small he was. But not powerless. Limited, perhaps, but there's always something that can be done. Everything can be adapted to.

The sun was higher now. It had even stopped raining. Joel caught sight of something yellow in the distance moving in his direction, the colour joyfully vivid against the grey of water and sky. It was an inflatable powering towards him. He considered phoning the emergency woman again to let her know he was on the roof. He punched in a number, but it wasn't the emergency services who answered because that wasn't who he'd called.

'Jen?' he said. 'It's me. Are you still there . . ?'

The Butterfly Effect

T he butterfly danced in the air like a charred flake of paper, its black wings barred with red and spotted with white as if it was still on fire. It was a Red Admiral, *Vanessa atalanta*, a migrant, but Adam never saw it again, nor any like it. Insects were rare in those days, migrants rarer still, and, after he'd seen the butterfly, he'd begun to wonder why. Years later, he was still wondering as he stared at a computer screen and juggled equations and models, charted population booms and extinctions, measured warming and cooling, and mapped the shifts in the great engine of the climate, trying to pin it down as one might pin a butterfly in a case. But he never could. There was always a black hole that lay beyond the known knowns and the known unknowns, a lacuna in which a butterfly could flap its wings and make anything happen. And, in the end, it did . . .

He's paddling towards the City although he's not sure why. He's a great deal older than the man who'd tried to pin down the climate, but he's still asking questions. It's close to dawn as he moves upstream through a low mist that hugs the water. He's keeping close to the southern shore in case he's seen, but there's no sign of life on either of the drowned banks, no smudge of smoke, no stock in the fields that have turned to grassland. No boat moves along the shore, and there isn't a single sail on the horizon. There's only his kayak arrowing its way towards the City on the flooding tide. Even the ancient stronghold of The Rock, an island now, is deserted, and it stands like a rotten tooth in the jaws of the river. The last time he'd passed this way a flag had been flying defiantly from the summit, but even the flagpole has gone, and the walls are fire-blackened, the place desolate and overgrown.

The morning is still. Somewhere in the world a butterfly has flapped its wings and sent the jet stream swinging south, trailing the swirling lows with it, and now the northern half of Britain is crushed beneath a high-pressure system. The City lies beyond the marsh where the airport used to be, floating above the mist like a mirage, serene in the early morning light. The last time he'd seen it the night had been on fire, the sky a red wound as the City burned. That was years ago now, but the signs of that conflagration can still be seen: the buildings blackened, their roofs fallen in. Some church spires still stand, but most are little more than a tracery of burnt timbers. Adam feels something that might be regret, or pride, or maybe exasperation, at the sight of this City of towers and spires, humbled by fire and flood and disease, still brooding over the shreds of its former glory.

He leaves the kayak hidden in a clump of willows that have sprung up beneath an overpass and walks north. It's fully day by now, but the City seems to pose no threat. Nothing moves but decaying plastic tumbling on the rising breeze and a swirl of starlings startled by his presence from their roost in a lime tree. A few roe-deer eye him warily from beneath the trees in what used to be a park, and something like a dog vanishes out of sight around a corner. The zoo had been ransacked, the animals set loose, and there are wolves in the mountains once more, bears in the forest, kangaroos in the grasslands. The dog might have been a jackal, but he doesn't see it again, nor hear any sound but his own footsteps as he walks down the long road to his old flat.

He doesn't know what to expect – a burned out shell in all likelihood – but it isn't that bad. The fire must have begun in the upper stories of the tenement, for only these are in ruin. The roof has fallen in, of course, but the lower stories are damaged only by smoke and looting and twenty years of rain, so when he reaches the door at the end of the darkened corridor it's as if he's returning home after only a day's absence rather than twenty years. It's as if, when he pushes the door open, he'll see Molly sitting there as she'd sat on the night when everything ended.

'I can't live like this any more.'

She was sitting in the dark, still wearing her coat, crouched over the two-bar electric fire, the one they kept for emergencies. But it never gave out much heat, and the place was cold and damp and stank of wet wool. The Spring had been wetter than usual, and it had been raining for days. Adam was soaked to the skin and shivering after cycling back from the University. Normally, if Molly got back before him, she'd light the wood-burning stove and start to cook, but that night she was sitting in the dark drinking Australian wine, the bottle on the floor beside her.

She looked up, saw him staring at her, and gave him a sour look. 'Don't worry. I'll recycle the bottle.'

'What's happened?' He was genuinely puzzled, since it had been as much her idea as his that they'd live as lightly in the world as they could. They'd buy nothing imported, nothing with a significant carbon footprint, no luxuries. They'd eat no meat and use as little electricity as possible. Something must have happened. Perhaps Molly knew, somehow, what he'd discovered only that day. But she just shrugged.

'The road by the river's flooded again and the bus didn't turn up. I had to walk all the way from the hospital, and I've had a bloody day. There were twenty more cases. I've had it, Adam. All of it.' She waved her hand about the cold pokey little flat. 'All this. I'm tired of freezing, not having a car, tired of being a vegetarian and not eating anything that's travelled more than fifty miles.' She poured herself another glass of the wine that had been transported half-way across the world. 'I'm *tired*.'

'I'm tired too.' His voice was sharper than he intended. He was cold and hungry, and he'd had a bloody day too. 'But if we're to survive we need to live like this.'

She laid down her glass and hunched herself deeper into her faintly steaming coat. 'The thing is, Adam, when you say 'us', you mean the human race. But when I say 'us' I mean Molly and Adam, and I don't think *we're* going to survive.'

'Listen.' He crouched down beside her, felt warmth on his face from the fire. 'We can't give up, especially now. Look at the weather, the way the river's rising. The Greenland icecap's melting faster than anyone predicted. I ran the model again today, plugged the new data in, and it just makes it all the more certain. The feedback loops are kicking in, Molly, each one driving the next. No-one's put everything into the model before, and now I know why. They were too scared. Now it's me who's scared, because it's years too late to do anything about it. All we can do is try to survive. Listen –'

'No!' She jumped up, almost knocking over the bottle, and began pacing to and fro, hugging her coat about her. 'I don't want to listen! I'm tired of your doom-mongering, and so is everyone else. No-one wants to listen to you. Don't you understand that? You know your trouble, Adam? You're just an observer, poking at something to see if it's dead. Well it is. *We're* dead.'

'For God's sake, Molly, I never said there wasn't any hope!'

'Hope? For what? Oh, you mean the human race again, don't you? Why do you even care? You don't have a stake in the world. All you have is your fucking model. You *want* everything to fall apart so you can say 'I told you so'.'

'Don't be ridiculous!'

'It's you who's ridiculous! *This* that's ridiculous.' She pulled a book from the shelf and threw it at him. It was 'Practical Self-sufficiency'. 'And this –' Another book narrowly missed him, then another. He backed up against the door as book after book flew towards him: all his ideas, their escape route, their chance of survival. 'And this –' She pulled the last one from the shelf, glanced at the title and let it drop to the floor. It was his well-thumbed copy of 'Surviving the Apocalypse'.

'Survive if you can, but count me out. It's over, Adam. I'm out of here.' She started to button her coat, and Adam began to feel colder and more frightened than he'd felt all day.

'No, you're not.'

What happened next shouldn't have happened. He tried to talk her out of leaving, tried to stop her with words, then lips and hands, but it spiralled out of control. Later he blamed it on his rising sense of panic, his need not to face what was coming alone. She fought back with a strange complicit desperation, but he was stronger than her. Afterwards he sat by the electric fire and drank the rest of the wine, listening to her cry as she packed, then to the door banging behind her. Only then did he get to his feet, pick up his books and put them back on the shelves. He washed out the empty wine-bottle and set it aside for recycling but never did get around to it.

The bottle's still there in the looted scavenged flat, but Molly isn't. She didn't come back after that night. He tried to find her at the hospital, but she'd been transferred to one of the others, and no-one could tell him which one. The outbreak was sweeping the city by then, and panic had set in. He didn't know it at the time, but the end was beginning.

In truth it had already begun. Somewhere, months before, probably in the far east, a disease had arisen and begun to spread. It would have been a chance event, a mutation enabling a virus to jump from animal to human, the one factor he hadn't allowed for in his model. It was the unknown unknown that had turned probability into certainty. Had Molly, as she'd walked back through the rain that night, begun to see what would happen? If the bus had turned up would everything be different now?

But the bus hadn't arrived, and so Molly had left. Days later, so had Adam, abandoning his model and, with it, the promising academic future that no longer existed. Instead, he set about building a different future, something he'd planned for years. He'd even marked the place, the one he and Molly had discovered when kayaking on the west coast, a rocky bay screened by birch and alder, invisible from the loch and the moorland above. There was a ruined steading on a raised beach where people had once lived and survived and would do so again. But turning the old steading into a place to live had left him with little time to listen to his wind-up radio, and, by the time he did, it was too late.

The epidemic was too virulent and too infectious to be contained. It had swept Vietnam then China, Africa, the United States, Europe, the entire world, killing the old and the young, the immune-compromised, the overweight, the undernourished: anyone, in fact, who wasn't completely healthy. And then it killed ninety per cent of those who were. The apocalypse had arrived, but not the one he'd expected.

Once he'd learned about the scale of the pandemic he'd gone back to find Molly, but the City had been sealed off. Later, from the hill above his secret bay, he'd seen the glow in the east and had watched the City burn. He'd smelled smoke on the air and worse than smoke. Not long afterwards the cracking transmissions from his radio had ceased. It was as if the world had been stunned into silence and, like a flower shrivelled by the first frosts of winter, had folded in on itself. The Age of Irony had begun, and Adam felt it keener than most. His model hadn't allowed for the pandemic, but he knew what would happen; everything would grind to a halt. The wheels of climate change would slow to a standstill. The feedback gears would poise, quivering, like a man tottering on the edge of a crumbling cliff, waiting for a gust of wind to push him back to safety or send him plummeting into the abyss. Waiting for a butterfly to flap its wings.

Only now, here in the flat where everything had begun to end, does Adam understand the human scale of what has happened – not at the level of a population, which might have been predicted, but in the lives of a single man and woman, which could not. They too had stood on an edge, but by what he'd done he'd sent them both into the abyss. She'd been as frightened as him that night. Why had it taken him all these years to understand something that simple? He'd never mentioned the black hole that lay beyond the known knowns and the known unknowns, and yet she'd understood it was there, since she'd lived in it as, day by day, the number of cases had risen. She'd gone back to the hospital knowing what they faced, because that was her stake in the world, and, in spite of her denial, she'd still had hope – hope that was the last spirit in Pandora's box, the gift of the Gods to mankind, consolation for ills not gifted but made.

He closes the door behind him and walks back to the kayak then leaves the City to its brooding silence. He paddles back down the river on an ebbing tide then heads north, eventually reaching the hidden settlement at dusk, his dark-stained kayak merging with the shadows so that his approach is secret, even from the others who'll be keeping watch. He's no longer alone for he's found other survivors like himself, and together they're eking out a wary existence. There are predators in the world now, and not just wolves and bears, but they've survived. There are even children, although none of them are his.

She's waiting for him. Her hair is darker than he remembers, her body thinner, and her eyes, in the flickering torchlight, have the wary regard of all survivors. She's younger than he remembers too. It is as if, for Molly, the wheel of time has, like the feedback loops, come to a grinding halt and reversed. This girl is eighteen or nineteen, older maybe – it's hard to tell – and so, of course she isn't Molly after all.

'How did you find this place?'

The girls shrugs as Molly had shrugged. 'My mother told me about it.'

His heart rocks. 'Is she . . ? The girl makes a swift gesture of negation and tilts her head to one side to watch his reaction. It's an observer's regard and, seeing that, his heart rocks once more. Hope, the last spirit in the box, has found its way home.

'My name's Vanessa,' she says. 'My mother told me you'd explain what that means. She said my father would explain everything.'

Somewhere, in the chambers of Adam's heart, a butterfly unfolds wings that are black and red and white, a butterfly that's ready to fly, ready to change the world.

Author's Note

I very much hope you've enjoyed reading these stories. If you have, I'd love to hear from you, so **please post a review on Amazon**. It needn't be an essay – a couple of lines would be fantastic. Reviews are particularly helpful for authors like me who're just setting out into the stormy waters of publishing. It would be great to know you've got my back!

If you read on, you can find out more about each of the stories and about me.

❧

If you've enjoyed these stories and would like to read another one, you can! Subscribe to my Newsletter to receive a **free short story**.

Subscribe at www.barbaralennox.com/subscribe

to also receive notifications of new blog posts and new content on my website, together with regular Newsletters about my writing journey.

Visit my website **www.barbaralennox.com** for more free stories, extracts from my forthcoming novels, sample poems, and lots of information about my Dark Age Trilogy, The Trystan Trilogy.

Appendix

The stories in this collection were all written at different times and for different reasons. Many have already been published (under another name) in small literary magazines, in other Anthologies, and/or have won prizes in Writing Competitions. In this appendix you can find out more about each of the stories.

Myths and Legends

The Man who Loved Landscape was written in 2004 and was inspired by a horror story I'd read a long time ago about a lonely spirit of the wilderness. It was set, I believe, in Canada, but similar spirits of place can be found in Gaelic mythology. These include the Each-uisge, the Water-horses who haunt lochs, and the Uraisg, a brownie-like spirit who haunts streams and other wet places. The Park in the story isn't named, although it was the Cairngorms I had in mind, perhaps on a bigger scale. The story was published in the Earlyworks Press Anthology, *Survival Guides,* in 2006.

Am Fear Liath Mór is the Gaelic for another of these spirits, the Big Grey Man. It was written in 2003 as an entry to the Scottish Mountaineering Article competition. It won first prize and was published in *The Scottish Mountaineering Council Newsletter* in June 2004.

Going Home was written in 2003 and was inspired by the story of Persephone, the daughter of Demeter, Goddess of the harvest. Persephone was supposedly abducted by the God of the Underworld, Hades, but returns to her mother for six months of every year. In *Going Home*, I've stuck pretty much to the story but have questioned the motivations of all concerned. This story won first prize in The Library of Avalon Short Story Competition in 2003.

Icarus was written in 2001 and was inspired by the Greek myth of Icarus, who flew too close to the sun and so fell to earth. I was less interested in the original myth than the idea of the colour white and how far a love of this colour might take someone. This story was published in *Peninsular Magazine* in April 2003.

Eurydice is a companion story to *Icarus,* in that it too explores obsession, in this case with black. It was inspired by the myth of Orpheus and Eurydice, in which Orpheus goes down to Hell to rescue his dead wife Eurydice but is ultimately unsuccessful. This story was first written in 1998 and was runner up in the FISH annual short story competition. It was published in 2001 in the FISH Anthology, *Asylum 1928 and other stories.*

What's in a name? is a light-hearted take on the myth of Perseus and the Gorgon. It was written in 2001.

Heartwood was written in 2006 and was inspired by the tales found in many cultures about the spirits of trees. Like many of my stories, it's about coming to terms with a loss and the discovery of another way of life.

The Gingerbread House was written in 2000 and was an attempt to rewrite a well-known fairy tale as a horror story.

The Lyall Bequest is one of the oldest of my short stories, having been written in 1994. It was inspired by the mediaeval Arthurian myth of The Grail and the older associated legend of the Fisher King.

The Skies of Kansas is based on the modern myth of the superhero. It was written in 2013 and published in the Anthology, *Dundee Writes 5,* in the same year.

Tales from a Riverbank

O ne Gold Ring was the first of my River Tay series and was written in 2005. This series was intended to be a number of linked stories in which the protagonist of each was a character from the previous story and the setting would move further down the river. This turned out to be more difficult than I'd anticipated, and some of the stories weren't strong enough to be included in this collection. *One Gold Ring* was inspired by learning about the gold-mine near the headwaters of the River Tay, and finding out that people still pan for gold in the river. The story has references to the Greek myth of King Midas, who could turn everything to gold. *One Gold Ring*, originally entitled *Headwaters,* won second prize in The New Writer Poetry and Prose Competition for 2005, and was published in *The New Writer* in 2006.

Feckless as Water features a character mentioned in *One Gold Ring*. It was written in 2005 and makes reference to the Scottish myth of the Water-horse, the *Each Uisge,* a creature that lives in certain lochs in the Highlands. The story won third prize in the New Writer Poetry and Prose Competition for 2006, and was published in *The New Writers' Collection* in 2007.

Being a Tree is the third of three linked stories, and is told from the point of view of the wife of the main character in *Feckless as Water*. It was written in 2006.

Imagining Silence concludes near the setting of *Feckless as Water*, in Crianlarich on the West Highland Way, a long-distance walking route from Glasgow to Fort William. This story was written in 2005, and was published as *Watershed* in the Earlyworks Press Anthology, *Rogue Symphonies,* in 2007.

Backwater takes place further down the river, at an unnamed location, and is about a couple coming to terms with the loss of their child. It was written in

2007 and won second prize in the New Writer Prose and Poetry competition for 2007. It was published in *The New Writer Collection* in 2008.

The Outing, which was written in 2017, takes place in the Botanic Garden in Dundee, within sight of the River Tay where it broadens out to an estuary. The story explores the loss of memory. It was published in 2020 in an Anthology to celebrate Dundee's Botanic Garden, *Our Botanic Garden – A Place to Bloom*.

A Room with a View also takes place in Dundee, and follows a young woman as she discovers the true nature of her relationship with an older man. It was written in 2007 and appeared in the Anthology, *Turn Back the Cover*, published by Nethergate Writers in 2007.

The Tower was written in 2014 and takes place on the tidal island, Lucky Scaup, which lies near the mouth of the river. An old lighthouse once stood there, but it no longer exists, having been undermined by the river. In my story I alternate between an old man's childhood memories and his present existence in a hospital or hospice.

A Bobble Hat in Blue was written in 2013 and takes place at Tenstmuir Point, at the mouth of the River Tay. There were always rumours that there were nudists out at the Point. The story appeared as *The Point* in the Anthology, *Watermarks,* published by Nethergate Writers in 2014.

The Fairway is set at the very mouth of the river where it becomes sea. The Fairway buoy is the last of the buoys that mark the channel of the River Tay, and the story follows a couple who are dealing with fear of the future and what it might bring. *The Fairway* was written in 2005 and was published in 2006 in the Earlyworks Press Anthology, *Islands in Mind*.

A Glimpse of the Past

*C*aught *Knapping* is a very silly story which was written in 2014. It was inspired by a BBC Listening Project broadcast in which two men talked about their enthusiasm for flint-knapping, an activity carried out by Stone age peoples to make weapons and tools. Sealed Knot, Pax Romana and Sparta Mora are re-enactment societies. Lewis McGugan played for Watford, also known as the Hornets, and their ground is Vicarage Road.

The Eagle and the Serpent was written in 2013 when I was researching the history of the Romans in Scotland for a forthcoming novel. *The Eagle and the Serpent* is set in AD 82 or 83 when the Legionary Fortress at Inchtuthil, on the banks of the Tay, was built and then abandoned. On excavation, a large horde of nails was found, and my story attempts to explain this.

The Knowing is also set in the early part of the first millennium, and it too is related to my longer fiction, *The Trystan Trilogy,* which makes reference to a rite of passage gone through by all young Caledonian warriors. Although I have set *The Knowing* in Circinn, roughly the county of Angus, and my unnamed character is a member of the Venicone tribe of that area, I had in mind the mountain of Schiehallion as the setting, since the name means Fairy

Hill of the Caledonians. This story was written in 2005 and it appeared in the Nethergate Writers Anthology, *Roots*, published in 2008.

Nechtansmere, a time-slip story, was written in 2008 in response to research I was carrying out for the novels of *The Trystan Trilogy* whose main character is half-Pictish. The little that is known about the Picts comes from their art, and this is explored in the story. The battle of Nechtansmere took place in 685 and was a decisive victory for the Picts against the Anglo-Saxons.

A Bohemian Christmas has been included in the historical section since it makes reference to a 10th century Bohemian saint, although it was actually inspired by a well-known Christmas Carol. The story itself is set after the end of the Cold War. It was originally written in 2001 and won first prize in a local Short Story Competition in 2011.

The Orb-weaver and the King was written in 2002 and appeared in the same year in the Anthology, *Weavers of Tales: A selection of Scottish Women's Short Stories*, published by 'Women of Dundee and Books'. I wanted to write a story in 2nd person viewpoint and chose Bruce's apocryphal spider as my narrator for the story of the 14th Century King, Robert the Bruce of Scotland.

The Washer at the Ford was written in 2004 and was inspired by the Gaelic folk tales of the *Bean Nighe*, a spirit seen to wash the grave clothes of those about to die. It's set in the North-west of Scotland at a place my mother, as a child, used to go to every summer to work on the family croft.

The Sparrow was written in 2014, the anniversary of the First World War, but the metaphor of the sparrow in the hall is a much earlier one and dates from the time of the conversion of the Anglo-Saxon King Edwin by St Paulinus in the eighth century.

Love and Loss

What She Would Have Wanted was written in 2008 and is set in Glen Clova in Angus. Jock's Road is an old right of way which runs from Glen Clova in Angus through to Auchallater and thence to Braemar in Aberdeenshire.

Stolen Away was written in 2005 and was inspired by a number of childhood memories, principally that of a Fair that came to my village every summer, my mother's suspicion of 'gypsies', and my fairy-tale-induced confusion about what and who these travelling folk were.

Like the Tide was written in 2001 and was published in *Peninsular Magazine* in 2004. It was the winner of the best of the non-competition stories.

Evidence of Ice was written in 2004. The metaphor I used throughout the story is that of the processes of glaciation. I was intrigued to learn that Scotland, once crushed beneath a mile of ice in the Ice Age, is, even to this day, still rising, a process known as post-glacial rebound. This story was published in *The New Writer* in 2006.

Bogeyman was written in 2002 and was inspired by a childhood memory of a man in my village we children referred to as 'The Bogeyman'. The idea of the outsider, the scapegoat, is a powerful one, and it is found in many cultures, as is the 'naming and shaming' by the media of people who may be innocent, both themes I wanted to explore in this story.

Looking for the Leonids was written in 2002 in response to seeing a shooting star. The Leonids are to be seen in November and are one of the more prolific annual meteor showers. Meteor showers are named after the constellations from which they emerge, the Leonids being from Leo. It won 2nd prize in the Litchfield and District Writers' Short Story Competition in 2006.

The Mushroom Pickers was written in 2001 and is set in my local forest. Together with *Looking for the Leonids*, it was commended in the Ayr 800 Short Story Competition in 2005. It appeared in *The Speakeasy Anthology*, published by Speakeasy Press in 2005.

Fogbound was written in 2005. I don't usually write dark stories but this one is certainly disturbing, and I don't know what inspired it.

Theophany was written in 2002 and appeared in 2002 in *Afterimage*, a magazine of creative writing published by the University of Dundee.

Appointment on Valentine's Day was written in 2002 and follows a clergyman as he wrestles with his relationship with both his wife and God.

Moving On was written in 2013 in response to climate change. It was published in 2013 in the Nethergate Writers Anthology, *A Long Way from Eden*.

The Butterfly Effect was also written in 2013 in response to climate change and takes place in a post-apocalyptic landscape, following extensive flooding and a pandemic, an unnerving foreshadowing of the events of 2020.

About the author

I was born, and still live, in Scotland on the shores of a river, between the mountains and the sea. I'm a retired scientist and science administrator, but have always been fascinated by the early history of Scotland, and I love fleshing out that history with the stories of fictional, and not-so-fictional, characters.

I've had a number of short stories published in various anthologies and magazines, and, in this collection, I've gathered together some of my favourites. Many of these are set in Scotland. A longer historical short story, *Song of a Red Morning,* which takes place in 6th century Scotland, was published by Amazon in 2019.

Song of a Red Morning is set at Dunpeldyr, the Iron Age Fort of Traprain Law in East Lothian. This is also the setting for the opening of my Dark-age Trilogy, *The Trystan Trilogy*, which consists of *The Wolf in Winter, The Swan in Summer* and *The Serpent in Spring. The Wolf in Winter* is my first full-length novel and will shortly be published in both e-book and paperback form.

Find out more about me and my writing on my website:

Barbaralennox.com

Connect with me on the following:

Twitter	twitter.com/barbaralennox4
Instagram	instagram.com/barbaralennoxwriter
Pinterest	pinterest.co.uk/barbaralennox58
Goodreads	goodreads.com/author/show/19661962.Barbara_Lennox
Amazon	viewauthor.at/authorprofile

Acknowledgements

I would never have written any of these short stories if I hadn't attended the 'Continuing as a Writer' classes, part of the University of Dundee's Continuing Education Programme. These classes were tutored by Esther Read whose support and encouragement has been unstinting and invaluable. Esther, I can't thank you enough. I'm also grateful to the other members of the class, and the Nethergate Writers Group, for their helpful and constructive criticism.

At home, Harry, Rambo and Oscar, the best cats in the world, were with me all the way, usually asleep.

Finally, but not least, I'd like to thank my husband, Will, for putting up with all the scribbling and not asking any questions.

Printed in Great Britain
by Amazon

60643157R00135